A SAFE HARBOUR

A SAFE HARBOUR

Benita Brown

headline

First published in 2005
by HEADLINE BOOK PUBLISHING

10 9 8 7 6 5 4 3 2 1

Cataloguing in Publication Data is available from the British Library

ISBN 0 7553 2325 4

Typeset in Times by Avon DataSet Ltd,
Bidford-on-Avon, Warwickshire

Printed and bound in Great Britain by
Mackays of Chatham plc, Chatham, Kent

Headline's policy is to use papers that are natural, renewable and
recyclable products and made from wood grown in sustainable forests.
The logging and manufacturing processes are expected to conform to the
environmental regulations of the country of origin.

HEADLINE BOOK PUBLISHING
A division of Hodder Headline
338 Euston Road
London NW1 3BH

www.headline.co.uk
www.hodderheadline.com

To Norman, as ever.
And also to my mother, who read to me and told me stories.
I know she would have been pleased that I grew up
to be a writer.

Our first married home was a two-room, three-hundred-year-old cottage on a cliff top overlooking the sea at Cullercoats. My husband was born in a cottage not far away, as were his father and generations of Browns before him. Even when we set up home the village was not what it used to be. And, now, with many of the old dwellings gone and the streets redeveloped, it would be difficult for a stranger to visualize the thriving fishing community the village once housed.

'Belle Vue Cottage' is still there, although that is not its name. I have the fondest memories of it. But I hope you will forgive me for taking small liberties with the lie of the land. After all, this is a work of fiction.

Chapter One

Cullercoats, August 1895

Eighteen-year-old Kate Lawson knelt by the bed and watched as her great-grandmother's eyes moved restlessly beneath closed lids. What did Sarah dream about? Was she a child again running barefoot on the white sand, with the clouds racing overhead and the gulls' harsh cries echoing round the bay? Or did she dream she was a young wife still, helping Rob bait the lines when their bairns were sleeping; here in this very cottage while night pressed down on the village? Or did her darkest grief come back to haunt her – was she reliving the torment when first her husband and then four of her sons were claimed by the sea, their drowned bodies brought back by the tides and tossed carelessly on the shore?

No one knew quite how old Sarah was, but they reckoned she must be over a hundred. Her skin was weathered and wrinkled and the few wisps of hair that strayed out from her bonnet had faded to sandy grey. The lustrous auburn it had once been she had bequeathed to her children and it would live on through the generations.

Kate remembered that when she and her brothers had been small children Sarah had watched over them while their mother went to the beach to help their da haul in the coble, the fishing boat the family depended on for their hard living. Sarah would tell them stories, sing the old songs, play counting games. She had been the only one who could make Kate sit still long enough to have the tangles combed from her long, abundant hair. Her wisdom and patience had been a source of comfort in difficult times.

Sarah was fully dressed. One of Kate's duties was to ease the old woman's brittle bones out of bed each morning, wash her as if she were an infant, and then help her into her skirt, jacket, shawl and bonnet.

And even put on her boots, which Kate's elder brother, William, would have cleaned the night before along with the others; although Sarah had not set foot outside for many a year. She spent her days lying on top of the eiderdown on the bed in the corner of the main room of the cottage, propped up among pillows, her rheumy eyes sometimes open and staring into the mid-distance, and sometimes closed as she surrendered to the dreams that maybe seemed more real to her than her present purposeless existence.

Her only pleasure now was her clay pipe, which she clamped between her toothless gums and sucked on ceaselessly. But the sucking noises had stopped and Sarah's snores had alerted Kate to the fact that the old woman was sleeping again. She leaned over and removed the pipe gently from the corner of her great-grandmother's mouth. The bowl was cold so, rising quietly, Kate took the pipe over to the fireplace and tapped it on the grate to empty the tobacco ash before placing it in the rack.

She stepped back from the hearth and turned to gaze around the room. It was still too early to light the lamps but the glow from the fire and the last of the evening sunlight slanting through the open doorway merged to bathe the interior of the cottage in a mellow light. Everything in this room was familiar to her and yet Kate willed herself to see with the eyes of a stranger, wanting to record and remember, for her father had told her that once she left the cottage to marry Jos Linton she would never be welcome here again.

Behind her the coals shifted and settled in the grate and the lid of the kettle rattled in the flow of steam. Along with the ticking of the clock and her great-grandmother's snoring, they were the only sounds to disturb the air. They were alone here, she and Sarah. Her father and brothers were digging for bait and her mother, Nan, was taking her ease for a while, and had moved a stool outside to sit in the lane and gossip with her neighbours. But even in this precious spare time most of them would be knitting as they talked, the needles clicking and the oiled wool flying through their practised fingers as the light faded over the farmland beyond the village to the west.

Kate had never learned to knit. Kind, patient Nan had despaired of the dropped stitches, the tangled knots and the hot, angry tears. Eventually she had given up trying to pass on to her only daughter a skill that was second nature to almost every other woman in the village. Even Kate's childhood friend Jane Harrison had mastered the intricate age-old patterns while she was still at school, and Jane's father was not even a fisherman.

Poor Ma, Kate thought as she listened to the low pleasant voices of the older women and the faint click of needles coming from the lane. Kate still felt ashamed when she remembered the day she had flung the needles and the yarn down on the stone-flagged floor and run out of the cottage.

She had fled down the bank to the sea shore red-faced and furious. Not because her mother was vexed with her – no one could have been more patient – but because she was embarrassed and angry with herself. She knew she wasn't stupid. Didn't she always come top in the weekly tests at school, even keeping ahead of the lads? So why couldn't she master four needles and a skein of wool? She'd taken refuge in one of the caves and stayed there while the light outside had faded and her twin brother, Thomas, had come looking for her.

'Hawway, our Kate,' he'd said as he peered into the dimness and saw her crouched on the fine white sand with her arms wrapped round her knees. 'You can't sit here all day.'

'Is Ma vexed with me?' she'd asked him.

'Not her. But you'd best come back before Da comes in.'

She'd entered the cottage hesitantly, content to let her brother lead the way for once, but there'd been no sign of the ruined knitting. Their ma had been setting the table. Wordlessly Kate began to help her. That had been years ago and her mother had never tried to make her knit again – although she hadn't been able to resist saying, only a few weeks ago, that she wondered who was going to knit Jos's ganseys.

'His ma will knit his jumpers and his boot socks too,' Kate had told her.

'And divven't you mind that?' her mother had asked.

'Why should I?'

'Most lasses want to look after their man themselves.'

'Well, I'm not *most* lasses!' Kate flared.

Her ma saw her chin go up and her eyes spark and she shook her head. 'Now, Kate, divven't gan crabby. I know you're not like other lasses. You're bright and you're bonny and I know you're going to be a good wife to Jos and a good daughter to Mary. And Mary will be pleased to let you do the cooking; she doesn't mind admitting that she hates it. And the rest of the Linton family'll be happy, too, I imagine, after years of Mary's burnt offerings.'

Mother and daughter smiled at each other and Kate laughed. 'I don't know about that. I like cooking but William and Thomas always pull faces at my efforts.'

'That's brothers for you. But you know they're only teasing. Fair tyrants they are. Heaven help the lasses them two wed!'

'It's your fault, Ma, you've spoiled them. You've spoiled all of us . . .' Kate faltered, an ache of grief in her throat and her eyes moist. 'Oh, Ma, I'll miss you.'

'Divven't fret, lass. We'll still be able to see each other.'

'But not here, will we? Not in my own home. Da said once I was married to Jos Linton I would never be welcome here again. Why does he hate Jos so?'

'You know fine well, Kate. It's not Jos your father hates, it's the whole family.'

'But that's worse! And for such a stupid reason.'

'To be fair to him yer da isn't the only one to frown on interlopers. They're country people – not fisherfolk – and they come and take our living from us.'

'There's a difference between frowning and hating,' Kate said, 'and the Lintons came here before Jos was born.'

Her mother sighed. 'Memories are long. And at least yer da hasn't forbidden the marriage. He could hev done, you know.'

'He's glad to be rid of me. He said so. He said I was a thorn in his side.'

'And isn't that true?'

Kate looked at her mother in surprise and saw that Nan was smiling. 'Yes, I suppose it is. It will be easier for you when I've gone, won't it? There won't be so much cause for him to lose his temper.'

Their smiles had faded and they had looked at each other solemnly, each woman remembering what Henry Lawson was like when the drink or his temper took him. Nan had put her arms round her daughter. They'd stood there without speaking, watched only by the faded eyes of old Sarah – who might have heard everything, or nothing. As ever, her wizened face had given no clue.

And now, one week before the wedding to her childhood sweetheart, Kate found that she was near to tears as she remembered that moment of closeness with her mother. Her vision was blurred as she took in the scrubbed table, the brown teapot reflecting the light of the fire on its rounded sides, the window beyond, whose small panes always sparkled even though this meant daily washing inside and out because of the salt air.

Nan Lawson was house-proud and fastidious. Mary Linton was careless and easygoing. Jos's father, James, was even tempered and tolerant. There were those who said he might have taken a firmer line with his two high-spirited sons, but the Lintons worked hard and respected one another. Kate knew that it was a very different household she would be entering as Jos's bride, but she also knew that she would be happy there. She would no longer have to live in fear of her father's unpredictable moods, his outbursts of rage and his drunken violence.

When she and her brothers had been children their father's favoured method of disciplining them had been to take off his belt and beat them. Nan had suffered beatings too, and they had only stopped when William had grown big enough to protect his mother and his younger brother and sister. Now, although William's presence kept a rein on Henry's worst excesses, Henry was still master here and the whole family lived under the shadow of his tyrannical authority.

'Kate!'

Kate blinked at the sound of her name and glanced towards the open door. A man's figure was framed in the doorway, a familiar silhouette against the afternoon light. Her spirits lightened. 'Jos . . . is that you?'

'Kate . . . you've got to come . . .' The voice cracked and Kate's smile vanished. She felt the first stirrings of alarm.

Not Jos, she saw as the figure moved forward falteringly. It was his younger brother Matthew, who had the same sturdy frame but was not so tall.

'Come? Where?' she whispered, with a nod towards the old lady sleeping on the bed against the wall.

Matthew glanced at the old woman distractedly. He had stopped on the other side of the table and he stared at Kate wildly. Her alarm turned to dread when she saw his clenched fists. She took a step towards him and found herself grasping the back of a chair. 'What is it?' she asked. 'What's happened?'

'It's Jos. He's not come back.'

'Yes he has. I saw him. I spoke to him. We're meeting later on the boat field.'

'No, Kate, he's missing. Him and Barty Lisle.'

'I don't understand.' Kate stared at her sweetheart's younger brother. The ticking of the clock on the mantel suddenly seemed louder as it consigned to the past the last few seconds when anything would make sense. 'They came back from the fishing hours ago.'

'I know. But they went out again. Two little lads playing on the beach saw them. They took Jos's boat – just Jos and Barty. The bairns saw them head for the harbour mouth and then they just sat there.'

'They must have dropped anchor,' Kate said.

'Aye, that's likely.'

'But why – what were they doing?' Kate asked.

Matthew shook his head. 'Who knows? The next time the bairns looked out, the tide was high and the coble was nowhere to be seen.' He came round the table and took her by the arm. 'Ma's down on the beach waiting. Please come.'

Kate was still trying to make sense of what she'd heard, but she let go of the chair and allowed Matthew to guide her out of the cottage and along the lane towards the harbour. She was aware that others were following; she heard her mother's voice among those of the other women, and the footsteps ringing out on the cobbles as they began to hurry.

Damn this skirt, she thought, as she tried to keep up with Matthew. Losing patience she wrenched herself free from his grasp and, stooping swiftly to grab hold of the folds of the deep-tucked hemline, she yanked it up above her knees. With her long slender legs freed from restraint she was able to keep pace easily.

Her heart was pounding, more from fear than exertion, as they ran down the slope from Bank Top to the beach. At the bottom, Kate almost fell as her feet sank into the soft sand still damp from the retreating high tide. She gasped, and cried out involuntarily. Matthew turned and steadied her.

She was aware of others gathering as the word spread that two men were missing, but Matthew was guiding her towards the figure of a woman silhouetted starkly against the grey of the sea and the sky. Mary Linton, Jos's mother, had drawn her shawl around her and was standing with arms crossed tightly across her body as if holding in her grief. The waves were lapping round her feet but she didn't seem to have noticed. As they approached, Kate could hear her ragged moans of distress.

'Stay with her,' Matthew said quietly. 'I'll hev to help Da with the search.'

'Aye, you go, Matthew,' Kate said. He turned and retreated up the beach to make his way to the high water moorings.

Mary Linton didn't turn her head when Kate gently placed her hand on her shoulder. 'Me bairn . . . me bairn,' the older woman moaned. 'Lord God give us back me bairn.' At those words Kate was seized with dread.

Jos was only a year older than Kate and their childhood friendship had grown into sweet first love. But it was a love which they had believed would endure for a life time. This couldn't be happening. Please God don't let Jos be taken from me, she cried inwardly.

Kate was aware of the water sucking and gurgling round her feet and she put her arms round Mary Linton's waist and drew her back slightly until they both stood on firmer ground. She scanned the sea, looking beyond the breakwaters to the horizon. She tried desperately to imagine some good reason why Jos and Barty would stay out for so long.

Earlier that day, after the beach auction of the fish, Jos had called by her parents' cottage and asked her to meet him on the boat field that evening so that they could discuss their wedding plans. The Lintons had prospered; they lived in one of the few two-storeyed cottages in the village, another reason why Kate's father hated them, and Jos and Kate were to be given a room of their own. A tiny room under the sloping eaves of the roof, but nevertheless they would sleep there alone together and not have to share a room with other members of the family as most of the villagers did.

Never allowed to cross the threshold of the Lawsons' cottage, Jos had taken her hand and pulled her along the lane. Seeing that they were alone he'd gathered her into his arms and swung her round until they were both dizzy and, not even giving her a chance to catch her breath, he had kissed her until her senses were racing as fast as the clouds high in the sky above them.

'Not long, now, sweetheart,' he'd murmured into the soft skin of her neck, 'not long, now, before we can be together every single night. Soon we'll be man and wife. Then I can make love to you in a nice warm bed instead of—'

'Whisht, Jos, whisht!' Kate had covered his mouth with the fingers of one hand and looked around. But there was no one to hear his words except a stray cat stretched out on the sun-warmed cobbles and a lone herring gull perched on the roof of a nearby cottage.

'Divven't fret, lass,' Jos had said and he'd prised her fingers away from his lips and, turning her hand, he'd kissed her palm. The faint rasp of his stubble had made her shiver with pleasure. 'Divven't fret,' he'd said again. 'We've done no wrong.'

Then Jos had told her that he was going to take Barty to the Queen's Head and treat him to a pint of ale, or mebbes two – Jos had laughed at Kate's frown – while he made sure the lad understood what his duties as best man entailed. He'd said nothing about taking his boat out again.

The evening air had cooled and there was a breeze skimming the foam from the tops of the waves. Kate hadn't had time to snatch up her shawl and she began to feel cold. She could hear the subdued voices of some of the women who had gathered on the beach behind them. They were no strangers to grief and they knew it would be best to leave Kate and Mary alone to support each other.

Matthew and some of the men had already launched their cobles and started the search. Perhaps the lads were in trouble of some kind beyond the harbour mouth. Whatever they were up to they would never have sailed willingly out of sight of the shore. Kate hoped and prayed that Jos's coble, the *Sea Quest*, would soon be found and that Jos and Barty would be in it, safe and well. But with every second that passed the knot of fear tightened inside her.

Other men had come running down from Bank Top and Kate watched as the crews, three men to each coble, manhandled the vessels on to wheeled axles and then pulled them over the soft sand into the water. Few words were spoken. They all knew what to do. Some had brought coals and kindling to light the fire-pans in the boats. The light from these braziers would be needed in the growing darkness.

There wasn't the slightest hint of disaster in the air, Kate thought. As the day faded the voices behind her died and the only sounds to be heard were the creaking and splashing of the oars as the cobles manoeuvred in the small harbour. Within the shelter of the breakwaters the sea was calm. Gently curling waves flopped innocently on to the shingle. But death was present; Kate sensed it in her bones.

Mrs Linton paid no heed to the activity on the beach or in the harbour. She pressed her bowed head into her hands as if to catch her sobs. Kate put an arm round her shoulders. She looked down at the thick, greying hair coiled neatly into a bun at the nape of her neck. The skin that showed above the high collar was weather-beaten and wrinkled. Mary Linton was only forty-two years old.

Mary was shivering. 'Do you think it would be best for you to wait at home, Mrs Linton?' Kate asked. 'It's cold here on the beach.'

The older woman's shoulders stiffened and she pulled away. She shook her head without turning to look at Kate. 'No, I must stay. I must be here for him.'

Kate looked away. It was distressing to witness the woman's anguish, especially as her own was growing with every passing minute. But of course Jos's mother would stay as long as the search went on, although Kate sensed she already feared that the men's efforts were in vain and that Jos was lost.

Kate shivered. 'Come away, Mrs Linton,' she tried again. 'Jos wouldn't want you to catch a chill.'

The older woman drew her shawl up over her head. 'I've telt you,' she said tersely. 'I'm staying. Get yerself home if you can't face the waiting. But my lad would expect his womenfolk to do their duty.'

Kate knew she had been rebuked. Useless to explain that she had only had the older woman's welfare at heart. To her dismay she felt the ache of grief in her throat grow stronger and her eyes begin to smart. Her vision blurred and she rubbed at her eyelids with cold fingers. It was not yet time for tears. She felt Mary Linton's arm come round her shoulders.

'I'm sorry, Kate, hinny,' she said. 'You're not much more than a bairn. Eighteen years old. About to be a bride. You shouldn't hev to face this.'

Mary and Kate stood together on the darkening shore and when the men in the cobles began to cast their grappling hooks into the water they groaned in unison. The *Sea Quest* had not been sighted and the men were searching the water for a wreck. Jos was never going to be a bridegroom. Now they must wait for the sea to give up his body.

The two women clung together as they looked out to sea. Light from the fire-pans in the cobles danced on the swell and illuminated the scene at the harbour entrance as the men searched. The fire-pans, which gave the men a bit of warmth and could boil a kettle, had different cut-out patterns so that each family's coble could be recognized from the shore.

The Lintons were there and George Lisle, Barty's father, and Kate could see her own family's coble although she knew her father was not on board. Her brothers had answered the call. Time and again the crews cast their grappling hooks into the blackness of the water, to no avail.

Kate turned to look up towards Bank Top. A group of villagers stood in line gazing down at the scene below. It was too dark now to make them out individually but Kate could see the women's skirts fluttering as the wind began to gust. Some of the men, not engaged in the search, stood with their womenfolk, wanting to see the outcome but not wanting to intrude. Many of those silent watchers would have been guests at my wedding, Kate thought.

'Here, lads, over here!' The words carried clearly to the shore on the strengthening wind.

Mary Linton gripped her arm and Kate turned and strained to peer across the water. Her elder brother, William, had hooked something and he was leaning over as he held his burden against the side of the coble. He was waiting for assistance. Already the other crews were beginning to row towards him.

Soon all the cobles were huddled together, nudging and bumping against each other in the swell, the light from the fire-pans illuminating the sea around them. William and Thomas heaved together and a dark shape rose from the water. The small boat rocked violently as the brothers dragged their burden aboard.

'Oh dear God . . . dear God.' Kate sank to her knees in the wet sand. She heard someone shout, 'Over here . . . here's the other one!'

Holding her head in her hands she began to cry.

Kate followed the sombre procession from the water's edge. The men tried to maintain their dignity but the bodies were made heavier by the water and those carrying them stumbled now and then in the soft sand. They laid them on the ramp that led up to the lifeboat house.

Jos and Barty looked peaceful in death. Jos's eyes were open and his mother reached down and closed them gently. Then she took off her shawl and laid it over her son's body, covering his face. His father and brother watched silently, approving her gesture. Kate stood beside her, helpless. There was nothing she could do for the man she had been about to marry. A little further up the ramp Barty's father, a widower, stood by his only son's body with a look of blank resignation on his face.

After a while the men came with a cart and took Jos and Barty up the bank. They were going home for the last time. Jos's family walked behind the cart. The way they clung together excluded her.

'Kate? Are you coming?' her mother's voice called through the darkness.

'Not yet. I need to be on my own.'

Nan didn't try to persuade her. 'Don't stay too long,' she said, then she set off up the bank after the others leaving Kate on the now deserted beach.

How quiet it was. Just the lapping of the waves on the shore and then the drag back across the shingle. Up in the village warm lights shone from cottage windows. Kate turned to look at the beached cobles. It wouldn't be long before the men returned, trudging down the bank in their heavy sea boots and oilskins. Their wives and children would come with them, helping to carry the fishing gear, the nets, the food, the water bottles.

The crew of each coble would push their boat on wheeled bogies into the water. Then they would row the boats out beyond the breakwater before hoisting the sails, which would flutter briefly before filling with wind and thrusting the bows of the cobles into the heavy open sea. Soon, all that would be seen on the far horizon would be a cluster of tiny specks of light coming from the fire-pans. The men would harvest the fishing grounds as they had for centuries. But Jos would not be with them. Jos would never go fishing again. She was waiting here in vain.

The forlorn screech of a herring gull roused Kate from her reverie. She turned away from the sea and made her way, slowly, up to Bank Top.

Chapter Two

At sunrise Kate was back on the shore.

She had not slept. She had been sitting by the fire in the cottage when her older brother William had come home from the grim task of taking the bodies of the two young men to the lifeboat house. There they would stay until daylight, when the undertaker would be called. Kate's father, who had taken no part in the recovery, had already left to prepare the coble for the night's fishing and Thomas had returned to the beach to help him. Kate's mother had been seeing to the old woman, feeding her a bowl of broth one slow spoon at a time.

'Kate, lass . . .'

She looked up mutely to see William's handsome face drawn and grey. His ashen features and the way he shook his head, almost in disbelief, sharpened her grief. She rose and moved towards him.

'Why, William? Why?'

'Whisht, lass,' he said with a glance over his shoulder towards the bed where their mother was tending to Sarah. Nan nodded gravely in their direction and continued with her task. William motioned for Kate to sit again and drawing up a chair sat beside her. He took both her hands in his.

'I'll tell you what I've learned from Constable Darling,' he said quietly. 'I don't want you to hear it from others. It seems the two of them had a drink or two.'

'Jos told me they were going to talk about the wedding.' Kate felt her voice break and she paused a while before she asked, 'Did they drink too much, is that it? Were they too drunk to know what they were doing? But why would they put to sea?'

'No.' William shook his head. 'They weren't mortal. It seems they drank just enough to make them merry. They must have decided to walk it off. They went up to Marden farm. They . . . they stole some apples.'

'Stole apples!'

'Aye, Farmer Bains saw them from his window. They'd climbed over the orchard wall and they'd found an old sack. They were gathering up the apples that had fallen too soon. They were laughing and pushing each other like two big bairns and it was only when one of them fell against a tree that Farmer Bains decided to chase them off before they did any harm. He came out hollering at them but, of course, the lads outran him.'

'So why did they put to sea?'

William gripped her hands more tightly. 'That's the tragedy of it. Mr Bains says he'll regret all his life what he said next.'

'What? What did he say?'

'He yelled after them that he'd get Constable Darling to arrest them and lock them up.'

'But they must have known he wouldn't do that – not for the sake of a sackful of unripe apples!'

'If they'd been sober they would have known that. A tongue-lashing from Farmer Bains or Constable Darling would have been the most they'd have to bear.'

'Oh, Jos, Jos . . .' Kate said. 'It would be him that decided to launch the coble, wouldn't it? Where Jos led Barty followed.'

'Likely,' her brother said.

'But what happened out there?'

'Some bairns who were playing on the beach watched them. They saw them drop anchor outside the harbour.'

'What were they doing?'

'Sleeping it off is my guess. And they must have been asleep when the tide came in.'

'Oh, no . . .'

'With the anchor down, caught on a rock, the other lads think, the tide swamped the coble and dragged it down. I doubt if either of them could swim; not many of the fishermen can. And God knows if they woke up before—'

'Don't!' Kate said. And then, 'How could he? How could Jos leave me like this for the sake of a sackful of apples?'

She rose to her feet angrily, not knowing what to do or where to go. Her brother stood and caught her, and held her in his arms until her grief and anger had subsided.

'Kate, I've got to go,' he said. 'Our da and Thomas are waiting for me. But you know how sorry I am, don't you?'

13

She nodded. Nan had come up behind them. The old woman was sleeping. 'Go now, William,' their mother said. 'I'll look after her.'

Nan gave Kate a bowl of broth and Kate did her best to eat it. They talked quietly about the story William had told until, still not making sense of it all, Kate persuaded her mother to go to bed. She would sit by the fire, she had said.

But she had not been able to take comfort from its warmth. There was no warmth in the world that could compensate for the loss of all her hopes and dreams. She rose, pulling her shawl around her shoulders, and crept quietly out of the cottage.

A light sea mist hung over the harbour, muffling all sound and enclosing her in her world of grief. She stood in the wave-ridged sand at the shoreline, the salt air cooling her tear-stained face and the dampness making her long russet hair cling to her neck in coiled tendrils.

Hugging her shawl around her body, Kate looked out towards the horizon to where the cobles rolled and pitched on the swell, their square red-brown sails appearing and disappearing in swirls of ghostly vapour. Despite the tragedy of the day before, the men of the village had gone out not long after midnight. They had their livings to earn and would be back for the morning fish auction on the beach.

The pale disc of the sun, still low over the sea, grew warmer and the mist began to lift. As the sky cleared the cries of the gulls grew more shrill. They spread their wings and rode the currents of air above the bay, their screams piercing the air. Kate put her hands over her ears. The old superstition that seabirds were the souls of drowned sailors and fishermen sprang into her mind. Had they come to greet poor Jos and Barty? Or were they scolding them for losing their lives in such a hare-brained escapade?

Suddenly a wave sped across the shore towards her. The whooshing sound roused her from her unhappy musings and she stepped back, but not before two or three rounded stones, tumbling in the lacy foam, washed up against her feet. She looked down and her eyes widened. The water retreated but the gifts it had brought stayed. And then another wave brought more. And she saw that they were not stones at all.

Kate looked out across the water. Under the mist trails, glistening fragments of light sparkled on the ever-shifting surface of the sea. And bobbing up and down as they drifted towards her were the apples that Jos had stolen. He'd meant them for her. As if in a dream, Kate sank down on to the wet sand and began to gather them up.

Jane Harrison and her mother sat at the table in the cosy, well-furnished room behind her father's workshop. Mr Harrison was a shoemaker and cobbler and he had prospered. And although, when she'd been small, Jane had run barefoot with the other village children it was not because, like many of them, she could not afford a pair of shoes. In fact she had the best her father's skill could provide and that was why her mother allowed her to take them off when she went to play on the shore. The cobbler's wife was sensible enough not to want the shoes ruined with salt water just for the sake of pride.

But now neither Jane nor her mother liked to dwell on those childhood days. Jane had done so much better than most of the other girls who had been in her class at school. In her mother's eyes Jane had risen so far above the village lasses that she was a better class of person altogether, and Jane would not have argued with that. Save for Kate. There was something about Kate Lawson, something indefinable, that defied anyone to try to put her in her place.

Jane had caught the first morning train home from Newcastle where she worked as a lady's maid in a big house in Jesmond. She always did this on her day off, even though it meant rising long before even the skivvy and the kitchen maid whose job it was to get the kitchen range going and set the table for the staff's breakfast. Jane preferred to spend as much time as possible at home. Her mother spoiled her. She would make breakfast for her the minute she arrived, but today Jane couldn't face the plate of poached eggs and bacon. She stared at her mother, horrified by what she had just heard.

'Drowned? Jos drowned?' she said.

'Aye, pet. And Barty Lisle, too.' Her mother sighed. 'And all for the sake of a few apples.'

'I don't understand.' Jane was both shocked and bewildered.

After hearing her mother tell the tale, she shook her head. Her friend Kate's sweetheart had made a habit of getting into mischief ever since he'd been a small boy. It had been harmless fun most of the time, although he had frequently strained Jane's sense of humour. She'd often wondered what Kate had thought about it, but then, Kate would never have criticized Jos.

'I must go to her.'

'Yes, I know you must. But you haven't eaten anything. Will you at least have a cup of tea? I'll sit and have one with you.'

Jane allowed her mother to fuss a little. In truth she was glad to stay awhile in the comfort of the parlour while she adjusted to the terrible situation. She wasn't sure yet what she would say to Kate, her oldest friend. She took a sip of her tea and smiled wanly at her mother.

'I was going to fit the dress today,' she said. 'Make the last adjustments.'

The two women stared at each other, their expressions solemn. 'Poor Kate,' Florence Harrison said. 'She'd have made such a bonny bride.'

'I had such a battle with her over that dress, you know.' It seemed as if the shocking news of Jos's drowning was too much for Jane to assimilate and she was hanging on to emotions and events she could understand – her recent tussles with her friend over her gift of a wedding gown.

'Wedding dress?' Kate had said, incredulously. 'No, Jane, I shall wear my best dress with a bit of lace here and there – you can sew it on for me – and a bit of orange blossom in my hair, just like the other lasses round here.'

'But you're not just like the other lasses round here!' Jane had exclaimed. 'And don't you know how beautiful you are? Besides, you're my friend, and I want to do this for you.'

'But the expense of it . . .'

'There's no expense involved. Mrs Coulson gave me the silk and the tulle that was left from Geraldine's wedding. I helped the dressmaker, you know. And I learned so much from her. Oh, Kate, do let me make you a wedding gown!'

'But I look dreadful in white!'

'Mm, perhaps you do . . . that flame-coloured hair of yours might be too much of a contrast.'

'Well, thank you very much!'

Jane remembered how Kate had flushed and, rising quickly from the sofa in the Harrisons' parlour, been about to flounce out. 'Kate, don't go,' Jane had said and she'd laughed at her friend's indignation. 'Your hair is gorgeous; it's your crowning glory with those shades of copper and bronze and even gold. And those green eyes make you look like . . . like a picture in the art gallery – you know, the one with the lady standing at the window of a castle?'

Kate had sat down again at this point, her eyes widening. No doubt she was remembering the day they had gone to the art gallery in Newcastle together and how much they had both admired that particular picture.

'Don't you know I'm teasing you?' Jane had continued. 'Oh, Kate, you're so quick to rise to the bait. But you must let me make a dress for you. I need to practise my skills.'

'So that's it. I'd be doing you a favour, would I? Especially as I'm pretty sure there's enough bonny fabric left to make a dress for my beautiful bridesmaid, too.'

'Well, of course.' They'd looked at each other and laughed. 'I've brought a piece home with me – let me show you.'

How long ago had it been, that day when they'd opened the brown paper parcel and spread the bits of fabric out on the parlour table? 'Look,' Jane had said, 'it's not true white – it's ivory; just perfect for your creamy complexion. And the tulle – see,' she'd held up something light and filmy, 'there's enough of this left to make you a full-length veil.'

'And cover my face to hide my embarrassment.'

'Embarrassment?'

'For goodness' sake, Jane, did you ever hear of a fisherlass getting married in a silken gown, with a veil of . . . what did you call it?'

'Tulle.'

'Well, did you?'

Jane had sensed victory slipping away. 'Proper wedding gowns are becoming fashionable, you know. They're not just for society ladies. You only have to look in Jerome's window in Newcastle.'

'The photographer's?'

'Yes. Go and have a look at the wedding portraits. Oh, Kate, why shouldn't you be the first in the village? Lead the way?'

And after that it hadn't taken too much persuasion. What young bride could have resisted the samples of fabric and the silk flowers she'd brought to show Kate, along with the sketches she'd made, copied from the latest fashion magazines?

'And now what shall I do with the dresses?' Jane asked her mother. 'Kate's and mine?'

'Sell them, I suppose.'

Jane was shocked by the matter-of-fact way her mother said this, but she knew she ought not to have been. Her mother was just as shocked as she was and just as sorry for Kate. She'd had tears in her eyes when she had broken the news to Jane. But Florence Harrison was a practical woman and she would not want to see such fine dresses go to waste.

Jane's parents had worked hard and they had scrimped and saved to make sure their daughter would never have to work as hard as they had.

Jane had gone to the village school with the rest of the village children, but she had had extras such as elocution and deportment lessons. And how Kate had mocked her when she had begun to 'talk proper' – until the day Jane had asked her to help with one of the little rhymes she'd been given to learn. Kate had enjoyed the novelty of it so much that Jane and she always did Jane's elocution homework together after that. Mrs Harrison had often mused ruefully that her husband's hard-earned money was paying for Kate Lawson to be made a lady, too. But impatient Kate would never have been able to learn to sew the way Jane had.

That had always pleased Mrs Harrison, who couldn't help being piqued that Kate, a fisherman's daughter, so outshone her own daughter in her school work. Jane had been a good little pupil who worked hard but never quite caught up with her brilliant friend – except in the needlework class where no one could match her.

Her mother had been overjoyed when Jane had shown she had an aptitude not only for plain sewing but for embroidery, too. Those skills along with her passion for clothes had deemed her suitable, in her mother's eyes, for work in a big house, and as a lady's maid at that. Well spoken and well dressed, Jane had had no trouble securing a position first as an upstairs maid and very soon as personal maid and companion to the daughter of the house. And now that Miss Geraldine had married and left home, Jane had become maid to Mrs Coulson herself.

The house where she worked was the Jesmond mansion of Ralph Coulson, an eminent Newcastle solicitor. Jane loved it there. And she never tired of bringing home tales of the beautiful furniture and draperies, the fine china and the paintings on the walls. Commissioned by a 'real' artist, she had told her mother.

'Well, one day, I may sell the dresses,' Jane said now. 'But meanwhile I'll sew them into a couple of old sheets and leave them in the cupboard in my room here.'

'All right, pet. But don't leave it too long. Fashions change, as you keep telling me. Let a respectable time go by and then you could advertise them in the newspaper. I've seen it done.'

'I suppose so.'

'And it would be a shame for such bonny frocks to be wasted – to never see the light of day – wouldn't it?'

'You're right.' Jane finished her tea and dabbed at her mouth with her napkin. Her mother had always set a nice table. Not for her the bare scrubbed table or the oilcloth to be found in the fisherfolk's cottages. Florence Harrison had poured all her energies into her home and Jane had been brought up in comfort and a certain amount of style.

Florence had seen how hard the other lasses of the village had to work and she was determined her daughter's life would be different. She hoped that in town there would be opportunities to meet a different sort of young man from the lads Jane had grown up with. Perhaps another servant, but a superior servant, of course. Or a shopkeeper who owned one of the smart little shops in Jesmond, or a clerk from Mr Coulson's office. She hoped that, eventually, Jane would see the advantages of such a marriage – if only her daughter could forget her old fascination with William Lawson, good lad though he was.

'Here,' her mother said, 'aren't you going to put your hat on?'

Jane stood before the mirror in the hallstand as she tucked in a stray wisp of hair. 'No, I don't think so. It's a little . . . a little frivolous, don't you think?'

She turned to smile anxiously at her mother. Florence Harrison held the small straw hat in her work-roughened hands and gazed wonderingly at the sprays of tiny artificial blue and white flowers and the matching satin ribbons. 'Yes, pet, I know what you mean.'

Jane turned back to the mirror and adjusted the hyacinth blue satin bow at the neck of her white blouse. The ribbon was the same shade as her skirt and the buttonless jacket, which was cut away to reveal the self-coloured rows of piping on the blouse.

'Gan on, you'll do.' Her mother smiled as she fell into the local way of talking. She didn't do it often as she had always striven to speak a little less broadly than her neighbours. Not because she was a snob – she never thought of herself as superior to the hardworking women of the village – but because she had wanted a better way of life for Jane and she'd believed it was no use paying good money for elocution lessons if she wasn't going to try to set some sort of example herself.

'Right . . . I'll go now. See if there's anything I can do to help.'

Everything looked so normal, Jane thought as she made her way to the Lawsons' cottage. It was still early and the men hadn't returned from the fishing, although it wouldn't be much longer now. Children played in the cobbled lanes and on the boat field on the headland. Cats slept, dogs foraged in the gutters and the gulls, as always, swirled and screeched above the cliffs.

The door of the cottage was open and Jane stood for a moment in the sunlight, her eyes adjusting to the dimness inside before she raised a tentative hand to knock.

'Come in, Jane, hinny,' a woman's voice said softly.

Jane stepped inside and saw that Kate's mother, Nan, was standing at the table rolling pastry.

'Meat pie,' she said and got on with her work.

Jane glanced round the room. So clean and neat, but so very different from her own home. And if she now felt out of place in her mother's modest but attractive parlour, how much more at odds with her expectations of life would a fisherman's cottage be? No . . . much as she loved Kate's brother William, she could never live as a fisherman's wife . . .

A slight sucking sound made her glance towards the bed against the wall. The old woman, Sarah, lay there as usual, her clay pipe moving up and down in her mouth; that was what the sound was. Jane was startled to see that she appeared to be staring at her. Her rheumy old eyes were open and focused instead of half closed. Her face was so wrinkled that there seemed to be no room to harbour an expression, either a smile or a frown.

It was hard to tell what old Sarah was thinking. Did she think about anything now? Perhaps she was simply staring into space, her mind adrift amongst a jumble of memories. But then Jane noticed that the old woman's bony fingers were picking restlessly at the ends of her shawl.

'You've heard, then,' Mrs Lawson said. It was a statement rather than a question.

'Yes. I'm sorry. It's dreadful.'

'Dreadful?' There was a hint of scorn in Kate's mother's voice as if 'dreadful' was too meagre a word to describe the situation.

Jane felt herself flush and she saw the lines of the older woman's face soften. 'Don't mind me, pet. Our Kate's taken it hard.'

'Of course she has.'

For a moment nothing was heard except the slap of the pastry on the tabletop and the rhythmic thump and roll of Nan Lawson's wooden rolling pin. She paused to dust her hands with flour before lifting up the pastry and draping it over the pie dish. 'Kate's on the beach,' she said. 'Will you go to her?' There was a break in her voice. Jane saw that there were tears in her eyes.

'Yes.'

'I canna help her,' the older woman said. 'There's nothing I can say, nothing I can do. But I don't want her to be alone. You're her friend.'

'I'll go,' Jane said. She turned swiftly and hurried out of the cottage.

A few minutes later she stood on Bank Top and stared down in puzzlement. There was a lone figure on the shoreline kneeling down and leaning forward as if washing something in the sea. Jane watched the jerky movements until a sudden toss of the figure's head revealed the red hair. It was Kate. Jane began to hurry. As she sped down the bank she began to call Kate's name, but her friend either didn't hear her or didn't care. To Jane's dismay she saw a wave wash right over Kate but still she didn't stop what she was doing.

Never as fleet of foot as Kate, Jane stumbled as she hurried over the rough sand and shingle and, mindful of the hemline of her skirt, she stopped just short of where the waves washed in. She stared in horror as she watched her friend lean forward again and again and, with both arms outstretched, make scooping motions in the water. What was Kate trying to catch? The waves?

'Kate!' she called. 'Kate, what are you doing?'

Jane lifted her skirt and walked gingerly over the damp sand. She tried not to think of the salt marks the water would leave on her shoes. She was relieved when Kate suddenly sat back on her heels and looked round.

'Jane?' she said. 'What are you doing here?'

Jane was shocked by the other girl's appearance. Kate's glorious hair had escaped all restraint and was hanging down in ragged witch's locks. Damp strands of it were plastered over her face, which held an expression of bewilderment tempered with rage. She didn't seem to care – or perhaps she wasn't aware – that the waves were washing around her, making the folds of her skirt float and lift as they rushed in and then receded.

'Get up,' Jane said. 'You're soaking wet.'

Kate didn't respond. Instead she turned away and looked out to sea, and then made that crazy scooping motion again.

'For heaven's sake, what are you doing?' Jane could barely suppress her irritation – and fright. Had her friend lost her mind? Was she crazed with grief? What should she do? Kate was taking no notice of her but she couldn't just leave her there, kneeling in the water.

She took a step forward and, abandoning any thought of saving her own clothes from getting soaked, she took hold of Kate's

21

shoulders. Kate flinched and then looked up. Jane was shocked by the sheer misery etched in her friend's face. But even more shocked by the tentative smile. What on earth was there to smile about?

'What have you got there, Kate?'

In answer the other girl dropped her head and indicated what she had collected in the folds of her skirt. Jane frowned. Apples? Had Kate been gathering apples from the sea? That was crazy.

'Jos sent them,' Kate said. 'He wanted me to have them. He must have opened the sack and sent them in on the tide.'

All at once it made sense. These were the apples that Jos and Barty had given their lives for. Jane stared down at them in despair. Barely ripe, some of them bruised, most of them clearly mis-shapen windfalls. Jane felt a sharp ache of grief gathering in her throat.

'No, Kate,' she said huskily. 'Jos didn't send them. You know that.'

'Then how . . .'

'The sack has come open of its own accord. The apples have floated free. Now, come along. You can't sit here.'

Kate's expression hardened. In spite of the glittering tears, Jane saw her eyes narrow. She knew that look of old, but she had had plenty of practice in dealing with her friend's wilfulness.

'Look, the men are returning.' She leaned forward and pointed out to sea to where the cobles had begun the familiar race home. 'The beach will be busy soon . . . the fish auction. You don't want people to find you like this. They'll laugh at you.'

'Laugh at me?' Kate sounded shocked but Jane felt no remorse for the lie. For of course no one would laugh. This close community would have only pity and compassion for this poor bereaved girl, but somehow she had to get Kate to get up out of the water. So she had appealed to her pride.

'Yes, laugh. And you don't want folk saying that Jos was better off drowned than married to a madwoman, do you?' For a moment Jane thought she had gone too far. Kate's face blanched and her green eyes grew huge with shock and pain. Heedless of her fine skirt Jane knelt down next to her friend and took hold of her shoulders. 'Come along, Kate,' she said gently. 'You would want Jos to be proud of you, wouldn't you?'

After a long moment Kate nodded and made an indistinct sound in her throat. Jane helped her to her feet but the other girl suddenly stopped and caught at her skirt in an attempt to save the apples.

'No, Kate.' Jane took hold of Kate's hands and stopped her. 'Let them go.'

She helped Kate shake her skirt until all the apples she had gathered fell into the sand-flecked foam and bobbed about with the sea-polished pebbles. Kate stared down at them and when a retreating wave began to take them back to sea she made a moaning noise.

'Hush,' Jane said softly. 'Now come back with me.'

'No – I can't go home.'

'It's all right. You can come to my house. You can stay with me today.'

Suddenly a wave, more forceful than the rest, pulled back and seemed to drag the wet sand away from beneath their feet. Kate stumbled and Jane put her arms about her friend and held her tightly. Then she turned her round and began to lead her away from the shoreline. Never, in all the years they had known each other, had Kate allowed herself to be led by anyone other than Jos. But now, weary with grief, she submitted to Jane's will. They walked up the gentle slope of the beach together hand in hand like the children they had once been.

'My mother thinks you are neglecting yourself.' Richard Adamson stood in the living room of the two-storeyed cottage his forebears had once lived in and glanced apologetically at his cousin, who was visiting from America.

Howard Munro, who was as tall as Richard himself, and whose careless way of dressing did not disguise the fact that his clothes were of first class quality, pushed a lock of fine brown hair back from his expressive face in a gesture which had become familiar. He smiled. 'Why should she think that?'

'Well . . .' Richard gestured helplessly. He wished his mother had not sent him on this errand. Howard was a grown man with a generous allowance from his parents and quite capable of looking after himself. Surely it should concern no one if he chose to subsist on bread and cheese in his artist's garret, as village gossip had it, rather than taking up Grace Adamson's offer of dining with them. 'Well, she promised your mother,' he continued, 'that not only would we let you have this cottage for the duration of your stay but she would also see that you ate regular meals and brought your laundry along to be taken care of at our house.'

Howard looked guiltily at the pile of rumpled linen bundled on the sofa, which also served as his bed. Then he pushed his hair back again and laughed. 'I'm sorry,' he said.

'Sorry?'

'You are a busy man, Richard. You have a fleet to command. You have better things to do than run around on errands like this.'

Now it was Richard's turn to smile. 'You make it sound grand . . . my fleet. They're just trawlers.'

'*Just* trawlers? No, not simple fishing boats, Richard. Your vessels are *steam* trawlers; your family are pioneers who have revolutionized the fishing industry and provided cheap fish in abundance. You've brought added prosperity to the river Tyne.'

Richard stirred uneasily.

'What is it?' Howard asked.

'What you say is true. But in doing so we haven't pleased everybody.'

'Ah, yes. Not everybody likes change. Especially if it affects their livelihood. The local fishermen resent what you're doing.'

'They'll have to adapt. They can't stop progress.'

'No. And now, not only am I taking up your valuable time, I've also angered you.'

'No, not at all.'

'It's kind of you to say so. But how can I make amends?'

The American's smile was so open and engaging that Richard relaxed. 'By putting on your jacket and coming back with me.'

'Now? So early?'

'Yes, now – for a substantial breakfast, designed to tempt a starving artist.'

'I'm hardly starving. I'm just naturally slim.'

'You'll have to convince my mother of that. Then, when I depart to go and command my fleet, you can stay and talk to my mother for a while and, perhaps, write a note to enclose in her letter to your mother. That way both our mothers will be satisfied.'

'Very well. As long as you will honour your promise.'

'Promise?'

'To let me paint your portrait.'

'Ah, you were serious, then.'

'Of course.'

Richard smiled ruefully. 'I'm no oil painting, as they say.'

'On the contrary. Your features may not be classical, but those dark intense looks are compelling.'

24

'Yes . . . well . . . you can paint the picture. But now . . .'

'I'll get my jacket.'

On the way from the simple fisherman's cottage that had become Howard Munro's studio to the large house in the imposing terrace where the Adamsons lived, the two men paused on the bank top and, leaning on the railing, looked out across the bay.

'Look,' Howard said, his voice expressing surprise.

'At what?'

'Out there . . . the fishing boats – the cobles.'

'Well?'

'The men went fishing.'

Richard smiled. 'That's what they do.'

'But the drowning – just yesterday. You heard about it?'

'Ah, yes.'

'Don't they care?'

'Of course they do, men and women alike. But the men must fish and, very soon, the women will come down to the beach and help to land the boats and unload the catch. The buyers will arrive and the auction will begin. They can't afford not to carry on as usual.'

Richard glanced at his cousin uneasily, waiting to be reminded that this was his fault, but Howard seemed to have lost interest in their conversation.

'Marvellous,' he said raptly. 'Just marvellous.'

'What?' Richard asked. He tried to look at the scene with what he imagined was an artist's eye. Perhaps his cousin was visualizing the composition of his next painting. 'Do you mean the cobles? The – er – the red sails against the blue-grey sky and – er – the sea? Is that it?'

Howard smiled distractedly. 'No, not the cobles, although they are quite an impressive sight, racing back to the harbour, cutting through the waves, the gulls streaming in behind them. Perhaps . . . yes, I will. But that wasn't what I meant.'

'What then?'

'The girls.'

Richard turned his head to look at the group of women making their way down the slope that led to the beach, where they would wait for the cobles to come in. Howard saw the direction of his glance. 'No, not them,' he said. 'I mean the two coming up towards us. Look, they're hand in hand. She's magnificent.'

'What? Jane?' Richard recognized the cobbler's daughter. As a child, his forays to the village had been restricted, and he had not formed

25

friendships with the fisherfolk's children. But he had sometimes been trusted to take the family shoes to Mr Harrison for repair, and he had observed Jane since he was a boy and she a mere infant, toddling confidently in and out of her father's workshop, knowing she would not be scolded. And what a beautiful child she had been with her pink and white complexion, her soft angel-fair curls and her dark-fringed blue eyes. Now she was a beautiful woman, he supposed, although he would not have referred to her as 'magnificent'.

'Is that her name? Jane?' Howard asked. He frowned.

'What is it?'

'The name. It doesn't suit her.'

'Why ever not?'

'That magnificent creature? Jane?'

'Magnificent? Little Jane? Of course she's very pretty, beautiful, even, but hardly *magnificent*.'

Howard was grinning. 'No, Richard, I didn't mean the pretty little thing in blue. I meant the other girl: that great tall fisherlass with the lion's mane for hair. Even in those simple clothes she's wonderful. Don't you agree?'

Richard looked at the girl. Perhaps because of those simple clothes, the drab, heavy skirt, the short jacket and the shawl that all the village girls wore, he had not given her a second glance. Jane's bright blue fashionable costume had taken his eye. But now that he did look at the fisherlass, looked at her properly, he saw that Howard was not exaggerating. She was magnificent.

Chapter Three

Both cortèges had left the church and were making for the burial ground on the headland overlooking the mouth of the river. Kate walked behind the first horse-drawn hearse with Jos's family. That morning Matthew had come for her, saying that his mother wished it. The black-plumed horses wound their way along the village streets through a fine mist of rain. Every cottage they passed had the curtains drawn. The heavy clouds hung low over the village and ahead of them the stark outline of the ruined priory looked gaunt and unwelcoming. The moisture had seeped through Kate's clothes to her skin. She could feel it running down the small of her back.

Kate had put on her best black skirt and jacket and pinned her hair back neatly. Her mother had lent her a black lace shawl to cover her head. She walked tall and tried to look dignified although she knew that her eyes were red-rimmed and the lids were swollen. When Matthew had called at the cottage that morning Kate had been weeping with rage as much as sorrow. Her father had announced that he would not be coming to the double funeral and nothing Kate could say would persuade him.

'It's well known I had no respect for the Lintons,' Henry Lawson said. 'I didn't care for the lad when he was alive and I'd be a hypocrite if I went to pray at his graveside.'

'What about Barty, then? Have you no respect for the Lisle family, either?'

'Whisht, lass,' her mother whispered fearfully. 'Divven't anger your da.'

But her father deigned to answer her, putting on his reasonable voice. 'I feel sorry for George Lisle,' he said, 'and that's the truth, but he should never have let his lad get so pally with Jos Linton. He should hev known that no good would come of it.'

'How can you say that? Apart from being a Linton there was nothing wrong with Jos. He worked hard. He helped his family and he had his own coble as well.'

'And no sense of responsibility.' Henry Lawson shook his head. 'Who knows? This might be fate.'

'What do you mean?'

'It's saved you from a bad marriage.'

'How can you talk like that with Jos drowned and my heart broken!' Anguish and anger made her raise her voice and she could feel her mother's fright.

'That's enough!' her father bellowed. His face began to purple. 'Ha'ad yer whisht before I'm angered.'

'But don't you care that people will think less of you?' Kate said. Her father's eyes narrowed and colour suffused his cheeks.

'Now, Kate, don't talk like that to your da,' her mother said anxiously, as William stepped between Kate and her father and tried to lead her away.

It was at that moment that Jos's brother had arrived with the invitation from his mother and Kate had gone with him thankfully. And now she was pleased that her mother and her two brothers were walking immediately behind her. But she found that she couldn't forget her father's words because, in her heart, she knew that there might be some glimmer of truth in them.

She would never forgive her father for seeming to welcome the drowning and yet, much as she loved Jos, she had been worried that his happy-go-lucky nature sometimes made him irresponsible. With his own coble he'd achieved independence from his father and he worked hard. He'd promised Kate that one day soon they would have a cottage of their own and not have to share with his family. Kate had been confident that he could achieve it. And then he'd thrown their future away for a sackful of apples.

At last the procession reached the graveyard, where the headstones seemed to shelter from the elements beneath the dramatic ruins of the ancient priory. The burial plots were only a stone's throw from the sea that had provided Jos and Barty with a living and cut short their young lives. The coffin bearers picked their way along the narrow paths. Generations of seafarers and fishermen were buried here. Many of the headstones bore engravings of ships and anchors and the inscriptions told sad tales of husbands, fathers and sons lost at sea.

The mourners gathered around the newly dug trench awaiting Jos's coffin; he was to be buried first. The dark soil, contrasting so vividly with the bright green sward, gave off the loamy smell of damp earth and Kate felt herself reeling when she glimpsed the writhing bodies of worms amongst the protruding grass roots.

No one spoke. The only sounds were the dull pounding of the rain on the turf and the crash of the waves on the rocks below the headland. The strong clear voice of the Reverend James Wheeler came almost as a shock. 'Ashes to ashes, dust to dust,' he intoned as Jos's coffin was lowered into the ground.

Overcome with horror, Kate let his words fade into the background of her consciousness. She reached into the pocket in her skirt and closed her fingers tightly round the wedding ring that Matthew had given to her that morning, as soon as they had left the Lawsons' cottage. 'My brother would want you to have it,' he'd said.

The sound of the heavy earth hitting the coffin was like a blow to her stomach and she felt a hot surge of nausea rise to her throat. Fighting to swallow the bile, she backed away from the graveside, where the proceedings seemed to become more and more unreal.

She saw one or two faces turn and stare at her but, fortunately, they left her alone. If any kind soul had tried to comfort her she might have broken down and told them that not only was she grieving for Jos and the happy future his foolish action had stolen from her, but she was angry with him too, and fearful. Fearful because he had left her to face the consequences of their loving alone.

The doors of the mission hall were open but Kate, who had avoided her mother's attempts to gather her into the family fold and walked back alone, was reluctant to enter. She did not want to mingle and talk with the mourners because she was acutely aware of her place – or rather lack of it. A sweetheart but not a bride. She was not part of the Linton family and now never would be, yet she had already distanced herself sufficiently from her own family to realize that she would always feel out of place with them.

Mrs Linton had organized the funeral tea along with Kate's own Aunt Meg, who had stepped in to help the widowed George Lisle. Margaret Lawson, her father's elder sister, had never married and often helped out at funerals, weddings and baptisms. Kate had always been fond of her aunt and her kindly presence was reassuring. Eventually Aunt Meg saw Kate hovering in the doorway and came to get her.

'I could do with a hand,' she said gently.

'But—'

'Mary Linton's useless with grief. I've telt her to sit down with her man.'

'Of course.'

Kate was aware of pitying looks as she followed her aunt through the hall past the long trestle tables laden with food. Once in the small kitchen she was glad to busy herself with washing and drying dishes, only half concentrating on anything her aunt said until the moment Meg took hold of her arm and said, 'Kate, I asked you to take those sandwiches in a good ten minutes ago.'

'Oh . . .' Kate turned from the sink and frowned. 'Sandwiches?'

'Yes. That plate there.' The older woman nodded towards the table where a meat server was piled high with ham and pease-pudding sandwiches. 'You can take them round, show yourself, and then, if there's any left, put the plate on the table.'

'But—'

'You've hidden away in here long enough, pet. You have to show your respect. I know it will be hard. Just this once, then you can come back here.'

'Please, Aunt Meg, don't make me.'

Her aunt sighed and shook her head. 'I know how you must feel, lass; as if no one could ever understand what you're going through. But I do.'

'Do you?'

'Why shouldn't I? I'm no stranger to grief, you know. Why do you think I never married?'

'I . . .' Kate stared at her aunt, disconcerted and momentarily shaken out of her self-pitying mood.

'I didn't always look like this, you know. I was once as bonny as you are, if I say it myself, and I had more than my share of chances. But I'd had a lad that was just as handsome as your Jos, and I'd lost him, just as you have. Only it wasn't a bit of daft carry-on that took him – he was drowned in a storm. They never got back to the harbour in time.'

'Aunt Meg . . . don't!' Kate felt her knees buckling and her aunt hurried to help ease her down onto a chair.

'I'm sorry, Kate. I shouldn't hev said that about the daft carry-on. But it has to be said that Jos might hev brought it on himself – and poor Barty, too – while many another good lad is lost while they're working hard for their families. But what happened isn't your fault. Here, dry your eyes.' The older woman took a clean man-sized handkerchief out of the pocket in her apron and handed it to Kate. 'It's a pity your friend Jane couldn't hev come today. You'd have had someone your own age.'

'They wouldn't let her have the time off.'

'Hard-hearted!'

'No, that's the way it is in those big houses. Jos wasn't a relative of hers, after all.'

'I suppose so. Now, how are you feeling?' Her aunt nodded towards the plate of sandwiches. 'I would take them in meself, pet, but I'm weary. I wouldn't mind sitting awhile.'

Kate looked at her aunt properly and saw that the elderly woman did indeed look tired. Her fading auburn hair had escaped from its neat bun and was hanging down her back. Her eyes looked puffy and her face was drawn.

'Of course. I'm sorry. I'll take these in and anything else that's ready.'

'There's nowt else. As I say, take these and then come back and we'll hev a bit to eat together in here.' Aunt Meg indicated two plates piled high with sandwiches, sausage rolls and a slice or two of plain cake.

'I'm not hungry.'

But even as she said it Kate knew that wasn't true. She was hungry. She was young and healthy and, in spite of her overwhelming grief, the fresh air on the headland and the walk there and back had given her an appetite. She was glad that her aunt was giving her the opportunity to eat in here, away from the public gaze. She had an idea that people would be expecting her to be too grief-stricken to eat. It puzzled her that she wasn't.

Before Kate had even left the kitchen her aunt had dragged another chair up to the table and sunk down. She poured a cup of tea and then reached into the pocket of her pinafore and pulled out a small flask. Kate paused in the doorway and watched as the older woman unscrewed the cap of the flask and tipped a generous measure of spirits into her tea. Aunt Meg looked up and smiled.

'Divven't frown, lass. Just a little gin to buck me up a bit. You can't say I don't deserve it. Now get away with you.'

Kate forced herself to smile gravely at the guests as she moved around the hall. Most of them murmured sympathetically that they were sorry for her loss. She realized that her aunt had been right to encourage her to do this. Her mother and her elder brother, William, looked pleased with her. Nan nodded towards where Thomas was sitting with some of the younger men round the fire burning in the big iron range.

'You can tell that lot not to hog the fire. Give some of the old folk a chance to warm their bones.'

'I will.'

Kate was beginning to feel chilled, as much from low spirits as because of her rain-damp clothing. She felt herself drawn towards the warmth of the fire where her twin brother sat with Matthew Linton and some of the younger men. She noticed that they were sitting in a tight group with their heads together, talking earnestly. They were too engrossed in their conversation to hear her coming. She was just about to call out to Thomas when something she heard shocked her into stillness.

'Jos said we should settle for the bastard,' Thomas said quietly, but the fury in his voice gave his words clarity.

'Jos said?' someone asked.

'Aye. Now that he's gone we mustn't forget.' She couldn't make out who had said that but the others were nodding in agreement. And they were clearly agitated.

'We must act together . . .'

'Show Adamson we won't be beat . . .'

'Sink the bastard . . .'

Kate heard further snatches of the conversation but then the cry of a child further down the hall made one of the men look round. He saw Kate, coughed and sat back. She had no idea how he had managed to convey that they were no longer alone but suddenly the tone and the content of the conversation changed. Matthew seemed to be telling the others about a strange and ugly fish he'd once caught. He'd taken it to the College of Science in Newcastle but nobody knew what it was. It was there still, pickled in a jar.

Suddenly the air of conspiracy had dissipated. *Conspirators?* Is that what they had looked like, Kate wondered? What in God's name had they been talking about? And if there was a conspiracy, what had Jos had to do with it? Good-natured, easy-going Jos. He'd shared everything with her, hadn't he? And yet now it seemed there had been secrets . . .

'Are those for us, Kate?' Thomas stood up and came towards her. 'Here, let me take them.' He reached for the sandwiches. 'Do you want to sit by the fire for a while? You look cold. Shall I get you a chair?'

'No, it's all right. The kitchen's warm and Aunt Meg has a plate waiting for me.'

32

'Are you sure?'

'Yes. I'd rather.'

Thomas made no further attempt to persuade her, and although everyone in the group smiled sympathetically at her, she had the impression that they were glad she had chosen not to join them. She thought her brother looked uncomfortable. He shot her a glance that she could only interpret as guilty before she turned and left them.

Thomas will tell me what this is about, she thought as she returned to the kitchen. Kate was the elder twin, and even though it was only by a few minutes she had always taken the lead. When they were children she had been the adventurous one who had as often as not led her more docile brother into trouble. As they grew she had still taken the lead. Brighter than he was, she had often helped him at school and now they were grown Thomas still came to her for advice.

That was why this was so puzzling. Thomas, like Jos, had never hidden any secrets from her. She decided she would ask her brother outright what the group by the fire had been talking about. She was confident that he would tell her.

Apart from Kate and her aunt, the Lintons were the last to leave. James and Mary Linton along with their surviving son, Matthew, stood together and acknowledged the murmured condolences of the departing guests. There was dignity in the way they held themselves but Kate, watching from the kitchen doorway, saw that Mary Linton was being supported by both her husband and her son. If they had removed their arms she would surely have fallen to the floor.

And then, when everybody had gone, they stood there alone, looking as if they weren't quite sure what to do next. Kate approached them. All three of them looked at her but they didn't speak.

'I . . . I'll come and see you, Mrs Linton . . . perhaps tomorrow,' Kate said.

'No. Don't.'

Kate's eyes widened. 'But why not? I don't understand.'

'Every time I look at you I'll remember. I'll remember the wedding we planned. The happiness. I just couldn't bear it.'

Mary Linton turned towards her husband and he put his arm round her and led her away. Matthew lingered. He looked at Kate helplessly. 'I'm sorry,' he said. 'She's taken it badly. Try to understand.' He left her without a backward glance and the door swung shut behind him.

Aunt Meg moved quietly about the kitchen. Kate stood alone in the hall as the shadows lengthened. It seemed she had lost not only Jos but the affection and companionship of his mother, too. She couldn't remember a time when she had ever felt so hurt and alone.

The high tide reached the mouth of the cave before retreating and Kate stepped over the usual jumble of seaweed tangled up with bits of driftwood. She rested her hands on the rough sandstone walls as she ventured further inside. The passage narrowed and the pale sand sloped upwards so that gradually there was less headroom. Eventually she came to the familiar outcrop of rock that formed a low platform wide enough to sit on. This had been their place.

When they'd been children they had gathered here, the four of them. Kate, Thomas, Jos and Jane. Even though the children of the village had to help their parents with tasks such as baiting the lines and spreading the nets to dry, there was sometimes a spare hour or two for play. They would gather here, bringing bread and cheese, a piece of cake (Jane usually brought that), a bottle of water or lemonade (Jane again), and candles and matches.

Jos had told them that the caves had once been used by smugglers and that, somewhere, there was a secret passage that led underground as far as the old priory where the monks had lived. But, although Kate and the two boys must have spent hours searching for it, scrambling over tumbled rocks and squeezing into narrow spaces until Jane called out to them in fright to come back, they had never found it.

It was years since the four of them had played here together but their names had remained, carved into the sandstone walls. As Kate's eyes grew accustomed to the dimness she ran her fingers along the uneven surface until she found the deeply grooved markings. She stared at them.

There it was, the heart with the names inside. Jos and Kate. Jos had carved them into the sandstone with the help of a nail and piece of rock. He'd told her that the heart and the names would be there for ever; that people in centuries to come would know that Kate and Jos had been sweethearts.

'Centuries?' Kate had questioned.

'Yes. Look.' Jos held the flickering candle closer to the wall of the cave and moved it backwards and forwards until he found the other markings. They were very faint, and although she peered at them intently she couldn't make them out.

'It's a list of names,' Jos had asserted.

'Are you sure?'

'Yes, old names. Names that aren't used any more. Many years ago – oh, a long, long time ago – folk used to live in these caves.'

'Live here?'

'Yes. You can tell by those soot stains. They were made by the smoke from fires.'

'Ugh! Fancy living here,' Jane had interrupted. 'How . . . how *primitive*!' And they had all laughed at the way Jane had wrinkled her nose.

The next time they had met in the cave Jane had found something else to make her curl her lip. Thomas had followed Jos's example and carved a shaky heart shape, and inside he had put his name and Jane's. He had not been so expert as Jos and the marks were mere scratches, but they were clear enough and Jane was cross.

'You had no right to do that,' she had told him. 'I don't want people to see my name along with yours.' And she'd picked up a rough stone and scratched away vigorously until the words were almost obscured. Then she'd flung the stone down and flounced off.

Even then Kate knew why Jane didn't favour Thomas. It was because she had set her young heart on Kate's elder brother William, who, in those days, had not taken the younger child at all seriously. Poor Jane had always contrived to be there when William was around, looking up at him as though he were a hero in a romantic story book.

Eventually Jane's devotion had been rewarded. One day William had looked at her and seen a beautiful young woman rather than a pretty child. He had fallen in love with her. Kate knew of their courtship although, for reasons best known to Jane, they had tried to be discreet.

But in those happy childhood days Thomas had never guessed that his elder brother was Jane's favourite and Kate hadn't had the heart to point out to him that he was wasting his young passion. Poor Thomas, how hurt and embarrassed he had been that day when Jane had spurned him by scratching out their names. Kate remembered how her twin had gone off in the sulks for the rest of the day, leaving her and Jos alone. They had looked at each other and laughed, then settled down to eat the bits of food they had brought. And talked. And talked.

An ache came to Kate's throat when she remembered how she and Jos had always had so much to talk about, even when they'd been children. And how he respected her opinions, not like some of the lads who treated the girls as though they were a lesser form of human being.

So why hadn't he told her what he and the other lads had been planning?

Kate remembered the disturbing snatches of conversation she had overheard at the funeral tea the day before. She had not yet had the chance to question Thomas about the incident. But she would. Anything that Jos had been involved in was important to her. Surely Thomas would understand that and put her mind at rest.

She realized that her head was aching. She had not been able to sleep last night. Her bed was a low truckle that during the day was pushed under the bed her mother and old Sarah shared. At night Kate pulled it out and eased it towards the hearth. Often she would stare into the flames and, on cold wintry nights, would be comforted by the glow and the warmth while the wind howled round the cottage and rattled the windows.

Last night she hadn't been able to find comfort in the pictures formed by the burning coals. She had finally stopped crying but she couldn't ease the ache of sorrow from her throat. She thought of the years to come. Would she be like Aunt Meg and never marry? Kate had believed her aunt when she'd told her that she'd had more than one chance to wed someone else but she'd never been able to give her heart again. Aunt Meg had remained single by choice. But Kate knew that she herself might not have any choice. There was a reason why no other man might ever want her now.

Kate sank down on to the rocky ledge and leaned back to rest against the wall of the cave. She remembered the day that Jane had flounced off and Thomas had skulked away not long after. He'd waited awhile to make it quite clear he wasn't running after Jane. And, after he'd gone, although Jos had smiled he hadn't made fun of Thomas, as many another lad might have done. He'd said, 'He doesn't stand a chance with pretty little Jane, does he?'

She knew what he meant but, prickling a little at his description of Jane, Kate had asked, 'Why not?'

'Because she's in love with William.'

Kate had been surprised. 'In love? But she's only a bairn, not yet twelve years old.'

'Makes no difference. She's given him her heart – not that he's noticed.' Jos had grinned. 'And, anyway, we're just bairns, too, and you're in love with me, aren't you?'

'Jos, don't!'

'Don't what?'

'Talk like that.'

'Why not? It's true. You and me are sweethearts, Kate. Always will be. And when we grow up we'll be married. That's why I carved our names in this heart.' He'd turned to the wall of the cave and run his fingers over the carving. 'This will last for ever. Even after we're dead and gone people will see our names carved here and know that we were sweethearts.'

Kate could hear his voice now, whispering through the dimness. And her own voice answering him, 'I don't like to think about that, Jos. Us being dead and gone.'

'Don't worry,' he'd said, 'that won't be for a very long time yet.'

But Jos had been wrong – at least as far as he was concerned. He had gone and left her and she would have to face the years alone. Kate closed her eyes as sorrow and weariness overcame her. She could hear the distant cries of the gulls and the never-ending rhythm of the waves advancing and retreating. It was a sound that she'd grown up with. The sound of the sea. Today it was calm and the song it sang was almost like a lullaby. She leaned back and was about to close her eyes when she became aware of a shadow moving on the wall of the cave.

She sat up quickly and turned towards the entrance. A man was standing there. With his back to the light she could not see his face clearly, but from the shape of the silhouette she knew he was not a fisherman. His clothes were well cut and seemed to hug his slender frame. He was tall enough to have to duck his head almost as soon as he stepped inside the cave.

'Are you all right?' he asked, and his speech revealed him to be a stranger.

'Yes, thank you, but why do you ask?'

Kate rose to her feet and immediately felt at a disadvantage because she had to stoop. She moved forward until she could stand upright and found herself closer to the stranger than she would have liked. He must have sensed her unease because he moved back into the sunlight.

'I beg your pardon. I did not mean to pry,' he said. 'But I saw you enter the cave some time ago and . . . you did not come out, so—'

'You were watching me?' Kate asked sharply.

'Only because I was concerned. I mean, I know what happened.'

'What happened?'

'Your sweetheart . . . the funeral . . . I'm sorry.'

37

'Sorry?'

'I mean, I am sorry for your loss.'

During this exchange Kate had realized who he was. This must be Howard Munro, the American artist, who had taken the two-storeyed cottage overlooking the bay. He called the upper room his 'studio', apparently, and, although he bought provisions at the village shop, he was often invited to the Adamsons' grand house for his meals. It was said he was a relative of theirs.

'That's . . . that's kind of you.' She was not sure how to respond to such formal speech but she was encouraged by the gentleness of his tone and his concerned expression.

And then he suddenly seemed to be as unsure as she was. 'Well,' he said, 'if you are sure that you are all right, I should go.'

'Yes. No. Wait!'

The American had already taken a few steps away but he stopped and turned to look at her. 'What is it?'

'Thank you. If you hadn't come when you did I might have fallen asleep.'

He looked at her questioningly.

'The tide's coming in.'

'I know that,' he said.

'But you needn't have worried,' Kate said. 'At this time of year the water rarely reaches more than halfway into the cave. The worst that could have happened was that I would have been trapped here for a while. I would have been cold and wet and hungry.' She paused. 'But nothing worse.'

'If you say so.' His expression was unreadable.

Kate smiled and then continued softly, 'When we were children we used to play here, and once Jos—'

'Your sweetheart?'

'Yes. Jos dared my brother Thomas to stay there with him,' she turned to point to the rocky outcrop, 'there on the ledge, while the tide came in. He said they wouldn't be there long until it turned and he had food and candles. He said it would be an adventure. But Thomas wouldn't.'

'And Jos?'

'Oh, yes.' Kate laughed. 'Jos stayed. And got a hiding from his father for his trouble. But he didn't care. He'd had his adventure.' She was quiet for a moment and then she smiled sadly at the American. 'So you see, Mr Munro—'

'Howard, please.'

'So you see, if I had woken up and found the tide had come in I would have been uncomfortable but safe.'

'But how was I to know that? I might have thought it necessary to wade in and rescue you – like a hero in a story book. And then we both would have been cold and wet – and miserable as well, no doubt.'

He was smiling broadly and Kate realized how attractive he was.

If this had been any other young man – any lad from the village – she might have thought he was flirting with her. But she had never met anyone quite like Howard Munro before. Perhaps people behaved like this where he came from. She found herself intrigued.

'I think you're teasing me,' she said.

He laughed. 'A little. But now if you look behind me you'll see that the waves really are advancing, so perhaps you would let me escort you back to the village.'

Kate nodded an agreement. What a strange thing to have happened, she thought. She glanced at the man striding beside her and wondered if they would meet again.

They didn't speak as they made their way to the sloping path that led up to Bank Top. Tall though he was, Howard found himself having to lengthen his stride to keep up with the long-limbed fisherlass. He was immediately aware of her natural grace, although he sensed that his mother would not approve of the way the girl strode more like a man than a 'lady'. He allowed himself a brief flight of fancy and imagined what it would be like to take this girl back to Boston with him. To dress her in silks and satins and present her to polite society. Surely her beauty and honesty would win all hearts. It would be an interesting experiment.

He saw that their progress did not go unnoticed. Two small lads squatting at the end of the southern breakwater glanced across and then went on with their fishing. A group of men loading lobster pots into their cobles also looked up and stared for a little longer than the lads had done. Howard suddenly felt out of his depth. He wondered if they would disapprove of his approaching Kate like this.

At home in America there were rigid rules of etiquette in the society to which his family belonged. These fisherfolk might also have conventions which should be observed. He glanced at the young woman now hurrying up the slope. She seemed unaware of the attention they had attracted. Or perhaps she had noticed and didn't care. Howard received the impression that this girl was confident enough to make her own rules. Even in her present state of unhappiness he sensed she had a life force that would not be quenched. He knew he must see her again, and more than ever he wanted to paint her portrait. But now was not the time to ask her.

When they reached Bank Top they parted. 'I hope to meet you again,' he said and wondered how she would interpret his words. But she seemed to be only half listening.

'Goodbye, and thank you,' she said.

'Why do you thank me?'

'For caring what happened to me.' Her smile did not reach her eyes. She turned and hurried purposefully away. It was as if she had suddenly remembered something she had to do.

Thomas was sitting on an old chair in the back yard of the cottage with a broken lobster pot over his knees. Kate stood in the doorway and watched as he expertly repaired the gash in the pot's netting. The yard was cluttered with old nets, two barrels for salting herring and a barrow with one of its wheels missing. Now and then William made some effort to get things shipshape but their father would tell him to leave things be. He claimed he knew where everything was, and maybe the nets *were* beyond mending, but they might come in useful for something or other.

Her brother was bent over the lobster pot so that she could only see the top of his head as he concentrated on his task. Kate hesitated. She was loath to disturb his concentration but now, the first time she had found him on his own since the funeral tea the day before, seemed a good time to question him.

Suddenly he looked up as if some extra sense had warned him of her presence. He smiled. 'How long hev you been standing there?' he asked.

'Not long.'

'What is it?' Thomas's smile faded. He must have sensed her agitation.

'I have to ask you something.'

He looked genuinely puzzled. 'Ask away.'

'What were you talking about yesterday – you and the other lads, when you were sitting by the fire in the mission hall?'

She was sure she saw his eyes widen with consternation before he shrugged and said, 'I can't remember.' He looked uneasy.

'I don't believe you. You were planning something.'

40

He tried to smile but it came over as a grimace of embarrassment. 'No, Kate, there was nothing like that.' They stared at each other and Thomas reddened. 'We were talking about some of the strange fish we've caught from time to time – and how the teachers at the College of Science like to pickle them and put them on display.'

'Yes, I heard that. But that was what you meant me to hear when you realized I was there. But I heard other things before that. Something about Adamson's trawlers – about not being beat.'

Thomas began to shake his head. 'You're mistaken—'

'Don't lie to me!' Kate felt a surge of anger. 'You were planning something. You said you must act together and that you mustn't forget what Jos had said.'

'And what was that?' Thomas said quietly.

'That you had to settle for the bastard. That's what I heard and it's no use denying it. You've got some kind of plan to cause trouble for Mr Adamson, haven't you?'

Thomas stood up slowly and hoisted the lobster pot on to the roof of the coalhouse where several others were stored. The action gave him time to consider his reply and Kate clenched her fists impatiently. He made a show of checking to see that the pot was stowed properly and then turned to face her, but he couldn't meet her eyes. Kate had never seen her brother look so perplexed.

Finally he said, 'You know well enough how bad the herring fishing's been lately.'

'Everyone knows that.'

'Some men have been forced to lay up their cobles and seek work crewing colliers out of Shields.'

'Yes. The coal ships.'

'Not long back a canny herring season would see us through the winter, but Adamson's steam trawlers have put an end to that.'

'Thomas, the steam trawlers won't go away. It's . . . it's progress, I suppose.'

'But, don't you see, the trawls on his damn boats take more than a man's fair share. He'll finish it for everybody.'

'I know, but it's not just Adamson's trawlers, is it? What about the Scottish boats?'

'Aye, and damn them. I'm sure Jos would hev had a plan to fettle them as well! But we were going to start with Adamson. He's supposed to be one of our own! Why, just a generation or two back the Adamsons were plain inshore fishermen and they lived in the village like the rest of us. Now look at them – living in that grand house and prospering while the rest of us scrape a living!'

'Thomas,' Kate said gently, 'that's hard to swallow, I know it is, but the old days are over. Don't you think we might all have to change?'

Her brother's face flushed. 'I'm glad Jos can't hear you talking like that. He'd be ashamed of you!'

'I understand why you're upset—' she began.

'Upset!'

'No, listen to me. I don't want to quarrel with you. Really, I don't. I just want to know what Jos was planning to do.'

'Why?'

'Because I have a right to know. Jos and I were going to be married. Don't you think he would have told me once we were man and wife?'

Thomas looked troubled. 'I'm not so sure.'

'Of course he would! You know how close we were. You know he didn't treat me like the other lads treat their womenfolk. We always discussed everything – we made all our plans together.'

'That's true.'

'Well then, I'm sure that now . . . now he can't tell me himself, he would have wanted you to tell me.'

'I've telt you. Jos said Adamson had to be stopped.'

'But how?'

'I've said enough, Kate. This isn't women's work.'

'Oh, for goodness' sake!'

'And it's no use you getting into a paddy. That's how you get your own way, losing your temper with folk, isn't it?'

'No!' Kate was stung to hear her brother criticize her.

'Yes, it is. You might not realize it, but you can fair frighten folk when yer bonny green eyes blaze like that.' Thomas was smiling now and Kate could see that she'd lost the battle. 'And I'm not going to let you get your own way this time.'

'This time?'

'Aye, as you have done ever since we were little bairns. I might be the lad but you've been the leader. But not any more. You'll just hev to believe me that Jos was right and what we're doing is for the best.' He raised his chin and stared at her but when he saw the way she was clenching her fists he looked down at the ground. 'Anyway, I've got to see Matthew now, so if you'll—'

'Wait a moment.'

'What now?'

42

'Does William know?'

'No. And you're not to tell him.'

'That's easy – I still don't know what this . . . this plan is, do I?'

'That's right. And you're not to bother William. Jos didn't want him involved. So if you respect Jos's memory, keep quiet and forget you heard anything.'

'I wish I hadn't!'

Kate stepped aside and Thomas went out into the lane without looking at her. She watched him go and then turned and crossed the yard, but she stopped at the open doorway. Inside the cottage she could hear her parents' voices. She couldn't make out what they were saying but her father's tone was harsh and, as usual, her mother's was conciliatory. It had always been this way. Never mind that what Henry Lawson said when he was in one of these moods was often nonsense, Nan would pretend to agree just to keep the peace and avoid a violent outburst.

Kate sat down on the chair that her brother had just vacated. She had believed that she was going to escape from scenes like this; that a new and happier life was about to begin in the Lintons' home. She leaned back against the wall of the cottage and closed her eyes. She was vexed and weary. She'd learned nothing from the conversation with Thomas and she realized that, for once, she wasn't going to get her own way. Her brother would tell her nothing.

She wished, now, that she hadn't heard one word of whatever it was they'd been plotting at the funeral tea. Ignorance would have been better than knowing that the man she was grieving for had been planning something that she suspected was unlawful and possibly dangerous. But she decided to let it go. Whatever they were going to do no longer involved Jos. He was beyond harm. Her brother Thomas would have to look out for himself.

Chapter Four

Kate would have liked to sit for a while and take pleasure in the warmth of the sun. How agreeable it would be to relax and let the summer heat soothe her weary bones. But through the open door of the cottage she could hear her father's voice rising in a crescendo of anger and her mother's responses sounding ever more conciliatory. Should she go inside so that her mother would not have to face him alone, or would her presence only aggravate him further?

What she heard next made her leap to her feet. She stood there, shaking, as her father burst out of the back door. He glanced at her balefully before he crossed the yard and stormed off down the lane. Kate wanted to rush in to her mother. She had heard her cry of pain, but she found that her heart was pounding. She had risen too swiftly. She turned and grasped the back of the chair, letting her head drop until the surge of her own blood subsided.

Then she went into the cottage. Her great-grandmother was sitting bolt upright on the bed mouthing barely articulate sounds. When she saw Kate, Sarah clutched her shawl tightly with one hand and with the other she pointed towards the floor where Nan was struggling to rise.

'Wait, I'll help you.' Kate knelt down and grasped her mother's arms. The two of them rose together. When they were standing Kate searched her mother's face. There was a red mark under one eye. 'He punched you.'

'Aye. But go and settle Sarah. Tell her I'm fine.'

Kate was reluctant to leave her mother, but her great-grandmother had started whimpering like a frightened child. Kate went over to the bed and took hold of Sarah's hands, little claw-like things with painfully thin fingers. They were trembling. Kate held them in her own and whispered soothingly that everything was all right, until, eventually, the old woman settled back amongst her pillows. Kate pulled the blanket up over her lap and went back to her mother, who had turned to lean with both hands on the table. Kate was aware that the old woman was following her movements with watery eyes. As they were always rheumy it was hard to tell whether she was crying.

'What was it this time?' Kate asked.

Nan Lawson looked over her shoulder at her and shook her head, wincing at the movement. 'Yer da's angered with William and Thomas.'

Kate was surprised. If her mother had told her that her father had found another reason to be dissatisfied with Kate's own behaviour that would have been nothing new. But since her brothers had grown to young manhood, Henry Lawson had settled into an uneasy truce with them. He needed his sons to crew the coble and he sensed that they were not in as much awe of him as they used to be.

'My brothers? What have they done? And why blame you?'

Her mother pushed herself away from the table and turned to face Kate. 'I might as well tell you, he told them not to go to the funeral yesterday. He thinks it's my fault they defied him.'

'Why your fault? Doesn't he think they've got minds of their own?'

'Apparently not. He thinks I encouraged them because . . . because . . .'

'What are you trying to say?'

'Because of you. He thinks I'm too soft with you and that I let you get all your own way.'

'I see.' Kate reflected fleetingly that this was twice today that a member of her family had suggested that she got her own way. It made her uncomfortable to think that this caused problems for her mother. 'Oh, Ma, will it ever change?'

Her mother managed a smile. 'You or your father, do you mean?' Then the smile faded when she heard Kate's suppressed sob. 'If you mean your father, no, Henry will never change.'

'I thought it might be better for you once I was married. Once I'd left home. And now . . . now . . .'

'Don't torment yourself, pet. Once you'd gone he'd hev found something else to displease him. Look at today – he's turning on William and Thomas.'

'But only because he thinks they came to the funeral to please me.' The two women stared at each other in despair. 'Go and sit by the fire,' Kate said. 'I'll make a cup of tea.'

'Aye, pet. We'll sit for a while.'

When her mother started to walk away from her Kate noticed

something lying on the floor. It was her father's tobacco pouch. She stooped to pick it up and place it on the table and that same feeling of dizziness overcame her. I need sleep, she thought.

The kettle was on the hob. Her mother used the poker to push it further towards the burning coals. It began to steam. 'Leave it,' Kate said. 'Sit down. I'll do everything. But first I'll get you a wet rag to hold to that eye.'

Kate crossed to the sink and stooped to move aside the flowered curtain strung on a wire below the bench. She took one of the clean rags that her mother stored on the shelf there and then rose to turn on the tap. As the cold water gushed into the sink it splashed onto her face and she realized how hot she felt; not burning heat, just warm and clammy. The feeling of nausea returned and she put her hands on the cool edge of the stone sink and leaned forward, eyes closed, to steady herself. She was still clutching the rag and she had some idea of holding it under the tap and using it to cool her own brow when, without warning, she felt her stomach heave.

'Kate, what's the matter?' she heard her mother ask, but she couldn't answer as she found herself emptying the contents of her meagre breakfast into the sink. When the spasm was over she tried to right herself, but she felt her knees give way. Then, before she could sink to the floor, her mother's arms came round her. Gratefully Kate leaned back against Nan.

'Oh, Kate, me bairn,' she heard her mother groan. 'What hev you done?'

Her mother led her to a chair and made her sit down. Kate sat miserably clutching the damp rag and twisting it round and round while her mother made the tea. Nan placed the teapot and the cups on the table, but before she sat down herself she busied herself mixing something in a bowl. 'Lard and vinegar,' she said, although Kate hadn't asked. 'Smells nasty but if I smear it on me cheek it might stop the bruising.'

She put the bowl on the table and, avoiding Kate's eyes, she began to dab the foul-smelling concoction on her face.

'I'm sorry, Ma,' Kate whispered.

'Tell me what I suspect isn't true,' her mother said. 'Tell me that you're just upset and weary.'

'I wish I could.' And then, as her mother poured the tea and pushed a cup across the table towards her, she whispered, 'I was supposed to be doing that.'

'Aye, you were.' Her mother's voice seemed devoid of all tenderness and Kate felt a stab of anguish.

'I'm sorry,' she whispered again, and this time she wasn't talking about Nan's bruised face, 'but I thought you would never have to know.'

'Are you far gone?'

'I've only just missed.'

'Then you'd probably have got away with it. Did Jos know?'

'No. Oh, poor Jos . . .'

'*Poor* Jos? What do you mean, *poor* Jos? He should hev behaved himself till you were wed.'

'I know. But I'm to blame as well, aren't I? He didn't force me.'

'Kate . . .' Her mother glanced across at the old woman but Sarah had closed her eyes and seemed to be sleeping.

'No, listen, Mother. I knew the risk we were taking. But I loved Jos so and the nearer it got to the wedding the more persuasive he became. He made me feel I was being cruel to deny him. Oh, please don't look at me like that. I know it was wrong.'

'I divven't know about wrong – although the minister would say so. No, what you did was plain daft. Now look at the trouble you're in.'

'But we didn't know this was going to happen, did we? And Jos said that we loved each other, so what we did wasn't a sin.'

'There you are! And you're trying to tell me he wasn't to blame!'

'Ma, please stop. It's done. I can't change things, and I said poor Jos because I wasn't sure, so I didn't tell him, but if I had told him he'd have been happy.'

'Happy!'

'Yes, of course he would. That's what we get married for, isn't it? To have children? And now my poor Jos is drowned and he never knew that he was going to be a father. Oh, Ma, I can't bear it!'

For a moment neither of them spoke. In the hearth the wet coal hissed and spat. Her mother spoke without looking at her. 'I love you, Kate,' she said. 'I love all me bairns but, God forgive me, you've been special, with your bonny looks and your bold ways.'

'I know you've always stood up for me,' Kate said, 'and I'm grateful.'

Her mother sighed. 'But I don't know how I can help you this time.' She was silent for a moment and then she said, 'I suppose you're sure of it?'

'I've never missed before. It's always come on to the day.'

Her mother sighed resignedly. 'How are we going to tell your father?'

47

The two women stared at each other. 'Does he have to know?' Kate's voice was hardly more than a whisper.

Her mother didn't answer at once and Kate frowned as she saw the older woman's expression change and suddenly become more guarded. Nan Lawson was shaking her head very slightly, her lips drawn together in a thin line and her eyes staring at a point behind Kate and above her head. Kate realized what this meant at the same moment that a hand came forward to take up the tobacco pouch from the table. Her father had returned.

She sensed rather than saw her father's meticulous movements as he filled his pipe. She could hear his breathing and smell the ale on his breath. Her mother remained sitting bolt upright and staring at Henry like a trapped animal.

'Well then,' he said eventually, and he strolled over to the fire. He took a spill from the container on the mantelpiece and leaned over to light it. Then he took his time lighting his pipe. Kate realized how much she hated the sucking noises he made. While he was occupied Kate's mother left her seat and came to stand beside her daughter. Once the pipe was drawing to his satisfaction Henry turned to stare at them.

'Well, then,' he continued as if there'd been no interruption. 'What is it Kate doesn't want to tell me?'

'It's nothing, Henry,' Nan said.

'Let the lass speak for herself.'

Kate felt her mother's hands on her shoulders. She reached up and pressed them before rising to face her father. 'I'm with child, Father.'

The words seemed to paralyse him. He removed the pipe from his mouth and clasped the bowl in his right hand. His left hand still held the spill. The end was smoking, Kate noticed. Henry stared at it as if it had offended him and then turned and hurled it into the fire. He turned back to face Kate and she blanched at the barely restrained anger of his expression.

'Jos Linton's bairn, is it?' He almost spat the words at her.

Kate felt her own fury flare. 'Of course! Whose else would it be?'

Taken aback by her defiant attitude, it seemed, Henry turned his anger on his wife. 'And you think that's of no consequence, do you?'

'What do you mean?' Nan asked.

'I asked you what it was Kate didn't want to tell me and you said it was nothing. You lying bitch.' Henry hadn't raised his voice but that made it all the more frightening. 'The lass is carrying Jos Linton's bastard and you think that's nothing, do you?'

Kate felt her mother begin to shiver and she risked a swift glance. Nan was terrified and clearly wished that she could be anywhere but here in her own cottage, facing her husband across the table.

'It's not my mother's fault,' Kate burst out and her father jabbed the hand holding his pipe towards her. Kate saw the smoke swirl and a few small fragments of burning tobacco fly into the air.

'Hold your tongue,' he said, still in that quiet menacing tone. 'Your words count for nothing here.' Kate was glad of the table that lay between them when her father moved forward. 'And furthermore, there's no room for you in this house.'

It must have taken all her mother's courage to say, 'But Henry, Kate is our daughter.'

'Mebbe so,' he said, 'but I'll not raise a bastard in this house. Especially not when Jos Linton is responsible. The Lintons have no place in this village. James Linton is a thief—'

'No,' Kate cried. 'How can you say that!'

'Because it's true. There's no other way to describe a man who steals other folk's livings from them. James Linton should get himself back to Burnmoor where he belongs and take that wife of his, a poacher's daughter—'

'You don't know that!'

'Kate!' her mother hissed. 'Be quiet. Let him speak.'

'As I said, a poacher's daughter who can't bait a hook to save her life.'

'And Matthew?' Kate asked, ignoring her mother who was tugging on her sleeve. 'Matthew and Jos were born here.'

'Makes no difference. Interlopers all. No real fisherman would hev behaved the way Jos did. Risking his life for a few green apples. And what's more he took Barty with him. You can't tell me the lad would hev acted so daft it he hadn't been egged on by Jos Linton.'

Kate would have liked to say that Barty was old enough to make his own decisions but she knew that what her father said was probably true. Often when they'd been bairns Jos had led them into pranks that even high-spirited Kate had balked at. The remembrance made her feel even more wretched.

'I see you've got nothing to say for yourself,' Henry Lawson continued. 'You know that what I say is true.'

Kate shook her head. Not all of it was true but she knew her father would never change his mind about the Linton family.

49

'Henry,' Nan said. 'Go easy on her. Kate's our bairn and she's in trouble. We hev to decide what to do.'

'*We* hev to decide?' her husband said. 'There's no we about it. *I've* already made me mind up. I've told you I'm not raising one of Linton's brats under my roof. She's got to go.'

'Where would she go?'

'Where? To the workhouse in Shields. That's where the likes of her go with their brats, isn't it? In any case, I divven't want to set eyes on her again.'

'For God's sake, Henry, you can't mean that.'

'Oh yes I can. And as for you, hold your tongue, woman, or you'll go out the door along with the slut. Now I'll give her until tomorrow morning but when me and the lads come back into harbour, I want her gone. And I forbid you to let her in this house ever again, as long as I live. Do you understand?'

Kate's father turned his back on them and spat into the fire. The phlegm sizzled and congealed on the bars of the grate. As far as he was concerned the matter was closed.

Sleep was impossible. Her mother had sobbed into her pillow and the old lady had muttered and tutted as if she knew what was going on – and maybe she did. But eventually they had both drifted off into an uneasy sleep marked by their tossing and turning, leaving Kate on her truckle bed near the fire to lie and listen to the constant sound of the sea breaking on the shore.

Kate was ready to leave well before her father would return from the fishing. She sat with her mother and drank hot, sweet tea while they talked, trying to comfort each other and discussing what Kate would do in the months that lay ahead.

'I'll come and see you, Kate. He hasn't forbidden that.'

'That's because he hasn't thought about it. What will you do if he does forbid you to see me?'

'Divven't fret. I can keep me own counsel.'

Kate knew what her mother meant. To keep the peace Nan Lawson had learned over the years that sometimes it was better to lie to her husband; or at least not to tell the complete truth. There was a difference. Most of the time it was to protect her children when they were young – hiding from Henry things they'd broken, perhaps. Replacing a dish or a jug and hoping he wouldn't notice. And, as they'd grown, the boys had learned to hold their tongues and keep out of their father's way. It was only hot-headed Kate who ever openly defied her father. Her brothers despaired of her.

Kate rose and went over to the bed where the old lady was still sleeping. She was dreaming again. Her brow was pulled into an anxious frown and there were traces of tears on her wrinkled cheeks. Kate bent down and kissed Sarah's brow. She cared deeply for her great-grandmother and she wondered if she would ever see her again.

'You'll let me know if . . . if . . .' she said to her mother.

'Of course.'

Kate had bundled her clothes into a shawl and now she picked it up and walked to the door. She hugged her mother and walked away from her childhood home.

Back Row was deserted, save for the black cat sleeping full length on the stone window sill. As Kate approached it opened one eye and then the other. It raised its head and stood up, stretching its lean body into an arch. Then it jumped down and approached her, purring loudly. She bent to stroke its head and then the sudden cry of a gull overhead made it skitter away with an angry yowl. But it crossed my path, Kate thought. And Jos had once told her that not only was it lucky to stroke a black cat, but if it crossed your path you could make a wish.

Kate closed her eyes. What I wish for most is impossible, she thought. I want to turn back time to the day before Jos drowned. I want the foolish prank that ended in tragedy never to have happened. Her brow furrowed. But what am I to make of what Thomas has told me about Jos's plans? I'm beginning to think I didn't really know the lad I'd promised to marry.

She looked down at the bay, its calm waters protected by the old stone piers. A safe harbour, she thought. That's what I need now, not just for me but for Jos's child. Then that is what I'll wish for.

Not much later she sat on one of the wooden benches outside the Look-out House. Her bundle was on the seat beside her. From here she could see the slope that led down to the beach and almost all of the harbour. The sea shimmered in the light from the eastern sky. The scene below was busy. The men had set out not long after midnight and now most of the village's eighty cobles had returned from the fishing, including her father's. Kate watched as the crews unloaded the fish and began to sort it into boxes ready for the beach auction. As soon as that was over the men would go home to bed.

Some of the women, the fishwives, were making their way down to the beach ready to buy. Once the fish was bought and sorted it was packed into their creels, the deep wicker baskets which they carried on their backs. When they were loaded up they might catch a lift on a cart if they were lucky, otherwise they set off up the slope so heavily laden that the ropes that kept the creels on their backs left permanent marks on their shoulders and upper arms. Most of them had a regular round of customers, and not all the customers were local.

At the bottom of the slope horses waited patiently while carts were loaded with boxes of crabs and lobsters as well as the fish to be sold at Shields. The first to arrive at North Shields Fish market would get the best prices. On a normal morning Kate would have been helping to unload her father's coble and then drag it up the beach. She wondered if he had told her brothers why she was not there. She wondered if they would miss her; dear reliable William and Thomas her impetuous twin. She would certainly miss them.

Kate shrank back against the wall of the Look-out House when she realized that she was not alone. Not far away, the artist Howard Munro was leaning on the wooden rail as he gazed at the scene in the harbour. Kate was glad that her seat was in the shadow of the overhanging roof. Mr Munro had been kind to care what happened to her, but would he be so concerned for her if he knew that, unmarried as she was, she was expecting a child?

To her relief he didn't stay long. Kate watched as he strolled away along the headland to meet another well-dressed gentleman. Kate thought it looked like Richard Adamson. She had observed that Mr Munro and Mr Adamson often walked out in the morning together, accompanied by Mr Adamson's dog. The two men were striding out and they soon vanished in the direction of the old priory with the dog bounding along ahead of them.

And then Kate saw the person she was waiting for coming up the slope. Her Aunt Meg was bent almost double under the weight of her fishwife's creel. Her father's older sister must be in her mid-fifties, Kate guessed, but she was tough and wiry. She worked hard on her round and asked help from no one, not even her brother. Kate's father did not get on even with members of his own family. But Aunt Meg had always been friendly with Kate's mother and had loved Henry's children, Kate and her brothers, as if they were her own.

When she reached the top of the slope Aunt Meg saw Kate and came towards her. She eased the creel off her back and lowered it on to the bench. Then she sat down. Her cheeks, naturally rosy, were even rosier than usual and she was out of breath.

'You could hev gone straight round to Belle Vue,' she said. Belle Vue was the name she had given her cottage. Her breathing slowly steadied, but Kate saw how strained she was. 'I left the back door open. I was going to call by before setting off on me rounds.'

'I didn't know that. And I wanted to be sure of seeing you. Make sure it was all right.'

'Of course it's all right. When your mother came to see me last night I telt her not to worry, you'd be fine with me. Didn't she say?'

'Yes. But you know my mother . . . did she tell you everything?'

'Yes, she told me why yer da wants to pack you off to the workhouse. Well, we can't have that.'

'I'm sorry.'

'What are you apologizing for?'

'For the trouble I'm going to cause you. After all, me da – well, he's your brother, and—'

'And he's a tyrant. Well, divven't fret. I'm not afeared of him; I never have been. Now, hawway, our Kate, we canna sit around talking. These fish won't sell themselves . . . What are you looking at?' She turned her head to look in the same direction. 'Oh, yer da. Divven't fret, him and yer brothers'll be down on the beach a while yet.'

Kate pushed herself forcefully up from the bench. 'I wish me da was dead!' she said, the emotion roughening her voice.

'That's wicked. And you don't mean it.'

'Yes I do. He's violent and cruel and he's made our lives a misery. I don't know why my mother married him.'

'I warned her that Henry was a bad bugger,' her aunt said. 'But she wouldn't listen. Oh, you should hev seen him when he was a stripling, Kate. Yer da was easily the best-looking lad for miles around. He could hev had any lass he wanted . . . well, mebbe not, not the sensible ones. And yer ma as well. She was right bonny but she had no sense at all, bless her. She was dazzled by him and, to be fair, his drinking was under control in them days. You know it's the drink that makes him bad, don't you?'

'Only too well.'

'It's like a disease, I think. He can't help himself.'

'Disease or not, no man should ever hit his wife and bairns the way our da has hit us.'

'Aye, I've seen the bruises on poor Nan. I know what she's had to

53

bear for the sake of her bairns. I telt her many years ago that when you were all grown she could leave him and come and live with me, but I don't suppose she ever will.'

'Why not?'

'Pride. Her own family begged her not to wed Henry Lawson but she was determined to have her own way. Does that remind you of anyone? It should. You're very like her, Kate. Oh, I know you get that stubborn streak from your father, but your ma's a proud woman and you're the same.'

Kate was speechless. The idea that her parents were once young and passionate was disturbing. And was that why her mother had been so supportive of her when she'd announced that she wanted to marry Jos? Because Nan herself had once been in the same position? She was suddenly overcome with anguish for her kind and loving mother. She had followed her heart and it had not brought her happiness. But I could have been happy, Kate thought. It would have been different for Jos and me, or at least I thought so . . .

Aunt Meg rose from the seat and began to strap on her creel.

'Here, let me help you,' Kate said, and she was surprised and dismayed to discover how heavy the basket was.

'Divven't worry' – her aunt must have seen her frown – 'I'm used to this. And I don't carry as much as I used to. I think I'm getting old.'

'Not you.' Kate smiled but she was worried. She wasn't sure of her aunt's exact age but she had noticed how tired she had seemed of late. 'I won't be a burden to you,' she burst out. 'I'll help you as much as I can.'

'I'm counting on it. I've promised yer ma that you'll be well looked after but you'll hev to earn your keep while you're with me. I hope you didn't think you were going to be a lady of leisure.'

'Of course not!' Kate flared and then she saw that her aunt was teasing.

'Eeh, Kate, you'll have to learn to keep that temper in check if you're going to bide with me. I'm a Lawson too, remember, and I dare say I could better you in a shouting match. Now then, we've gossiped long enough and Albert will be setting off soon.'

'Albert?'

'Albert Brunton. It's Wallsend for me today and Albert will take me as far as the old milestone. Now hawway, we'll take your bundle along home and pick up me crabs and lobsters.'

Before they set off Kate stooped swiftly and kissed Aunt Meg's cheek. Her aunt's skin was whiskery and Kate could smell gin and snuff. Snuff, her aunt's secret vice. At least, she thought it was a secret, but the brown stain just below her nose gave her away. As long as Kate could remember Aunt Meg had smelt of gin and snuff, although there was also a very faint trace of her favourite rose and lavender hair rinse. Aunt Meg had the distinctive Lawson hair, and even though the colour was fading she was still proud of her abundant tresses. She started each morning by dressing it carefully, no matter that by the end of the day most of it would have escaped the tortoiseshell combs and be hanging down her back.

And Aunt Meg's face, though weathered, still bore traces of her former beauty. Kate's mother had told her that Meg Lawson had once been considered the bonniest lass in the village and all the lads had wanted to dance with her when the Scottish band played at the salmon supper.

Once back in her cottage Aunt Meg wasted no time. She took an empty wicker basket and put it down on the bench next to a large iron boiling pot. She lifted the pot into the sink and gently tilted it so that the cooked crabs and lobsters it contained spilled out. Soon they were packed neatly into the basket.

'Here, take this,' she said, holding the basket out. 'You can start earning your keep straight away.'

It was only a short walk along a rutted dirt track to Albert Brunton's timber yard, which backed on to the small Quaker burial ground at the end of Marden Lane. The yard was cluttered with assorted junk; bits and pieces of metal and off-cuts of wood. Sawdust was mulched into the dried mud underfoot and the sweet smell of resin hung in the air.

Mr Brunton must have been sawing and cutting since first light and the cart was loaded and ready to go. 'Here, girl, here . . . steady now, steady!' Kate watched as with practised gentleness the timber merchant manoeuvred the big, good-natured bay into the shafts. 'Aye, you're a good girl, Bess,' he said as he patted the mare's neck and then checked the bit.

Albert Brunton was a quiet man. The wags had it that his horse got more words out of him than his wife did, but Mrs Brunton smiled at him nevertheless as she crossed the yard to help him pull open the big wooden doors. Tilda Brunton said good morning to Aunt Meg and shot Kate a sympathetic smile. She didn't question her presence, and neither did Albert. He simply nodded to Meg and then helped both her and Kate up onto the cart, lifting the creel and the basket up after them.

As her aunt settled herself she made a show of huffing and puffing. 'Eeh, I'm getting on a bit for this kind of life,' she said. 'It's a good job I've got my niece to help me. And she's only too pleased to,' she added after a slight pause. 'It'll take the poor lass's mind off things.'

By this evening, Kate thought, everyone in the village will know that I've moved into Belle Vue cottage and my aunt, God bless her, has tried to provide a believable explanation. It will be months yet before the truth becomes plain for all to see. But before then my father will surely come and demand that she throw me out. I believe Aunt Meg is strong enough to stand up to him – so long as he is not drunk and violent . . .

Soon the cart with its heavy load of bagged logs and its two passengers swung out into the lane. 'We'll be a good half-hour, so you lean back and hev a bit shuteye,' Aunt Meg told Kate who did so willingly, although it was difficult to find a comfortable position amongst the bags of logs.

'Here you are.' Her aunt had found an empty sack. 'Fold this up and put it behind your back. I'll wake you when we get there.'

Kate closed her eyes and tried to sleep, but her mind was churning. So much had happened; so much had changed. Just a few days ago she had been looking forward to marrying a man who had his own coble. And although they knew that at first they would have to live with his family, they had plans to buy their own cottage.

And now here she was about to begin life as a fish lass selling fish from door to door. From under half-closed lids she looked at Aunt Meg, who seemed to be resigned to a life of toil and was totally uncomplaining. Her aunt's cheerful expression made her smile. But as she watched, the older woman slipped a hand into a pocket in her voluminous skirt and brought out the familiar flask. As the cart trundled along Aunt Meg raised the flask to her mouth, took a swig and wiped her lips with the back of her hand. She slipped the flask back into her pocket and settled back with a satisfied sigh. Kate's smile faded. She had not realized that her aunt had started to drink so early in the day.

Chapter Five

Kate stared at the lump of weathered stone, almost obscured by a tangle of grass, while Mr Brunton helped Aunt Meg lift the baskets of fish, crabs and lobsters down from the cart. It must be very old, she thought. The inscription was barely legible and those letters she could see did not look like parts of English words. Local people said the Romans had put the stone there centuries ago, to tell the Roman soldiers how far they were from somewhere or other. Rome was in Italy. Kate had learned about the Roman Empire at school.

The Romans had come here and built a wall between England and Scotland, and much of it was still there. It started over on the west coast and ended here, in Wallsend. The schoolbook said that was how the town had got its name. The teacher had once asked Kate's class to write a letter as if from a soldier to his mother in Rome; telling her about the beautiful countryside and asking her to send him some little treats. Kate had wondered whether the wild northern hills could be compared with somewhere as exotic as Rome but she had entered into the exercise with enthusiasm and had ended the letter by asking for some warm socks.

While she'd been daydreaming, Albert Brunton had deposited the baskets on the ground at Aunt Meg's feet. He grabbed the reins of the impatient horse, who seemed to know that it was time for them to be getting on their way. 'Whoa there, lass!' he said, and climbed nimbly back on to his seat. 'Now mind, Meg, don't keep me waiting. I'll be back at the usual time to water Bess at the trough in the Plough's yard yonder. And if I'm not in sight you might find me taking a gill in the bar.'

This was the longest speech Kate had ever heard Albert make. When he'd finished talking he grinned and flicked the reins. Bess set off at a steady trot, harness jangling as they headed for the town.

Kate could see the houses on the horizon, smoke rising from the chimneys and hanging like a pall over the crowded rooftops. The giant cranes in the shipyards formed monstrous shapes against the sky. And up and away from the river bank the pit wheels rose above the crowded streets. Here men toiled underground hewing the coal to keep the fires of faraway London burning. Coal was also needed for the railways and for steamships such as Richard Adamson's new trawlers.

Kate was puzzled. 'Why doesn't Mr Brunton take you all the way into town?' she asked.

'Because I hev a few calls to make before I get there. First that inn at the crossroads over there, the Plough, then Jackson's farm and a smallholding or two. The country wives pay well and they like first pick.'

Kate offered to carry the creel with its six stones of haddock and codling instead of the wicker basket, but Aunt Meg shook her head. 'No, pet, there's a knack to it. I'll get you a creel of your own and instruct yer proper, but not today. And besides, I would feel lost without it after all these years. I sometimes think I was born with a creel on me back.' Meg settled her burden properly and headed for the inn.

Even though she was carrying the lighter load, and taking into account the amount of gin Aunt Meg must have put away, Kate had a job keeping up with her. The cook at the Plough was expecting her and Kate was relieved to see how much fish she bought. She took half a dozen crabs and a lobster from Kate's basket, too. Mrs Butterfield was a cheerful, talkative woman and obviously would have liked them to stay and gossip for a while.

'I'll try to get back early,' Aunt Meg told her. 'Me niece and me will sit with you in the yard, if we hev time, and perhaps hev a sup of ale. But now I must get on.'

Kate didn't speak either at the inn or at the farm and the small-holdings. At one dwelling she stood and watched a bunch of white chickens scratching around in the dusty soil until her aunt nudged her with her elbow. It was the nearest the kindly woman got to admonishing her. Kate mouthed the word 'sorry' and began to pay attention as her aunt smiled and cajoled her customer into buying more than she might have planned to. Kate realized she had a lot to learn. Aunt Meg knew everyone's name and all about their families, but Kate sensed that her interest was strictly businesslike. It was all to do with selling fish.

After the last smallholding it was a short walk into town. Her aunt headed for a pleasant area, well away from the river, and looking almost like a park with its stretches of grass and graceful trees. 'The toffs live here,' Meg told Kate. 'Just look at these grand houses.'

'Who can afford houses like this?' Kate asked.

'The bosses from the shipyards and the mines, a shipowner or two, lawyers, doctors, them kinds of folk.'

When she called at these houses Meg did not go to the front door but found a back door or, in some cases, went down the area steps to a small yard and a semi-basement. As she negotiated one such set of steps Meg lost her footing. Kate saw her begin to fall, but before she could do anything to help, her aunt had saved herself by grabbing the railings.

'Are you all right?' Kate asked. Her own heart was pounding.

'Why, of course. That step's worn; I should hev remembered.'

As Kate followed her aunt down into the yard she looked at all the steps closely. She didn't think any of them looked worn. Meg's demeanour was different now. She was just as pleasant but not quite so jolly. More respectful, in fact, although none of the women who answered the door were the ladies of the house. They were all servants, but they seemed to think they were a better sort of person than a mere fishwife. Kate wondered if she would ever be able to deal with people like this and voiced her doubts to her aunt as they walked on.

'Remember, Kate, hinny,' her aunt told her, 'you can't let your pride stand in the way of business. You hev to act respectful.'

'That must be hard sometimes.'

'No, it isn't.' Aunt Meg laughed when she saw Kate's doubtful expression. 'Oh, some of them put on airs and graces and look down their noses at you because they think they're superior. But that's not the reason you're being polite to them.'

'Then what is?'

'The reason is that in spite of being a fish lass *you* are a lady, you and me both, and we would never demean ourselves by behaving like some of those who think they're ladies – whether mistress or servant – but don't act like such.'

Soon they had done with that part of town and were going door to door in the terraced rows that led down to the river. The wives of the working men greeted Meg with smiles and gossip just like the country women, although the humour was sharper and the attitude not quite so easy-going.

Soon Meg's money pouch hung heavily and clinked as she walked. Both baskets were nearly empty and this made the going easier, but even so Kate's arms were protesting so much that she felt they might drop off. Her aunt seemed to have the lifting power of a packhorse. She didn't appear to be tired but her face was bright red. Unfortunately this wasn't caused only by hard work.

Every now and then Meg had stopped to take a sip from her flask. The first time she did it she had glanced at Kate awkwardly and muttered something about needing fortifying. Kate had kept quiet. She had no idea what she could have said, and after that her aunt had been quite open about it.

The drinking didn't seem to affect her behaviour. It was true her gait was a little unsteady as they walked back to meet Mr Brunton, but, unless you knew she had been drinking, this could have been put down to weariness. Kate was pleased to see the timber merchant waiting by the milestone. She was glad that her aunt would not have the opportunity to return to the Plough and 'hev a gill'.

Mr Brunton was happy. He told them he'd had a good day. The colliery had taken all the pit props and he'd had no trouble selling the bags of logs. Prudent folk, it seemed, never thought it too soon to stock up for the winter. He hoisted Aunt Meg up on to the cart, grinning at Kate as he did so. Kate flushed and looked away. It was obvious that he knew that her aunt was the worse for drink and he thought nothing of it. Kate tried to fight down a surge of embarrassment. She loved her aunt and didn't want anyone to think the less of her.

They hadn't gone more than half a mile on the journey home when the older woman collapsed on to a pile of empty sacks and fell asleep. She began to snore, but Kate didn't think Mr Brunton could hear her because of the noise of the horse's hoofs and the clatter of the wheels. She hoped not. Without its load of wood the cart jolted wildly on the uneven and rutted surface of the tracks, but even when the wheels left the road altogether Aunt Meg did not wake up.

Kate found herself clinging on to the sides of the cart for dear life. She began to feel sick and the bile rose hot and sour into the back of her throat. The sound of her heartbeat seemed to pound in her head to the same rhythm the horse's hoofs made as they struck the road. She knew she was tired and she knew that these days of sickness would not last. If she felt wretched now it was only to be expected. But she would not complain to Aunt Meg. She had assured her aunt that she would not be a burden to her and she was determined to keep her promise.

When the cart finally pulled in to the timber yard Meg smiled and opened her eyes. Amazingly she looked none the worse for wear. 'Well, Albert, how much do I owe you?' she asked once Mr Brunton had helped her down.

'Nowt,' he said. 'You know I don't want payment.'

'Well, will you take a bit of fish?'

'If you insist. Tilda would like that.'

While they had been talking Mrs Brunton had appeared in the doorway of the shed that served as an office, holding a plate. She walked towards them and held out the plate, and Meg reached into her creel and took out most of the fish that was left. She slapped it on the plate. Kate realized even before her aunt glanced at her and winked that this was a ritual.

'Hev you enjoyed yerself today?' her aunt asked as they walked home to Belle Vue Cottage.

'Very much,' Kate said with as much enthusiasm as she could muster.

'It's been grand having you along,' Aunt Meg continued. 'Someone of me own to keep me company. And never fear, Kate. You're a clever lass – you'll soon pick them up, the tricks of the trade.'

Kate was sure she would. And she was genuinely glad that her presence was making her aunt happy. Even though her heart was aching she was determined to make the best of things. Not just for her own sake, but also for the baby she was carrying, who was all she had left of Jos.

Her mother was waiting at the door of the cottage. 'How'd you get on?' she asked.

Kate couldn't have expressed how pleased she was to see her there. 'You'd better ask Aunt Meg.'

'The lass did very well,' her aunt said. 'But hawway in; we'll hev a cup of tea.'

The fire had been banked up and it didn't take long to stoke it up a little and get the kettle boiling. The day had been warm but it was cool inside the cottage and although her mother and her aunt sat companionably at the table Kate drew her chair to the fireside and savoured the cheery glow.

'Lissen, Kate,' her mother said, and she looked troubled. 'There's no one else knows yet that you're expecting. Just you, me and Meg here.'

'And my father.'

'Oh, aye, not forgetting your father.' Her mother sighed. 'And he's the reason I want to keep this quiet. If word got round and if he thought there was gossip about you he would . . . he would be angry.'

61

Kate knew that was an understatement. 'And he would take it out on you,' she said.

Her mother didn't reply, but there was no need. All three of them knew that it was true.

'So yer ma and I agreed that we'll let folk think you've come here to help me,' Aunt Meg said.

'It's for the best, Kate, believe me,' her mother added. 'It'll be our little secret.'

'That's all very well,' Kate said, 'but the secret won't keep, will it? What happens when I begin to show? What happens when the bairn is born?'

The two older women looked at each other and Kate thought her mother looked unhappier than ever. 'Shall I tell her?' Aunt Meg asked.

'Aye, you'll hev to.'

'I'll write to your Aunt Winifred,' Meg said. 'I'm pretty sure she'll take you in. In fact she'll be pleased to.'

'Who is Aunt Winifred?'

'My little sister. She's a couple of years younger than your father.'

'Why don't I know her?' Kate asked.

'Because she ran away long before you were born.'

'Ran away?'

'Aye, and it was your father's fault.' Aunt Meg sighed. 'When your grandfather was drowned along with our eldest brother, your father, although just a lad himself, became the man of the house and started laying down the law about what Winifred and me could do – our ma, too. Well, Ma just gave in to him and I did too, to keep the peace. But Winifred was just like you, Kate. She spoke up for herself and wouldn't give in. Our poor mother had a lot to bear and I'm sure that's why she followed our father to the grave only a year later. Then your father became worse than ever, a proper tyrant, so Winifred ran away.'

'Where did she go?'

'We didn't know – not for years. And your father wouldn't hev her name mentioned. But eventually I got a letter from her.'

'She sent it to me,' Kate's mother said. 'It was before your father and I were married so the letter was safe coming to my parents' house.'

'And I've been writing to her ever since,' Aunt Meg continued. 'Your da doesn't know anything about it. Eeh, Kate you're so like her. I know she'll take you in.'

'But that's marvellous,' Kate said.

'Well, yes and no,' said her mother.

62

'What do you mean?'

'It means it might be years before I see you again. You see, your Aunt Winifred lives in America.'

'America?' Kate stared at her aunt and her mother, unwilling to take in what this might mean.

'Yes, pet, in a place called New York. And although I don't want to lose you,' Nan said, 'I know that you'd be well looked after. Winifred has married well: she was working in a shoe factory and she caught the boss's eye. Well, Winifred wouldn't settle for anything less than a ring on her finger and, the last time I heard, she was helping him run the business. Designing fashionable boots for ladies, if you please.'

'That's right,' Aunt Meg said. 'Poor Winifred.'

'Why do you say that?' Kate was startled.

'Well, it seems that try as they might her and Herbert just can't have children. It's a grief to them both, the last I heard. So, you see, I think she'll be overjoyed to have you – you and the bairn. And divven't fret, Kate, lass, you'll be well looked after.'

'But I'd be so far away!' Kate felt the tears pricking at the back of her eyes.

'Whisht now, don't upset yourself,' her aunt said. 'It's bad for the bairn. And it won't be for a while yet, anyways. For the time being you and me will live here happily together. All right?'

'I just don't know. I'll have to think about it.'

'Of course, but I'm sure you'll see it'll be for the best,' her mother said. 'And Kate . . .'

'Yes?'

'Meanwhile it's best not to tell anyone about the baby.'

'Who would I tell?'

'I thought you might tell Jane. Then Jane might tell her mother . . .'

'She wouldn't. Not if I asked her not to.'

'Perhaps not. But it's better to be safe than sorry. And then there's William.' Her mother paused. 'I know you confide in him sometimes. Well, I think it's best to keep him in the dark about this.'

'My brothers don't know?'

'No.'

'Why do they think I've left home?'

'I told them you'd angered your father once too often. It was easy for them to believe that.' Nan gave a faint smile.

'But why can't you tell them? They wouldn't condemn me!'

'You can't be sure of that. Lads are funny.'

'Oh, aye,' Meg said. 'Lads are funny, all right. They do their best to sweet-talk a girl into giving in and then, if anything goes wrong, it's all the lass's fault.'

'My brothers aren't like that. They wouldn't think less of me. In fact they'd stand up for me.'

'That's what I'm afeared of,' her mother said. 'Thomas sometimes acts without thinking first. If he stood up to your da – quarrelled with him because he'd thrown you out – it would be me that would get the worst of it.'

'Aye, we're back to my devil of a brother again,' Meg said. 'All roads lead to him. So, Kate hinny, just do as your ma tells you for the sake of a quiet life.'

Kate sighed. 'I will.'

'Good lass,' Aunt Meg said. 'And now your ma had better get along home and leave us to hev a bit supper before we gans to bed. We'll be starting work tomorrow as soon as the boats come home.'

Jane stirred in her bed, frowning before she had even opened her eyes, and wondered what had woken her. It was early; too early, for now that she was Mrs Coulson's personal maid she did not have to get up at first light like the other domestic servants. She raised her head from the pillows and looked around the room. There was nothing there to disturb her except that the curtains were blowing a little, and now that she concentrated she could hear rain spattering on the window. A moment later the window panes rattled as the wind gusted and Jane realized what it was that had roused her from her slumbers.

Reluctantly she pushed back the bedclothes and kneeled on the bed to reach up and close the window. She didn't want the rain coming in and soaking the eiderdown. She pulled the lower half of the window down then reached up and secured the catch. Then she paused to gaze out over the garden. The view always delighted her. And the birdsong. She loved the sound; the sweet notes were so different from the harsh crying of the gulls at home in Cullercoats.

Once when William had brought her home she had shown him round the grounds of the house, sure that he would be impressed, and she had been dumbfounded when he had remarked that it looked like a public park. Then she had looked up at him and had understood from the admiration in his eyes that he had meant it as a compliment. So she'd told him that gardeners were employed all year round and that there was a large glasshouse where all sorts of exotic flowers

64

were grown so that there was always something pretty for the table arrangements.

Now, as she gazed out over the rain-drenched lawns and the dripping trees, she marvelled as always that this house was so near the centre of Newcastle and yet there wasn't another house to be glimpsed over the treetops. Even in winter when the branches were bare there was enough cover to hide the nearest roofs, although not the sight of smoke rising from the chimneys; that was always present.

But whatever time of year it was there was always something in bloom in the Coulsons' garden, or a display of colourful leaves to cheer the eye. Now, in the first week of September, some of the leaves had started to change colour and the heavy rain had brought a few of them down. They would be swept up from the lawns before the family had even come down to breakfast, however, and if one of them should happen to glance out of a window, everything would be tidy and neatly ordered. Perhaps William had been right, after all, when he'd said the grounds reminded him of a park. But, if so, it was a very grand one.

In fact Mrs Coulson was planning what she called a water feature. Jane had asked her if she meant a fountain but her mistress had assured her it would be more original than that. A grotto would be created with rocks and a tumbling waterfall; wild flowers would be planted and everything made to look like a sylvan grove.

Jane let the curtains fall back into place and settled back amongst the bedclothes. This bed was so comfortable, unlike the maids' beds in the attics where poor Dora, the tweeny, claimed she had a flock mattress so thin that the springs of the bed left angry patterns on her bum. Jane smiled when she remembered how Mrs Roberts the cook-housekeeper had scolded Dora for being so coarse as to use that word when there was a perfectly respectable one available: posterior. And she had pointed out that at least Dora had a bed, whereas Iris, the scullery maid, slept on a truckle under the kitchen table.

And I have this lovely room of my own, Jane thought. I don't have to share. I have rugs instead of bare floorboards, an oil lamp instead of a candle in a saucer, and a fire in the hearth that Dora has to clean and keep burning for me. And I'm allowed a kettle so that I can make myself a cup of tea.

Jane pulled the bedclothes up to her chin and tried to make herself comfortable. Now that she was awake she could feel where some of the curling rags were digging into her head, and she put up a delicate finger to try to ease them away from her scalp a little without loosening the

65

knots. How lucky Kate is to have hair that waves naturally, she thought. And whatever way she wears it, whether she puts it up, lets it fall free, or drags it back and ties it with a piece of ribbon like a schoolgirl, she looks beautiful.

Am I jealous? she wondered. No, of course not. Kate may be striking at first glance but her looks are too unusual to be really fashionable like . . . well, like me. Jane reached over to her bedside table and took up the letter she had received just the day before. She opened it and held it in the light that fell across her bed from the window.

Dear Jane (the letter began),
I'm sure your mother will have written and told you that I am living with my Aunt Meg. I have angered my father once too often and, for my mother's sake, we thought it best that I should leave home. And now my father behaves as though I don't exist. If he catches sight of me on the beach he seems to look right through me.

And I have to go to the beach for I'm learning how to be a fishwife, can you believe that? My aunt is teaching me how to sell fish from door to door.

Well, then, as a fisherman's daughter, I thought I knew as much about fish as anyone would ever want to know but I was wrong. I go down to the beach with Aunt Meg in time for the auction and she's teaching me what to buy. Once the fish is sorted the heads are cut off – I can just imagine your expression, Jane, but this, at least, is nothing new to me. I've helped my mother with this task ever since I was old enough to be trusted with a knife. My aunt has taught me how to pack my creel – yes, I have a creel of my own now – with the fish lying in different directions so that more can be packed in.

Oh, Jane, it's so heavy that the rope seems to cut into my flesh! I've seen the marks on my aunt's shoulders and upper arms when I help her to bed at night. How long will it be, I wonder, before I have marks like that? But at least the load gets lighter as the day goes on. My aunt has a regular round and she's very popular with her customers. Sometimes we catch a lift with Mr Brunton to Wallsend, and sometimes to Whitley. One day a week we get the train to Gosforth Village and you can imagine how the other passengers on the train turn up their noses and edge away from us. I don't blame them.

66

As soon as we get home I strip off and wash myself and every piece of clothing – every day. My aunt and I have at least three sets of everything, but, even so, I imagine that I will never completely get rid of the smell of fish.

By the way, those fish heads. They don't go to waste. We parcel them up and sell them as pet food. And one of our best customers for this is that American, Mr Munro. You know, he's the artist who lives in the cottage where the Adamson family used to live and have never sold. Well, it seems that not long after he moved in there he took pity on a stray cat and the next thing, it seems – or so he told me – is that the wily creature (his words) brought his friends home, and now Mr Munro has a bunch of hungry lodgers to feed.

One morning as Aunt Meg and I were setting off for Brunton's wood yard to catch our lift, I saw Mr Munro sitting on a little stool facing the windows of his lodging and making a sketch. I was curious and I stopped and looked to see what he was drawing. It was one of the cats, a tabby, sitting inside on the sill next to a pot with a geranium and looking out of the open window through narrowed eyes as he warmed himself in the morning sun.

And do you know that cat looked so lifelike that I could imagine it suddenly yawning, stretching and jumping right out of the picture. Does that sound fanciful? Well, you must blame Mr Howard Munro. I think he must be an exceptionally good artist.

Well, Jane, I hope it won't be too long before I see you again. I do miss you and our chats. I had to write because you haven't been home for a week or two and I wondered what William had been telling you about me. Yes, I know that you and William are still seeing each other even though your mother and mine are being kept in the dark about it! William disappears every now and then. Always on a Sunday. My mother doesn't suspect a thing but I worked it out, and I'm thrilled for you. But one of these days I'd like you to tell me when you are going to make up your mind and put my poor brother out of his misery.

Well, you weren't expecting that, were you?

With love from your friend,

Kate.

Jane slipped the letter back into its envelope and put it in the shallow drawer set in her bedside table. She knew she would not be able to get back to sleep now. She had too much to think about. So Kate knew her secret, did she? Well, how much of a secret was it? She and William were not promised to each other. She doubted if they could even be considered a courting couple. To be that, both parties would have to be of the same mind, wouldn't they?

She had adored William ever since she was a small child. He had been kinder than the other boys of his age and handsome in spite of his red hair. In fact, just like Kate's, the hair was actually an advantage: a wonderful, rich red that went well with his greeny-blue eyes. She had been ecstatic when he had at last seemed to take notice of his younger sister's friend, offering to walk her home if she and Kate had talked too long and night was falling; not just being polite but talking properly to her and asking her questions about her work in the big house in Jesmond.

And how difficult it had been for her. For the more she learned of another way of life, the more she knew she could never become the wife of a fisherman. Had she really dreamed, when she'd been a small girl, of marrying William and living in one of the cottages on the cliff top? Perhaps she had thought that her life as William's wife would be no more onerous than her mother's life as the wife of the village shoemaker and cobbler. But she had been wrong.

Kate's letter had demonstrated vividly how hard the life of a fisherman's wife could be, even if she didn't have to sell fish from door to door. And the cottage. Even if she kept it spotlessly clean there would always be that smell of fish and wet sea boots. It would get in her clothes and in her hair; she would never be free of it. And as for her hands . . .

Jane got out of bed and pulled on her robe. First of all she removed the cinder guard and built up the fire a little, then she placed the small kettle on the hob. She would make herself a cup of tea. While she waited for the kettle to boil she prepared the tray and pulled the velvet-covered armchair nearer to the fire. It was only a small chair, she acknowledged, but it was well upholstered, stylish and extremely comfortable. Even her mother didn't have a chair as fine as this, and in the cottage where William lived there were only wooden chairs and nowhere to sit in peace and take your ease.

No, she could never live that way. Not after what she had become used to. And she didn't intend to go on living as a servant either. There was something she hadn't told William when he came up to town and they went walking together. She had a plan. As she sipped her tea she wondered bleakly whether William would agree to it. She knew that he loved her, for he had told her so. But she doubted very much whether he would agree to what she had in mind. And where would that leave them?

Jane held the porcelain teacup with both hands, her delicate fingers spread across the pattern of rosebuds. Outside the wind gusted and a pattering of raindrops fell down the chimney, making the coals splutter and hiss. She closed her eyes. What on earth was she going to do? She sensed the time was coming when she would have to choose between the life she had planned for herself and the man she loved with all her heart.

Chapter Six

Kate pushed the shop door open and the bell above it danced and jingled on its spring. Mrs Willis hurried from the back room, blinking as a shaft of sunlight fell through the opening. By the time Kate had shut the door behind her, the village shopkeeper had taken up her usual pose, hands resting on the counter.

The shop in Front Street was on the ground floor of what had once been a large house. Large, that is, if compared with the fishermen's cottages. A wooden extension had been tacked to the front of the building so that it jutted out into the street, creating a sizeable front and back shop.

Charlie and Alice Willis lived here alone and worked together although, these days, Charlie was seldom seen. Every now and then he could be heard coughing and spluttering and Alice would hurry through to tend to him. Charlie had been a miner and, although he had left the pit when he was still relatively young, he had not escaped unscathed. Everyone knew his lung condition had been brought on by years of breathing in coal dust. Now it was a matter of how long he had left.

'Well, then, you're up early. What can I do for you?' Alice asked. She managed a smile but Kate thought she looked tired.

Kate looked round the display of stock. Alice sold everything from pegs and hairpins to beans and barley – that is if she could find anything that was asked for amongst the jumble. The shop was still reasonably clean, Kate thought, but disorder was taking over. Sometimes it was easier to leave Alice a list and call back when she'd had time to put the purchases together. And as she didn't have much time that was just what Kate had decided to do.

'Here's my aunt's order,' she said, placing Aunt Meg's neat list on the counter. 'There's not much. Tea, sugar, a bag of flour, some candles and some lamp oil. I'll come back later. And here's the rent money.'

'Thanks, pet. Have you got the book?'

Kate handed over her aunt's rent book and watched as Alice made the entry. In former days Mr Willis used to go the rounds of the few cottages they owned and collect the rent, but now their tenants obliged by bringing the payments to the shop.

'How is Mr Willis?' Kate asked.

'Not so bad.' That was all Alice ever said and you could only judge from the anxiety in her eyes what the truth of the situation was. 'And Miss Lawson?'

'She's fine.'

'All the better for having you to help her, I suppose.'

'Well, yes.' Something in Mrs Willis's tone caused Kate to frown.

'Aye, I thought it was about time she had someone to keep an eye on her.'

Kate was so surprised that she spoke without thinking. 'What do you mean?'

Alice gave her what her mother would have called 'an old-fashioned look' as if trying to make out whether Kate really didn't know what she was talking about. Then she said, 'I could tell your mother was worried about Meg. I mean, she's getting on, isn't she? She probably thought it would be good for both of you. You lost your sweetheart, and it's no secret your da was at odds with you, so your ma did a wise thing asking Meg to take you in. She probably pretended it was for your sake, didn't she?'

'Yes.'

Kate had finally understood what Mrs Willis had been hinting at. It seemed it was no secret that Meg Lawson liked a tipple, and the shopkeeper and no doubt others in the village seemed to believe that Kate had moved into Belle Vue Cottage in order to keep an eye on her Aunt Meg rather than because her father had thrown her out. She wondered if her mother had guessed this would happen.

For her aunt's sake she would have liked to have told Mrs Willis the truth, but she couldn't. And now she realized she had something else to worry about. Her aunt was a popular figure in the village and if folk believed she needed someone to keep an eye on her then she probably did. Aunt Meg had written to her younger sister, the mysterious Aunt Winifred who had run away to America and done well for herself. As soon as they got a reply the plan was that they would make the news public. Or rather they would say they'd had an unexpected letter from Winifred who, after all these years, wanted to make it up with her family, so Kate was going to go and visit.

Kate had accepted that she would be going to America, even though she knew it would break her heart to leave her mother and her brothers. Not to mention her aunt, whom in these few short weeks she had come to love almost as much as she loved her mother. But if Meg really did need someone to keep an eye on her, what would happen when Kate was gone? Kate resolved to speak to her mother about it.

'Are you not out with your aunt today?' Alice asked.

'No, she's left already. We're going our separate ways today.' Kate smiled. 'Aunt Meg trusts me to go round by myself at last. I hope I won't lose her any customers.'

The village streets were quiet. Back from the night's fishing, the men would be settling in their beds now, while their womenfolk got on with their allotted tasks. On the way back to the cottage to pick up her creel Kate reflected on all that her aunt had taught her. Not just how to sell the fish but also how to bid for them at the beach auction. Until today they had gone the rounds together but Meg had decided that now there were two of them it would make sense to try to find some new customers.

'That way we can save a bit money towards your passage to America,' Aunt Meg had told her. 'Mind you, I'm pretty sure Winifred will provide for that, but I don't want you to arrive in America a pauper.'

So today Meg had set off for new territory in Monkseaton leaving Kate to do an easy round. She was to visit the long terraces of big houses facing the sea right here in the village. 'I have a few good customers here,' her aunt had told her, 'and it's not too far to walk. When you've done you can go home and put your feet up for a while.'

Until now Kate hadn't accompanied her aunt to these houses. She'd stayed at home and caught up with some housework in the cottage. A short while later, when she set off, she realized she felt apprehensive. These people lived in the village and yet they were not part of it. They were business people from North Shields and Newcastle. One of the houses was owned by a London merchant who used it as a holiday home for his large family of small children.

All the houses were imposing but the largest and most imposing of all was that of Richard Adamson, who owned the biggest trawler fleet that fished out of North Shields. The Adamson house was double-fronted with a massive stone-pillared entrance porch.

She was more confident with the selling now and she was pleased to find that most of the servants who answered the doors to her were local girls, even some she'd been at school with. But her aunt had warned her that that would not be the case at the Adamson house.

'Mr Adamson will come to the door himself,' her aunt had told her. 'They're most particular about their fish. He'll be expecting you. I try to go at the same time every week.'

'Why doesn't Mrs Adamson come to the door?'

'Creaky old bones.'

'I beg your pardon?'

'The only Mrs Adamson in that house is his ma and she's getting on. And, in any case, she used to be a schoolteacher afore she married. Real bonny lass she was, but she knows nowt about fish. Mind you . . .' Aunt Meg had tilted her head to one side and frowned, 'I'm saying she's old but she's probably only about the same age as meself.'

Kate had smiled. She had no idea of Aunt Meg's correct age and she was sure that the older woman would never tell her.

Meg hadn't noticed Kate's amusement and she went on, 'So there's no young Mrs Adamson, although I've heard there might be soon, and from a very grand family. I shouldn't imagine she will answer the door. And furthermore, coming from the kind of background she does she'll probably persuade Richard that it's the cook's job to buy the fish like in the other houses.'

'Richard? You call Mr Adamson Richard?'

Her aunt had smiled broadly. 'Aye. Well, not to his face, but him and me are old pals.'

'Really?'

'Divven't look so amazed. It goes back a long way, to when he was a little lad.' Aunt Meg had settled back in her chair to tell the story. 'He was coming back from the village shop one day – he'd bought himself a bag of boiled sweets – when some of the village lads set about him.

'I found them in the back lane. They were calling him names – making mock of his fine clothes and his shiny boots. They had no shoes at all, of course.'

'I can't believe they would do that,' Kate had interjected.

'Aye, well there was hard feelings about the Adamsons even then. Folk don't like people to get above themselves, do they? It didn't matter that the Adamsons had worked damned hard for their success. Anyway, one of the lads had grabbed the bag of sweets but young

Richard wasn't going to give it up that easily. He hung on to it and the bag tore. There were pear drops, sour cherries and pineapple cubes scattered all over the lane. I can see them in my mind's eye now – all the bonny colours.

'Well, it was too tempting; most of the lads went after the sweets, but it looked as if two of the bigger ones were going to do Richard harm, so I dashed forward, picked him up and ran all the way to his house with him.'

'He must have been grateful.'

'Was he heck! He yelled all the way that I should have left him to sort it out. He kicked and screamed and wriggled like an eel. Finally I set him down and walloped him.'

'You what?'

'I tapped his behind. He got such a shock that he stopped yelling, and after a while he had the grace to thank me. We've been pals ever since.'

Now Kate stood at the bottom of the steps that led up to the front door. Her aunt had told her not to go down to the servants' entrance in the half-basement. She hoisted the creel on to her shoulder and took firm hold of her basket. She had never spoken to Richard Adamson, although she had often seen him striding along the cliff top or the beach with his dog. These days he was often accompanied on his walks by the American. Kate knew the men to be cousins and yet they looked quite different. Mr Munro appeared to be quite at home in his fashionable clothes but Mr Adamson, for all his wealth, had the rugged air of his hardy forebears.

She wondered why the Adamsons, mother and son, continued to live in the village when they knew how much they were despised. Even their generous donation towards the building of the new lifeboat house hadn't eased the situation. Some of the older fisherfolk could remember when Richard Adamson's grandparents lived in the house now occupied by the American artist and how his grandfather had fished out of the tiny harbour in his own coble, struggling to make a living like the rest of them.

Perhaps his grandson felt that the family were still part of the community. It was sad, Kate thought, that it didn't seem as if they were going to be forgiven for working hard and making life easier for themselves.

There was a short path leading to the door. Briefly Kate noticed that the small garden area on each side of the path was laid to lawn, with a rock border and a few close-growing plants that could survive the winds that blew in from the sea. She climbed the steps but hesitated before pulling the bell knob. Then, conquering her nerves, she gave it a tug and was startled to hear the resulting clanging echoing from inside the house. As the bell's reverberations died away they were replaced by approaching footsteps.

When the door opened Kate found herself staring up into the surprised eyes of a tall man of about thirty. Kate was taller than most of the village lads, including her brothers; Jos and she had been the same height. She couldn't remember having to look up into anyone's face since she had been a child.

The eyes that were staring at her were grey and they were set in a strong-featured face that somehow did not match the fine clothes Richard Adamson wore. His dark hair was neatly combed and barbered but it looked as though it had been a battle to tame it.

'Good morning,' he said at last. 'I'm sorry if I seemed to stare but I was expecting Miss Lawson.' His voice bore hardly any trace of the local way of speaking.

'Miss Lawson is my aunt. She asked me to come today.'

'Is she well?'

Kate knew she had benefited from Jane's elocution lessons but, nevertheless, she took care to form what she thought might be a correct reply. 'Thank you, sir, she is in good health.'

'I'm pleased to hear it. But there's no need to call me sir. Your aunt never does.' Richard Adamson smiled and Kate noticed how attractive and almost boyish it made him look.

She remembered her aunt's tale of how she had once picked Richard Adamson up and carried him home and walloped him into the bargain. She found she couldn't meet his gaze. 'I'm helping her,' she said.

'I'm glad of that. Meg is . . . Meg is getting on in years. It pleases me that her family think enough of her to want to help. But it's a hard trade you've chosen to follow.'

Kate felt her blood rising. Without warning her easily roused temper prompted her to tell him that it was all the harder since his trawlers had plundered the fishing grounds. No matter that reason told her you couldn't stand in the way of progress, there was something about being here, in the doorway of this grand house a mere stone's throw from the humble dwellings of the men whose trade was dying, that taught her for the first time how hatred could grow.

75

Richard Adamson could not have known anything of the battle that raged within her because he said, pleasantly, 'Shall we see what you have to offer?'

Kate swung the creel from her shoulder and placed it on the doorstep alongside the wicker basket that contained the crabs and lobsters. She felt her brief flash of fury subsiding but she couldn't stop herself saying, 'Why do you buy fish from my aunt?'

'I don't understand.'

'You own a fleet of trawlers. Surely you can bring as much fish home as you like.'

Kate was aware that her tone had not been as respectful as perhaps it should have been and she waited uncomfortably for his reply. Her eyes were fixed on her baskets but she had the impression that he was scrutinizing her carefully.

'I do,' he said at last. 'I bring home anything I fancy. But it pleases me to buy from your aunt. She's one of those people who brings something to life. I fear I'm putting this badly, but she can cheer up your day. Don't you feel that?'

Kate was surprised by his answer but it made her smile, because no matter that he thought he'd put it badly she knew exactly what he meant. 'Yes, I do,' she said, and was relieved to find that the awkwardness that had arisen between them seemed to have vanished. I'd better get on with the business of selling fish, she thought.

She lifted the lid, which also served as a filleting table, from the top of the creel, and pushed forward the basket containing the crabs and the lobsters.

After a moment Richard Adamson said, 'I'll take four of the codling and two of the lobsters.'

Kate took her filleting knife from its slot in the creel and picked up one of the codling.

'No,' Richard Adamson said, 'leave the filleting. The cook will do that.'

Kate was relieved. She would have felt uneasy carrying out the tricky task under the watchful eyes of Mr Adamson. More than likely her nerves would have made a fool of her. 'Very well, s— I mean Mr Adamson.'

But, in spite of her nervousness, she realized that she didn't feel overawed by this man. There was a warmth in his eyes and he had a ready smile. Yet for all that, she reminded herself, he must surely have a ruthless side to his nature to account for his success in business. She

76

must not forget that agreeable as he had just been he was causing untold misery in the village.

She reached for wrapping paper from the wad she kept under her blouse at her back where it absorbed moisture from the fish and acted as a cushion between her spine and the creel.

'No,' Richard Adamson said again, 'wait a moment.'

He turned and walked to the hall table where a large willow-pattern dish, probably a meat server for a huge roast, Kate thought, was waiting. When she'd placed his purchases on the dish and slipped the payment into the money pocket in her apron, she hoisted the creel on to her back once more. She was conscious that Richard Adamson was watching her every move – and that he was frowning, although she couldn't fathom why.

Kate thought he looked odd standing there in his smart and no doubt expensive business clothes clutching a dish of fish and lobsters. She suppressed a smile at the idea that his dignity was somehow being undermined by a dish of codling.

'What is it?' he asked.

'I beg your pardon?'

'You were smiling.'

'Was I?' Kate managed to inject deep surprise into the question. She saw him frown. 'Well, that was probably because I'll be going home soon. I'm almost finished selling fish for the day.'

'Hm.' He didn't look convinced. 'And will you be calling again next week?'

'I don't know. Whatever my aunt decides.'

'Give Meg my regards, won't you?'

'I will.'

Kate turned to go when he called, 'Wait a moment. I don't know your name.'

'Kate. Kate Lawson.'

'Good day, then, Kate.'

'Good day, Mr Adamson.'

She realized that the leave-taking had been awkward and she wasn't sure why the constraint had returned. As she walked down the steps she had to fight a powerful desire to turn to see whether Richard Adamson was still standing there. She had not heard the door close. I won't look back, she thought. There's no reason to. She realized that the encounter had left her feeling thoroughly unsettled.

Richard watched the tall, fiery-haired girl walk away from him. It's like a disguise, he thought: the drab clothes and the heavy working shoes. But the clothes can't hide her beauty, nor her work as a fish lass hide her spirit. And then an unsettling idea surfaced. She was laughing at me. I'm sure of it, but I don't know why.

He stood and watched until he saw her turn and go down the area steps of one of the other houses, then he shut the door. It was time he gave the fish he'd bought to the cook, said goodbye to his mother and set off for his business premises on North Shields Fish Quay. He thought perhaps he might walk there today. It was only a couple of miles away and perhaps the wind coming off the sea would help clear his head and blow clean away the image of Kate Lawson's troubling secret smile.

Jane leaned towards the mirror on her dressing table, and turning her head from side to side she smoothed her blond ringlets, pulling each one down a little and letting it bounce back into place. Unbidden, her friend's voice echoed in her memory.

Torture! Kate had once exclaimed when Jane had explained to her her nightly routine of curling rags, followed by help from the curling tongs the next morning. *Sheer torture. I could never put up with all that discomfort and fiddle-faddle!*

It was all very well for Kate, Jane thought now. Her hair needed no more than a thorough brushing to make it look good. Jane hardly liked to admit it but she was a little jealous of her friend's looks. She told herself she shouldn't be. After all, Kate's beauty was very different from her own.

Kate was tall whereas she was small; Kate although slender and shapely enough did not have the truly womanly curves that Jane herself possessed. Jane knew that she would have to take care not to become plump – not to say stout – like her mother. And Kate, being out in all weathers, would have to take care that her naturally clear complexion did not become wind-roughened and tanned like an Amazon's.

Jane had read in one of Mrs Coulson's *Lady's Journal*s that women should compare themselves to delicate flowers and aim to look pale and interesting. Pallor could be induced by drinking vinegar and avoiding fresh air. A pale skin was a mark of gentility. It meant that a lady could afford not to work outdoors getting suntanned, which was to be considered vulgar and coarse. And a lady's crowning glory was her hair.

Jane looked in the mirror thoughtfully. Kate's hair was certainly glorious – but she wondered if red could be considered a fashionable colour? Probably not. And as for the matter of skin colour, Jane's own complexion was pale with a delicate hint of rose in her cheeks. One thing she had not told Kate, or even her own mother, was that she had taken to helping this faint rose blush with the tiniest touch of rouge. She had picked up this trick while helping Mrs Coulson at her toilette, and she had also learned how to apply a dusting of powder to stop her nose looking shiny. These days she always carried a tiny book of *papier poudré* in her reticule. Each little book contained leaves of coloured paper impregnated with floral-scented powder, just sufficient to remove the shine from nose, cheeks or forehead if the need arose.

Jane sat back, pleased with the arrangement of her hair, but she paused before reaching for her hat. Her eyelashes were satisfyingly dark but she wondered if she would ever dare darken them further. She had long ago discovered that the burnt matchsticks in the little glass dish on Mrs Coulson's dressing table did not mean that her mistress had taken to secretly smoking cigarettes.

No, one evening when Jane was helping her dress for dinner her mistress had laughed and told her that she might as well confess. Jane had watched in awe as Mrs Coulson struck a match, waited for it to go out and cool a little and then applied the tip to her eyelashes. So far Jane had been deterred from trying it by the knowledge that tiny specks of soot sometimes fell on to Mrs Coulson's cheeks where they became smeared as the evening wore on.

No, for the moment she would be satisfied with a discreet touch of rouge and the lightest dusting of powder. And she didn't think she would ever have to drink vinegar. When she'd been a child her father had delighted in calling her his little china doll and her mother had encouraged her to believe that her pale complexion, dark-fringed blue eyes and angel-fair hair added up to a ticket that would carry her away from the village and secure her an altogether different existence in town.

So far her mother had been right, although Jane knew how much she owed her parents for paying for the deportment and elocution lessons and encouraging her skill with the needle. Jane had accepted that, no matter how attractive she was, no handsome prince nor even a 'gentleman' was likely to want to marry a girl from a fishing village. But she was enough her parents' daughter to have the determination to succeed in her own right. If her plan came to anything her mother and father would be pleased with her. They would not be pleased if she married William Lawson. But she had decided to try with all her might to make both her dreams come true.

With her hat firmly pinned in place Jane smiled at her reflection. She was being sent into town in the carriage to look at the new fabrics in Bainbridge's. Fabrics suitable for autumn and winter clothes – and for London. Mr Coulson had political ambitions and had met Mr Gladstone. Soon there was to be another meeting and Jane was going to help her mistress look as elegant as possible. For, she had told Jane, the master may stand for Parliament and we will have to have a house in London. Mrs Coulson had made it plain that although she wanted Jane to go to London with them, nevertheless she would not stand in the way of Jane's plans.

Jane made her way down the wide, Turkey-carpeted, mahogany staircase. The measured tick from the long-case clock on the first-floor landing echoed from the high walls of the hall. Dust motes danced in the coloured shafts of light that fell through the stained-glass window in the wall behind her. The light cast jewelled patterns on the tiled floor of the hall below and the smell of lavender polish surrounded her.

When she reached the bottom she turned towards the rear of the house. At the end of the passage she pushed open a door that looked as though it was part of the oak panelling. The other side of the door was covered in green baize. She stepped through the doorway and hesitated. This door separated two worlds: the world of servants and the world of masters. Jane, as a lady's maid, had achieved an uncomfortable place between the two. Uncomfortable because although she never wanted to go back to the world of servants, realistically she knew she would never be part of the grand world of masters either. Not if she married William.

The backstairs were uncarpeted, cold and unlit. She hurried down as quickly as she could and along the stone-flagged floor that led to the stable yard. She was slightly irritated that the carriage had not come to the front entrance of the house for her, but as soon as they were bowling along on the way to the city she could sit up straight and enjoy the admiring glances of the passers-by. She knew she looked every inch a lady.

That night Kate lifted the tin bath down from the nail in the wall of the back yard. She didn't care how many kettles of water it would take to fill it; she longed to lie back and soak herself in some sweet-smelling water.

When she had finished her round, Kate had called at the village shop to collect her aunt's order and on impulse had asked Mrs Willis if she had any bath salts. She had stood there, hot and weary, while Alice obligingly searched her dusty shelves.

'You're in luck,' Alice had said eventually, and she handed Kate a fancy glass bottle full of pale pink crystals. 'That'll be one shilling.'

'Oh,' Kate said. She had already seen the price on the side of the bottle.

There had been no need to say more. Mrs Willis must have seen the disappointment in her eyes. 'Although, mind,' she said, 'that bottle's been sitting on the shelf over a year now. How's about if I offer it half price?'

'Thank you. I'll take it.'

So after they had eaten their teatime meal together Kate had asked her aunt if she could have a bath instead of the usual bowl of water in the sink.

'Why, of course, pet. We'll both hev one. It'll ease me old bones.'

As well as the kettle they boiled pans of water and when they judged there was sufficient hot water in the bath Kate added some cold from a jug and then took the jar of bath crystals from her pocket. She read the label. It was faded but she could just about make out the directions.

'What does it say?' Aunt Meg asked, perhaps alarmed by Kate's frown.

'Fragrant Bath Salts,' Kate replied.

'I know that, you daft ha'p'orth! I meant that smaller writing underneath.'

Kate began to read in an exaggeratedly refined manner. 'These superior salts, added to an ordinary bath or wash-hand basin of water, will instantly soften the hardest water, rendering the skin beautifully clear and soft, and also produce a most exhilarating and invigorating perfume!'

'My, my, all that for a shilling!'

'Mrs Willis let me have it for sixpence.'

'Better still. How much do you have to use?'

Kate read the directions. 'A teaspoonful for a wash-hand basin and two tablespoonfuls for a large bath.'

'So it'll last a while,' Aunt Meg said.

'Do you think I've been extravagant?'

'No, pet, divven't fret. You need a little treat – the way you are, and considering everything that's happened to you. Now hurry up. I'll lock the doors and fetch the screen. Then I'll sit beyond and be ready if you need me.'

'Need you?'

'Aye, pet. You never know, you might come over dizzy. In your condition, you know.'

When Kate had stripped to her shift she spooned the pink crystals into the water and both she and Aunt Meg savoured the delicate scent that arose in the swirls of steam.

'Mmm . . .' Meg sniffed appreciatively. 'Carnation.'

'No, I think it's rose,' Kate said.

'You may be right. I've probably ruined me sense of smell after all these years of snuff-taking. But whatever it is, it smells lovely.'

Kate heard the longing in her aunt's voice and looked at her kind old face. 'Aunt Meg, I think you should go first.' She hoped her aunt wouldn't guess how much it cost her to say that.

'No, pet, you first. I'll hev the kettle ready with some more hot water, and if you like you can add another spoonful of them crystals before I get in.'

'Of course I will.' Kate didn't argue although she felt guilty.

'Gan on, I won't look.' Her aunt grinned as she gestured to Kate to take off her remaining clothes. Eyes averted, she offered her hand for Kate to grasp as she stepped into the fragrant water. 'Lower yerself slowly. Are you down?'

'Mm.'

'Then I'll sit with me knitting for a while. Give a shout if you need me.'

Kate had pinned her hair up for the moment although she intended to wash it later. She settled down, lying back against the slope of the bath, her arms stretched out along the sides. She closed her eyes and gave herself up to the soothing warmth of the water and the scent of roses. She could hear the crackling of the coals in the fire and the click-clack of her aunt's needles. She could never remember her aunt knitting before and wondered who the garment could be for. William or Thomas perhaps? No doubt her aunt would tell her.

Outside the cottage she sensed a stillness as a mist curled in from the sea. An old superstition held that it also brought the wraiths of dead mariners. She could hear the muffled thuds of the waves beating on the shore and the sound of foghorns from the ships waiting to enter the Tyne on the turn of the tide. She could also hear the mournful clanging of the bell on the Black Midden rocks near the mouth of the river. Over the centuries many a vessel had come to grief on these rocks.

Centuries . . . Jos had liked to speak about centuries and the passing of time. Jos . . . Kate tried to remember her sweetheart as she had last seen him, smiling his carefree smile, the corners of his eyes crinkling. But for some reason the picture wouldn't form in her mind's eye. She felt a twinge of panic when she realized that the features she had known so well seemed to be evading her. How could that be? She concentrated extra hard and then almost cried out in shock when instead of Jos's face she saw another face; older, stronger, with a gaze that was both compelling and unsettling. It was the face of Richard Adamson.

Guilt surged through her. Breathing rapidly, she reached for the wedding ring she wore on a piece of ribbon round her neck and willed the disturbing likeness to go away. As she fingered the smooth circle of gold the image faded and she began to breathe more easily.

She never took the ring off and now, in the bath, the ribbon was wet and seemed to stick to her damp flesh. Kate felt a slight discomfort when her arm caught the side of her breast. She looked down and saw that the flesh around her nipples was darker than it had been and the breasts themselves were slightly more full. Only slightly, she thought. She smoothed her hands over the flat plane of her belly. Was there a slight roundness? No, she decided. No one could tell that I am with child.

Her mother had told her that, tall and slender as she was, her pregnancy might not be obvious until the fifth month – and perhaps not even then if she carried the baby 'high'. Of course she would have to let out her clothes and maybe be clever with an extra fold or two of material. She'd be wearing warmer clothes, anyway, come December, but hopefully they would have heard from Winifred long before then and Kate would be on her way to America.

Sighing, she took up the flannel and soap and washed herself. When she took the pins out of her hair and leaned forward to wash it she called for her aunt to help. Kate held a flannel to her eyes while Meg knelt down by the bath and helped by scooping up jugs of water.

When she had dried herself she put on her nightdress and then it was her turn to help her aunt. The older woman had kept a shift on – for modesty's sake, she said – but, even so, Kate could see the tracks the ropes of the creel had left in the skin of her shoulders and upper arms. Kneeling by the bath in the soft glow of the firelight, helping with something so personal, Kate had never felt closer to her aunt. She realized that, much as she loved her mother, they very rarely shared moments like this.

Her mother was always busy. If they had a bath it had to be when the men were out fishing and there was always something else to do, some task to finish, so they could never linger.

While Kate emptied the bath bucket by bucket and then dragged it to the yard to tip out the last fragrant suds before hanging it up on its nail, her aunt made a cup of tea, and then they sat by the fire to drink it. Both of them brushed their hair until it was dry. That night, soothed by her bath and comforted by her aunt's presence, Kate slept more soundly that she had done for weeks.

They were down on the beach as the first cobles came in with their catches. Kate was now doing some of the buying although she felt nervous when the bidding started. Her aunt knew what price to pay down to a farthing.

'Divven't fret, Kate, I'll give you the wink if the price is going too high. Keep an eye on old Martha over there. When she drops out it's time to stop.'

'Did I do all right?' Kate asked when the auction was over.

'Aye, lass, you did. You've nowt to worry about. You're learning fast.'

They sat on the low wall near where the cobles were moored and packed the fish they'd bought into their creels.

'Right, Kate, do you think you can manage the Wallsend round on your own today? I'll go along to Whitley.'

With the two of them sharing the business it was essential to find new customers and Aunt Meg was the expert at that. Kate didn't think she was ready yet to knock on the doors of strangers and persuade them to buy fish. So she agreed to go to Wallsend, hitching the usual lift with Albert Brunton.

The day went well, although many of her customers asked after Meg, concerned that she might be poorly. More than one of them said how pleased they were that the old fishwife now had a strong young helper. 'By the end of the day, she's right weary, isn't she?' one kindly woman said. 'Aye, bone weary,' the woman's neighbour added, 'and a bit unsteady.'

Kate wondered if they knew that it wasn't weariness that made her aunt unsteady on her feet but the contents of her flask. She assured anyone who asked that her aunt was quite well and that no doubt they would be seeing her soon. She sold almost the entire contents of her creel but she remembered to keep a respectable parcel by to give to Albert's wife, Tilda, when they returned to the timber yard.

Then she set off for Belle Vue Cottage, eager to tell Aunt Meg how well the day had gone. The walk home took Kate down Marden Lane towards the sea. At the bottom of the lane she turned left to walk along to the village and as she walked past the grand villas on Beverley Terrace she looked up at Richard Adamson's house. The front door was closed and the large windows were obscured by lace curtains. She wondered if Mr Adamson was at home – but, of course, that was unlikely; he would still be at his business premises on the quayside at North Shields.

There was the usual activity on the top boat field. One of the cobles was being painted blue and white. At least, it was half painted – the pots of paint were there but there were no painters. And the nets were spread out ready for mending but no one was mending them. Instead a group of men was huddled over by the cliff top.

Kate was curious. No one in the village stopped work without good reason. She made her way across the boat field and frowned when she realized that the men were not staring out to sea – they were peering down over the cliff. She edged her way through the group. Someone, she didn't register who it was, tried to stop her. He took hold of her arm but she shook herself free.

'It's Kate Lawson,' she heard another man say.

'For God's sake stop her.'

'Wait, lass! Divven't look down.'

But it was too late. Kate had reached the cliff's edge and she looked down and saw what it was that the men were staring at. The figure of a woman lay sprawled at the foot of the cliff. The woman's neck was twisted at an unnatural angle and a dark stain was spreading out from under her head and seeping into a rock pool.

Kate felt her knees give way. 'Look out!' someone cried, and the men at each side of her caught her arms and held her steady.

'No . . . no . . . no!' Kate was hardly aware that it was she who was crying out in grief and terror at the sight of her Aunt Meg lying like a broken doll on the rocks below.

Chapter Seven

Kate had scrambled down the rocks with no thought for her own safety, and now she knelt and cradled her aunt's head in her arms. Blood had seeped into the rock pools. Kate stared at the crimson ribbons curling through the water, staining it with the colours of death. Surely Aunt Meg couldn't be dead – she was still warm. Kate looked up at the faces of the men surrounding her for reassurance. Unable to stop her, some of them had followed her down to the beach. They saw the anguished question in her eyes and one or two of them shook their heads gravely.

Kate felt tears well up. She blinked them away and lowered her head to gaze desperately into the face of her beloved aunt. Meg's eyes were wide open as they stared up at the wide blue sky and the seabirds circling above the bay. But the old fishwife could neither hear the harsh cries of the gulls nor see their graceful flight as they caught the currents of air to lift them even higher. Behind the eyes there was nothing; emptiness. Aunt Meg was no longer there no matter how much Kate wanted her to be.

Kate began to rock backwards and forwards, still cradling her aunt and crooning to her as if she were a baby. She heard the onlookers begin to mutter worriedly. Fragments of their conversations pierced her dazed state.

'Crazed with grief . . .'

'No wonder . . .'

'Poor lass. First her sweetheart and now her aunt . . .'

'And so soon after . . .'

'Has anyone told Henry? After all, he's Meg's brother.'

'Aye, I sent young Davy.'

Kate heard her father's name mentioned but she didn't care. Let him come, she thought. She was aware of movement in the crowd around her. They parted as someone pushed their way through.

'Stop that,' the newcomer said roughly. 'That will do no good at all.'

The speaker knelt down and took Kate in her arms. 'Now come away with me, before your father comes,' her mother said. 'Do you hear me? Lay her down. Lay her down gently. That's right. Come along – I'll help you up.'

Reluctantly Kate did as she was told. She stared at her aunt's poor head lying on the rocks with the dark blood matting her once splendid hair. She leaned forward again and eased her aunt's shawl up so that it lay under her head like a pillow. Then, rising, she allowed her mother to lead her away.

A week later the two of them sat facing each other across the table at Belle Vue Cottage. Her mother had taken the old cocoa tin down from the mantelshelf and now she opened it and shook the contents out on to the scrubbed surface. Kate watched as some of the coins rolled towards her and then clattered to a stop.

'Should we be doing this?' Kate asked.

'Why ever not?'

'It's Aunt Meg's money. Her savings.'

'She can't spend any of it where she's gone.'

'Don't say that!'

'It's true. And I know Meg would want you to have it now. She told me that she was going to give you a tidy sum to set you up in America. She didn't want Winifred to think we were paupers.' Her mother gazed at the coins on the table and began gathering them up and putting them in neat little piles. She sighed. 'Poor Meg. I don't think she'd counted it lately.'

'Why do you say that?'

'Because she led me to believe there was much more than this. By the time I've settled up for her funeral there'll be precious little left. I don't understand. Unless . . .'

'What is it?'

'Well, Meg was over-fond of her gin, wasn't she?' Nan held up her hand when she saw that Kate was about to protest. 'No, Kate, we all knew about it. And she was the soul of generosity. I telt her many a time not to listen to hard luck stories, especially if she'd had a drop or two, but she didn't heed my advice. You know what I think, Kate? I think she'd got herself into a right muddle. I don't believe she had any idea how much money there was left in the tin. And that's what I'm going to tell your da.'

'Why do you have to tell him anything?'

87

'Because Meg worked hard and had a canny business. Your father is sure that she had some savings. He telt me to come and get them. He said, as her brother, he was entitled to anything she left.'

'Give him the money, I don't care.'

'No, I'm not going to do that, at least not all of it. He'll only spend it on drink.'

The two women stared at each other, their expressions grave.

'Drink . . .' Kate said. 'Drinking too much is a family failing, isn't it?'

Her mother looked as though she wished she could deny it. She nodded slowly as she said, 'I'm afraid so.'

'Well, what about my brothers? Don't you fear for them?'

'I don't know, lass.' Her mother looked bleak. 'William doesn't seem to like the drink very much. I don't know whether he finds it distasteful or whether he's been put off by your da's behaviour. But Thomas . . .' Nan's voice trailed off and she stared ahead without really seeing anything. 'I sometimes worry about Thomas. He's a hothead to start with and when he's had a drink he's impossible.' Nan pushed about half of the coins across the table towards Kate. 'There's as much as I dare give you. Your da will have to be satisfied with the rest.'

'But how will you convince him that's all there is?'

'I'll say she's been spending it on drink. That's partly true. And he'll have to believe it because it was the drink that killed her, wasn't it?'

Kate flinched. She'd been told how Meg had been laughing and joking with some of the lads on the boat field. She'd had a good day and had already been back to the cottage to leave her creel and basket. Then, seeking company, perhaps, she had strolled out into the sunshine.

If only I'd got home earlier, Kate thought now. If only I had not made any attempt to gossip with the customers the way my aunt did. She had tortured herself with such 'if onlys' ever since the day of the accident. But she hadn't been home when Meg had returned to the cottage and her aunt had gone out seeking 'a bit chat' as she would have called it. After a while she had set off for home, taking the cliff-top path. Nobody saw the exact moment when she stumbled. No one was near enough to reach out and prevent her falling. And it must have happened only a moment or two before Kate had walked that way. So there was another 'if only'.

The hateful vision returned. Kate tried to banish from her inner eye what she had seen when she had gazed down at the rocks below. Meg's twisted body, the eyes staring up in surprise, the ribbons of blood spreading out across the rocks and into the pools of salt water.

'Shall I put this money back in the tin?' Her mother's question brought Kate back to the present.

'I suppose so,' she said. 'What are you doing?'

'I'm hiding the tin at the back of this drawer in the dresser. Just in case your father gets it into his head to come looking.'

'Do you think he will?'

'Not if I do my job properly, but we'll be safe rather than sorry, shall we?'

Kate nodded dumbly. She was surprised and grateful that her mother could be so practical when she herself was still too stunned with grief even to think straight.

'What's this?' her mother said as she picked something up from the dresser. 'There's something wrapped up in this clean tea towel.'

'Bring it over. I'll show you.'

Wordlessly Kate unwrapped the bundle that her mother placed on the table before her and they both stared at what was revealed.

'*Your* work?' her mother asked. Her eyes had widened in disbelief.

Kate smiled. 'Hardly. No, it's Meg's.'

'But it's beautiful. And I didn't know Meg could knit anything more complicated than a simple shawl.'

'It is a shawl,' Kate said, 'or at least half of one.'

Together they stared at the soft white wool and the delicate lacy pattern of what looked like tiny seashells. 'For the baby,' her mother breathed.

'She wouldn't let me see what she was knitting. I found it after she died when I was looking for – for clean things for the undertaker. It was wrapped up just as you found it and hidden among her petticoats.'

'I'll finish it,' her mother said. 'But we'll keep it here. Whenever I can I'll come round and spend some time with you. Are you going to be all right here on your own?'

'I'll manage.'

'And you'll be able to pay the rent?'

'Yes, Aunt Meg taught me well. I'll do as much of her round as I can, although I might have to let the new customers go.'

'Then I can only hope that we'll hear from Winifred soon. I don't want anything to happen.'

'What do you mean?'

'In spite of the trouble you're in, the poor bairn is an innocent soul. I wouldn't want you to lose it.'

Kate's hands went instinctively to her abdomen. As yet there was no visible sign of Jos's child and she had felt no movements. But it was there, her child was there, safe within her, and a wave of love so powerful that it left her gasping overwhelmed her. 'No,' she whispered and she knew she was shaking. 'No, I mustn't lose my baby.'

'So work hard if you must,' her mother said, 'but whenever you can you should rest. Put your feet up, eat properly. I'll bring you food from home when I can. A drop of broth, a bit of stew. And make sure you drink plenty milk for the little 'un's bones and teeth.'

'But what will my father say about you bringing me things from home?'

'He'll never know.' Her mother pursed her lips and suddenly looked old and tired.

'What is it?' Kate asked. 'Is something wrong?'

'No more than usual. Although your father's drinking is getting worse. I don't know how he would manage without your brothers – particularly William. You know, Kate, I've come to rely more and more on your elder brother. And I know that's not fair. He'll want to get wed one day and then what will I do?'

'Come with me to America!' Kate said it impulsively and she saw her mother's eyes light up briefly, but the light was soon extinguished.

'No, pet. I took my marriage vows and I'll see them through. And there's Thomas. Big as he thinks he is, he still needs his ma.'

Her mother insisted on filling the coal scuttle and seeing to the fire before she took her leave. 'Will you be down at the beach auction in the morning?' she asked.

'Of course.'

'Then have an early night. Go to bed now. You've no one to please but yourself. I half envy you.'

But Kate didn't go to bed. She was too restless. She knew she wouldn't sleep so she got the writing set from the drawer in the dresser and sat at the table to write a letter to her friend – who still didn't know what the true situation was. But she could tell Jane of her sorrow and how much she missed her beloved aunt. It would give her comfort to pour out her heartache, knowing her friend would sympathize. She picked up her pen.

A while later she finished the letter with a request that Jane should try to come home for a visit soon. She blotted the pages carefully, put them in an envelope, sealed it and attached a stamp. She left the envelope lying on the table and rose from her chair. But making a sudden decision she snatched her shawl from the back of the door and seized the letter. I'll walk along and post it now, she thought. I need some fresh air and the village will be quiet at this time of night.

After she had posted the letter Kate stood for a while on Bank Top and let the light breeze from the sea cool her face and lift her hair. It was soothing. The surface of the sea, like grey silk, rippled in the breeze and the moon had laid a pathway of silver across the water in the bay. Kate clutched at the rail and stared at the dappled water. She could hear the waves slapping on to the beach and then pull back across the shingle.

'Beautiful,' someone said softly.

She recognized the voice and didn't even turn when the speaker came to stand beside her.

'Yes, isn't it?' she replied. 'The moonlight on the water...'

'I didn't mean the moon light,' Howard Munro said. 'I meant you.'

Kate was shocked. 'You shouldn't speak to me like that.'

'Forgive me. I meant no disrespect.' He laughed softly. 'I'm an artist, remember? Sometimes we don't behave like gentlemen. But then people don't expect us to. Am I forgiven?'

Kate smiled tentatively and nodded her assent.

'Good, because I've been meaning to ask you, may I paint your portrait?'

'*My* portrait? Why?'

'It will be one of a series of pictures of this village and the people who live and work here,' he said. 'I hope to exhibit them in a gallery in Boston – my hometown.'

Kate was nonplussed. She didn't know what to say.

He must have seen how puzzled she was because he smiled encouragingly. 'I will tell you what to wear...' Kate backed away a little. 'Don't worry, I want you dressed pretty much as you are now in your dark blue skirt and bodice with your neckerchief and your working shoes. And, of course, carrying your – what do you call it? Your basket.'

'Creel.'

'Yes, your creel. And you will have to be patient and stand still and it will be like work, so I shall pay you a proper fee, as I would any model.'

'Model...' Kate had heard about artist's models and she was not sure if they were respectable.

'And you won't be the first person here to pose for me. I've already started work on some sketches of Martha Smith, standing right here on Bank Top, holding her creel.'

'But Martha is so old!' Kate couldn't help saying. 'All those wrinkles . . .'

'And those piercing blue eyes. And all that wisdom in her face. Marvellous!'

'So it's not my beauty you want me for, then,' Kate said.

'I beg your pardon?'

'If you're looking for models like Martha . . .'

'Kate, you're teasing me. So, will you pose for me?'

'I don't know. I'm not sure I could be bold enough to stand here on Bank Top and allow myself to be gawped at by the world and his wife as they pass by.'

'You have a wonderful turn of phrase, Kate, but that won't be necessary. I am used to being gawped at and I will stand here alone to make sketches of the background. You will come to my studio where it will be more comfortable and you will be safe from curious onlookers.'

'Your studio?'

'Yes – in the cottage Richard has loaned to me.'

'In your cottage . . .'

'If you are worried about the proprieties let me tell you Martha has been twice already. She brought her granddaughter Betsy to act as chaperone. You could bring your mother – or a friend, perhaps.'

'I can't answer you now.'

'I'll pay you well. After all, I may sell the paintings some day.'

'Money is not my concern.' Kate could not disguise her flash of fury and the artist looked abashed.

'Of course it isn't. And now I've managed to insult you again. But promise me you'll think about it.'

'I will. But now I must go. I have to be up early in the morning.'

'Oh, no. I've kept you talking and I know how hard you work. May I see you safely home?'

Kate laughed. 'It's not far and the only creatures about are a few cats.'

'Some of them mine, so I'd better come along to protect you from them. After all, we are going the same way.'

They fell into step but didn't speak again until Mr Munro bade her goodnight just a few steps from her door. Once inside Kate got into bed as quickly as possible. She lay for a while and tried to make up her mind about Mr Munro. He had a disconcerting way of speaking but she thought there was no harm in him. But did she want to pose for him? Did she want her likeness captured on canvas for anyone to see? The idea was unsettling but not altogether unpleasing. She had promised him she would think about it. But not now . . . she was too tired. Then, just before sleep overtook her, a disturbing image flickered in her mind. That of a curtain twitching at one of the windows as she and Mr Munro walked by.

As they hurried along Heaton Road William glanced at his reflection in the rain-speckled shop windows and hardly recognized himself. Jane had told him long ago that he must never meet her in town wearing his fisherman's gansey, even his best one, and he had turned up today wearing the jacket and trousers he wore at church. He had also put on his best shirt and his only tie. It pleased William to keep Jane happy. He was wise enough to know that she only wanted the best for him – as he did for her. His mother had smiled knowingly when he left the cottage but she hadn't asked him where he was going. He was pretty sure that she knew.

He had called at the servants' entrance of the Coulsons' house and had been slightly aggrieved that Jane hadn't seemed to notice the effort he'd made. She'd asked him in, which was unusual – in fact almost unheard of – and immediately directed him to a sort of cloakroom and told him to change into the clothes he would find waiting there.

He did so uncomplainingly and had presented himself for inspection. His darling had both smiled and frowned. He'd watched her changing expressions with fond amusement. The suit had been made for a less muscular man but Jane said it would have to do. The waistcoat was so tight it made breathing difficult and the shirt collar cut so sharply into his neck that he found it almost impossible to turn his head. Then there was the hat: the 'bowler'. He thought he would rather go to the Afghan frontier than walk the streets of Cullercoats with that perched on his head. But as they were going to be walking the streets of respectable suburbs he guessed that he wouldn't be too out of place.

William was walking on the outside as Jane said he must and reflected alongside him was the trim, elegantly dressed figure of Jane. She looked so self-assured as she hurried along holding her umbrella to protect herself from the sudden shower. But even his admiration of her and pride in her could not quell his doubt.

'Do I look all right?' he asked.

'William, your appearance is every bit that of a gentleman, so please will you remove that pained look from your face.'

He stopped, and Jane turned to glare at him. William did not respond. He was looking up at the sign written in large gold letters above the shop. It said: C. & M. HOGG, LADIES' AND GENTLEMEN'S OUTFITTERS. The C stood for Cyril, but he was long deceased. The M stood for Mabel, the widow Hogg, who wanted to retire and go to live with her daughter who had married a draper with a thriving business in Leeds. Or so Jane had told him.

'Now remember, William, when we go in I will do the talking, but I shall look to you every now and then to make sure that you agree.'

'Would it matter if I didn't?' William grinned. Jane was used to getting her own way and he'd never minded. He respected her quick brain and he considered himself a lucky man that a lass so dainty and beautiful – like a Dresden shepherdess, she was – would be content to walk out with him.

'Of course it would.' Jane's tone didn't carry conviction but the look she slanted up at him through her dusky lashes sent his senses reeling, as usual.

William felt himself flushing and he ran his forefinger along the inside of his collar to ease it away from his neck. 'You said it was all done and dusted,' he said.

'It is, as far as the shop itself is concerned, but there's the stock to consider. My father has been very generous in agreeing to set me up in business and I want to make sure we spend his money wisely.'

'We?' William had a nightmare vision of himself serving behind the counter, selling socks perhaps, or neck ties, or collars as uncomfortable as the one he had been forced to wear today.

Jane's smile was thin. 'I said "we" because Mrs Hogg is expecting an engaged couple. Even though she has run the business by herself for years it seems she is unwilling to sell to a single woman. Ridiculous, isn't it?'

'If you say so.'

'I do. And, William . . .' Jane's tone softened and she raised her umbrella higher and moved closer to him, looking up into his face with those amazing blue eyes. 'We are an engaged couple, aren't we? I mean, I know I haven't got an engagement ring – and I don't mind, really I don't – but we are promised to each other, aren't we?'

'Jane . . .' He stepped closer and put his hands on her waist.

'William, not now, people will see us.' The umbrella trembled, sending a scattering of raindrops down on both of them.

'The street is Sabbath quiet,' William said. 'All the shops are closed. There's no one in sight.'

'Somebody could be looking from an upper window. Many of the shopkeepers live above the shop – as . . . as . . .' She bit her lip and hurried on. 'Now.' She glanced cursorily at the display in the shop window as she shook her umbrella and furled it. There were ladies' blouses, gentlemen's shirts, children's smocks, socks and gloves all arranged in no particular order. William saw her frown. He guessed that should her plan to buy the shop be successful – and it looked as though it would be – the window would be sorted out very quickly. 'Now,' she repeated, 'Mrs Hogg will be waiting for us.'

The notice hanging in the door said 'Closed' but as soon as they knocked the door opened. Mrs Hogg proved to be a tall, spare, wrinkled woman with wire-framed spectacles that always appeared to be sliding down to the end of her long nose. But her smile was welcoming.

William followed Jane in, smiled politely when he was introduced and then stood back while the two women discussed business. Jane kept looking at him questioningly and he remembered to smile or nod wisely. He had no idea what they were talking about, since he had lost track long ago, but he seemed to be making the right responses because Jane was looking happier and happier.

He was glad about that. He wanted Jane to be happy, but as he looked at the rails of ready-made clothes sheathed in protective covers and the bolts of cloth stacked neatly on shelves behind the counter, he saw no place for himself. Then he sensed that Jane and Mrs Hogg had stopped talking and when he looked up he found they were both staring at him.

'What is it?' he asked.

'I should ask you that question, William dear,' Jane said. 'You uttered such a sigh just now.'

'Did I?'

'Please don't worry, Miss Harrison,' Mrs Hogg said. 'I think I know what the matter is. We've been talking so much that I'd quite forgotten poor Mr Lawson. I should have realized that he will want to talk to you . . . and perhaps advise you. I'll tell you what I'll do. I'll go upstairs to the flat so that Mr Lawson may express his opinions freely, and return in a quarter of an hour.'

The woman shot him a genuine smile. Whether or not she believed that Jane needed to consult him, she was willing to go along with the idea that the man was the master. She pulled a curtain aside at the back of the shop and vanished behind it. They could hear her mounting the stairs.

'I'm sorry,' William said. 'Was I rude?'

'No.'

'Then tell me why you look so cross.'

'I'm not cross. Just disappointed. I thought you'd be interested in my plans.'

'I am. But . . .'

'But what?'

'Well, mebbes I had plans too.'

Jane stared at William. She was at a loss how to proceed. William loved her, she was sure of that. She had hinted for long enough that she never wanted to go back to live in the village and he had seemed to accept it. But perhaps he never had. Perhaps she had made it too obvious how very much she loved him and perhaps he had therefore believed that she would give in to him in the end.

If only I could have forgotten about William Lawson the minute I left Cullercoats and came to work in town, she thought. But she had not been able to forget him and her plans for the future had always included him. He didn't know yet what part he was to play. She hoped he would approve, but first she must show him how happy owning this outfitter's business would make her.

She looked at him now. So tall, so handsome – so like a Viking, she imagined fancifully – with his strong features and firm jawline and his red-gold hair. But his expression was bleak. She acknowledged he looked uncomfortable in Mr Coulson's cast-off clothes but, nevertheless, they were better than his own. It had been kind of Mrs Coulson to pass on her husband's clothing and she had instructed Mrs Roberts, the housekeeper, to allow Mr Lawson to change in the staff cloak cupboard. Jane had expressed her gratitude, but it was a pity she hadn't had time to alter the suit William was wearing now, for, although he didn't know it yet, there was another more important meeting ahead of him.

She moved closer to him, gently pressing the length of her body against his. She rested her head on his chest for a moment and then undid a few buttons of his waistcoat. She slipped her hand inside and rested her palm on his smooth, white shirt. She felt his heart begin to race.

'You do love me, don't you?'

'You know I do.'

'And you want me to be happy?'

'I do – but I want us to be happy together.'

'We can be.'

'I don't see how. With you setting up in business here in town and me living at the coast.'

'Be patient. As soon as we've done here I'll explain my plan. But now why don't you kiss me?'

She raised her head and William claimed her lips eagerly. She could feel his passion rising and her own pulse began to race. In a sudden movement William put his hands to her waist and lifted her up on to the counter.

'That's better,' he said. 'You're such a little thing.'

'No, William. Stop. We mustn't. But maybe we won't have to wait much longer.'

She placed her hands on his shoulders and pushed him away. She knew her face was flushed and she turned away from him, swinging her legs up over the counter and down on the other side. For his sake as much as her own she was glad to keep the solid wooden structure between them.

'Look at all these lovely fabrics,' she said. 'Such a variety. There's taffeta, cotton, poplin, muslin, even organdie. And look – look at these glass-fronted drawers. All the trimmings I need: lace, ribbons, belts, buckles, buttons as well as tapes, threads, pins, hooks and eyes.'

'Jane, stop! I can see you're pleased but you might as well be talking a foreign language.'

Jane sighed but continued determinedly, 'Well, this is in English, plain to see. Can you read this notice?'

William obliged and read the words printed on the card in the fancy frame standing on the counter: 'ALTERATIONS UNDERTAKEN.'

'That's the side of the business I'm going to develop,' Jane said. 'That and dressmaking. And, William, I won't even have to advertise for customers. Mrs Coulson is going to tell all her friends about me. She'll tell them about the work I've done for her and her daughter, and how pleased she is. My reputation should grow by word of mouth, and— William! What are you doing?'

William had pulled a chair forward and was sitting down. He proceeded to take one of his shoes off and knead his foot. 'These shoes might be long enough but they're not wide enough,' he said. 'If you don't mind, Jane, I'll give them to me da when I get home. They should fit him.'

'I don't mind at all if you give them to your father.' She stressed the last word. 'But now you'd better put your shoe back on before Mrs Hogg comes back.'

Jane felt like crying. William had managed to spoil her happy mood by his sheer lack of interest. No, that wasn't fair. He loved her and he was pleased for her but he was troubled and she knew why. She walked round the counter to stand beside him. When he had finished tying his shoelace he started to stand but she pushed him back on to the chair gently and sat on his knee.

'Are you vexed with me?' he asked. He looked so contrite that she would have forgiven him anything.

'No. I'm vexed with myself. I brought you here to see what I planned to do and I didn't explain things properly.' She paused and took a deep breath. 'William,' she began, 'you want us to be together, don't you?'

'You know I do. I want us to be married and I don't see how we're going to manage that if I'm in Cullercoats and you are running a business here in Newcastle.'

Jane knew that she had to convince him that their future lay away from Cullercoats. Fishing was a hard life and getting harder. With the competition from Adamson's steam trawlers and the Scottish boats, the catches were getting smaller and smaller, the men returning after hours of gruelling work with half-empty cobles and grim faces. Some of the fishwives had stopped buying from the beach auction and were going early in the morning to the fish quay at North Shields to buy their herring.

Her mother's last letter had told her that some of the men didn't think it was worth going out any more. They had either sold their cobles or left them untended and were seeking work as labourers in the building trade. Jane didn't want that to happen to William so she'd convinced herself that it wasn't for entirely selfish reasons that she had thought of another future for him.

'I know,' she told him. 'And I do have a plan. I wanted it to be a surprise after we'd seen the shop. I wanted you to see what a marvellous opportunity this is. I thought you'd be pleased for me.'

William looked uneasy. 'I am, I suppose.'

Jane dabbed at her eyes with her handkerchief, a tiny square of embroidered linen, but managed to smile through her tears. 'Oh, William. This is my fault. We should have gone there first.'

'Gone where?'

'Wait and see.'

Jane took his large, handsome face between her kid-gloved hands and kissed his brow, his eyes, one after the other, and then his mouth. He responded as he always did and the resulting embrace left her breathless.

'You smell gorgeous,' he said when at last they pulled away from each other. 'Like a summer garden.'

'And you smell delicious, too. Like a real gentleman.'

The lime-scented brilliantine she had combed through William's hair before they came had not been salvaged from Mr Coulson's dressing room. Jane had bought it at Bainbridge's along with a matching aftershave lotion. William had been genuinely pleased with her gifts and Jane had averted her eyes guiltily, not wishing him to know that her primary concern was that, when they met Mrs Hogg, he would not smell of fish.

'Er – hum!'

Startled by the sound of a cough, Jane rose hurriedly and so did William. The widow Hogg was smiling.

'Don't worry,' she said. 'I'm not shocked. Strange as it may seem to you young folk, I can remember what it was like to be engaged to be married. But, now, have you any more questions?'

Jane assured her that she was perfectly satisfied and that she wanted to go ahead. 'My father will be coming to see you,' she said. 'As soon as possible.'

When they left the shop they found that the rain had stopped and the sun was trying to shine. Jane took that as a good omen.

Chapter Eight

'Well?'

Jane looked up at William uneasily. They had stopped outside another shop. It was closed and the window blinds were pulled right down so that there was only the merest glimpse of a marbled counter to be seen. William hadn't said a word, and she couldn't tell from his expression whether he was pleased or affronted. He glanced up at the smart blue façade with the gold-painted name and then, eventually, he turned and looked at her.

'You want me to work in a shop?'

'Not just a shop. A fishmonger's.'

'A shop assistant?'

'Not just an assistant. Mr Rennison is expanding the business and he's looking for a buyer. He no longer wants to depend on taking deliveries from a fish merchant. He needs someone with the right knowledge. Someone who could go to the fish quay in the morning and do the buying for all his shops. Someone who would know how to choose the fish and would know the proper price—'

'There's no proper price.'

'What do you mean?'

'It depends on the weather – the size of the catch – the demand.'

'Exactly!' Jane became a little less anxious. 'Mr Rennison knows that and he wants someone he can trust.'

'How do you know this?'

'He supplies the Coulson household and most of the other big houses in Jesmond, Gosforth and Heaton – the better class of customers.'

'Better class?' William raised his brows.

'You know what I mean.'

'No, tell me.'

'William, don't be difficult. You know very well I mean the richer customers. The ones who are above sending the cook out to the fishwife on the corner.'

For a moment she thought she had angered him but to her relief he smiled.

'The more fools they,' he said. 'The fish they would buy from the creel would be just as good and mebbes even fresher. But don't worry,' he said when he saw her frown, 'I have no objection to rich folk spending their money and keeping poorer folk in business. But you still haven't explained how you know he's looking for someone.'

'Mrs Coulson's housekeeper is Mr Rennison's sister. He sometimes visits and I overheard them talking in the kitchen. It's no secret. I haven't done anything wrong.'

Jane had decided not to tell William of the months she had spent going round the shops in her brief hours off duty, asking questions and hoping upon hope that such an opportunity might arise. The fact that just a week or two ago everything had seemed to fall into place didn't mean that she hadn't been agonizing over William's future for some time and now she saw this development as no more than she deserved. Surely nothing could go wrong – if only he would agree to the plan.

Although the rain had stopped, a nasty little wind had sprung up and Jane shivered. Usually this would have brought a quick response from William but today he didn't seem to have noticed. She decided not to be hurt for she saw the speculation in his eyes and hoped that he might be reaching the right conclusions.

'How do you know he'll take me on? *If* I apply for the position, that is. After all, I'm only a fisherman.'

'Don't speak like that! You are honest and clever and hardworking. Mr Rennison will recognize those qualities straight away.'

There was something else that Jane thought better to keep to herself: that Mrs Coulson had promised to speak to Mr Rennison and recommend William most highly. And the fact that the fishmonger was a member of the Liberal Club along with Mr Coulson would also help.

'So you'll think about it?' she asked hesitantly.

'Maybe I will.' He nodded slowly as he said it but then he frowned. 'What is it?'

'There's my father to think of. I'd have to be sure that he and Thomas could manage without me.'

'I've thought of that.'

'You have?' He sounded astonished.

'My mother told me that Mr Lisle has taken Barty's death very badly.'

'Of course he has. Barty was his only son.'

The wind gusted and Jane reached up to hold her hat steady. She felt it lift and the hatpin drag at her hair. 'I understand that Mr Lisle has sold his coble and is working for anyone who needs an extra man.'

'That's true.'

'Then why shouldn't your father take him on?'

William looked doubtful. 'I'm not saying he wouldn't consider it, but he wouldn't be pleased with me for leaving him.'

'Oh, William!' She wanted to scream at him that he was a grown man and that other men's sons were leaving Cullercoats to work on the colliers, or even going deep sea. Or labouring in the building trade. Or emigrating to all parts of the Empire.

'It's not as if you'd be moving to a different part of the country,' she said. 'We could live above the shop – my shop – and, oh, my darling, it's such a cosy little flat, and you would catch the train early in the mornings down to the Fish Quay, supervise the buying and have the fish packed and sent off to the shops. And you'll never have to risk life and limb again and break my heart by getting drowned. William, you'll have a chance to use your brain!'

'Don't you think it takes brains to be a fisherman?'

Jane felt her heart thud against her ribs. Had she just spoiled everything? She bit her lip and slanted a worried glance up at him. William was smiling. He was teasing her. She felt like crying with relief.

'I promise you I'll think about it, sweetheart,' he said. 'It's true the fishing is dying fast. There's less fish to go round and I don't want to find myself scraping a living. Not if I have a wife and family to keep.'

'Family?'

'Well, I suppose there's room for a bairn or two in that cosy little flat above the draper's shop, isn't there?'

'Of course . . . but . . . I mean, I want children, I do really. But not at first, perhaps. I'll want to get established.'

'Don't look so worried, Jane. I know what you want and I don't mind waiting a year or two for a family. But I hope to God I won't have to wait much longer before I have a wife.'

'So will you meet Mr Rennison and talk things over?'

'Aye, but not today, I hope.'

Jane tried to hide her irritation at his use of 'aye'. William didn't speak 'rough', but there was no denying that he didn't speak as well as Kate did. She hoped that when he moved away from the village and started mixing with other tradespeople he would gradually drop some of the words he used now.

'No, my love. Not today,' she said. 'I'll let you know when Mr Rennison is ready to see you. He's going to tell . . . he's going to tell his sister, Mrs Roberts, and she'll tell me.'

That was another white lie, as Jane preferred to think of it. In fact Mr Rennison had promised to let Mrs Coulson know when he wanted to interview William, but Jane was worried that William might think he was only getting the job because of some sort of patronage. Jane had enough faith in him to believe he would get the job anyway.

'So what are we going to do now?' William asked.

'We'll go home, shall we?'

'Home? You mean . . .'

'Yes, back to Cullercoats. We've been keeping folk guessing long enough. Although I must say Kate hasn't been fooled. William, I want you to come and visit my parents. My mother always cooks too much lunch on a Sunday, especially if she thinks I'm coming home.'

'Do I have to keep these clothes on?'

'Well . . .'

'I wouldn't be able to do justice to your mother's cooking if I was worried about popping the buttons on this waistcoat.'

Jane couldn't help smiling. 'All right, we'll go back to Jesmond and you can change. But, perhaps, you should keep that tie on. It's . . . it's a little newer than yours.'

William took her arm and began to walk away briskly, obviously relieved and happy to be going back to Cullercoats. And apparently not at all nervous about the meeting with her parents. He had known them all his life. Not only because his sister and Jane were friends but also because everyone in the village knew Jane's father, the village cobbler. Jane wondered whether he had understood what she'd meant. Did he realize that she wanted folk to accept them officially as a courting couple? She hoped so but, just in case he didn't, she would prime him on the journey down to the coast on the train.

'Please don't walk so fast,' she begged. 'I can't keep up with your long legs.' He smiled an apology and slowed down. Next time she spoke she was a little breathless. 'Then after lunch,' she said, 'we'll visit your parents, shall we?' Her voice faltered. She liked William's mother very much but the thought of facing Henry Lawson was frightening. Especially if he'd had a drink or two. 'Perhaps we won't stay too long there.' She paused to gauge his reaction. He was still smiling. She hurried on, 'Because I think we should spend the rest of the day with Kate. She must be lonely living in that cottage by herself and it's time I visited her.'

'Anything you say, sweetheart.'

William grinned and Jane realized that he had understood what she'd meant, after all. Perhaps he didn't altogether approve of her plans for their future, but she thought that the fact that she was prepared to go with him and tell their families that they were going to be married had lifted his spirits.

William was still smiling. He was happier than he'd been for a long time.

'Jane, I'm very happy for you.'

William had been summoned to the boat field by Thomas, who said that a few of the lads wanted to ask his advice about something, so Kate and her friend had taken their chairs into the back yard of Belle Vue cottage in order to catch the evening sun while they gossiped.

'I hoped you would be,' Jane said. 'And I'm determined to make a success of it, you know.'

'I should hope so. You'll have me to answer to if you don't. And my mother, probably.'

Jane frowned. 'Well, it's nice of you to say so but I didn't get the impression that your mother was very keen on the idea. No, not very keen at all.'

Now it was Kate's turn to be puzzled. 'I'm sure you're wrong. For as long as I can remember she's wanted you and William to get married.'

'Oh, dear.' Jane looked abashed. 'We've been talking at cross purposes.'

She didn't have to explain; Kate understood immediately. 'I meant I was happy that you and my brother are going to be married—'

'— and I thought you were happy about my shop. Are you, Kate? Are you pleased about my new venture?'

'Does it matter what I think?'

'Of course it does.'

'Why?'

'You're my best friend – my only friend – and you are William's sister. So of course it matters what you think.'

Kate turned her head to find Jane staring at her intently. 'Do you want me to convince William that your idea is the right one? Is that what you really mean?'

'No . . . I mean yes . . . oh, this is difficult. Yes, I'd like you to talk to William but only if you really think it's the best thing to do.'

Kate smiled. 'Well, I certainly can't see you as a fisherman's wife. You have no idea how to bait the lines, or gut a herring.'

Jane pursed her lips with distaste. 'I should think not! Oh . . . I mean, I know you have to . . . I'm sorry.'

'Don't worry. I'm not offended. I'm not ashamed of being a fish lass, but you have other skills – and you should be proud of them. And I'll tell William so. But after that it's up to him what he decides to do.'

'Apart from my parents, who are pleased about it, you're the only one who knows about William's . . . William's new position.'

'If he gets it.'

'Well, of course. He didn't want to tell your mother because she might tell your father. William thinks it better to wait until things are more definite.'

'Very wise.'

They looked at each other solemnly, both knowing very well that Henry Lawson would oppose most strongly the idea of William's leaving home.

'Your father wasn't at home when we called,' Jane said.

Kate smiled. She guessed that Jane would have been relieved to find that so. 'How was my great-grandmother?'

'She was sleeping, I think. She was very quiet.'

'I miss her.'

'Kate, why can't you go home? Whatever you did to anger your father, surely he'll have forgotten about it by now.'

'He won't forget.' Kate rose from her chair before Jane could respond. 'But William will be coming back soon and I promised you some kind of meal. Shall we go in and see to the table?'

When Jane and William had arrived Kate had been pleased to see them but mortified that she had nothing much to offer in the way of refreshment. She knew without looking that the larder contained an oven-bottom bread cake, some cheese and three salted herrings. She supposed that would just about do but then she had noticed that Jane was carrying a basket.

'Your mother sent this,' her friend had told her. 'She said if William is going to have his meal with us she felt obliged to contribute.'

The basket contained a small joint of home-boiled bacon, a dozen plain scones and half a pound of butter. Kate had silently blessed her mother for trying to spare her embarrassment. But in any case, she'd thought, Jane has probably never had to think about what's in the pantry. She can have no idea of what it's like to live from day to day as I am doing now.

With a choice of ham, cheese and salt herring to be followed by the scones, the table didn't look too meagre, and when she heard William crossing the yard Kate lifted the kettle from the hob and poured boiling water into the teapot.

Jane's smile was brilliant when he entered but Kate thought her brother looked troubled. He didn't speak, and after a while Jane's smile faded. 'What is it?' she asked. 'Has something happened?'

'No,' William said. But his expression didn't alter.

'Then why do you look so grim?'

'Grim?'

'Yes, grim!'

There was an impatience in Jane's tone, an expression of irritation that Kate's mother would never have dared use when dealing with Henry. Kate watched them and wondered how her brother would react. He seemed to shake himself before he framed an answer.

'There's nothing wrong. It's just Thomas and his hot-headed friends. They talk a lot of nonsense. I . . . I worry about them.'

A picture from the recent past sprang into Kate's mind: Thomas sitting by the fire in the mission hall with Jos's brother Matthew and a group of their friends.

'*Jos said we should settle for the bastard!*' That had been Thomas, his voice tight with fury.

And then someone else spoke . . . '*Now that he's gone we mustn't forget.*'

'*We must act together . . .*'

'*Show Adamson we won't be beat . . .*'

'*Sink the bastard . . .*'

The voices faded. Kate looked at her brother, who was trying to convince Jane that nothing was wrong. William hadn't been part of that group at the funeral tea so why was she so sure that that was what was troubling him?

Kate asked them to sit at the table and began to pour the tea. Suddenly

William looked as though he'd come to some sort of decision. 'Kate,' he said, 'have you become friendly with the American artist?'

This took her so completely by surprise that she found herself sitting down quickly. The teapot wobbled in her hand and Jane reached over and took it from her. She noticed that her friend looked as surprised as she was.

'Why do you ask?'

'There's gossip.'

'Gossip?' Kate raised her chin and her eyes flashed.

William wasn't intimidated by her angry stare. 'You've been seen talking to him.'

'And where was that, exactly?'

'On the beach. And one night . . .'

'Yes?' Kate's chin went up and she could feel the heat rising. 'One night?'

'One night you were seen walking home together – alone.'

Kate saw that Jane's eyes were round with surprise. William, on the other hand, looked uncomfortable. So uncomfortable that, although her temper was racing, she took pity on him and took a deep breath before saying anything.

'Who saw us?'

'What do you mean?'

'That's not a difficult question, William.' Her ire was rising again. 'Who saw me walking home – *alone* – with Mr Munro?'

'I don't know.'

'Then who told you about it?'

'Jos's brother.'

'Matthew?'

'That's right. Before you ask, I don't know who told him. But apparently more than one person has noticed . . . has noticed . . .'

'Noticed what?'

'You and the American. They're of the opinion that you're over-friendly.' At this point William raised his hand and extended it, palm out, towards her. 'And before you fly off the handle,' he said, raising his voice, 'just remember that I'm your older brother and I have every right to bring this matter up. I wouldn't do so if I didn't care for you.'

'What does caring for me have to do with it?'

'You're a woman living alone; you must know that you'll have to guard your reputation. And if this gossip ever got to our da there'd be hell to pay. Our mam would suffer for it and, furthermore, I wouldn't be able to protect you if he caught you alone here.'

Kate put her hands flat on the table at each side of her plate. Grown woman though she was, the thought of her father in a rage was intimidating. When she'd been a child he had terrified the family with his shouting and his violence, and although nowadays he relied less on physical violence and more on shouting, that did not mean his nature had changed. If the drink was on him his behaviour was dangerously unpredictable. Fortunately William and Thomas were able to keep an eye on him and help shield their mother, but now that Kate lived alone in this cottage she might not be able to rely on her brothers' protection.

She controlled her anger. 'So this gossip has not yet reached our parents?' she asked.

'No. You have friends in the village, Kate. People feel sorry for you. Not only because you lost Jos, but also because our father turned you out at such a sad time in your life. They also admire you for trying to make a living for yourself. Our father . . .' he paused, 'our father has angered many people in the past. He's not well liked.'

'But my "friends" in the village did not hesitate to tell Matthew Linton?'

'No, but they weren't being malicious.'

'Really?'

'No, Kate. They feel you are innocent—'

'Of course I'm innocent!'

'Let me speak. They feel that you don't realize that Mr Munro might be taking advantage of you.'

'Well, he's not. He's just being kind. The first time he spoke to me it was because he was worried about me.'

'Worried about you? Why should he be worried about you?' Jane was unable to keep silent any longer. 'Why should a perfect stranger be worried about you?'

'Because he knew what had happened and . . . and he saw me go into the cave one day and he doesn't know about the tides. He thought I might drown and he wanted to make sure I was all right.' Both Jane and William looked at her doubtfully. 'It's true,' Kate said. 'Mr Munro is an artist. He's not like the people we grew up with.'

'Of course he isn't.' Jane sounded scornful.

'But neither is he like the rich folk, the gentlemen. He said that people don't expect him to behave like them.'

108

'What nonsense has he been spinning you, Kate?' her brother demanded. 'In my opinion Matthew is right to be worried about you. Mr Munro obviously wants . . . something.' Suddenly William couldn't meet her eyes.

'And what is that, exactly?'

'You know,' William said in the direction of his plate.

And, of course, Kate knew very well what her brother meant and she felt a hot flush of shame. She disguised her embarrassment by trying to sound cold and haughty.

'Kate . . .' Kate was surprised at how sympathetic Jane sounded. 'William is right to be worried about you. You should be grateful that he cares.'

'I am. But he's mistaken. And the people who have spread this gossip must have evil minds. It's always been the same in this village – everyone prying into other people's lives and taking a delight in spreading rumours. As if . . . as if I didn't have enough to worry about.'

Kate couldn't disguise the break in her voice. Here she was defending her reputation as far as the American was concerned and neither her brother nor her best friend knew that there was much more in her life that the village troublemakers could gossip about.

'Enough to worry about?' Jane asked.

'Of course I have. Living here alone, trying to make enough money to pay the rent. Do you think it's easy?'

When William spoke his voice had softened. 'Of course it isn't easy. That's why I'm warning you.'

'Warning?'

'Not to make things worse for yourself.'

'Does Mrs Linton know about this?'

'Matthew said no one wanted to tell her. She would be upset if she thought Jos's sweetheart had forgotten him so soon.'

'No!' Kate cried out in anger and pain. 'Of course I haven't forgotten Jos! How could I? But you're wrong about Mr Munro. He means no harm. He doesn't want to seduce me—'

'Kate!' Jane breathed in shocked tones.

'He simply wants to paint me.'

William and Kate stared at her. William's face remained stern but Jane had forgotten her manners so far as to be open-mouthed with surprise.

'Paint you?' her brother said at last.

'Yes, my portrait.'

'But why would he want to do that?' Jane asked.

Kate didn't know whether she should feel insulted by the incredulity evident in her friend's tone. 'Don't worry, it's not for my beauty,' she said wryly. 'Mr Munro intends to paint other folk who live here; both men and women, in their working clothes. I think he intends to exhibit them in some gallery.'

Jane was still looking astonished but William was looking doubtful.

'It's true,' Kate said. 'In fact he's already made a start.'

'He's painting your portrait?' William asked.

'Not mine. Not yet. He's started with Martha Smith.'

'Old Martha!' Jane shook her head as if what she was hearing was getting more and more strange. 'But she's—'

'I know.' Kate smiled. 'She's incredibly brown and wrinkled. So you see, I meant it when I said Mr Munro hardly wants me for my beauty. It's just because I'm a fisherlass. And furthermore, don't you go thinking that he's going to lure me into his studio for any other purpose than to paint me.'

Jane gave a shocked gasp.

'Don't talk like that in front of Jane,' William admonished.

'For heaven's sake, just listen to me. It's all quite respectable. He said that Martha Smith takes her granddaughter with her and I could have my mother as my chaperone.'

Kate stared at them defiantly. It seemed that neither William nor Jane knew what to say. Eventually William spoke; he still looked troubled.

'Have you talked to Ma about this?'

'No, because I haven't decided whether I want to do it. Although I could do with the money.'

'Money?' Jane's eyes grew even wider.

'Yes. He pays the people who pose for him. He says it's only fair because one day he might sell the painting.'

'And this is all that's between you?' William asked. 'This talk about painting?'

'Do you think I would lie to you?'

'No, of course not.'

William's words made Kate feel guilty. Not because she had lied about Mr Munro, she hadn't, but because at this very moment she was deceiving William and Jane and everyone who knew her, apart from her parents, about her true reason for leaving home. She hadn't lied, but, because her mother had begged her not to, she hadn't told the whole truth.

'Well, I don't suppose there's any harm in you posing for a picture so long as you take our mam along,' William said.

'So why do you still look uneasy?' Kate asked.

'Because none of this explains why you were seen coming home with him very late one night. He walked you to the door.'

'So that's it.' Kate remembered the night she had posted the letter to Jane and the curtains of one of the cottages twitching as she walked by. Her anger surged again but suddenly she was too weary to express it. 'I couldn't sleep. I went to post a letter – to Jane. Mr Munro was out walking – well, just looking at the sea. That's when he asked me to pose for him. And he walked me home. I don't suppose I should be surprised if the busybodies want to make more of it.'

'No, you shouldn't.' If William had noticed the faint trace of sarcasm he decided to ignore it. 'I don't want to quarrel with you, Kate. I believe you're more intelligent than most folk round here, but sometimes you're not very wise. For my sake, for our mother's sake, please be more careful.'

In that moment Kate saw what a good man William was and how seriously he took his duties as the older brother. 'I will, I promise.'

'And will you have your portrait painted?' Jane asked. Kate could see that this was bothering her friend.

'I haven't decided yet. But, if I do, I'll talk it over with my mother. Now I'm going to have to make another pot of tea. This one is cold.'

The atmosphere lightened a little as they ate their meal. Jane chattered happily about her plans for the future and William tried to humour her, but his responses seemed to be half-hearted. At first Kate believed this was because he didn't really want Jane to open a dressmaking shop. And whether he wanted to work for a fishmonger she couldn't tell. She sensed William was uneasy about the upheaval that lay ahead.

But then Kate remembered what William had said when he'd returned to the cottage just now. Something about their brother Thomas and his 'hot-headed friends'. And, suddenly, she remembered how sure she had been that Thomas had called William to the boat field not to repeat gossip about herself and Mr Munro, but to discuss something much more serious.

And she knew that if she were to ask William what that was, he wouldn't tell her. She was not the only member of the Lawson family to have a secret.

111

Chapter Nine

Kate set off for the beach carrying her creel, her basket, and her scrubbing brush. Halfway down to the shoreline, she stopped and turned to look back at the village spread out along the cliff top. The white-washed fishermen's cottages were clustered on her right, their red-tiled roofs reflecting the late afternoon sun. The tall brick-built houses of Beverly Terrace straggled along the headland to the left, as if trying to distance themselves from the more humble homes.

Seeing them like this, Kate was suddenly more aware than she had ever been of the gulf between those who lived in comfort bordering on luxury and those who worked almost every hour God gave them to win some sort of living from the sea. And, of late, men like her father and her brothers were losing the battle.

She turned back to her task, and found a pool deep enough to immerse the creel and basket and give them a good soaking. After swilling them round she dragged the creel from the pool, water pouring through the basketwork, and scrubbed it as hard as she could to remove the dried fish scales, the scraps of fish and the sand and grit that was trapped inside.

When she was satisfied that the creel was as clean as she could make it, she set it aside on a flat rock and worked on the basket. When she had done, she set the basket next to the creel and had started to stand up when the world seemed to spin. The clouds raced, the sound of the waves grew distant and the cries of the gulls echoed from some faraway place. Nothing seemed real. She felt as though someone had tied a ribbon round her forehead and was pulling it tightly. Her heart was beating fast and the breath caught in her throat. She knew she had straightened up too quickly and she closed her eyes and placed a hand on her chest, gulping in shallow breaths until her heartbeats were less erratic and the pain in her head eased.

Kate had always been healthy so she guessed this was something to do with being pregnant – and working too hard, and not getting enough sleep, and probably not eating enough either. I must take care, she thought. I don't care what happens to me but I would never forgive myself if I harmed my child.

As soon as the world had righted itself Kate got to her feet slowly and stood for a moment looking out to sea. The tide had turned and the waves were already lapping the rocks. The sun sparkled on the water and a slight breeze lifted the foam from the crests of the waves and blew it into the air. Spindrift, Kate thought. That's what it's called. She had always thought the name romantic. How can I leave all this? If I go to America I will leave my whole life behind.

Kate tossed the scrubbing brush into the basket and, taking care not to move too quickly, she picked up both the basket and the creel. She cast one last glance across the waves and breathed in slowly, savouring the tang of the salt air, then turned reluctantly to go.

Something unusual caught her eye. Some movement on the cliff top. Something was happening in front of one of the grand villas. With the basket hooked over one arm Kate raised her hand to shield her eyes against the westering light and tried to make out what was going on.

As far as she could tell a large group of people had gathered and more were joining them. They came from the direction of the cottages and joined the others outside the house with the pillared porch: Richard Adamson's house.

Then she became aware of the sound. An angry sound. Men's voices, haranguing and shouting. At first she thought it was a drunken brawl but dismissed that thought quickly when she realized that the shouting seemed to be orchestrated. The noise assaulting the early evening stillness had not been prompted by drink. The men who had gathered outside Richard Adamson's house were bellowing with rage.

Kate made her way up the slope to the watchtower. She left her basket and creel on the wooden bench that circled the seaward side of the building. Then she turned left to walk along past the boat field towards Mr Adamson's house. The noise grew louder as she approached and she saw that most of the younger men of the village seemed to be there. They were crowded together on the pavement. Some of them had ventured a little way up the path. A few of the village women were watching from a short distance.

When she was near enough Kate looked at the faces in the crowd; they were filled with hate. When she saw who was at the front she felt a tremor of fear. She was unsure whether to stay or slip away. Her brother Thomas and Matthew Linton were standing on the steps that led up to the front door of the house and they had turned to face the other men. Thomas was waving his arms about, exhorting the crowd, conducting their voices in some kind of rhythmic chant. Matthew was holding a roughly made placard. It read: ADAMSON STARVES BAIRNS!

She could see two other placards being held high and, as they waved and turned, she read: ADAMSON CLEAR OFF! The other had no words, just a crude picture of a gallows and a body swinging on a rope. The rest of the men were waving their fists and shouting.

'Come out, Adamson!'

'Come out and face us!'

'Let's drown Adamson!'

Kate stood near to, but apart from, the other women. Had she seen her mother, or Jos's mother, she would have joined them. But, after scanning the group anxiously, she was pleased to see that neither of them was there. Both of them would have more sense – and more dignity – than to be part of this. For even the women, silent as they were, had malice on their minds. They stood with arms folded across their bodies, hugging their excitement close, their eyes wide with speculation.

She glanced across at the house. Lace curtains covered each of the panes of the large bay window on the ground floor. Was anyone standing behind those curtains, watching and listening to what was going on?

The silence from the house, the lack of reaction, incited the demonstrators to further fury. A voice angrier than the rest yelled out, 'Hang Adamson!'

Others took up the chant. The home-made banners swayed furiously. Kate prayed that the men would soon wear themselves out. That they would be satisfied that they had made their point, that the shouting and fist-waving would stop and they would go home. If not, where would it end? The law had little mercy on rioters. They were imprisoned, transported or worse. They could be hanged themselves, never mind wanting to hang Adamson.

Then suddenly the shouting stopped and Kate held her breath when she saw why. The door was opening. Thomas and Matthew backed slowly down the steps, not taking their eyes off the door. Then everyone seemed to sigh on one breath and there was a collective growl of barely suppressed fury when they saw who was standing there. Richard Adamson.

He was formally dressed, and looked very grand in contrast to the men gathered before his house who were mostly in working clothes. Kate noticed, too, although she didn't know why, that his hair was neatly arranged. His face showed no emotion, neither fear nor anger. Perhaps he was waiting for absolute silence before he spoke. But if that was the case, he didn't get the chance. The crowd began to shout insults.

'Coward!'

'Adamson's yellow!'

The chanting grew louder and Richard Adamson raised his hands as if to silence them. Someone shouted, 'Go on then, speak!' and the chants died away.

'I have been part of this community for as long as you have,' Richard said, and the men began to mutter. He raised his voice, 'Our interests are the same. To make a living from the sea—'

'If that's the case,' someone shouted, 'why are you stealing our livings from us?'

'Your only interest is greed,' another man shouted.

And another, 'Aye, you take all the herring with your damned trawlers and leave us none.'

'Listen to me—' Richard began.

'No, you listen! Will you feed our bairns when there's no money coming in?' This time it was a woman who shouted.

'You can't stop progress—' he began but, again, he wasn't allowed to continue.

'Will progress pay the rent?' the same woman countered.

The crowd became restive and Kate thought Mr Adamson glanced towards the side window in the bay. Did she imagine it or had the lace curtain twitched? By now everyone was shouting again, even the women, and Kate edged away from them, wanting to distance herself from what was going on.

When she looked back at the house she received a shock. Richard Adamson was staring straight at her and, although she had no idea why, she found that disturbing. Did he think she was part of this? Was his look questioning or accusing? Almost immediately, she thought, Why should I care? These men and women have the right to feel aggrieved – to be angry. What could he possibly say to justify what he is doing?

The men were pushing forward now, with Thomas at the fore. Kate didn't know whether Thomas meant to go up the steps or whether the force of the shoving had propelled him, but the next moment he was

115

confronting Richard Adamson face to face. The crowd fell silent. They stared at each other, Thomas defiant, Richard Adamson grave. Then, perhaps distracted by the twitch of the lace curtain, Richard turned away. Thomas must have thought that he was going back into the house for he grabbed his shoulder and swung him round.

Kate would always believe that her brother meant only to talk to him – well, to shout at him, perhaps – but Richard Adamson must have thought he was under attack because he pushed Thomas away with all his might. Thomas went hurtling back down the steps into the arms of his fellow conspirators.

The resulting hush was momentary. For an instant she lost sight of Thomas, but he appeared again swiftly and she saw him raise his arm above his head. It was only when he drew his arm back for the throw that she saw he held a large stone. He must have taken it from the border of the garden.

Kate was horrified. She wanted to shout and tell him to come to his senses. To plead with him to think of their mother. Ask him if a few creels of herring were worth risking prison for – and maybe his life. But it was too late. The stone had already left his hand.

He didn't aim at Richard Adamson. If he had, he couldn't have failed to hit him. Kate saw at once that he meant only to attack the man's property, not his person. When Thomas released his missile she held her breath, then watched in dismayed fascination as the stone arced through the air and crashed through the side pane of the bay window.

The angry voices faded. All heads turned towards the window. The glass had shattered and all but one large shard had fallen into the room. Kate could see splinters caught in the lace curtain. The remaining shard hung like a large dagger from the window frame. It swung backwards and forwards for a few seconds and then it fell outwards and shattered into fragments on the wide stone sill.

Richard Adamson stood as if frozen, staring at the broken window. The next moment the lace curtain was pulled aside. The woman who appeared there was not Richard Adamson's mother. She was young and beautiful.

She was tall, maybe as tall as Kate herself. She wore an emerald green evening dress and a necklace of jet fashioned like a lace collar with a tassel falling down to nestle between the curves of her breasts. All this Kate took in in an instant. She also saw how pale the young woman's complexion was. Maybe it seemed so in contrast to her raven-black hair, or maybe she was sick with worry. Certainly her voice betrayed her anxiety, although Kate thought she was making an effort to control herself when she called, 'Will you come in now, Richard?'

Instead of answering he frowned and gestured towards the men below as if he wanted to stay and talk.

She said somewhat shakily, 'You're bleeding, you know.' Kate realized that a piece of glass must have caught Richard when the window shattered.

The woman's voice carried clearly and, hearing her words, some of the people on the outer fringes of the crowd began to melt away, including some of the fishwives who had been standing on the cliff top. Kate saw Richard Adamson take a handkerchief from his pocket and begin to dab at his cheek.

'I think your mother would be much happier if you came in and cleaned the wound. You can talk to these men another day.'

Nobody knew what to do. Thomas hadn't moved since he'd thrown the stone but the other men were beginning to draw away from him. However, they stayed within earshot, compelled to watch the drama being enacted on the top step. Suddenly a large man pushed his way through to the front. Kate noticed some of the men glance at each other furtively. They began to slip away.

The newcomer gripped Thomas roughly by the shoulder and spun him round. Her brother found himself looking up into the face of Constable Darling. Without releasing his grip on Thomas, the constable addressed Richard Adamson.

'Are you all right, Mr Adamson, sir?' he called.

'Yes, I'm fine, thank you, constable.'

Mr Adamson continued to dab at his face and now Kate could see the blood staining his handkerchief.

'I would go inside like the young lady said, sir, if I were you. I can deal with this lot.'

With these words, and still holding on to Thomas, the constable turned to face the men who remained. Amongst them Kate recognized her twin brother's circle of friends. Matthew stood the closest although he no longer held his banner aloft.

'This is an unlawful assembly,' the constable said in ringing tones. The other banners were lowered quickly. 'And this man has committed a serious assault. He's under arrest.'

The men groaned. Kate wanted to rush forward and plead with the constable for the release of her brother. She must have made a movement in that direction for she felt the person standing behind her grip her arm.

'Now get yourselves away home or I'll be forced to lock you up with this one.'

None of the fishermen was prepared to argue with the constable. Not only did he represent the law but they knew this huge powerful man could floor any one of them if they disobeyed him. Constable Darling was both respected and feared. A few of the men muttered under their breath, but their will to continue the demonstration was broken. They headed back towards the cottages in small groups.

Kate remained where she was. Soon she was the only one left except for the person standing behind her. She turned to find it was William, and she realized that it must have been he who had grasped her arm to prevent her from springing forward. Without speaking the two of them drew closer together, both anxious to see what fate awaited their brother.

Constable Darling was holding Thomas by the neck of his gansey. Her brother looked sullen but far from contrite. Richard was still dabbing at his cheek, his handkerchief now more red than white. While he folded it and tried to find a clean place, the dark-haired young woman came out of the house and offered him a clean hand towel. He smiled his thanks.

'Please come in now,' she said. 'The constable will deal with this hooligan.' And then her tone became more urgent. 'You must allow me to bathe your wound.'

'I'm coming,' he said. 'But first a word with the constable. Go inside, Caroline, I won't be long.'

For a moment it looked as though the young woman was going to protest. She stared at Richard and, eventually, gave a strained smile and a nod and went back into the house. Kate sensed that her action had taken a deal of self-control and she found herself admiring her.

Constable Darling waited until she had gone before speaking. 'I'm sorry you've had this trouble, sir. This one here,' he jerked Thomas forward, 'won't be fishing for a long time. Five years or more he'll get for this.'

Kate felt William's arm come round her and was glad of his support. 'Can't you do something?' she asked quietly. 'Say something?'

'I'm not sure what I can say,' William said just as quietly. 'Perhaps plead his youth? Worth a try.' He dropped his arm and was just about to walk forward when Richard Adamson spoke.

'No,' he said.

'No?' The constable frowned. 'I don't know what you mean, Mr Adamson.'

'I don't intend to prefer charges. Let the man go.'

Kate could hardly believe what she was hearing. She had expected that Thomas would be taken to prison and kept there until the next assizes. And Constable Darling had probably not been exaggerating when he'd said Thomas would get five years or more. Not only had he instigated an unlawful assembly, but he'd actually assaulted and wounded a gentleman.

The constable looked perplexed. 'I want you to know that would be against my better judgement, sir,' he said.

'If you're worried about what your superiors will say, I can assure you I'll take full responsibility. I'll tell them that you did your duty.' He paused. 'Eventually.'

'Eventually?' The constable looked uneasy.

'We'll talk about that in a moment. But now I suggest you let the fellow go.'

Reluctantly Constable Darling released his hold on Thomas. 'Skedaddle,' he said. 'And don't come near Mr Adamson's house again. Not you nor your pals. Understand?'

Kate willed her brother to show even the slightest gratitude for being given his freedom. But he didn't. He turned his back on Mr Adamson and the constable and walked away towards the village. The two men watched him, the constable shaking his head, and then they went into the house.

William pressed her hand. 'Go home, now, Kate,' he said, 'it's over.' He hurried after Thomas.

Kate looked over once more to the Adamsons' house. A servant girl had come out and was sweeping up the glass. Another was performing the same task inside. Kate could see her because the lace curtain had been taken down. Somewhere inside the room lamps had been lit but Kate couldn't make out much because of the activity at the window. A manservant appeared carrying boards of wood.

They'll board it up tonight, Kate thought, and tomorrow a glazier will come. They may have to buy a new lace curtain, but that and the new glass will be the sum of their inconvenience.

And was this the end of the matter? She thought not. She and Thomas had shared their mother's womb, they had shared a crib and they had grown together. She had been the first to learn to speak, and until

119

Thomas mastered his words she had been the only one who could understand him. She knew him better than anyone else did.

No, Thomas would not be satisfied with what had happened today. After all, what had he and his friends achieved? They had made their feelings plain but they had effected no change. How could they? Had they even expected to? As Kate turned to walk home she had a sense of foreboding that chilled her through and through.

Constable Darling had never been inside the Adamsons' house before, and as he followed the trawler owner up the richly carpeted stairs to the first-floor study he glanced surreptitiously at the oak panelling, the figured wallpaper and the gas lamps set in brackets on the walls.

He wasn't invited to sit. Mr Adamson, still holding a towel to his cheek, took his place behind a large, highly polished desk that was strewn with papers and open ledgers. He must have seen the constable's surprised stare for he gave a small smile and said, 'Yes, I know it's untidy. I'm glad my mother doesn't visit this room very often.'

'It will be different when you're married, sir.'

'I beg your pardon?'

'Well, my wife would never allow me to leave my desk in such a state, and quite rightly. I would never be able to find anything.'

'I know where everything is. That's all that matters.'

Adamson's smile had vanished to be replaced by a troubled frown. Constable Darling suspected that he was not going to like what came next. 'Yes, sir, I'm sure,' he said in an attempt to delay, if only for a few seconds, what Mr Adamson was going to say.

'I know you disapprove of my decision not to press charges against that young fisherman.'

'Thomas Lawson.'

'Lawson? The brother of the girl whose sweetheart drowned?'

'Yes, sir. Thomas is Kate's twin. There's an older brother, too, William. You can't mistake the Lawsons.'

'You mean the hair?'

'Aye, and the temper to go with it. They get it from their father. Although, to be fair, I've never known William to cause any trouble.'

'Do you think the girl was part of it today?'

'I shouldn't think so. Kate would have more sense.'

'She was there watching.'

'Mebbes she just wanted to see what was going on. But I can't answer for any of them.'

'I thought you knew the villagers well.'

'I thought I did.'

'And you have become part of the community?'

Constable Darling flushed. 'I know what you're getting at, Mr Adamson, but I had no idea what was going to happen today.'

'You mean you didn't know it would go so far? You thought they would just come along and wave their placards and shout for a while.'

'I didn't know anything about it.'

'Your house is in John Street. Less than five minutes' walk away. It took you a long time to get here. If you had arrived sooner things wouldn't have gone so far, would they? You could have prevented Thomas Lawson from acting so violently. In fact you could have broken up the gathering almost immediately. Isn't that correct?'

'Yes, sir.'

'Couldn't you hear the shouting?'

'I wasn't at home. They planned that, too.'

'You'd better tell me.'

Constable Darling shifted his weight from foot to foot and, at last, Mr Adamson took pity on him. 'Draw that chair up and sit down.'

'The bairns came to my door,' he said and then he paused.

'Some children came to your door. Go on.'

'They said they'd been playing in the ruins – the priory – and that Lucy Green, little Lucy, she's only four, had wandered off. They were afeared she'd found the secret passage.'

'There isn't one.'

'I know that, but the bairns think there is. Well, anyway, they couldn't find her. I went with them to look for her. I was afeared she might have fallen over the cliff top, to tell the truth, so I ran hell for leather.'

'Did you find her?'

Constable Darling sighed. 'Aye.'

'And she was safe and well?'

'Yes, she was.'

'The children had tricked you.' It wasn't a question.

'Aye.'

'But you don't believe it was their idea?'

'Not now I don't. The lads put them up to it, didn't they? In fact it's just the sort of thing Jos Linton would have thought of.'

'But he's the lad who drowned, isn't he?'

'Aye, but him and Thomas Lawson were thick as thieves – and Jos's

121

younger brother Matthew, an' all. I think this has been planned for some time.'

'And that is why I don't want the lad prosecuted.'

'I don't understand. That would put an end to it.'

'I don't think so. They're angry.'

Constable Darling would have liked to say that they had good cause to be angry but it wasn't his place to side with anyone – neither the rich nor the poor. His job was to uphold the law.

'And locking Thomas Lawson up in prison might make things worse,' Mr Adamson said.

'Do you think they'll think better of you for going easy on him?'

'No, there's no hope of that. I only want them to understand that I'm willing to listen to what they have to say. And I have some suggestions to make. We'll get nowhere if I bring the might of the law down on them.'

'I see.'

Richard Adamson smiled. 'I'm not sure if you do. But I want you to know that what you've told me today will go no further.'

'What do you mean?'

'I won't let anyone – especially not your superiors – know how the children tricked you today. I would have done the same as you.' Mr Adamson was smiling as he rose from his seat. 'And now I'm supposed to be taking my mother and Miss Travers to the theatre.'

'Well, sir, if you don't mind my saying so, you'd better change your shirt.'

'What?'

'It's got blood all over it.'

Richard Adamson sighed and Constable Darling speculated that, masterful though he was, he might have met his match in Miss Caroline Travers. Her father, Jacob, owned the biggest fleet of colliers in the Tyne and his family had been shipping coal to London for more than three generations. They were immensely wealthy. But there was no son to inherit the business. Furthermore, Caroline was an only child.

If Mr Adamson was marrying the girl for her beauty, good luck to him. There was no denying she was a corker. And if he had another motive then good luck to him again. Fish and coal. Fortunes had been made from both of them so why shouldn't two of those fortunes unite in matrimony?

'Get home for your evening meal, constable. I've kept you long enough.' Mr Adamson was smiling and pleasant, as if everything had been settled satisfactorily.

But as Constable Darling made his way home to his house in the village he couldn't help wondering if he ought to have stood up to Mr Adamson and insisted on arresting Thomas Lawson. He knew the feeling in the village better than the trawler owner did. And he felt in his bones that there was more trouble to come.

'Sorry. Does it sting?'

Richard opened his mouth to say he was all right and breathed in a whiff of pungent iodine fumes. He gasped and shut his mouth quickly. He felt his eyes stinging and blinked to clear them. He nodded, hoping that his strained smile would satisfy Dr Phillips, who had just put a couple of stitches in the wound in his cheek. Now the doctor was dabbing it with more iodine before applying a dressing of gauze. The doctor's paraphernalia was spread out on Richard's already cluttered desk. If Constable Darling could have seen the state of it now he would have been even more disapproving.

'It's not a very big wound but the glass cut deep,' the doctor said. 'Facial wounds often bleed a lot. Look worse than they are. However, your mother was right to telephone me.'

'Mm.' Richard guessed that the call had been prompted by Caroline. His mother was terrified of the telephone.

'And now the sticking plaster . . . hold still . . . there. Won't do much for your appearance, I'm afraid. I'm told you're going to the theatre?'

'Yes. The Theatre Royal in Shields. Some melodrama or other that the ladies wanted to see. We'll miss the dinner, though.'

'Were you going somewhere special to eat?' Dr Phillips smiled sympathetically as he washed his hands in the bowl of water and dried them on one of the numerous clean towels that Caroline had seen fit to provide. Sam Phillips and Richard had been at school together and had remained friends.

'Depends what you mean by special.' Richard grinned and then grimaced as the stitches pulled at the flesh of his cheek. 'Ouch!'

'Sorry, should have warned you. But the dinner?'

'With Caroline's parents at their house in Tynemouth.'

'It's getting serious, then?'

'What do you mean?'

'Dinner and the theatre with Ma and Pa. And your mother, too.' Sam smiled as he snapped shut his medical bag.

'Mm.'

'I'm not prying, but I didn't see an engagement ring on the young woman's finger.'

'Yes, you damn well are prying. And I'm not going to say more because – at the moment – there's no more to say.'

'Ah!'

'And what does that mean?'

'It means that one of you, either the beautiful Caroline, or you, Richard, has not made up their mind.'

Richard laughed. 'You always were a nosy little beggar, Sam. Always wanting to know the whys and the wherefores.'

'True, and no apologies. It's my curiosity about life and the universe that's made me a damned good doctor.'

'And modest, too.'

They both laughed as they shook hands. 'I'll call in tomorrow to change the dressing, shall I? After office hours.'

'If you think it's necessary.'

'It is. I must make sure that the wound is kept clean. We don't want an infection to take hold. As it is I'm afraid there's going to be a scar. Let's try to keep it as small as possible.'

'Very well. And you'll have dinner with us afterwards?'

'That's what I hoped you'd say. Yes, please.'

Richard would have seen his friend to the door himself but he knew Caroline was hovering and anxious to speak to him, so he pulled the bell rope and asked the parlour maid to see the doctor out.

Caroline and his mother were in the first-floor sitting room at the front of the house. The room commanded a magnificent view of the sea and was furnished in the grand style. This pleased his mother, but Richard often longed for something more homely.

'All right, dear?' his mother asked.

She was sitting by the fire. These lofty rooms facing the sea and the north winds needed fires even at the height of summer and now, in September, the evenings were growing cool. Grace Adamson was getting old; the black clothes she had worn ever since she was widowed emphasized how thin she had become, and even though it was still possible to see how beautiful she had once been, her fine-boned features were beginning to look gaunt and her skin was parchment pale.

'I'm fine, Mother. There's no need to worry. Sam's coming again tomorrow and I've asked him to stay for dinner. I know you like him.'

His mother nodded and smiled. She glanced away and stared into the mid-distance as if remembering something that pleased her. Perhaps some episode when Sam and I were lads, Richard thought.

Caroline rose from the chair at the other side of the hearth and came to meet him. 'I've telephoned my father to say that we'll meet them at the theatre,' she said. 'Naturally my parents are concerned, but I have assured them that you are all right, even if – even if . . .'

'Even if you think a blow to the head has affected my judgement.'

'I didn't say that.'

'No, but I believe you think me foolish for allowing the lad to go scot-free.'

'What should I think? I'll wager that the man showed not one jot of gratitude for your generous action.'

'I didn't expect him to.' He smiled. To Caroline, life was straight-forward. It was a long time since her father's family had been humble working men and her upbringing was a world away from the lives of the fishing families. Her father was not a hard master. The men who worked for him were paid adequately and he had set up a welfare fund for their widows and orphans, but he would not have tolerated what had happened today. He would have urged Constable Darling to uphold the law.

Richard knew it would be difficult to explain to Caroline that he could identify with the hopes and fears of the people in this village, and understood why they had behaved as they had today. There was no benefactor to provide for them when times were hard, as they were now.

And it was not so long since his own forebears had fished from this harbour in a simple coble. He still owned the cottage in which his grandfather had lived with a wife and family of four children to feed; all boys. All but the youngest of them, Richard's father, John, had been lost in the same storm. Their father, Nathaniel, had survived, and had sworn that he would make life better for himself and his surviving son, who was still a child.

Grief combined with poverty had been the spur and Nathaniel Adamson had prospered. By sheer hard work he had founded the modest fortune that had enabled his son, John, to succeed even further. And, now, Richard, who was John's only child, owned a fleet of trawlers and was prosperous enough to be courting the daughter of Jacob Travers.

Richard and Caroline had met because their mothers were members of the same ladies' reading circle. As well as recommending books to each other, some of them began to socialize. Richard suspected that his mother, who liked Caroline enormously, had from the moment she first

125

met her seen her as a suitable wife for her son. Richard had been amused to see the engineering that went on to get the two of them together, but he had not objected.

He watched Caroline now doing battle with herself. She had a sharp brain but she did not have the skill to hide what she was thinking. The struggle to drop the subject played itself out on her lovely face. No matter how much she would have preferred to carry on the argument, good manners and breeding won.

'Well,' she said, 'what's done is done. But now, do you still want to go to the theatre? Would it be better to stay at home and rest?'

'No, I'm perfectly all right, and if you can bear to be seen with me looking like a ruffian, I think we should go. My mother would be most upset to miss this performance of *East Lynne*. She read the book and cried copiously, and now she wants to see the dramatization and cry even more. She has a dozen handkerchiefs at least in her evening bag, isn't that right, Mother?'

'Don't tease,' his mother admonished. 'But, yes, I do want to go to the theatre. Have you read the book, Caroline?'

'No, but my mother and I saw a version of the play when we were in London.' Caroline put one hand on her breast and raised the other to place the back of the wrist on her forehead. She raised her eyes heavenwards and declaimed, 'Dead! Dead! Dead! Dead! And never called me Mother!'

Grace Adamson tutted and shook her head, 'That line does not appear in the book. Poor Mrs Wood, to have her novel traduced so.'

'Do you disapprove?' Caroline asked.

'I suppose I do . . . well, I know I *ought* to disapprove, especially as Mrs Wood did not want her novel to be adapted for the stage.' Then Grace Adamson smiled. 'But nothing will stop me seeing the play.'

The two women looked at each other fondly and Richard acknowledged that Caroline brought a breath of fresh air into this rather sombre mansion that his father had aspired to. Caroline was young and vital and she seemed to be genuinely fond of his mother. Today she had arrived early so that she would be able to help Mrs Adamson dress for the theatre. She had brought her own evening clothes with her and they had got ready together with as much laughter and gossip as schoolgirls. Richard acknowledged that Caroline contributed to his mother's well-being.

And would she be good for *me*? he wondered. She was beautiful, accomplished, well read; she played the piano competently and she sang tolerably well. And, unusually for a woman, her knowledge of politics matched his own. And she was brave. When the commotion had begun outside the house she had wanted to come out with him to face the crowd. He had convinced her that it was her duty to stay with his mother. But, going by her calm manner, she had proved she would be good in a crisis.

So why was it that he was still hesitating over taking the courtship further? Caroline would make a marvellous wife. He watched now as she helped his mother into her cloak and donned her own.

'Are you ready to go, Richard?' she asked. 'My father has ordered a carriage for us and I think I can hear it arriving now.'

Richard moved the lace curtain aside and looked out. 'You're right,' he said.

The carriage was just drawing up. The carriage lamps were lit and shone through the smoky dusk of the September evening. He looked beyond and saw a damp mist curling in from the sea. It hovered a few feet above ground level, making the boat field a mysterious place. The outlines of the cobles seemed to waver and the figures of one or two of the fishermen appeared and disappeared like ghosts.

The wound on his cheek had begun to sting and pull against the stitches. He felt weary. Richard closed his eyes and leaned his head against the cool window pane. Immediately another figure appeared to his inner eye and seemed to burn its image on to his eyelids. Kate Lawson, tall and slender, standing with the crowd and yet apart from it as she watched what had gone on today. It was natural that she should be there, for her brother seemed to be the ringleader. But had she been cheering him on or had she been merely anxious about what would happen?

Richard remembered the moment their eyes had met. Relived the shock he had experienced when he realized that this woman's estimation of him was important. Was that the reason he had been lenient to her brother? No. He really believed that it would have been the height of folly to exacerbate the matter by throwing the lad into prison.

And yet . . . The image of the girl refused to fade. She had taken up a place in his consciousness and she was not going to go. He didn't want her to go.

'Richard?' It was his mother's voice.

'I'm coming.'

Richard Adamson turned and smiled at the two women who were waiting for him. It was time to leave for the theatre.

Chapter Ten

Kate sat by the fire in the cottage cradling a mug of tea. The warmth helped ease the joints of her fingers, which were stiff and sore from the constant scrubbing and immersing in water. She preferred her tea black but, with her mother's admonitions in mind, she had forced herself to add milk. Anything for the good of the bairn, she thought.

She stared into the flames broodingly. She had hoped that William might call by and tell her whether he had managed to talk any sense into Thomas – or at least if this was going to be the end of it. She understood very well what had driven the men to act as they had, but she didn't see how they could have achieved anything. Richard Adamson was hardly going to give up his fleet of trawlers. As he'd tried to tell them, you can't stop progress.

But, in that case, what were the men like her father and her brother going to do? Thanks to Jane, William might have a future away from the village. An interesting and comfortable future if her friend was to be believed, but who would employ her father? Or hot-headed Thomas? William was thoughtful and intelligent; Kate knew he would be able to adapt to a new way of life, but Thomas . . . She couldn't see him taking orders from anyone except their father. He would find it hard to learn to work for any other employer.

What had Mr Adamson said? *'Our interests are the same . . . to make a living from the sea . . .'* They hadn't let him continue. Was it possible that he had thought of a way of helping them? They had not allowed him to speak.

And what of her own plans? Aunt Winifred had not yet replied to Aunt Meg's letter and Kate was beginning to fear that either it had gone astray, or something had happened to Aunt Winifred. What if she couldn't go to America as her mother and her aunt had planned? Part of her hoped that the invitation would never come, and yet, if it didn't, what would she do?

She was barely keeping body and soul together now. She couldn't bear the thought of remaining at Belle Vue. Not only would she bring shame on her family by having a child out of wedlock, but there was no way she would be able to afford to keep herself and a bairn. And if no one could help her she would have to go to the workhouse – indeed she could be ordered to go there. And that was unthinkable.

She knew she ought to be getting ready for bed. She had another long day ahead of her. Aunt Meg had taught her well and she had worked hard, but life was getting more and more difficult. She could still buy white fish at the beach auction if she wished, but the crabs and lobsters were dwindling at the end of the summer, and as for the herring . . . No, she had made the decision. Tomorrow she would go to Shields and that meant she would have to get up even earlier than usual.

She rose from her chair and stood for a moment with one hand pressed into the small of her aching back, then crossed to the sink to rinse out the mug. She glanced out of the window and was shocked to see that the earlier mist had thickened into fog. She couldn't even see the wall of her own back yard. She wondered if it would lift in time for the men to go fishing.

While she was seeing to the fire she heard a knock at the door and her spirits rose. She was careful not to rise too quickly, and then, wiping her hands on her pinafore, she hurried to the door and opened it. Mist swirled around the dark figure who stood there.

'William!' she said. 'I hoped you would come.'

But it was not William who stepped into the warmth and light of the cottage. It was her father.

After a moment's appalled silence Kate said, 'What are you doing here?'

Henry Lawson's face was flushed and his eyes were narrowed to pinpoints of rage. 'What am *I* doing here?' He swayed slightly as he spoke.

He's been drinking, Kate thought. But he's still sober enough to cause trouble. Fearful for the child she carried, she kept very still. She had no wish to provoke him.

'What am *I* doing here?' he repeated, and he took a step towards her.

Kate clenched her fists and moved back. She glanced beyond her father towards the open door. He saw her look and he turned and caught the edge of the door with one hand and slammed it shut. 'Oh, no, miss,' he said. 'You'll not escape me. You're going to hear what I have to say.'

The door hadn't closed properly and she could hear it rattling the sneck, but now that he'd seen her there would be no getting round him. Kate faced her father and waited for the onslaught.

He raised an arm and jabbed an angry hand towards her, his forefinger pointing. 'The question ish . . .' His words slurred and he stopped as if to gain control of his tongue. 'The question is, what are *you* doing here in Meg's cottage?'

'I'm living here.'

'I thought I telt you to get out.'

'I did. I left home.'

'Don't try to be clever. You know fine well what I meant. I won't hev you living here in the village and bringing shame on the family. Meg must hev been crazy to take you in. Now pack your bags and get yourself off to the workhouse before your condition's plain for all to see.'

Kate decided to try to placate him. She didn't want him taking his temper out on her mother when he got home. 'I will go, Father, soon.'

'Not soon. Right now. Go on, pack your bags. I'll stay here and see you off.'

'No, Da, not tonight. That's unreasonable.'

Henry stepped towards her and Kate saw to her horror that her words had tipped him over the edge. She backed away but he caught her by the shoulders and dragged her towards him. 'Don't you defy me,' he said, pushing his face towards hers. She could smell the beer and tobacco on his breath and she began to gag.

His fingers were digging into the flesh of her upper arms. She tried to twist free but he grasped her all the more tightly. 'Please, Da. Let go,' she gasped.

'Let go? You want me to let go?' His voice was so loud that Kate's ears hurt. She cringed away from him, which made him bellow all the louder. 'I'll let go of you when you promise to do as you're told.'

'No. You'll let go of her right now!'

The voice came from the doorway and Kate glanced over her father's shoulder to see Howard Munro standing there.

'Wha . . .' Henry spun round. 'Who the hell are you?'

'Never mind who I am. Let Miss Lawson go immediately.'

A look of amazement crossed her father's face. Still hanging on to Kate with one hand he stared at the newcomer. 'I know who you are,' he said. 'You're one of Adamson's kin. You're the American. Now clear out of here. What I say to my daughter is no concern of yours.'

'She may be your daughter but it is my concern if you hurt her. Let her go.'

Henry Lawson sneered. 'Or what?'

'Or I shall make you.'

Without warning Henry turned back towards Kate and with one swift movement he twisted her round, holding her arm up behind her back in one of his powerful hands. 'Come on, then,' he called over his shoulder. 'Let's see if you can make me.'

Kate was terrified. The American artist would be no match for her father even in this semi-drunken state. Her arm was hurting so much that her eyes blurred with tears and, in that instant, she saw her would-be rescuer start moving towards them. In desperation she acted instinctively and brought one leg up to kick her father in the shin as hard as she could. She still had her boots on and Henry gasped with pain and shock. His grasp loosened and she twisted free.

Immediately, Henry launched himself against the intruder. Kate could hardly credit what happened next. At the very last moment Mr Munro stepped aside and her father stumbled forward, propelled by his own momentum. Simultaneously his opponent seemed to twist round and push him with one hand. Henry Lawson fell to the stone-flagged floor. It was a hard fall and he lay there winded. Kate and her rescuer looked down at him. Groggily he sat up and clasped his stomach. Oh, no, Kate thought, he's going to be sick.

'Get out,' Mr Munro said. 'Now.' Her father glared up with a mixture of rage and bafflement but he didn't argue. He got to his feet, still clasping his stomach, and made for the door. 'I shall report what happened tonight to the village constable,' the American said. 'If I hear you've come here again I'll have you arrested for assault.'

Henry stumbled out of the cottage and it wasn't long before the sound of violent retching could be heard. Mr Munro shut the door.

Kate was staring at him in astonishment. 'How did you do that?' she asked.

'Long ago I realized I was never going to be the school boxing champion so I learned other ways to defend myself,' he said with a laugh, but then he looked at her with concern. 'Are you all right?'

'Yes, thanks to you. But how did you happen to be here?'

'I was on my way home. I heard you shouting.'

'You didn't hear why my father was angry with me?'

'No, and there's no need to tell me. I've heard enough about him from local gossips to know that it doesn't take much to anger him. But now I'm here there's something you should know. May I sit down?'

'Of course.' Kate indicated the easy chair beside the fireplace but he shook his head and drew up a chair from the table.

'No, you sit in comfort,' he said.

Kate complied, wondering what he was going to tell her. He looked very grave.

'I have been to Newcastle tonight,' he began, 'to a lecture at the Literary and Philosophical Society. And, Kate, I'm sorry to say the audience were paying less attention to the wood engravings of Thomas Bewick than to the rumours of the riot in Cullercoats today.'

'It wasn't a riot!'

'No, I don't think it was. But news, especially bad news, travels fast. And I'm afraid the newspapers have got wind of it. I imagine your brother will feature as the ringleader. I can only hope that he has learned his lesson.'

She stared at him bleakly. She didn't imagine for a moment that Thomas had learned his lesson but she could hardly say so to Richard Adamson's cousin.

'I'm sorry to have had to tell you this,' he said. 'But at least now you are prepared. And remember, if you need a friend – if your father should come here again – you must tell me. I meant what I said about informing the constable. Do you think the warning will be sufficient?'

'It may be. My father is a violent man but he has respect for the law. And I imagine he won't want to risk being bettered by you again. It would hurt his pride.'

Kate became aware of the crackle of coals in the fire, the ticking of the clock on the mantelshelf and Mr Howard Munro sitting facing her across the hearth like an old friend. She marvelled that she could feel so at ease with him.

'I suppose I had better go,' he said reluctantly. 'I imagine you get up early.'

'Yes, I do. And thank you for what you did tonight, Mr Munro.'

He was about to rise but he hesitated and said, 'Kate, will you do something for me?'

'If I can.'

'Then I would be very much obliged if you would start calling me Howard.'

'Very well. I'll try.'

They smiled at each other.

132

Kate rose as he did and walked with him to the door. There he turned and smiled. 'And something else – have you decided whether you will sit for me?'

'Sit?'

'Pose. I still want to paint your portrait.'

'Yes, I've decided I will.'

'But that's wonderful!'

Kate shut the door behind him and leaned against it for a moment. She wondered whether she'd done the right thing, but knew it was the least she could do for the man who just might have saved her life tonight.

After his mother had gone to bed Richard told the staff to do likewise, lowered the lamps in the first-floor sitting room, and sat by the fire with a glass of whisky and a cigar. Prince, his dog, sensing there was no one now to stop him, had padded upstairs and sneaked into the sitting room behind him and now lay on the hearthrug with his head resting on his paws, his eyes closed. The firelight shone on his smooth black coat.

Richard settled back and let his mind review the last few hours. The ladies had enjoyed the play and, despite her sensible nature, even Caroline had been moved to cry a little, while her mother and his had cheerfully sobbed into their numerous handkerchiefs throughout.

Caroline's parents had taken a box. Not even the dress circle would do for the Travers family. They wished to be well away from the odours of pomades, cheap scent and something baser that drifted up from the stalls. They were already ensconced and partaking from a tray of dainty sandwiches and a jug of lemonade when Richard's party entered. Richard settled his mother and Caroline into their seats and glanced curiously down into the auditorium, which seemed livelier than usual.

The house lights revealed a mass of excited people. The musicians in the orchestra pit, who were playing for all they were worth, might as well not have bothered to take up their instruments. Nobody could hear them. At first Richard thought the mood was engendered by the fact that the players they were about to see were an eminent troupe from London, but he soon understood that that was not the case.

It didn't take him long to notice that people kept staring up at the box where he was sitting, some of them even pointing. 'The sooner the play starts the better,' Caroline's father said. 'Then everyone might settle down. They're all talking about what happened, you know. Come here and sit by me.' He was seated behind the ladies. 'You and I will have to have a chat in the first interval. Would you like a drink? A proper drink, I mean.'

Richard declined but the man who it seemed would be quite happy to become his father-in-law insisted. 'Well, I'm going to have one so you'd better join me. I'll send for some whisky. You look as though you could do with it.' He paused to pull at the bell rope on the back wall of the box. 'Does that hurt?' He indicated the dressing on Richard's cheek.

'No, not really.'

'Not really? What kind of an answer is that?'

Fortunately they were interrupted by one of the theatre staff who took the order for the whisky and returned in next to no time.

Soon after that the orchestra had stopped playing, the lights had dimmed, the curtain had risen and the play had begun. Richard had not been able to concentrate. It seemed that what had happened outside his house today was proving as much of a melodrama as the unlikely tale of murder, mistaken identity, bigamy and adultery being enacted with gusto below.

During the intervals Jacob Travers had questioned him keenly about what had happened and, as Richard had known he would, expressed disapproval at Richard's decision to be lenient. But Richard had managed to convince him that it was not through weakness. He was not backing down before the bullies; he wanted to resolve matters peacefully, even help the men if possible.

'Help them?' Caroline's father had asked. 'You think you can?'

'Maybe.'

Jacob Travers had had to be content with that, although he left Richard in no doubt that, in his opinion, what had happened was dangerous and unlawful. And now, Richard thought, how was he going to sleep tonight? His cheek was hurting and his mind was in turmoil. Suddenly his cigar, one of his favourite Bouquet Imperials, held no appeal. He took it from his mouth, stared at it unseeingly, and tossed it in the fire. It sizzled for a moment and sent sparks flying. Prince raised his head, looked at him reproachfully and edged back a little.

'Sorry, boy,' Richard said.

The events of the day had shaken him. Not because of the fishermen's protest. He had been expecting that. But he had not expected it to turn violent. And he had not expected that his emotions would become involved. In this village he had become the enemy. He knew that. And, until today, he had accepted it. He had been prepared to face the angry faces, the hatred even. It was the price he, and others like him, would have to pay for progress. But nothing could have prepared him for the way he had reacted to the look in Kate Lawson's eyes. Did she hate him, too?

He tried to tell himself it didn't matter but he knew it did. No matter that Caroline Travers was beautiful, accomplished and suitable in every way. Richard knew that Kate Lawson was the truer, the greater prize, and he doubted if there was any chance of winning her.

Jane looked with horror at the headlines of the morning paper on Mrs Coulson's breakfast tray. She would have liked to sit down right here on the stairs and read it, but she couldn't. Some instinct told her that it would be better if nobody in this house guessed how concerned she was about the happenings in her home village. After all, her father wasn't a fisherman and she was supposed to have moved on, moved further up the social scale. The affairs of the villagers should not concern her.

Mrs Coulson was sitting up in bed, waiting for her breakfast. Jane poured her tea and left her with the tray while she got out the clothes her mistress would wear that day. Mrs Coulson never had much to eat in the morning. A cup of tea and a bread roll with honey was about as much as she could manage.

Soon she yawned and said sleepily, 'Take the tray away, dear. I think I'll rest for a while longer. Come back in an hour's time.'

'And the newspaper?' Jane asked. It was lying unopened on the eiderdown.

Mrs Coulson waved a dismissive hand. 'Take it away,' she said. 'I can't be bothered with such gloomy events. Riots, indeed!'

After she had taken the tray down to the kitchen Jane went up to her room. She was free for an hour. She would read the newspaper. But she had hardly got past the headlines when she began to cry. Thomas Lawson was named as the chief perpetrator of the scandalous event.

She scanned the rest of the story as quickly as she could through her tears and by the time she had finished reading it she was a little comforted. William had not been mentioned. Jane sent up a fervent prayer of thanks. But she knew Thomas of old and she couldn't believe that would be the end of it. She must move quickly and get William away from the village before anything else happened.

Two days after the incident outside his house Richard Adamson took delivery of another steam trawler. This latest addition to his fleet, the *Tyne Star*, built to higher specifications than any that had gone before, was now docked at the fish quay and Richard and his chief clerk, Len Dawson, were admiring it.

'There's nothing like another boat to increase profits,' Dawson said, 'and the more of the fleet we convert from sail to steam, the better it will get for us.'

Richard nodded. It was true. His catches, particularly of herring, had increased to record levels. As Dawson said, profits were good and they were well ahead of the competition.

'It's not the Scotch boats you're fretting about, is it, sir?'

'Fretting?'

'Well, if you don't mind my saying so, you're frowning when you should be smiling.'

'No, Dawson. The Scottish lads are no match for us.'

A large fleet of Scottish trawlers followed the shoals of herring south to the Northumberland fishing grounds and Richard knew many of them were now being towed to and fro by steam tugs. But he was confident that his new trawlers could run rings round them.

'Aye, well,' Dawson said, 'they'll be in tomorrow morning sharp, so we'll see the size of their catch soon enough.'

'Yes,' Richard said, 'and when the crews come ashore, there'll be more ale drunk along Clive Street than would float the *Tyne Star*.' His attempt at jollity fell flat. He remembered that his chief clerk had signed the pledge and was a member of the Temperance League.

He wished he could take back his words but the good man shook his head and said, 'No doubt, sir, and more's the pity. I can't respect a man, no matter how hard he works, who spends his money on drink before he puts food on the table for his wife and bairns.'

Richard was saved from having to reply by a warning bellow that rent the air. 'Clear the way there!' Dawson and he leapt aside as a horse and cart loaded high with barrels rumbled past over the cobbles. They watched as it pulled up a short distance away and the barrels were unloaded and stacked in long rows. As soon as the task was completed another cart arrived. The barrels were there ready for the herring.

The herring season was nearly over, but until then fish lasses from Scotland would join the local girls to gut and barrel the slippery silver fish. They would stand at long wooden troughs all day cutting and slitting, earning a few pence for each barrel they filled. It could take a week to ten days to fill the barrels with fish and salt and, when they'd finished at Shields, the Scots girls would follow the fleet, moving on by train to the next fishing port down the east coast.

Richard, whose mother had been a teacher in a school for young ladies in Newcastle, knew very well that women in previous generations of his father's family had been fish lasses, either working on the quayside or selling fish from door to door like . . . like Kate. His expression grew gloomy again.

'Is that cheek hurting, sir?' Dawson was looking at him with concern.

'No. Why do you ask?'

'Well, forgive me for saying so, but you haven't been yourself today and I wondered if the wound was bothering you.'

'No.' Richard fingered the dressing on his cheek. 'It's fine, I assure you. And now I suppose you'd better get back to your ledgers, Dawson. I won't be long. To tell you the truth, my head is aching so I think I'll walk a little.'

'I thought there was something, sir. Why don't you walk down to the river mouth? The sea breeze will do you good.'

As soon as Dawson had left him Richard allowed his mood of melancholy to return. He knew he should be jubilant today. The *Tyne Star* was a magnificent vessel, built to his own specifications. Furthermore, he loved the work he was engaged in. He had more than doubled the turnover since he had taken over the company on his father's death five years before.

And his hard work had not just benefited himself. Each trawler needed a crew of ten to fifteen men, and he made sure that everyone who worked for him was paid well and treated fairly. In addition, his growing business meant he had to employ people such as Dawson and the young clerks in the office. Then, indirectly, the other quayside workers prospered – the carters, the labourers and the coopers – and the money they earned spread through the town. No, he didn't think he had done anything to be ashamed of.

Richard walked along the quay, past the warehouses and ships' chandlers, away from the crowds and the bustle. Eventually, he passed the last of the moorings and came to Sand End. This river beach was where children played. It was here, also, that women came to wave goodbye to their husbands and sweethearts sailing from the Tyne. The crews would shout last messages and hope, if the wind was right, they would be heard on Sand End. If they were sailing to foreign ports it might be two years or more before they would see their families again.

The sand at the river's edge was dry and fine and a passing boat sent rippling waves up on to the shore. But Richard was oblivious of his surroundings. There was a gentle breeze blowing upriver. It carried with it the tang of the sea – the same tang that was always present at home in Cullercoats.

He had grown up there and some things never changed. The sound of the waves on the shore, the cries of the gulls, the sun sparkling on the sand and in the rock pools in the summer, the fog that rolled in without warning and the howling winter gales. For as long as the village existed these things would be constant.

What was changing was a way of life, and he knew that he was, to some extent, responsible. The whole nature of fishing had changed with the coming of the steam trawlers, and no matter how many stones they threw at his windows there was no going back. The nation had to be fed. Fishing under sail was slow and inefficient and soon all the boats, not just his, would be steam-powered.

Richard picked up a flat stone and skimmed it across the water. He watched it bounce four times off the surface and then sink. If I dropped dead tomorrow, he thought, it would not make a scrap of difference. Someone else would take my place and continue what I have started. Progress, if that's what it is, will continue in the fishing industry. Much as he sympathized with the men in the village, he could not turn the tide for them. They would have to look to the future and he would help them if he could.

When he turned to go back to his office on the quayside he felt no better than when he had started out. He had a premonition that heartache and strife lay ahead. He prayed that his fear was unfounded.

Chapter Eleven

October

Surely the twenty minutes would be up soon? Kate's neck was beginning to ache and her shoulders, too. She was standing facing the window in the room Howard called his 'studio' but she was not looking directly into the light. 'That would make you squint,' Howard had explained. The first time she came he had asked her to bring her creel and her basket but he had soon decided not to use them, thank goodness. It was bad enough simply having to stand still all this time without having to hold on to anything.

Kate had worn her working clothes as the artist had requested and let her hair hang loose. When he had explained that the finished painting would show her standing on the cliff top she had laughed and told him it had better not be a windy day.

'I don't understand,' he'd said. 'You'll be here in my studio.'

'I mean in the painting. Look – in that painting over there, you've got the wind whipping the waves up and tossing the gulls across the sky, haven't you? Well, that's just what would happen to my hair if I didn't tie it back.'

Howard – as she had learned to call him – had smiled. 'Clever Kate. No, it won't be a windy day in this painting, although the sky will be what I call troubled. You will be standing on the cliff top gazing out to sea.'

'Why?' she'd asked. 'You must give me a reason why I'm standing there and tell me what I'm looking for, otherwise I won't know what expression to have on my face.'

Howard had raised his eyebrows. 'I can see I'm going to enjoy working with you enormously.' And then he had hesitated and looked at her uncertainly.

'Well?' Kate had asked. 'The reason?'

He had taken her hand and led her towards the window. 'This is the cliff top. You're standing here, looking out to sea, waiting . . . waiting anxiously for the boat to come home.'

'Whose boat?'

There was a pause before he replied, 'Your sweetheart's boat – I'm sorry, Kate!'

'No, it's all right. It hurts, of course. But it's not as raw as it was. If that's what you want, I'll do it. But you'd better tell me what I should do with my hands.'

'Here.' Howard had draped her shawl around her shoulders. 'Bring your hands up to clasp the folds of your shawl as if you are keeping it close to your body.'

'Not because of the wind on the cliff top, I hope?' Kate had teased.

Howard had laughed. 'No, there's no wind – well, perhaps a slight breeze to lift that marvellous hair of yours – but I want you to hold your shawl like that simply because it looks good. But you must stand very straight and proud—'

'Otherwise I'll look like a hunched old woman?'

'That's right.'

And again he had given her that appraising look that turned into a smile of approval.

And so she had stood here at the window, imagining it was the cliff top, and gazed out as if she was willing Jos to come sailing back to her. Howard had explained that she must stand slightly sideways so that he could position the easel to get a full view of her face. That was why her neck and shoulders were aching.

It was with relief that she heard Howard say, 'Betsy, would you go down and make a pot of tea for us, please?'

Kate lifted her shoulders up and down to ease them and then dropped her head to loosen the muscles in her neck. She was aware of Howard wiping his hands on a piece of rag, and then he came forward and took hold of her hands.

'Are you all right?'

'I'm fine.'

'Your hands are cold.'

'Are you surprised? There's no fire in this room and the north wind has been rattling the windows all the time I've been standing here.'

'Let's go down and sit by the fire.'

In the room downstairs there was a good fire going and Betsy Smith, old Martha's fourteen-year-old granddaughter, had already placed the teapot and cups and saucers on the table.

'Do you know where the cake is, Betsy?' Howard asked her.

'Yes, Mr Munro.'

'Could you fetch it for me?'

Betsy grinned and went to the pantry. A moment later she brought back a plate with a large raisin cake on it. 'Shall I cut it, Mr Munro?' she asked.

'That would be most kind of you.'

The girl giggled at his words and set about cutting the cake with an expression of intense concentration. Betsy Smith had long sandy ringlets and a dusting of freckles across her pretty face. Her eyes were blue and slanted almost like a cat's, but there was nothing much to be read if you looked into them. She was a good child, always willing to help, and hardworking, so long as the task she was given was not too difficult. At an age when her contemporaries were already assisting their families with the business of fishing, or leaving home and going into domestic service, Betsy was judged only to be capable of 'helping out'. And that's what she was doing now.

When Kate had told her mother that she was going to pose for Mr Munro and asked her to come with her to act as chaperone, Nan Lawson had refused. 'It's not that I wouldn't like to,' she'd told her daughter. 'It's just that I can't spare the time. Besides . . .' She hadn't finished her sentence but from the look on her face Kate had guessed what she'd been thinking. Her mother obviously believed that Kate's father would not approve. And if he didn't approve he might cause trouble.

Kate hadn't told her mother that Henry had come to the cottage and that Mr Munro had sent him packing. She hadn't wanted to worry her. Now she realized that if her father was provoked further he would only take it out on Nan.

'Well, that's that, then,' Kate had sighed.

'Why don't you ask Betsy Smith to go with you?' her mother said. 'I'm told she loved going along with her grandma and she made herself really useful.'

'Betsy?' Kate had looked doubtful.

'Listen, she may be a bit slow, but she's not stupid,' her mother had said. 'There's a difference.'

'All right. Do you think she'll agree?'

'I do. Especially as Mr Munro pays her a copper or two for her trouble.'

So it had been settled. Betsy was Kate's chaperone and, whether or not the girl understood exactly what a chaperone was, she certainly never took her eyes off what was going on. She was obviously taken with Mr Munro and interested in everything he did.

Betsy pushed a tea plate bearing a large slice of cake across the oilcloth-covered table towards Kate. Kate fell on it gratefully. She had noticed that her appetite had increased lately. Her mother had told her that that was natural but that she must try to eat food that would be good for the bairn. Kate wasn't sure if this meant raisin cake, but there was no way she could deny herself this treat. She noticed that the piece of cake Betsy gave to Howard was even larger and she smiled at this naïve favouritism.

'Hev I cut it right, Mr Munro?' Betsy asked.

'That's perfect, Betsy. Now be sure to cut a good piece for yourself.'

While Betsy bit her lip and gave her attention to cutting another slice, Howard glanced at her and smiled at Kate. The smile was in no way mocking; he was obviously enjoying Betsy's pleasure in the situation. He had made the child feel important and Kate admired him for that.

She thought about their growing friendship and how unlikely it seemed. It was obvious that Howard had led a privileged life and that he came from a level of society far above that of the fisherfolk. And yet he treated everyone the same. He respected the elders and was patient with the children. He was a good man. He would make a good friend.

Nevertheless, Kate suspected that he had never really been put to the test. That was not his fault, but perhaps it had always been made easy for him to be good natured and charming. She wondered how he would have dealt with the problems that his cousin Richard was now facing. Would Howard act with the same tolerant and yet steely forbearance? No, much as she liked Howard, and admired the unfaltering way he had dealt with her father, Kate found it difficult to imagine him being able to withstand such a crisis.

'My Aunt Adamson sent the cake along,' Howard told Kate. 'She has promised my mother that she will see to it that I eat properly.'

'Are they sisters?' Kate asked. 'Your mother and Mrs Adamson?'

'Yes. My mother is the younger sister. She married my father, an American architect who was visiting Newcastle. She's never been back to England, though I have a suspicion she still regards it as home.'

'Does that make her sad?'

'Not coming back to England? I don't think so. She has made a new life for herself in America.'

Kate was incapable of replying. The thought of the course her life might be going to take suddenly overwhelmed her. She took refuge in the raisin cake. As they drank their tea and enjoyed the cake she noticed that Howard's fingernails were splashed with paint, as was the old shirt that he wore while he was working.

It had taken her a while to get used to the smell of the room upstairs. Howard had explained that it was the oil in some of the paints he used and went on to say that he painted in watercolours, too. That first day she could tell that he would have loved to explain more about his work, and she had had to remind him that her time was limited.

'Of course,' he'd said.

'How often will I have to come here?' Kate had asked.

'I need about twenty hours of your time.'

'Twenty hours!'

'We'll do it in two-hour sessions.'

'Will I have to stand still like this for two hours?'

'No, twenty minutes at a time will do, and then we'll have a short break. Don't worry, I'm not a slave driver.'

And so far Kate had managed very well. The slight pains in her neck and shoulders eased if she shrugged her shoulders and rotated her head for a while, but she was more worried by the pain in her back. Each time it was a little worse. She hoped she wasn't harming the child she was carrying.

'Do you think you can manage to tidy this table and wash the dishes, Betsy?'

When Kate heard those words she knew it was time to go back to the cold room upstairs. Sometimes, depending on the weather, they did not manage to work for a full two hours. Howard needed daylight. He'd told her that there was nothing better for an artist than a room facing north because that way you got a cool clear light with no harsh shadows.

But if the storm clouds gathered, or the fog rolled in, they had to stop work. 'Don't worry,' he'd told her the first time this happened. 'It's going well. I'm sure we'll manage.'

He hadn't let her see the portrait yet. 'Soon,' he'd told her, adding, 'I don't want you to be disappointed by the early stages.'

They left Betsy to clear the table and wash the dishes. On a previous occasion Howard had remarked that, as the girl was supposed to be Kate's chaperone, he ought to tell her to leave everything and come up to the studio with them. But they both knew that, in her innocence, Betsy would not understand the implication and, moreover, she would be disappointed to be deprived of the small tasks that made her feel important. So they let it be.

Today it was about ten minutes before Betsy came upstairs and joined them. Kate glimpsed her from the corner of her eyes as she tiptoed in and sank on to a pile of old cushions on the floor. Kate had to work hard to suppress a smile. She knew exactly what Betsy would do next. She would draw up her knees and wrap her arms round her legs and then watch Howard intently, never taking her gaze from him or anything he did.

When the day's session was over Betsy insisted on walking home with Kate because Howard had told her she must. Kate suspected that it was a way of protecting her reputation. Anyone who might be watching would see Kate and Betsy leaving Howard's house together. And, once at Belle Vue Cottage, Betsy had got into the habit of coming in with Kate and asking if there was anything she could do to help.

Today Kate was pleased to let her do a little dusting and sweep the floor. She didn't feel guilty because the girl seemed to like to be busy. But when she had finished, as usual she wanted to stay longer. Poor little lass, Kate thought, she's lonely. Nevertheless, she had to be firm and send her home so that she, Kate, could get to bed. She was exhausted.

Before climbing into bed she pressed the folds of her nightdress against her body and looked down. Surely she wasn't imagining the raised curve of her belly. During the day her clothes hid the thickening of her waist. Her mother said that, if she was lucky, she might go another month or more before her pregnancy showed.

It's so wrong having to hide it like this, she thought sadly, and once under the bedclothes she pulled a pillow down and wrapped her arms round it, seeking comfort in its feathered softness. She should have been allowed to be proud of the baby she was carrying instead of having to pretend it didn't exist.

The next morning Kate was up early in order to walk to the fish quay at North Shields. She had to be in the auction shed at eight o'clock at the latest. She took only her creel. The supply of crabs and lobsters was dwindling. It wasn't worth haggling over them when she could be away on her rounds. It was her day to go to Wallsend but after she bought her fish she knew it would be no use returning to the village to beg a lift with Mr Brunton. He would have left long before she could get back there. So she took the train – and that cost money.

She no longer started her round at the Plough Inn and Jackson's farm. When she left the station it was easier to begin at the rows of workmen's houses that led down to the river and the shipyards. At first her customers had been surprised to see her so early, but they soon got used to the new routine and were often waiting for her with their dishes and plates.

The first time she'd seen them after her aunt's accident they'd been shocked and sympathetic. Kate was sure that many of them had spent more than they usually did because they were sorry for her. But now they were back to normal and they expected Kate to laugh and gossip with them just as Meg had done. And the trouble was she couldn't. It wasn't only because her moods seemed to be swinging violently these days; she had to acknowledge that she didn't have Meg's gift with people.

Often she found her customers' chatter boring, whereas her aunt would not only have joined in but have remembered everyone's name and those of their children and husbands as well. And sometimes she found it hard to hide her shock at the sort of gossip they repeated and at their crude sense of humour. She sensed they were losing patience with her and she'd already lost a customer or two.

It was no better in the avenues and squares in the better part of town. She'd watched in wonder when her aunt had put on a respectful manner to deal with the cooks and maids in the grand houses and she'd tried very hard to imitate her.

'*Remember, Kate, hinny, you can't let your pride stand in the way of business. You hev to act respectful,*' her aunt had told her. Aunt Meg's words had stuck in Kate's mind.

'*In spite of being a fish lass* you *are a lady, you and me both, and we would never demean ourselves by behaving like some of those who think they're ladies – whether mistress or servant – but don't act like such.*'

Unfortunately, Kate was finding it harder and harder to remember Aunt Meg's advice and once or twice she'd retorted sharply when one or other of the servants who had answered the door had been uppity with her. Once she had lost her temper and asked a young maid with a soiled apron and untidy hair escaping from her cap just who she thought she was! The next time she went to that house the door had been opened and then slammed in her face. Another customer lost.

I must control my temper today, Kate told herself, no matter how I am provoked. With that thought running through her head she turned the corner into a pleasant square. The sun was warm and a slight breeze rustled through the leaves of the trees, which were already taking on the colours of autumn. As Kate watched, a leaf shook loose from its branch and drifted down to land in her hair. That's supposed to be lucky, she thought, and she reached up to take the leaf but it blew away to land in the garden of one of the houses.

At that moment Kate heard the sound of horses' hoofs and turned to see a carriage and pair turn into the square and begin to make its way towards her. She didn't pay much attention to it until it was almost alongside her. Then she saw that there were two ladies sitting in the carriage, and in another instant she realized that one of them was Jane.

Her old friend looked every bit the lady, sitting there in the carriage with an older woman who Kate presumed was Mrs Coulson. In fact, Jane looked more ladylike than her mistress. Mrs Coulson was attractive enough but her tightly fitted plaid jacket emphasized her rather overblown charms and Kate thought that a woman of that age ought not perhaps to wear quite so many brightly coloured flowers and ribbons on her bonnet.

Jane, on the other hand, was dressed in plain dark blue with a small neat hat perched on top of her upswept hair, its only decoration being an even darker blue clutch of feathers that trembled with the motion of the carriage. All this Kate took in as the carriage drew alongside.

'Jane!' Kate called out. 'Hello there!'

Jane swivelled her head towards Kate. Her eyes opened wide and Kate thought she saw an expression of dismay before her friend turned away again.

She doesn't want to speak to me, Kate thought. Sitting there in that carriage all dressed up like Lady Muck. Does she think she's too good for me? Kate felt a surge of anger.

The carriage had drawn up outside one of the houses, and Jane and her mistress were preparing to get out. The coachman had dismounted and had come round to help them down. Kate gave her creel a hitch so that it was comfortable across her shoulders and strolled over.

'Jane!' she called. 'Don't pretend you don't recognize me.'

By this time the two women were standing on the pavement, shaking out and smoothing down their skirts, and Jane kept her head down, although she could not have failed to hear. But her mistress looked up

146

and stared at Kate. She turned to Jane and said, 'This young . . . fish lass . . . seems to know you, Jane.'

'Yes, Mrs Coulson,' Jane said, and redeemed herself by adding, 'this is my friend, Kate Lawson.' Although she still did not look too pleased to see her, Kate thought.

Mrs Coulson smiled and astonished Kate by saying, 'I'm pleased to meet you, my dear.' She turned to Jane and said, 'Would you like a few minutes to talk to your friend? Just come into the house with me and get me settled, and then you can come out and talk to Kate. But you mustn't stay out in the street for too long or they'll think I don't know how to treat my servants!'

Jane didn't answer but she looked a little flustered. Mrs Coulson laughed and Kate realized that Jane's mistress was what they called unconventional, while Jane herself was not.

Kate watched as the two women mounted the steps to the front door. The coachman had preceded them and rung the bell before retreating to the carriage. After Jane and Mrs Coulson entered the house – ushered in by a smart maidservant – the door was closed again and Kate was left feeling foolish as she waited on the pavement.

Eventually, the door opened again and Jane came to join her. They stared at each other for a moment and it was Kate who spoke first. 'She's nice, your Mrs Coulson,' she said.

'Yes, she is.'

'And she doesn't mind your coming out to speak to me?'

'Not at all.'

'So it wasn't because you were worried about annoying her just now?'

'What are you talking about?'

'You ignored me when I called to you.'

'Well . . . it's not quite the done thing, I suppose.'

'We've already agreed that Mrs Coulson didn't seem to mind. So please explain why you weren't at all pleased to see me.'

'I am pleased to see you, Kate, really I am. It's just that . . . well, you know, since the riot . . .'

'It wasn't a riot.'

'Well, the demonstration or whatever you want to call it. Oh, Kate, I've been so worried!'

'Why?'

'About William of course.'

'Ah, of course.'

147

'I just don't want him to get involved.'

'Of course you don't. But you don't need to worry. He's got more sense.'

'There's something else.'

Jane looked so miserable that Kate wanted to put her arms round her and comfort her. But that wouldn't do. Jane was all dressed up like a lady and she, Kate, was in her working clothes that reeked of fish even when they had been washed and hung out on the line to blow in the wind.

'What's troubling you, Jane?'

'We want to get married.'

'Well, I know that!'

'No, I mean soon. If I am to take over the shop and William is to live there with me, well . . .'

'Of course. You'll have to be married. What's the problem?'

'William hasn't told your father that he's going to leave home.'

'Oh.'

'You see why I'm worried?'

'Listen, Jane. You can't have your own way about everything. No – I mean it. You're very clever, you deserve to succeed, but you can't expect William just to do as you say all the time. You're very lucky to have William as a sweetheart, I hope you know that. He'll make a fine husband.'

'Of course I know that. But—'

'No more "buts". You can trust William to do the right thing. I'm sure of that. He loves you and he'll judge when the time is right. Be patient.'

'I suppose I'll have to be.'

Her friend's look was so bleak that Kate resolved to have a word with her brother as soon as possible and urge him to set his sweetheart's mind at rest. Good man though he was, he didn't always think it necessary to explain things, to let other folk know what he was thinking. She realized how infuriating this must be for a girl like Jane.

'Why are you smiling?' Jane asked.

'Oh, nothing.'

'Kate!'

'All right. I was thinking what a fine pair you will make, you and my brother. And what a handsome couple on your wedding day. Have you planned your wedding dress?'

148

Jane smiled. 'Oh, yes. It's . . .' She stopped and shot Kate a look of dismay.

'What is it?'

'Kate, I was going to tell you this . . . ask you if you'd mind . . . but I thought I would adapt the dress I made for . . . for . . .'

'For my wedding to Jos?'

'Yes.'

'My wedding dress?'

'Oh, no! Not that! The dress I was going to wear as your bridesmaid. I might add a train, but apart from that it wouldn't take much work. I have some new lace and some seed pearls – oh, Kate, do you mind?'

'Of course not.' They stared at each other and Kate realized that they both had tears in their eyes. 'So long as you will do whatever it takes to turn my gown into a bridesmaid's. You are planning to ask me to be your bridesmaid, I hope?'

'How could you doubt it?' Suddenly Jane reached up and took Kate's face in her hands, drawing it down so that she could kiss her brow. 'I must go,' she said. 'Mrs Coulson has more calls to make today. She's visiting people who might be helpful to her husband in his attempt to enter politics.'

'Politics, eh? My, what a grand world you move in!'

'Don't I just!'

The two girls grinned at each other and Jane turned and hurried up the steps of the house to be let in by the same maidservant, who didn't look too pleased and sniffed audibly.

Kate stood for a moment after the door closed behind her friend. She had just told Jane that she was lucky to have William. William was 'a good catch' as the girls in the village all knew. He was a fine figure of a man and handsome. He was also hardworking, intelligent and honest. And, in spite of his fiery red hair, he did not seem to have inherited their father's quick temper – as Kate herself and Thomas had, she acknowledged ruefully.

But, in her heart, she knew that William was lucky, too. Jane would make him a good wife. She was beautiful, elegant and clever – and as hardworking as William was. Surely, together they would prosper. Kate hoped their wedding day would not be long delayed.

And then she realized as she began to walk away that she had a very specific reason for wanting this wedding to be soon. If they don't get on with it, she thought, Jane will have to be a true expert with the needle to adapt my gown to disguise my condition. I don't suppose either she or my brother would want to be disgraced by a pregnant bridesmaid!

'I think we've earned ourselves a cup of tea, what do you think, Betsy?'

'What do *I* think, Mr Howard?'

'Yes, you, child.'

'You want me to go down and make tea?'

'Yes please.'

'Then why didn't you say so?'

Howard smiled. 'Quite right. Please, Betsy, would you go down and make a pot of tea for us? We'll be down in a minute.'

Betsy scrambled up from her customary place on the assortment of old cushions and hurried downstairs. Kate stretched her aching limbs and relaxed her pose. She had been surprised to find that standing still could be so tiring. The thought crossed her mind that lifting her creel and walking for miles with it was less tiring than posing for an artist.

'Don't you mind Betsy talking to you like that?' she asked Howard as she eased her shoulders.

'Not at all. I find her delightful.'

'Some would say she was impertinent.'

'Because she says what she thinks?'

'Well, yes.'

'But don't you see, she's not being rude or cheeky. It's the way her mind works.'

'Poor Betsy.'

'Why do you say that?'

Kate looked at him in surprise. 'Isn't it obvious? Her mind . . . well, her mind doesn't work as well as other people's, does it?'

'It doesn't work the same way, certainly. But who are we to say that it's inferior? In many ways Betsy is much more straightforward than the rest of us. Her reasoning process follows a direct path. She sees no point in not saying exactly what she means.'

'You're very patient with her.'

'Why shouldn't I be?'

'Not everyone is.'

Howard's face clouded. 'I know. I think sometimes she is beaten because she doesn't behave as her family think she should. They don't know what to do with her. That's why I'm glad I can give her gainful employment here with you – and that you allow her to spend some time with you at home.'

'What will she do when this portrait is finished?'

'I'll ask her to help with my next sitter. But after I go back to Boston I don't know what will happen to her. Unless . . .'

'What?'

'Unless you could find something for her to do. She loves to help you.'

'But I won't . . . I mean, I couldn't pay her anything.'

'I don't suppose she'd mind. She'd be happy just to spend the time with you rather than being at home. What about it, Kate?'

'I . . . I don't know.'

Kate couldn't tell him that she might be going to America, too, as soon as her aunt's letter came. She could see he was disappointed.

'I know another solution to the problem,' he said.

'What's that?'

'I could take you both back to America with me.'

'That's impossible.'

'Why?'

'Your family – your mother – what would you tell your family?'

'I'd say, "Mother, Father, I'd like you to meet my wife, Kate, and this little person is her friend and maidservant." '

Kate began to laugh at the joke but when she saw Howard's expression she stopped. She realized that he was in earnest.

'Your wife?'

'Don't sound so amazed – or is that alarm I see in your eyes? I'd make a very good husband, I assure you. I work hard, I've achieved a modicum of success; you won't starve, Kate. And furthermore, I've fallen in love with you.'

Kate stared at him in consternation. 'Please don't say that.'

'Don't tell me you didn't know.'

'I had no idea.'

But even as she spoke Kate wondered if that was true. Since she had been coming here to pose they had fallen into a way of talking and laughing together like old friends. As far as she was concerned, the friendship had begun that night in Belle Vue Cottage when Howard had saved her from her father's wrath. She remembered sitting by the fire with him afterwards and feeling completely at ease. And she remembered how reluctant Howard had seemed to leave . . .

'Howard,' she said hesitantly, 'I thought we were friends.'

'Of course we are, and that makes falling in love even more wonderful.'

151

She knew she ought to have been aware that his feelings for her were changing, deepening. Perhaps she had been, but she had been unwilling to admit it because it was not what she wanted.

'But I don't . . . I don't . . .'

'Love me?' He finished the sentence for her. 'Well, I admit that I'm disappointed, but I could teach you to love me, I'm sure of it. Marry me, Kate. Give me the chance to make you happy.' He took her hand and raised it to his lips.

Kate looked at his bent head as he kissed her upturned hand. This gesture should have stirred her senses but it only convinced her all the more that she could never love Howard in the way a woman should love a man if she were going to marry him.

Nevertheless, the intimacy of the moment allowed the image of another man to take her by surprise. Hastily she snatched her hand away and tried to suppress the thought of how she would react if it was Richard Adamson instead of Howard who had just pressed kisses into her palm.

Howard could not have guessed her thoughts. He straightened up. 'I'm sorry. I may have spoken too soon. But at least you know how I feel.' He smiled and Kate saw that somehow the smile made him look vulnerable. 'I will not speak of this again until your portrait is finished,' he said. 'All I ask is that you consider my proposal. Will you promise me that, Kate? Will you think about it?'

'I will.'

She made the promise but she knew what her answer would be, would always be. And she felt sad for him. She hoped this wouldn't affect their friendship. But it seemed she did not need to worry.

'Would you like to see the portrait before we go down?' he asked. The tone of his voice and his manner had changed completely, as he had promised they would.

'I thought I wasn't allowed to?'

'That was just in the very first stages. People expect too much and they are often disappointed. It's still pretty rough – but you will be able to see what I intend.'

Kate walked over to the easel, not daring at first to look at the painting. She knew if she showed the slightest hint of disappointment, Howard would be deeply hurt. She allowed him to position her in front of the canvas.

'You would see it better if you opened your eyes, Kate.'

'Oh, of course. It's just that I'm nervous.'

'Well, so am I. Now please open your eyes and look.'

Kate did so and what she saw took her breath away. She could see that the painting was in its early stages and yet every line of the girl's body depicted anguish and tension as she looked out to sea from Bank Top. The girl ... was it really her? The fine-boned face – still unfinished; the hair lifting slightly in the breeze as Howard had said he would paint it. All the light in the painting's sky seemed to be reflected in that hair.

'Well?' Howard asked.

'Do I really look like that?'

'No, you are more beautiful. This doesn't do you justice – although I will endeavour to improve it. I wish I had time to paint another portrait of you, Kate, and another, and another. I think I would never tire of painting you.'

'The tea's getting cold,' someone said from the doorway and they turned to find Betsy standing there. She looked cross.

'I'm sorry. We'll come down now,' Howard said.

'No don't,' the girl told him. 'I'll hev to make another pot anyway. You've got visitors.'

'Visitors?'

'Aye, two of them. It's Mr Adamson and his lady friend. They want to come up but I telt them to wait until I'd asked you.'

Chapter Twelve

'My goodness, Howard, the child guards you as fiercely as Cerberus was said to guard the gates of Hades!'

The dark-haired young woman who had swept into the studio ahead of Richard Adamson looked even more beautiful, if that were possible, than the first time Kate had seen her. Her cherry-red jacket of rich velvet was nipped in at the waist and her grey skirt hugged her slim hips before flaring gently and smoothly to the floor. Her dark hair was piled up in glossy coils that flattered the shape of her head and a hat that Kate's mother would have called 'a daft bit of nonsense' was perched on top. Earrings that looked like diamonds glittered when she moved her head.

Kate was suddenly conscious of her own workaday clothes. The skirt with its tucked hemline fell to just above the ankles so that her sturdy unfashionable shoes were plain to see. Her hair, which Howard had insisted must hang free, looked slightly windblown. Howard had asked her not to tame it too vigorously. And as for the young woman's hands inside the kid gloves as smooth as a second skin, Kate was certain they would not be reddened and work-roughened like her own. She found herself thrusting her hands deep into the pockets of her skirt and then a moment later wished she hadn't.

'Caroline, I'd like you to meet my model, Miss Kate Lawson,' Howard said. 'Kate, this is Miss Caroline Travers.'

Kate realized this was a formal introduction and she pulled her hands out of her pockets quickly as she came forward to shake hands. She needn't have bothered. Caroline Travers merely glanced at her with an unfocused smile before turning her attention back to Howard. Kate stood for a moment debating with herself whether she ought to thrust her hand towards the young woman and say 'How do you do' very loudly, but she decided that, if she did, it would probably be she herself who was left looking foolish.

'And I think you've already met my cousin, Richard Adamson,' Howard said.

Kate nodded and Caroline Travers turned towards Richard in surprise. 'When did you meet Miss Lawson?' she asked.

Before Richard could answer, Kate, no doubt prompted by her own particular devil, said, 'I sell fish from door to door. Mr Adamson likes to choose his own.'

Caroline wasn't at all put out. She smiled at Richard. 'I didn't know that,' she said. 'How interesting.' Then she looked at Kate. 'Of course, you're a fish lass, that's why Howard is painting you, isn't it?' Without waiting for an answer she turned to Howard and said, 'Richard has told me that you're making many studies of the village and its people and I persuaded him to bring me here. I may want to buy one.'

'I'm very flattered,' Howard said.

'I'll be honest with you. I'm told that you're going to be famous; that you're already sought after. It would please me to say that I had bought one of Howard Munro's paintings – from the artist himself.'

Kate wondered how Howard would take that. To this young woman, it seemed that buying a painting was merely a matter of wanting to own something valuable rather than seeing the value in the painting. But Howard was smiling.

'Please look around.' He gestured towards the door and across the landing to an area which had once served as the only bedroom for four growing boys. 'That's my gallery through there, although nobody has visited it yet. You must be the first.'

Kate turned away from them and walked over to the window. Caroline Travers had made it clear that she, Kate, was not to be included in the conversation. Why should she be? She was only a fish lass, after all. She rested her forehead against the cool window pane and looked down into the bay. The conversation continued behind her.

'Will you come with me and help me choose?' she heard Caroline Travers say.

'Certainly.'

And then she heard their footsteps on the bare wooden floorboards as they walked into the room, little larger than a decent-sized cupboard, that Howard called his 'gallery'.

It was draughty by the window and Kate was aware that the tip of her nose was cold. She was tempted to pull her shawl up over her head but that would mean combing her hair again and, with her wild curls, that

155

always took some time. Instead she pulled the shawl more tightly round her shoulders and tucked her hands into its folds.

'It's plain to see why the village has such a fascination for Howard, isn't it?' Richard Adamson spoke from just behind her, making her gasp with fright. 'I'm sorry. Did I startle you?'

'Yes, you did. I thought you'd gone with the others.'

'There's hardly room for three in there and, besides, I've seen most of the paintings already.'

Kate glanced at him curiously. 'And do you like them?'

'Very much.' He came to stand beside her. 'And, as I said, I can see why he is so inspired. Look down there – the steep cliffs, the harbour, the two old breakwaters. A group of fishermen talking on the beach. A coble or two bobbing on the swell. The gulls circling over the bay.'

'It's beautiful. But there's tragedy there too,' Kate said.

'I know that. My father lost three brothers to the sea. One storm took them all.'

'I'm sorry.'

'I didn't know them. But my father never forgot. It was that tragedy that drove my grandfather and then my father to make a better life for themselves.'

'But men still die in your trawlers, don't they?'

'I try to make sure that they don't. My crews are not exposed to so much danger as they would be in a small coble. Many inshore fishermen have realized this and come to work for me. Kate . . .'

'What is it?'

'My business is expanding. I could find work for others . . . your father . . . your brothers . . .'

'You would find work for Thomas? Even after what happened?'

'Yes.'

Kate shook her head. 'He wouldn't work for you. And I doubt if my father would either.' She didn't mention William because there was no need. It seemed Jane had already plotted the course that William's future would take.

'They wouldn't have to work for me,' Richard Adamson said. 'There are other trawler owners, or other work on the quay – carters, labourers. There are the smoking sheds. I could find work for most of the men in the village.'

'What if they don't want to leave a way of life that's familiar to them?'

'Then I can't help them. You can't force men to change.'

156

They were silent, not looking at each other, but simply staring down at the tranquil scene below. A scene that gave no hint of the turbulence that lay under the surface.

They could hear Howard and Caroline talking about the paintings. They sounded animated.

'Do you enjoy posing for Howard?' Richard asked.

'I suppose I do, although standing still is harder work than you might imagine.'

'You will have to tell me how you manage it. I've agreed to sit for Howard. Silly, isn't it to call it "sitting" when I shall probably be standing the whole time.'

'He wants to paint you?' Kate moved away a little and turned to look at him.

'He does. I can't think why. I'm not exactly a maiden's dream.'

'Oh, but . . .'

'But what?'

'You're certainly not ugly.'

'Thank you.' He grinned and Kate felt herself flushing.

'I'm sorry. Have I been impertinent?'

'No, of course not. You must say what you think. Go on, tell me more.'

'Are you sure?' He nodded. 'You have such an interesting face,' she said. 'Strong features . . . compelling . . .'

Richard raised his eyebrows. 'That's almost what my cousin said. Almost his very words.'

'Well, then, it must be true.'

Kate smiled and was relieved to see that Richard Adamson smiled, too. The tension that had existed earlier when they had been talking about the situation in the village had eased. But her sense of relief was momentary. Kate realized that another sort of tension was beginning to grow and coil inside her. It was something to do with the way Richard Adamson was looking at her.

And also something to do with the way she was looking at him – and what she saw. The way a lock of hair always looked as if it were ready to flop forward, the slightly lopsided smile, even the scar on his cheek – why did these imperfections add up to make him so much more attractive than Howard who was conventionally good looking?

'Richard, do come and tell your cousin that he must allow me to pay for this painting!'

Richard Adamson turned as Caroline and Howard came into the room. Howard was carrying a small painting, a watercolour. It was of

157

three children standing at the end of one of the breakwaters. They were looking out to sea. But they were smiling. Kate imagined that what they were seeing was their father's boat coming home.

'I don't want payment,' Howard said. 'This must be a gift. A wed—' He stopped and looked awkward. 'A gift from me to Caroline,' he ended.

'I think you had better agree, Caroline,' Richard said. And did she imagine it, or did he sound embarrassed?

'Very well. And thank you,' Caroline said. And she too had lost her poise.

Howard meant it to be a wedding present, Kate thought. That's what he was going to say. So why did he stop himself? And why do both Richard and Caroline look so ill at ease?

'Would you like to go down, now, and I'll ask Betsy to make tea?' Howard said.

'That would be charming. Tea in an artist's studio.' Caroline's smile was forced. 'But before we do, may we have a look at your work in progress?' She moved towards the easel.

'I'd rather you didn't.' But Howard's words came too late. Caroline Travers was already standing looking at the half-finished portrait of Kate. Richard went to stand behind her. They were both silent.

'Well?' Howard asked eventually.

'I'm sure it's going to be very nice,' Caroline said and turned as if to leave the room.

'Nice?' Richard said. 'It's magnificent.'

Howard laughed. 'You know nothing about painting, Richard. But I must say I'm pleased with it so far and I'm glad you like it.'

Caroline had already left the room and they could hear her going down the stairs. Then her voice echoed up from the room at the bottom. 'Oh, there you are, child. Mr Munro wants you to make us a pot of tea.'

'I'm sorry,' Richard said to Howard.

'Sorry? Why?'

'Caroline does rather take charge of things, doesn't she?'

The cousins smiled at each other.

'Am I allowed to say she'll make a marvellous wife for an important businessman? No? Am I speaking out of turn?'

Richard remained tight-lipped.

'Well, if you don't mind,' Howard said when it became obvious there was going to be no reply, 'I'd better go down ahead of you and make sure that Caroline hasn't ruffled Betsy's feelings.'

Kate and Richard were left alone in the upper room. After an awkward moment or two he asked, 'Are you coming down? My mother sent along another cake, Madeira this time, I believe, and some cheese tartlets, too. She has promised my aunt that she will not allow Howard to go hungry.'

'Does your mother bake the cakes herself?'

'Not any longer. She has had to agree that she just gets in the way in the kitchen. But she used to enjoy baking and the cook uses her recipes.'

'Those I've tasted are very good.'

'Then shall we go down and enjoy today's offerings?'

His smile was easy again and somehow the awkwardness had eased away. So much so that Kate felt able to say, 'Miss Travers ought not to have compared Betsy to Cerberus, you know.'

Richard frowned. 'Why not?'

'There was a book on the classroom shelves at school. It was called *The Children's Book of Gods and Heroes*. It retold the ancient Greek legends—'

'I had that book when I was a child,' Richard interrupted with a smile. 'My mother bought it for me. Have you read it?'

'From cover to cover. Anyway, you'll know that Cerberus was a monstrous dog with three heads. Betsy doesn't look a bit like that.'

'No, she doesn't. But I have noted her devotion to Howard and I suspect that if anyone was to harm him – or anyone that she loved – she could be just as fierce.'

'Are you two coming down for your tea and cake?' Betsy stood in the doorway. They had not heard her coming up the stairs and they glanced at each other self-consciously, wondering how much of their conversation the girl had heard.

'Yes, Betsy, we're coming.'

Betsy glared at them, nodded, and descended the stairs again. Kate and Richard looked at each other and tried hard not to laugh out loud at the girl's ferocity. When they entered the downstairs room, still smiling and at ease in each other's company, Kate noticed that both Caroline and Howard looked up at them in surprise. And neither of them smiled.

Kate and Betsy had hardly left the artist's cottage when Thomas appeared before them. He stopped directly in their path. His eyes were blazing and his face was contorted just like their father's when he was in one of his rages.

'What the hell's your game?' he snarled.

Kate backed away. She was aware of Betsy moving in close behind her and clinging on to her skirt. 'What are you talking about?' she asked her brother.

'Don't play the innocent with me. You know well enough what I'm talking about. Where have you just been?'

'I've been to Mr Munro's house. You already know that because you must have watched me leave.'

'And what exactly have you been doing there?'

'I don't have to stand here and answer these questions. If you really want to know ask our mother.'

Kate tried to step sideways but Thomas moved too. Her answer had obviously puzzled him and he frowned. 'What does Ma know about it?'

He looked so angry that Kate could imagine him storming home and bellowing at their mother, who already had enough to deal with. She decided she'd better explain.

'Mr Munro is an artist – a painter,' she began.

'I know that.'

'Well then, you probably know that he's been painting scenes of the village. Not just the cottages and the harbour but the people, too.'

'Aye, I know that as well. So?'

'He's been painting me.'

'So why were you upstairs?'

'I beg your pardon?'

'I saw you by the window.'

'That room is his studio – the room where he paints.'

'Oh, aye. His studio, is it?' Thomas's eyes narrowed. 'So what were you doing there with Mr Adamson?'

'What do you mean?'

'I saw you. I saw the pair of you at the window. Mighty pally you looked. What were you doing there with him? Talking about the price of fish, were you?' The look in Thomas's eyes was one of rage tempered with contempt.

'How dare you!'

Thomas glowered at her.

'I know what you're suggesting and I'm ashamed of you. I'm your sister, Kate Lawson, remember? How dare you suggest that there is anything improper between Mr Adamson and me!'

'No . . .' Thomas was still angry but, faced with Kate's own rage, he was less sure of himself. 'No, I didn't mean that.'

'Then what did you mean?'

'When I saw you there, in the window . . . well, at first I couldn't believe it. And then I saw that you were talking to him just like – I mean, as if you were friends. That made me angry, and you're a fool if you can't see why.'

'You hate Mr Adamson.'

'And so should you. After what he's doing to us.'

Kate knew there was no answer to that. She supposed she should hate Richard Adamson, just as many of the villagers did, but she saw no point to hatred. Anger, yes, but not hatred. Hatred didn't solve problems; it only made things worse. Her silence gave Thomas the confidence to attack her again. His eyes narrowed and his scowl deepened.

'And in any case what was *he* doing in the artist's house?'

'The house belongs to Mr Adamson. Howard is his cousin. He's staying there as a guest.'

She realized too late what she'd done when she saw her brother's face twist with fury. 'Howard, is it? Mighty familiar with the American, aren't you?' Suddenly he seized her wrist and pulled her arm up between them. 'For God's sake, are you right in the head? How can you be stupid enough to pose for a picture painted by one of Adamson's kin?'

Kate saw now exactly why her mother had not wanted to come with her to the studio. She would have had to tell Henry; and Kate's father would have reacted in the same way as Thomas had. Nevertheless, she still tried to reason with him.

'Sitting for a picture has nothing to do with the fishing—' she began.

'It's got everything to do with the fishing. He's painting the village, isn't he? And the men and their cobles, and the women helping on the beach, and even the children watching for their fathers coming home. I've seen him out along Bank Top with his drawing book.'

'But what's wrong with that?'

'Because his cousin – Adamson – is trying to put an end to all that. To destroy the village, to put paid to our way of life. If he has his way, all that will be left is a set of pretty pictures painted by his fine American cousin. Is that what you want? To be a picture in a history book?'

Kate stared at her brother. Thomas had neglected his school work but he had never been stupid. Kate had always known that. And now, in his rage, he had expressed most eloquently his fears for his livelihood – and that of all the families who had fished out of this harbour for generations.

He didn't wait for an answer. He kept hold of her wrist with one hand and, raising the other, he jabbed a finger towards her face. 'Now

161

listen to me,' he said. 'There'll be no more posing for this picture, understand?'

'You can't tell me what to do.'

In spite of the drama of the moment Kate felt like laughing when she remembered all the times in their childhood when her twin brother had tried to impose his will on her.

They stared at each other, neither giving way, and then a spasm of frustration crossed his face before he said, 'What if I tell our da?'

'You won't do that.'

'What makes you so sure?'

'Because if you do our mother will suffer for it. And you don't want that, do you?'

She watched his face purple and suddenly his grip on her wrist tightened until it was painful. His other hand swung back and, determined not to show fear, she prepared herself for a blow. But it never came. Like a small fury Betsy erupted from behind Kate's skirts and kicked Thomas hard in the shin. He yelped with pain and immediately let go of Kate's wrist.

'Leave her alone!' the girl yelled, and raising both her skinny arms she hit out at Thomas, the blows landing on his chest and probably doing no damage at all except to his pride.

Thomas let out a groan of rage and despair, and turning on his heel he left them abruptly as he had arrived. There was anger in every stride.

Kate rubbed her wrist as she watched him go. She heard a small sob and glanced down to see that Betsy had tears streaming down her face.

'Don't cry, Betsy,' she said, putting her arms round the child and drawing her close.

'I didn't want him to hurt you,' the girl said, her voice breaking with emotion.

Kate drew a handkerchief from her pocket and dried the child's tears. 'Let's go home now,' she said. And as they set off for Belle Vue Cottage she recalled what Caroline Travers had said earlier, and wondered if she had acquired her own small Cerberus.

Kate thought that Alice looked subdued and she wondered if Charlie's condition had worsened, but she knew that the shopkeeper didn't like people to ask. Perhaps she's trying to pretend that there's nothing the matter, Kate thought.

'What can I get you?' Alice asked. She was staring down at the counter.

'Not much. A bit of butter for a start, please.'

The mound of butter sat on a shining stone slab. Alice broke a piece off and shaped it into a rough square with wooden pats, then dropped it on to a piece of greaseproof paper on the scales. She seemed to take longer than usual.

'I must be losing my touch. That's a bit over, but I'll only charge you for half a pound.'

Kate was surprised. She doubted if Alice was losing her touch. Whatever she weighed out – butter, cheese, flour, sugar or lentils for the soup – she always got it right. It was almost as if she had a pair of scales in her head that ruled her hand and her eye.

'Anything else?' She still didn't seem to be able to look Kate in the eye.

Has she heard that I'm posing for Mr Munro? Kate wondered. And does she disapprove too?

'I thought I'd make a pan of soup,' Kate said. 'So I wondered if you have any bacon bits?'

'No problem.' Alice hurried through to the back shop. Kate heard her bustling about and a moment later she was back with a plate of bacon bits that she emptied on to another square of greaseproof paper and wrapped up. She handed them to Kate. 'I was going to hoy these out. There's nowt wrong with them – just didn't have any use for them.'

Kate didn't believe her. She had the strongest impression that the bacon had come from Alice's own pantry. Another puzzle. 'How much is that?' she asked.

'Just pay me for the butter. As I said, I was going to throw the bacon out. Now, hev you got onions, carrots, lentils? You'll need those if you're going to make soup.'

'I've got the vegetables, although they're a bit wrinkly,' Kate said. 'That's why I thought of soup – to use them up. But perhaps I need some more lentils. Half a pound would do.'

Alice put the blue paper bag on the scales and shovelled the lentils in. Once more, Kate thought she was over-generous, but when the shopkeeper put the bag on the counter and folded the top over she said, 'There you are, half a pound.'

Kate decided that the generosity was deliberate and she felt uneasy saying, 'One more thing. I need candles.' But at least she could insist on paying for every single one of them.

Mrs Willis disappeared again into the storeroom. Kate could hear her rummaging amongst the jumble of stock and she wondered whether she ought to go through and help her. She stood, undecided and suddenly weary. She didn't know how much longer she could support herself by selling fish from door to door. It wasn't that she was incapable of the sheer hard work required, even though the winter months would be hard. It wasn't even the fact that she was pregnant. She was young and fit and she knew of women older than herself who kept on working right up to the moment their bairns were born.

No, the problem was that she was losing customers and she simply wasn't making enough money to pay the rent and keep herself properly. Howard had promised to pay her the same rate as the folk he called professional models, but he hadn't parted with a penny yet. She was sure this wasn't an oversight on his part. He probably thought it would be easiest to pay her when the portrait was finished and he could total up the hours she had worked. She had considered asking him for some kind of advance but, so far, had been too embarrassed.

She was jolted out of her miserable daydreaming by a cry of dismay and the sound of something falling. She was just about to lift the flap in the counter and go to investigate when Alice reappeared, looking dishevelled.

'Here's your candles, pet,' she said. 'The damn things are on a top shelf and that would be no problem to a fine tall lass like you, or even anyone of a normal height. But a dumpy little body like me needs the cracket and I couldn't find it. Then I saw that Charlie had his feet up on it and he's asleep and I didn't want to disturb him.'

Kate was intrigued by this glimpse of chaos. She would have liked to ask the shopkeeper why the candles were kept on the top shelf when they were such an everyday object and Alice couldn't reach them without standing on a stool, but she decided the arrangement had probably been made years ago when both Charlie and Alice's daughter Susan worked in the shop and no one had ever thought to reorganize things.

'So what did you do if you couldn't use the stool?' she asked.

'I put me foot on the bottom shelf and pulled meself up,' Alice said. 'I reached for a bundle of candles and brought the lot down. Heaven help us if I've broken any – Charlie will go mad.'

She gave a thin smile and tried to make a joke of it. But Kate knew very well that, even if Mrs Willis told her husband what had happened, he would not 'go mad'. The Willises' marriage was one of the happiest Kate had ever come across. Charlie had been a miner until they had saved enough to open a little shop. Alice had wanted him out of that hellhole, as she called it, and was prepared to work night and day to make sure he never had to go back to it.

Kate paid for her purchases and turned to go. She wasn't altogether surprised when Mrs Willis said, 'Wait a moment, Kate.'

She turned to face her. She wasn't sure what she expected but the shopkeeper's attitude ever since she had entered the shop had given her the feeling that something was wrong.

'Listen, lass, I'm not being personal, but is there any chance of you making things up with your da?'

'None at all!' The response came without thought. That was the last thing Kate had been expecting.

'Are you sure? I mean, if you apologized and promised not to try his patience in future?'

'He wouldn't take me back.' Kate couldn't tell her that it was not a matter of an apology. 'You . . . you know what my father is like.'

Alice sighed. 'Aye, he's unforgiving.'

'So why do you ask?'

Alice Willis shifted her position uneasily. She began to fold and unfold a piece of greaseproof paper that was lying on the counter. Outside the sky was darkening and the oil lamp hanging on a chain above the counter didn't shed enough light to reveal the expression in the shopkeeper's eyes. Kate suddenly felt very weary. She was sickened by the combined odours of cheese and bacon mingling with the fatty smell of stew drifting though from the kitchen in the back shop.

Her shopping bag, with hardly anything in it, suddenly felt heavy and she was aware that she must concentrate very hard on keeping upright. There was a wooden chair at this side of the counter placed there for the convenience of the customers but she did not want to sit down. That was not in her nature. Whatever it was that Alice was going to say, Kate would face it standing upright.

'The truth is, Kate, I need the cottage.' Alice's words tumbled out as if she hadn't been able to bottle them up any longer.

Now Kate really did sway. She placed one hand on the counter to steady herself. 'Is it a matter of more rent?' she asked. She tried to calculate how much an increase was likely to be. She was already finding it difficult, what with losing customers on her fish round and trying to put something by for her journey when word came from Aunt Winifred.

'No, hinny, it's not a matter of the rent. I need the cottage. Our Susan wants to come back here. Her man got a good job at the smokehouse at

Craster but they've never settled there. Seth's going to try his luck in North Shields. Mr Adamson has promised me he'll help him.

'Well, you can see they couldn't live here, not Susan and Seth and three little bairns – one of them a baby. I'm sorry, Kate. You'll have to move out of the cottage.'

'When?'

'Not for a week or two. They've got affairs to settle. But it was only fair to give you warning.'

'Right. If you don't mind I'll go now,' Kate said angrily.

She already had the door open and the bell was jingling above her head when Alice called out to her. 'Shall I ask around if anyone wants a lodger?'

'No, don't bother. I can see to it myself.'

She gave the door an extra hard push and heard the slam and the rattle with a perverse satisfaction. In truth Kate had no idea what she was going to do. She could never go home and she hated the very idea of becoming a lodger with a family here in the village. In all probability that meant she would have to share a room, and even a bed, with one or more of the daughters, or perhaps the old grandmother. How long would she be able to keep her condition secret in those circumstances?

She hurried down the street in a fury, almost tripping over one of Howard's stray cats as she went. It arched its back and spat at her before yowling and fleeing. She felt hot and was pleased to feel a light spattering of raindrops on her face. She could smell the smoke from all the chimneys of the village as folk built up their fires for the evening. She felt enclosed by it. Trapped. She longed for a keen wind from the sea to blow the smoke and all her troubles away.

Once home in the cottage she dumped her shopping bag on the table and then sat down and stared at it. I shouldn't have been so angry with poor Alice, she thought. She has every right to want the cottage for her daughter. She's not a bad woman. She's hardworking and kind. She gave me those bacon bits for the soup even though I suspect she was going to use them herself.

Kate reached over and tipped the shopping on to the table. She didn't feel like making soup. Her mother had urged her to cook nourishing meals for herself and she had done so – for the bairn's sake. But what was the use of nourishing meals when very soon all she might be entitled to was the meagre fare in the workhouse? Unless her mysterious Aunt Winifred answered Aunt Meg's letter and offered her a home.

Then a new idea occurred to her. Aunt Winifred hasn't answered because she doesn't want to offer me a home. She's not answering because she doesn't know what to say.

Kate stood up and looked around wildly at the place where she had found a refuge for a while, first with her beloved aunt and then alone, in sad but welcome peace. She clenched her fists and closed her eyes. Her screams were silent but left her shaken all the same. Jos, why have you left me to face this alone?

Hardly knowing what she was doing, Kate snatched up her shawl, pulled it hastily round her shoulders, and ran from the cottage. She sped along Bank Top and then down the slope to the beach. She would go to the place where she and Jos had had their happiest times, and where, in the warm dimness of a summer evening, their child had been conceived.

Chapter Thirteen

'Leave the bairn alone, Ann.' Martha Smith remonstrated with her daughter-in-law. 'You know she can't help it.'

'I swear she does it on purpose. Just to annoy me.'

'She's not doing anything wrong.'

'Yes she is. Just sitting staring like that. It doesn't look right.'

'She's thinking, that's all.'

'Thinking? And what's she got to think with?'

'Lissen, she doesn't think the same way we do but that doesn't mean she hasn't got a brain.'

All the time her mother and her grandmother had been talking Betsy had been sitting placidly as if their conversation had nothing do with her. This infuriated her mother even more. 'For goodness' sake, Betsy,' she said, her voice cracked with anger. 'Take yourself off to bed afore I clout you one.'

Betsy, suddenly focusing, saw her mother's half-raised arm. She got up quickly. The chair she'd been sitting on fell over. Ann Smith gasped with exasperation and brought her hand down hard across her daughter's face. Betsy turned and fled to the door. She pulled it open and ran out into the rain.

When she reached Belle Vue Cottage she found the door open. This was wrong. She knew that. She stepped inside hesitantly. The rain had been blown in by the wind and there was a damp patch across the stone-flagged floor. One of Mr Munro's cats, the ginger one, must have found the open door before her and was sleeping on the cushioned chair near the range. The black one was on the table. But Kate wasn't at home.

Richard trod carefully as he went upstairs to his study. Prince kept him company. The dog seemed to know that caution was called for and he kept his body low and his head cocked so that he could keep his eyes on his master's face. Richard grinned and put his fingers to his lips as if the dog could understand the gesture. And perhaps he did.

The Ladies' Reading Group was meeting in the first-floor sitting room and Richard had no wish to be called in to socialize. He would do his duty when the meeting came to an end, see the ladies to their carriages or call cabs for them if necessary, but he had excused himself long ago from handing round the teacups and small cakes that his mother always provided. Caroline had taken over that duty.

The overhead gas lamp was already lit but Richard put a match to the three oil lamps that were placed around the room and then closed the heavy velvet curtains. Crossing to the fireplace, he removed the cinder guard and built up the fire himself. He had observed that at the Traverses' house not one of the family would do this.

Not Caroline, nor her mother, nor even her father who was certainly capable of shovelling a few bits of coal into the fire. But Richard could not bring himself to pull the bell rope and summon one of the maids from the kitchen to do something he could easily do himself.

Prince watched his actions with interest and then flopped down on the hearthrug with a contented moan. Richard lifted his coat tails and warmed his backside for a moment before crossing to his desk, which was set at right angles to the hearth. He settled himself to deal with some paperwork. The scar on his cheek began to nag a little. It felt as though some invisible person was poking at it with hot needles. He opened a drawer in his desk and reached for the bottle of brandy and a clean glass. He poured himself a generous measure and, nursing the tumbler with one hand, turned the pages of his ledger with the other and set to work.

She couldn't find them. Kate sobbed with frustration. Although her eyes had become accustomed to the shadowy interior of the cave it was too dark to see the inscriptions carved into the wall. She began searching with her fingertips, running them over the sandstone walls, sure that sooner or later she would find the grooves that formed the names enclosed in the heart. The heart that Jos had carved to enclose the two of them within their own world for ever.

But her fingers, often sore and swollen these days, must have become too work-roughened and insensitive to find the carvings. She was sure she was searching in the right place. I should have brought a candle, she thought, as she sat down wearily on the ledge. Jos told me people used to live in these caves hundreds of years ago. Why shouldn't I make my home here now? She smiled at the thought. It would be like children playing houses.

She remembered when she, Jos, Jane and Thomas used to do just that, bringing jam sandwiches and a bottle of water. If she listened hard she could almost hear those long-ago childish voices over the pounding of the waves on the shore and the wind-driven rain. She sat down on the ledge and leaned back against the wall of the cave and closed her eyes.

The Smith family sat at the table eating supper together. When her daughter-in-law placed her bowl of soup before her on the table Martha asked quietly, 'Aren't you going after the bairn?'

'No.'

'She didn't take a shawl. It's raining.'

'You know fine well where she'll be. With Kate Lawson. She's not daft enough to stay out in the rain.'

'Don't you mind?'

'Why should I? If the Lawson lass is willing to put up with Betsy she's welcome to her. Now whisht.' She glanced towards her husband and two sons who had started eating. 'We'll have our meal in peace for once.'

But Martha wouldn't be silenced. 'Betsy's no trouble. You get yourself upset over nowt, if you ask me.'

'I'm not asking you,' her daughter-in-law said. 'Now sup up before I decide it's too much trouble keeping *you* here and pack you off to the workhouse.'

There was a knock on the door and the dog yelped but didn't wake up. He must have thought it was part of his dream. Richard had watched in amusement as the black paws twitched and the tail wagged. Whatever Prince was dreaming about he was enjoying it.

Richard glanced at the clock on the mantelpiece and was surprised to see how long he had been working. Here, in his study at the back of the house, there was only the crackling of the coals in the hearth and the sleepy whimpering of the dog to disturb the peace.

The knock sounded again. Firmer and more demanding. Richard sighed, drained his second glass of brandy, and called, 'Come in.' When the door opened he was surprised to see Caroline enter the room. He got to his feet. 'Are the ladies ready to go?' he asked.

'They went some time ago,' she said.

'Why didn't you come for me?'

'Your mother thought we shouldn't disturb you.'

Richard wasn't sure if he believed her. His mother had never minded interrupting his work before tonight. In fact she had objected forcefully when Richard had started bringing his books and papers home. Grace Adamson believed that all that should be left at the office and a man should relax in the evenings. It was a battle that she had won with Richard's father who, as a consequence, had started to spend more time in the office on the quayside, coming home later and later. Richard had asked her what she preferred. That he stay out late at night or bring his work home. He had won the argument.

Caroline must have mistaken the look of doubt in his eyes, or at least attributed it to the wrong reason. 'I managed perfectly well,' she said. 'The carriages arrived on time and I telephoned for cabs for the others.'

'Then I must thank you. But has your carriage arrived yet?'

He observed a fleeting look of irritation before she replied, evenly enough, 'My carriage will be here in just under an hour's time. I thought you would like us to spend some time together.'

'Oh, of course. Shall we go and join my mother?'

'We can go to the sitting room, if you like, but your mother has gone to bed. We have just finished reading Mr Hardy's *Tess of the D'Urbevilles* and most of the group found it quite distressing. Your mother said she wished to retire with a cup of hot chocolate, a ratafia biscuit or two, and one of Mrs Braddon's sensation novels which, no matter what the heroine is forced to suffer, will at least have a happy ending.'

Richard couldn't help responding to Caroline's light-hearted tone even though he sensed her gaiety was somewhat forced. He was a little surprised and even shocked that his mother had gone to bed leaving Caroline alone with him. In their world, servants didn't count, it seemed. He suspected that his mother, tired of his indecisiveness, might be trying to force the issue. She liked Caroline and thought it high time Richard was married.

He saw that Caroline was in the act of closing the door. 'Why don't we stay in here?' she asked. 'It's warm and cosy and I have no wish to disturb you.'

Richard laughed. 'But don't you think you have disturbed me by coming here?'

Her eyes opened wider for a moment but she saw that he was joking and responded, 'I meant by dragging you along the passage to another room.'

'Hardly a fearsome journey.'

They both laughed and Richard found to his surprise that he was enjoying himself.

'Let's sit by the fire,' Caroline said.

There was an armchair by the hearth, a high winged-back affair that kept the draughts away from your face. As Caroline settled herself in it, Richard picked up the chair from behind his desk and brought it round. He placed it so that he was facing her, with the dog lying between them.

The firelight shone on Prince's black coat and Richard noticed that the dog had begun to pant. He was either too deeply asleep or too lazy to move, so Richard stretched out one leg and tried to edge him further away from the fire. Prince opened his eyes, lifted his head to look reproachfully at his master, growled half-heartedly and then raised himself unwillingly to flop down about a foot away. He eyed the bowl of water that Richard kept for him at the side of the hearth but then closed his eyes. Richard smiled. The dog would drink if he needed to.

Caroline remained silent. Richard often wondered whether she altogether approved of Prince. She had certainly expressed surprise the first time she had found him wandering about the upper floors of the house.

Richard glanced at her but her expression told him nothing. Caroline had sat well back but he could see that she was gazing into the fire. He allowed his eyes to enjoy her beauty. The dark hair framing the classically oval face. The gentle slope of her shoulders and the curve of her breasts beneath a white blouse. She had lifted her feet up on to the small footstool and the tips of a pair of velvet embroidered indoor shoes protruded from her skirt's voluminous grey folds. He felt desire stir as hot and as potent as the French brandy he had recently consumed.

No doubt becoming aware of his gaze, Caroline looked up. What did she see in his eyes that caused her to blush? He knew that the reflected firelight had nothing to do with the flush that spread over her ivory complexion. But whatever she saw, she was not displeased. She smiled at him, her lips parted and her eyes shining. Her smile was inviting him to imagine what it would be like to make love to her.

He allowed the fantasy to play in his mind. But to his consternation, he had barely reached the moment when he would have taken her in his arms when the black hair changed to shining coppery red, the dark eyes to the greeny-blue of the summer sea. The face in his dream dissolved and formed again into something stronger: high cheekbones, a generous mouth – and was there just the faintest scattering of freckles – sun

172

kisses – across the bridge of the nose and her cheeks? The illusion was so strong that it left Richard shaken. He knew very well whom the face belonged to.

Richard closed his eyes and kept them closed until the vision had gone. He was aware of a shadow crossing before him and opened his eyes to find Caroline looking down at him.

'Are you all right?' she asked.

'Yes, I'm fine.'

'You don't look all right.'

'Blame the brandy.'

'I beg your pardon?' She sounded shocked.

'It's all right. I'm not turning into a drunkard but my scar was hurting and perhaps I had a glass too many to ease the pain. And after a long day . . .' He was aware that he was floundering. But if he couldn't blame the brandy what could he say? That he had become obsessed with Kate Lawson – a fish lass? He could never tell Caroline that.

'Oh, poor Richard.'

The concern in her voice filled him with guilt and what she did next took him completely by surprise. She knelt down before him and took his face in her hands. Then, leaning forward, she placed her soft lips over the scar on his cheek and kissed him gently. 'There, let me kiss it better,' she said.

Richard reached up for her hands and held them both in his. 'Caroline, you shouldn't . . .'

'Have I been forward?' Her voice was soft, teasing. He realized to his consternation that she was seducing him.

'We are alone here,' he said.

'So?'

'Your reputation . . .'

'For goodness' sake, Richard,' there was an edge of controlled temper to her voice, 'this is not a romantic novel. I am not some milksop heroine and you the dastardly villain. This is real life. We have been friends for over a year, and your mother knows perfectly well that we are "alone" ' – she emphasized the word as if holding it up to ridicule – 'together. In fact she encouraged— Oh!'

Caroline had risen swiftly, stepped backwards and trodden on Prince's tail. The dog yelped and leapt to his feet, causing Caroline to stumble. But Richard saved her. He rose quickly and caught her in his arms. She was trembling.

'I'm sorry,' she said.

173

'It's all right. Prince isn't hurt. Look, he's forgiven you. He's wagging his tail.'

The dog, now thoroughly awake, ambled over to his water bowl but Caroline barely glanced at him. 'Oh, good,' she said. 'But I didn't mean Prince – at least, I'm sorry I stood on his tail, but I meant . . . oh, dear . . .' She stifled a sob.

Richard put the fingers of one hand under her chin and raised her face. She was crying. 'Please don't cry,' he said. 'There's nothing to apologize for.'

'Isn't there?'

She sounded so unlike herself. So vulnerable, like a child almost, that Richard put both his arms round her and held her close. Her nearness meant nothing to him. There was no leap of desire, now, no welling up of tenderness. Just a feeling of sympathy. Gradually her trembling ceased and she uttered a deep sigh.

'I'd better get ready to leave, I suppose. My carriage will be here soon.'

'Yes. I'll ring for Joan – no, it's late, I'll go and get your things myself. Why don't you sit down?'

Richard had decided to fetch Caroline's cloak and shoes not so much out of consideration for the young housemaid as for the fact that he needed to get away. And he suspected that Caroline, too, would appreciate a moment or two on her own to get over her embarrassment.

As he left the room he looked back and saw that she was sitting and gazing into the fire again. Prince, always ready to forgive, had lumbered over to her and placed his head on her knee. He was looking up at her as if to ask what the matter was.

By the time Richard returned Caroline had regained her composure. She changed her shoes, slipping her indoor shoes into her slipper bag, and stood up so that he could help her into her cloak. The cloak had a velvet-lined hood which Caroline pulled up and forward so that her face was in shadow.

'Your carriage is here,' Richard told her.

Neither of them spoke as they went down the stairs. Richard didn't ask when she was to visit his mother again and Caroline didn't offer the information. He took an umbrella from the stand and saw her into the carriage.

'Goodnight, Richard.' Caroline's tone was formal. Something about her attitude suggested to Richard that she may have forgiven herself for what had just happened but she had not forgiven him. Pity was not the emotion she had meant to arouse.

'Goodnight.'

He stood and watched as the carriage drew away. Then, as he turned to go back into the house, a gust of wind seized the umbrella and turned it inside out before tearing it from his hand and hurling it up into the air. Prince, who had followed them down, began to bark with excitement. Richard watched as the umbrella flew up towards the moon and the racing clouds, sailed over the boat field, and then plummeted down over the cliffs. Prince couldn't contain himself any longer and dashed away across the road.

'Heel!' Richard shouted and the dog stopped in his tracks and came back, head down but eyes slanted upwards, watching his master's face to see if he was in trouble. 'That's all right, boy,' Richard said and patted his head. 'You've been patient. I'll take you out now. How about if we go down to the beach and see what's happened to that umbrella?'

When Richard had donned his waterproof coat, he and the dog set out, turning towards the village to go down the slope to the beach. Maybe it was because poor patient Prince had had to wait longer than usual for his evening walk, or maybe it was the wind ruffling his coat that excited him, but he soon took off and raced ahead of his master. Richard wasn't unduly worried. Prince knew where they were going; Richard had uttered the magic word 'beach'.

Clouds sped across the sky, often obscuring the moon, but there was enough light from the gas street lamps strung along the seafront road to light his way. But when he reached the old part of the village he realized that he had lost track of Prince. Usually the dog waited at the top of the slope for the command to go down to the beach. But he wasn't there.

Then Richard heard a low growl, then a hiss. Prince must have disturbed a cat – probably one of Howard's motley crew.

'Prince! To heel!' he called but it was too late. The sounds of a furious chase echoed from the darkness of one of the narrow streets behind him. Prince was barking cheerfully but the cat was yowling as if its last days had come. Then there came a yelp of surprise. Richard realized that Prince must have been bitten on the nose or scratched for his pains.

He followed the sounds. Lamps shone dimly from behind curtained cottage windows. Now and then the moonlight reflected from the wet cobbles. There was an open doorway a little way ahead; a small figure was framed in the light.

'Go away!' the figure shouted. 'You shouldn't frighten little cats!'

As he drew near he saw it was Betsy, Martha Smith's granddaughter who had accompanied the old woman to Howard's studio and now seemed to be acting as chaperone to Kate Lawson. The child was holding a squirming bundle of black fur to her body with one hand and pointing at Prince with the other. The dog backed away but began to wag his tail as if trying to convey that he'd meant no harm; he'd only wanted to play.

Richard had reached him by now and added his reproaches to that of the child. 'Bad dog!' he said. 'What have you done?'

Prince looked utterly forlorn. He came towards Richard, his tail drooping, and Richard told him to sit and stay. Then he approached the child in the doorway. He was disconcerted to see that tears were streaming down her face. 'Is the cat all right?'

Betsy sniffed but didn't answer.

Richard's heart sank. He hated the thought of any animal in pain and distress. 'Here, let me have a look.'

The girl used both hands now to hold the cat even more closely to her body. Richard was afraid that, in its frightened state, it might claw her face.

'All right. You keep hold of the cat, but why don't we go inside and I can have a look at the poor thing, see if it needs patching up. You want to help it, don't you?'

'Yes!'

Betsy backed into the cottage. Richard commanded his now thoroughly miserable dog to stay where he was and followed the girl into the cottage and closed the door. He was struck by the neatness and cleanliness of the place, and also by the fact that apart from the girl, the cat she was holding and another one asleep on a chair near the fire, there was no one else there.

He knew very well that whole families crowded into cottages like this. Yet the girl was here alone. The weather was bad tonight. There was wind and rain and even with the door closed he could hear the sounds of the sea; it was running high. Had the men decided to go fishing despite the weather? Were they already down on the beach preparing to set out? But where were the women? Maybe they were with the men helping to launch the cobles. But surely Betsy's grand-mother, old Martha, should be here?

'Here, look.' Suddenly Betsy thrust the cat towards him. It seemed she trusted him.

That was more than the cat did. Richard grabbed the poor beast and tried to soothe it, stroking and petting it as gently as he could. He was rewarded with a scratch on his hand. But he held on tightly and was eventually able to assure Betsy that there didn't seem to be anything wrong with it. He placed it as gently as he could on the hearthrug from where it glared up at him balefully before beginning to wash itself vigorously.

'It scratched your dog's nose,' Betsy said.

Richard couldn't tell whether she was pleased or sorry. 'Don't worry,' he told her. 'The dog deserved to be put in his place.'

'You're not angry?'

'No. Well, yes, I am. With my dog, Prince.'

Betsy nodded as if this pleased her, but after this momentary distraction she sighed and began to look miserable again. Soon she was sobbing out loud.

Richard didn't like to leave her in this state. 'What is it?' he asked.

'I don't know where she is,' Betsy said puzzlingly.

'Who? Your grandmother?'

'No, Kate. She hasn't come home.'

Memory stirred. Of course. Kate had been living here with her aunt. Meg Lawson had been teaching Kate how to sell fish from door to door. Richard had assumed that she had moved in to keep the old woman company and had gone home to her family after Meg had died.

'Where is she?' he asked.

'I telt you,' Betsy said, 'I divven't know!' Her tone was sharp.

Richard suspected she was near to panic. He tried to calm her down. 'Perhaps she's gone to visit her mother?'

The girl shook her head violently. 'He won't let her. Her da – he won't let her go home.'

'Why is that?'

'Because he's a bad 'un.'

Richard realized that whatever the reason was Betsy did not know it. He was perplexed. He didn't know what to say.

'Me ma was shouting at me,' Betsy told him, suddenly becoming voluble, 'so I came to see Kate. She's kind. The door was open and the rain had blown in. The ginger cat was on the chair. The black one was on the table eating the bacon. I chased it out. I couldn't find Kate so I thought I would just sit here and wait for her. I divven't know how long

I sat here.' She glanced towards the clock on the mantelshelf. 'I can't tell the time. Kate's teaching me – big hand and little hand.' She paused and smiled at what must have been a happy memory. 'But I forgot to shut the door, and then that one flew in again.' She nodded towards the black cat who was now curled up on the hearthrug. 'All wet and spitting. Your dog came in after it but the cat turned and scratched his nose. I chased the dog out. You know.'

Richard assumed that she meant he knew the rest of the story. 'Yes, I know.'

'And Kate hasn't come home.' Betsy frowned; she looked as if she was thinking hard about something, trying to puzzle it out. Then her frown cleared and her eyes widened hopefully. 'Do you think she might have gone to Mr Munro's?' she asked.

'Why would she go there?'

'Well, he's painting her picture, isn't he – and they're friends, aren't they? I mean, they always laugh and smile a lot when he isn't telling her to keep still. Perhaps she's gone there to talk to him.'

Richard examined her suggestion and, although he found it an unlikely explanation, he was surprised at how disturbing the idea was. More than disturbing – the thought of Kate Lawson and his cousin laughing and talking and being friends was almost unbearable. Richard shied away from speculating why that was so, but it was.

'Mr Adamson – will you answer me?'

'Sorry. What did you say?'

'I knew you weren't listening. I asked you if I should go and see if Kate is at Mr Munro's house. I could tell her to come home because it's late.'

Before Richard could form an answer there was a knock at the door.

'Kate!' Betsy cried out and flew to open it. 'Oh,' she said, 'it's you, Grandma.'

Martha Smith was obviously surprised to see Richard there. She looked round the room quickly and then asked, 'Where's Kate?'

'I don't know,' Betsy said. 'The door was open.'

Richard added, 'And I found your granddaughter here. I think she's worried about Kate – Miss Lawson.'

Martha turned to her granddaughter. 'I wouldn't worry, pet. Kate has probably gone to visit her friend.'

'What friend is that?' Richard tried hard to sound as if he was expressing a casual interest.

'Jane – Jane Harrison.'

'The cobbler's daughter? But she works in town, doesn't she?'

'Aye, in a grand house in Jesmond. But she's home visiting her mother, and staying overnight. I saw her arrive with her little carpet bag.'

'Nothing much is missed in this village, is it?' Richard said wryly.

Martha laughed. 'What do you expect? Everyone knows everyone and we like to know what's going on.'

'Are you sure Kate is at Jane's house?' Betsy said.

'Well, I admit it's a guess but I think it's a good one. After all, the two lasses have been friends since their schooldays, haven't they? They always visit each other when Jane comes home. And talking about home, I think it's high time you came home with me.'

'All right. But if Kate has gone to Jane's house why would she leave the door open?'

That stumped Martha. 'I didn't think of that. But maybe she didn't. Maybe she was in such a hurry to visit her friend that she was careless when she pulled the door shut after her. Maybe the sneck didn't catch properly so the door blew open again.' She paused. 'What do you think, Mr Adamson? After all, there's a high old wind blowing tonight.'

The old woman looked at him keenly and Richard realized she was appealing to him for help. 'I think that's possible,' he said.

'Do you?' Betsy asked him and he nodded. 'And do you think she's all right?'

'Why shouldn't she be?' her grandmother said. 'Right now, your friend Kate will be sitting having a good old chinwag with her friend Jane Harrison, take my word for it. Now come along home. And you, too, Mr Adamson. Come out and shut the door. That poor miserable dog of yours is getting wetter by the minute out there.'

'What about the cats?' Betsy said suddenly and Richard could see that her grandmother was getting impatient.

'Don't worry about the cats,' he said. 'I think we should leave them here. I'm sure Miss Lawson won't mind. She wouldn't like to think of them being put out in the rain, would she?'

'But they might want to go home. Back to Mr Munro's house.'

'Why don't we open a window?' Richard said quickly, before Martha became more irritated. 'Look, that one above the bench. Just the top half. I'm sure the cats are clever enough to jump up and small enough to squeeze through.'

Betsy grinned. 'They come in that way sometimes.'

'Right, then. I'll open it now.'

Betsy seemed satisfied with that. The window opened, Richard followed Martha to the door. He paused to look round the clean and well-ordered room and wondered what it might be like to sit here with Kate by the fire.

'Come along, Mr Adamson, sir,' Martha said. 'Me and the bairn is getting soaked standing here.' It was obvious that she wanted to close the door herself and make sure it was secure.

After doing so, she said goodnight to him and she and the child hurried away along the rain-drenched street. Richard watched them go, then turned to look for Prince. The dog was huddled as close as possible to the wall of the cottage.

'If I could have trusted you to behave yourself, I would have allowed you to come in,' Richard said and Prince turned his head on one side as he listened. Then he got up and walked towards his master, wagging his tail experimentally. He pushed his nose into Richard's hand.

'All right, you're forgiven,' Richard said. 'But no more running off and no more chasing cats, right?'

Prince, no doubt eager to redeem himself, stayed close to heel as they set off for the beach.

Was Kate with her friend Jane? Richard wondered. Had she been so eager to get there that she had been careless about shutting her door properly? Or had she been equally eager to visit someone else? He stopped outside Howard's two-storey cottage and looked at it. The windows were dark and there was no light showing under the door. His cousin must be in bed. Kate wasn't here unless . . . No, he refused to let his thoughts take that path.

'All right – off you go!'

At the top of the slope Richard gave Prince permission to run ahead and the dog raced off as though the wind was behind him. The beach was deserted. Any fisherman who had decided to risk the weather had already set sail, but the row of cobles beached high above the waterline told Richard that many, wisely, had decided to stay at home tonight.

The tide was coming in and it seemed unusually high. It had reached the outcrop of cliff that cut the bay into two at high water. There wasn't much beach left for Prince to romp on but he was making the most of it, racing round ecstatically as the wind ruffled his coat and barking at the loose pebbles that scuttled by.

And then he started barking at the sea, running after the retreating waves and dodging backwards when they advanced again. Inevitably he got caught by a wave that surged further than he was expecting and Richard called him to heel.

'I don't want to spend the rest of the night rubbing you down, old fellow,' he said. 'It's too cold for a dip tonight.' Prince rewarded him by shaking himself vigorously. Richard laughed and jumped out of the way of the flying droplets. 'I think we'll go home now,' he said.

He set off for the slope that led up to Bank Top and was halfway there when he realized that Prince was not following him. He turned in exasperation and saw that the dog was nosing his way along the curving cliff face towards one of the caves. The water was already surging into the cave mouth and – Richard had to strain to see it – it looked as though something was floating in the water, going in and out with the waves.

Prince stopped sniffing and stared at the object. Then, without warning, he made a dash into the water and grabbed it with his teeth. It was obviously unwieldy but the dog would not let go. He turned, was buffeted by an incoming wave, struggled to keep his feet, and, half swimming by now, tried to make his way back to his master.

Now Richard saw what it was: his umbrella, turned inside out, the torn fabric trailing in the water. And there was something else, something that looked like a large piece of seaweed caught up in the spokes, making it difficult for Prince to manage his unwieldy trophy.

'Here, Prince!' he called. 'Leave it!' But his words were snatched away by the strengthening wind.

This is partly my own fault, he thought. I told the poor beast that we would go and look for the umbrella. Another wave, stronger than those that had gone before, knocked Prince sideways again and Richard had just decided that he must go into the water and drag the dog to safety when the wave receded and Prince scrambled up and lurched forward to drop the umbrella at Richard's feet.

'Good dog,' Richard said weakly.

He bent to fondle Prince's ears and realized that he would have to take the umbrella home, no matter what state it was in. After all, his faithful companion had risked his life to fetch it for him.

Richard picked it up and started to disentangle what he had thought was a clump of seaweed. It was a woman's shawl. Left near the mouth of the cave, no doubt, by one of the village women and then forgotten about. Richard shook it and decided to leave it on some nearby rocks well away from the waterline. Whoever had lost it would find it in the morning.

But as he spread it out and secured it with a heavy stone, a memory surfaced in his mind. What was it that Howard had told him? Something about making a fool of himself by going into a cave to rescue a young woman who told him in no uncertain terms that she didn't need rescuing.

And that young woman had been Kate. Kate Lawson, who had also told Howard that she and Jos, the lad who was to become her sweetheart, often played in that cave when they were children. And according to Betsy Smith Kate was missing. Had left her cottage without securing the door properly. Or had been in such a state of mind that she had left it wide open ... suddenly he knew for certain – Kate was in trouble. For some reason, she'd gone to the cave.

He didn't stop to think any further. Telling Prince to stay and guard the shawl and the umbrella, he plunged through the rising tide, feeling his way along the cliff face until he found the cave's mouth.

Wherever you were in the village you could hear the sound of the sea; it even became part of your dreams. Kate stirred in her sleep, came half awake, but was too tired to open her eyes. She couldn't remember ever being so tired. The mattress seemed hard and lumpy. She would have to drag it into the yard and hang it over the washing line and give it a good beating.

The room seemed cold. Had she built up the fire before coming to bed? She couldn't remember. And it was draughty, too. She must have left the window open; the window above the bench. Drat. One or more of Howard's cats would be bound to sneak in. They were always waiting, lurking, ready to trip her up if she opened the door, or jump down on to the bench from the window and seek out any tasty titbits she might have left uncovered.

It was strange, though. She was usually particular about all those little tasks, especially since Aunt Meg had died and she had been living here alone. Memory stirred and brought with it a sense of anguish. She was going to have to leave the cottage. Where would she go? What would become of her baby if she couldn't find somewhere for them to live? Would they take the baby away from her?

Sleep receded as her anguish grew and she turned violently, flinging her arm sideways. Her hand landed on the floor. But how could it have done? The bed was too high for that to happen. Kate tried to rouse herself but her head was hot and she felt groggy. Still struggling to swim up from the depths she realized that the floor where her hand lay was cold ... not just cold, but wet. And the water was lapping, backwards and forwards like the tide.

As the horror of her situation finally penetrated her feverish slumbers she forced her eyes open and sat up and banged her head on the ceiling. But, of course, it wasn't the ceiling of the cottage; it was the roof of the cave. She had fallen asleep on the ledge in the cave and the tide was coming in.

The water dragged at his clothes. He should have taken his coat off, he realized, but it was too late now. He had to go on.

Soon he had to stoop as the cave narrowed and the roof became lower. The moonlight barely lit the way now but his eyes adjusted to the dim light and he peered ahead. He could see the ledge and something lying on it. Someone. It couldn't be anyone but Kate and his heart almost stopped when he saw how still she was.

But then the figure stirred and one arm flopped over into the water with a faint splash. Richard hurried forward, forgetting to stoop, and banged his head on the rocky roof just as the figure sat up and opened her eyes wide.

'Kate!' he said, and her expression of terror turned to one of bewilderment as she stared up at him. He knelt down, heedless of the water now rising almost to his waist, and gathered her into his arms. 'For God's sake, Kate,' he said. 'Are you trying to break my heart?'

Chapter Fourteen

A shaft of watery sunlight fell across Kate's closed eyelids; she turned her head away. She wanted to sleep for just a little while longer. But, now, irritatingly, her tired brain stirred and presented her with a puzzle. Had she really fallen asleep in the cave and only awakened when the tide came in? No, it couldn't be. It must have been a dream – a nightmare – for now she was warm and comfortable in her own bed. The trouble was, she did remember going to the cave but had no recollection of returning to the cottage.

She sighed and stretched her limbs. How soft the mattress was, how snugly the down gave way and fitted itself round her body. But how could that be? Aunt Meg's feather bed was old and lumpy, her sheets, although clean, were rough and patched. These bed sheets were soft and smelled of lavender. Had she died and gone to heaven?

Feeling the stirrings of unease, Kate curled her body into a ball and pulled the bedclothes high over her shoulders. She had to think about this. Then a familiar sound made her open her eyes. It was the sound of a coal falling from the grate. Did they have fires in heaven? Kate suppressed a hysterical giggle when she remembered it was the other place where fires were supposed to burn.

She pushed the bedclothes down again and sat up cautiously. Wherever she was it was early morning, and the pale light that had woken her was sneaking through a crack in the curtains; not her curtains. The curtains in the cottage were made of blue and white gingham whereas these had a pattern of impossibly bright flowers. Furthermore they were long, falling to the floor where the hazy morning light threw the shadows of raindrops on to the bold colours of a richly patterned rug. And even though she was disorientated she could see they were at the wrong side of the bed.

Kate peered round the room. Her eyes were drawn to the fire. This was no workaday fire complete with oven range, but a pretty little fireplace with glazed tiles and a brass fender. The small lump of coal that had fallen and startled her was smouldering harmlessly on the hearth.

Her eyes travelled back from the fireplace across the oriental rug to the bed and the fine eiderdown, the silky folds of which she was clasping in her hands. And then she noticed the full broderie anglais frilled cuffs of the nightdress she was wearing. A fine linen nightdress that, like the bed sheets, gave off a pleasant odour of lavender. Lavender and rosemary, Kate thought, remembering her aunt's favourite hair dressing.

How did this happen? Kate probed her sluggish mind, trying to remember how it was that she was dressed in a fine nightgown and sleeping in a warm bed in such a well-furnished room. A glimmer of what had taken place had just begun to stir in her memory when she was almost startled out of what remained of her wits by the opening of the door.

'Awake at last,' a young woman in a maid's uniform said. Kate recognised the girl from her schooldays. The maid sniffed audibly and Kate took in her disapproving expression.

'Joan . . . Joan Donkin, isn't it?'

'Yes, that's right.' The sour-faced young woman shut the door and came into the room, going straight to the fire. She knelt to rake it, then swept up the ashes and, using the tongs, built it up with coal from the scuttle. Kate stared at her disapproving back. Joan had never been her friend.

The maid dusted her hands on a rag she took from her apron pocket and stood up. She turned to face Kate. 'Mrs Adamson said you could stay until the doctor's seen you. Mr Adamson has already telephoned him. But I could tell the mistress wasn't pleased. She looked even more out of sorts than when he brought you home last night.'

Memories began to flow in like the tide. 'Yes . . . he said he would take me home but I thought . . .'

'What did you think?' Despite her obvious hostility Joan's small eyes betrayed her curiosity.

'I thought he meant to the cottage . . .' Kate raised one hand to her forehead and found it hot.

Joan Donkin walked towards her. 'You're feverish,' she said. She picked up a jug from the bedside table and filled the glass, splashing the water carelessly. 'Here, drink this.'

Kate began to gulp the water down. 'Stop that,' Joan admonished.

185

'You'll make yourself sick and I don't see why I should clear up after you.'

'Sorry.' Kate stopped drinking. 'Joan,' she said, 'you and I were never friends, were we?' Joan's answer was another sniff. 'And I can see that you resent having to look after me,' Kate continued.

'You see right.'

'But please will you tell me what happened last night?'

'Don't you know?'

'Part of it. But I feel so hot – and tired – and, oh, I don't know . . .' To Kate's consternation she felt hot tears prick at the back of her eyes.

Fortunately Joan didn't notice. 'Tell me what you do remember,' she said.

Kate placed the glass of water on the bedside table and stared ahead. She frowned. 'I was in the cave . . . I sat down . . . I must have fallen asleep. And Mr Adamson found me there.'

'That's right.' Joan sounded disappointed as if she had wanted to hear a different story. 'He said it was thanks to Prince.'

'Prince?'

'His dog. I heard Mr Adamson telling his ma some rigmarole about a lost umbrella and Prince going after it and leading the way to you instead. Mind you, from the way his ma was questioning him, I could tell she was finding it hard to swallow.'

'But why shouldn't his mother believe him?'

'Oh, I think he convinced her. After all, why on earth should a gentleman like Mr Adamson have a rendezvous with a fish lass?'

'A rendezvous?'

'Aye.' Joan laughed scornfully. 'His poor ma thought the two of you were up to something in the cave and you'd got so carried away that you didn't notice the tide coming in.'

'But that's dreadful! Did she say that?'

Joan looked abashed. 'Well, not exactly. But I could tell the way her mind was working.'

Kate would have liked to say that that was because that was the way Joan Donkin's nasty mind worked but she controlled her rising anger. She must not antagonize the girl now, not when she needed an ally – even a reluctant one.

'And where was I when all this was going on?' Kate asked. 'Oh . . .'

'What is it?' Joan asked. 'Have you remembered?'

'Yes, it's coming back. I was in a bath . . . and someone had tried to undress me.' She looked Joan in the eyes. 'None too gently!'

186

The maid shrugged. 'Well, I'd gone to bed when Mrs Adamson came to get me. The poor lady had already retired and Mr Adamson woke her up when he brought you home dripping like a piece of wet codfish.'

'Codfish! Thank you!' Kate found the strength to glare but Joan was unabashed.

'Anyway, I filled the bath and got the soap and towels – and one of Mrs Adamson's own nightgowns – and then when I began to take your clothes off you had a proper paddy. I got a right mouthful for my pains.'

Kate felt uneasy. She remembered shouting and she remembered why. 'I just wanted to tell you that I could manage to undress myself,' she said.

Joan sniffed. 'Well, the upshot was that I had to sit out on the cold landing until I heard you stumbling about. When I came in you'd dried yourself and put the nightgown on.'

'I'm sorry. You were trying to help—'

'Only because I'd been told to.'

'That makes no difference. I was rude and ungrateful. But I wasn't myself, was I?'

'No, that's true,' Joan said grudgingly and Kate was relieved to see that her old enemy seemed to accept the explanation. For Kate had remembered only too well why she hadn't wanted anyone to see her naked. The bairn didn't show yet, but her breasts were bigger and another woman might have been able to tell . . .

'But now,' Kate looked around the room, 'where are my clothes?'

'I took them downstairs to be laundered. And I found you a dry bit of ribbon for the ring.'

'The ring . . .' Kate's hand flew to the neckline of the nightgown.

'Don't worry, it's there hanging round your neck. Is that the ring Jos bought?'

'Yes.'

'I thought so.'

Joan turned her back on her and began to sort out a small cupboard in the corner which Kate took to be a washstand. She was the last person that Kate would have wished for to help her when she was feeling weak and disorientated. The sooner she could leave this house the better.

'I suppose I'd better bring your breakfast.' Joan turned to face her. 'Mr Adamson says you're to have your breakfast in bed and stay there until the doctor's seen you.'

'Oh, no. If you get my clothes I'd rather go home now.'

187

'Impossible. I've told you your clothes are being laundered and, besides, if you don't do as I say you'll only get me into trouble with the master.'

'All right. I can see I'll have to stay.' Something occurred to her and Kate frowned. 'Joan . . . I wonder . . .'

'What is it?' Joan had reached the door and she turned impatiently.

'How did I get up here? To bed, I mean. Did you carry me?'

'Not likely. A great tall lass like you! No, Mr Adamson was waiting in his study. I went to tell him you were ready and he came and carried you up. You were real feverish by then. I don't think you knew what was happening.'

'I didn't,' Kate said, but Joan was already halfway out of the room. Kate could have sworn she heard the words 'Lady Muck!' before the door slammed behind her.

But now she had something else to worry about. The flush that spread over Kate's face had little to do with her fever. The mention of Richard Adamson's carrying her up to bed had opened the floodgates to another memory, of how he had carried her out of the cave and how, once they were safely on the beach above the tideline, he had put her down gently and they had both breathed deeply, gasping for air.

Then, looking at each other, they had moved together, wordlessly, and he had taken her in his arms. He had held her close to his body in the moonlight, the constant roar of the sea ringing in her ears, but not so loud as the beating of her heart. She had clung to him as if for dear life. 'Kate,' he had murmured before his lips had closed over hers.

Kate lay back amongst the pillows, her senses racing. How natural it had seemed, there on the moonlit beach, to be embraced by the man whose image had been invading her unquiet thoughts for some time now.

But last night had been no daydream. And this time she would not be able to push all thoughts of him away. For how could she ever deny the thrill she had experienced when she gave herself up to his kiss?

Jane looked up from the table as Martha Smith's granddaughter burst into the neat living room behind the cobbler's shop, Jane's father close behind her.

'Is Kate here?'

'I'm sorry, lass,' Jane's father said through a mouthful of tacks. 'She just dodged under the flap in the counter and ran through. Shall I chase her out again?'

'Don't worry,' Jane said. Even though she should be used to her father's ways by now she could never shake off the fear that one day he might swallow some of the tacks. 'I'll see what she wants.'

'I want to know if Kate is here,' Betsy demanded almost before Mr Harrison had gone back to his work. 'I've already telt you,' she added and her glare was baleful.

'Yes,' Jane said, 'and if you weren't so rude I might answer you.'

'Don't be hard on the child,' Jane's mother said as she bustled through from the back scullery with a plateful of scrambled egg on toast. 'She doesn't mean to be rude. It's just that she's not quite right in the head.'

Betsy turned to look at her and scowled. Then she looked at Jane again. 'My grandma said Kate was here.'

'Well she isn't. Why on earth would your grandma say that?'

Betsy's scowl turned into a worried frown. 'She said it was a good guess. But if she isn't here, where is she?'

'How should I know?'

'You're her friend, aren't you?'

Jane and her mother looked at each other helplessly. Then Florence Harrison placed the plate of scrambled eggs on the table and said, 'Eat this before it gets cold. There's nothing worse than cold scrambled eggs.'

'But what about this?' Jane waved a helpless hand towards their unwelcome visitor.

'Let's sort it out over a cup of tea,' her mother said. 'Would you like a cup of tea, Betsy? And a piece of toast, perhaps?'

'I'd rather have bread and dripping.'

Jane raised her eyebrows as, without waiting to be asked, the strange child took her seat at the table. Her mother shook her head but she managed a smile. 'Bread and dripping it is, then,' she said. 'But mind you let Jane get on with her breakfast. She has a train to catch.'

Mrs Harrison poured Jane's tea before she went back into the kitchen. Jane began to eat the eggs, which were as soft and buttery and delicious as only her mother could make them. Neither she nor Betsy spoke and Jane became aware of the rain pattering on the window panes and the cheerful crackle of the coals in the fire behind her. She tried not to notice that the child was staring at her, and was relieved when her mother returned with the bowl of dripping.

'Here you are.' Mrs Harrison placed the bowl on the table and set about cutting a thick slice of bread. She put the bread on a clean plate and reached for a knife.

'I like the jelly,' Betsy said.

'Do you, pet?'

Mrs Harrison broke the surface of the dripping and reached down to scoop up some of the rich brown jelly from the bottom of the bowl and spread it on top of the dripping. The child watched hungrily. I wonder if her mother bothers to feed her properly, Jane thought.

Betsy added some salt and pepper herself before beginning to eat. Mrs Harrison poured three cups of tea. 'So why are you here so early, Betsy?'

'I'm looking for Kate.'

'So you said. But why did you think she was here?'

'She isn't at home.'

'You mean the cottage?' Mrs Harrison asked.

'Yes.'

Jane's mother glanced at the clock ticking on the mantelpiece. 'She's probably on her way to the auction shed at Shields.'

'But she wasn't there last night – and the fire's gone out.'

'Oh, dear.' Mrs Harrison sighed. 'Can you explain a little more clearly, child?'

Betsy looked at her long and hard before she began to speak. Jane realized it must have taken great effort for the girl to sort out the muddle that was in her mind but, slowly and clearly, she began to tell them the story of what had happened the night before. Her mother's bad temper causing her to run from her own house to Kate's, finding the door swinging in the wind, Mr Munro's cats and Mr Adamson's dog and, finally, how her grandmother had come for her and persuaded her that Kate was safe at the cobbler's shop and Betsy must come home.

'And Mr Adamson shut the door,' she said. 'But he left the window open a little for the cats.'

At this point Florence Harrison reached for the teapot and poured them all another cup of tea. Betsy stirred two teaspoonfuls of sugar into hers and drank it greedily. 'I was thirsty,' she said. 'All that talking.' For the first time since she had arrived there was a hint of a smile. 'So are you going to help me?' she asked.

'Help you to do what?' Jane said.

'Find Kate.'

'But, really, Betsy, I don't think she's lost,' Jane told her. 'As my mother said, she'll have set off for Shields.'

The girl shook her head. 'No. I telt you. I went in. The fire's out and the cats are still there. And so's her creel and her basket. She wouldn't go to buy fish without her creel, would she?'

'No, she wouldn't,' Jane said, and at last she began to feel a shiver of worry. 'Did you go to her mother's house?'

'She won't be there. She never goes home to her ma. Her ma comes to the cottage to see her.'

'Well, nevertheless, I think you should go and see.' Then Jane surprised herself by adding, 'And I'll come with you.'

'You'll miss the train,' her mother said.

'Well, I'll just have to be late back for once.' Jane finished her cup of tea and rose from the table.

'Put your coat on.' Mrs Harrison rose, too, and opened the under-stair cupboard that served as a cloakroom and general tidy hole.

'Mother, I'm not a child. Of course I'll put my coat on and I'll take my umbrella too. And while you're fussing like this why don't you get that old coat of mine, the one that's too small, and give it to Betsy? It's raining harder that ever and that shawl of hers won't provide much protection.'

'Can I keep this?' Betsy looked down at herself as she buttoned up the coat.

'Yes, you may,' Jane told her. 'But now, let's go and find out what's happened to Kate.'

A little later, when Jane returned, without Betsy, her mother was still at the table enjoying a slice of toast. 'Well?' she asked.

Jane shook her head. 'She's not with her mother.'

'You didn't say anything to worry Nan, I hope.'

'No. I'd thought about that. I told her that I'd wanted to see Kate before I went back to work and that I must have missed her – she must already have set off for the fish quay – but I'd called in the hope that she might be there.'

'What did Nan say?'

'She said she hoped Kate wasn't thinking of working on a day like this and that she'd probably gone to Mr Munro's house.'

'The artist?'

'Yes. He's painting her picture. Well, Betsy insisted we go there, but we hadn't got far when we met Joan Donkin. She was on her way to the Lawsons' cottage; she'd been sent with a letter to Kate's mother. It seems she's at the Adamsons' house. She's been there all night.'

'For goodness' sake, why?'

'Mr Adamson brought her home. He said he'd found her on the beach – in a bad way. They've sent for the doctor.'

'Oh, poor lass,' her mother said. 'If only I hadn't stopped you going round to the cottage last night. You would have seen there was something the matter with her and you could have brought her here.'

'Don't feel guilty, Mother. You wanted us to have some time together. It's my fault – I'd have gone if I'd really wanted to go. But I was hoping that William would call by – and he did.'

Jane knew the guilt was hers alone. God forgive her, she had been too taken up with her own plans to give time to her dearest friend. William would have been only too happy to go with her to visit his sister but she had been content to allow her mother to persuade him to sit by the fire and eat the iced fancies and raisin cake she had baked for Jane's visit home. And her father had laughed teasingly when William had expressed the hope that Jane was as good a cook as her mother.

And while they had spent the happiest of evenings her friend must have been in some kind of trouble. What on earth had Kate been doing on the beach late at night when the weather was so bad? And how strange that Mr Adamson should have been there, too, and that he should have been prepared to take troublemaker Thomas Lawson's sister into his home no matter how sick she was.

Joan Donkin had made a point of telling her that, in her opinion, Kate was suffering from nothing more serious than a feverish cold. But if that was the case when had the cold started? And there was something else . . . something Kate's mother had said that lingered uneasily in her mind. She brought those words to mind now, '*I hope Kate hasn't gone to work on a day like this,*' Kate's mother had said, '*not in her con— I mean, she'll get soaked to the skin, won't she?*'

Nan had stumbled over her words and then hurried on to say that Kate was probably at the artist's house. Then she told Jane not to be a stranger, and that William was down at the lifeboat station catching up with some necessary repairs, and would be sorry he'd missed her.

Jane had stopped her in full flow. She didn't say that she already knew William's whereabouts because he'd told her what he would do if the weather remained too bad for the fishing when he'd called round to her parents' house the night before.

'So where is Betsy?' her mother asked now.

'Goodness knows. As soon as she'd heard what Joan had to say she took off – without a word of thanks, by the way.'

'Don't think too badly of her, Jane. Apart from old Martha, nobody has a kind word for her except Kate. That'll be why the poor bairn's so agitated.'

'Well, I'm surprised Kate has any patience with the girl. You know how quick-tempered she can be.'

'I do. But she has a good heart, and she'd never lose her temper with someone like Betsy. You must realize that.'

Jane sighed. 'I suppose I do. I wish I could go and see Kate, but I'll have to rely on you for news now.'

Her mother smiled. 'William will tell you, no doubt. Now here's your bag. It's time you went or you'll miss the next train, too.'

Jane submitted to a hug and a kiss then went through to the shop to say goodbye to her father. He held the door for her, murmuring, 'Watch where you're treading, pet. I don't want you ruining those good shoes.'

But the wind made it difficult to hang on to the umbrella and also watch out for the puddles, and Jane was soon out of breath. She arrived at the station with time to spare and was grateful for the fire burning in the waiting room. What a day, she thought. As she sat down for a moment and caught her breath, she allowed her mind to return to that moment at the Lawsons' cottage door and what Kate's mother had said – or rather had stopped herself from saying.

Sitting by the fire and toasting her toes Jane completed the sentence for her now. '*I hope Kate hasn't gone to work on a day like this . . . not in her condition.*'

'It was good of you to come at such short notice, Sam.'

'That's all right, Mrs Adamson. Richard more or less insisted, you know.'

'Hmm.' Her tone was disapproving.

'Er – he said you'd give me breakfast after I'd done my duty and examined the patient.' Dr Phillips's attempt to lighten the atmosphere was rewarded with a slight smile.

'Of course. In fact I was hoping you would join me. Come along – we'll go to the dining room at once.'

Grace Adamson had received her son's friend in the grand first-floor sitting room overlooking the sea. A cheery fire crackled in the hearth and reflected light played along the highly polished brass fender. Although the sky was heavy with rain clouds, the room was not quite dark enough for the lamps to have been lit. This put Sam at a disadvantage because he could not quite make out the expression on Grace Adamson's face.

Sam knew better than to offer to help his friend's mother rise from her chair. She reached for her walking stick and he looked away, but not before he had seen the grimace of pain as she eased herself up. Grace Adamson did not like to admit that she was getting old and that in the mornings her joints were stiff and painful. Sam busied himself opening the door so that he would not witness her awkward progress across the room.

She would not even allow him to help her on the stairs as they went down to the formal dining room on the ground floor. As Richard had taken an early breakfast and left for the office several hours ago, Sam imagined Grace Adamson could have made life easier for herself by ordering a tray to be brought to her room. But it was clear that she was going to make no concessions to her age or her creaking bones.

Good for her, Sam thought. More than a few of his women patients much younger than Grace Adamson, some barely past forty, had taken to their beds, or the chaise longue, and passed their days as semi-invalids simply because they enjoyed being waited on hand and foot, either by servants or by some poor unmarried daughter or other dependent female relative.

After holding Grace's chair for her and settling her at the table Sam glanced out of the window. The rain seemed to be hurling itself in from the sea and he could see the waves crashing over the breakwaters and cascading down into the bay. A day for the inhabitants of the village to stay at home, he thought, whether in the fishermen's cottages or in the grand houses strung along the promenade. Only folk such as he, a man of medicine, would have to brave the elements in such weather in order to visit his patients; or determined men of business like his friend.

It had still been dark when Richard had telephoned him earlier this morning. He had told a garbled story of finding one of the village girls in a cave and bringing her home because he suspected she was ill. He had asked Sam to come along and have a look at her but he hadn't told him why he was so concerned. And concerned Richard most certainly was, judging from his strained manner of speaking – although he hadn't actually said anything particularly revealing.

'Just make sure she's all right,' he'd told Sam. 'If you don't think she should be moved persuade her to stay here. You can telephone me at the office if you think there's anything I ought to know.'

'Such as?' Sam had asked.

'Whether she needs any pills – any medicine, you know.'

'And if she does?'

'Just prescribe them. Obviously, I'll pay your bill.'

Now, as Sam took his breakfast plate to the sideboard where a delicious array of food lay waiting on hotplates, he wondered about the word 'obviously'. Nothing had been obvious about this morning. He had known Richard since they were boys and he had learned long ago that his friend was not exactly secretive but was good at keeping his own counsel. There was a reserve about Richard Adamson that made you wary of questioning him. So Sam had decided to tend to the fish lass and then wait and see if Richard would explain any further.

Once she was seated Grace Adamson had directed him to the tasselled bell cord by the fireplace and asked him to pull it, and now a mature and homely serving woman appeared. Sam recognized her as Mrs McDonald, the cook-housekeeper. He must have shown his surprise that such a senior servant had answered the summons for she smiled at him.

'I like to make sure that Mrs Adamson has a proper plateful,' she said. 'If she tells Joan that she doesn't want much the lass gives her not much more than a poached egg and mebbes one slice of bacon. And Mr Adamson asked me to make sure that his mother ate a good breakfast seeing as how she won't eat much more until he comes home.'

Sam understood now why Richard had been pleased for Caroline Travers to visit his mother so often. No doubt the young woman's company would encourage Mrs Adamson to eat luncheon. He watched as Mrs McDonald filled her mistress's plate with egg, bacon, a slice of black pudding and a couple of grilled kidneys. On the table were already set bread rolls, toast, butter, marmalade, a teapot, a coffee pot and jugs of hot water and hot and cold milk.

'Go on, sir, fill your plate,' the cook-housekeeper told him. 'Why not take a couple of those lamb cutlets? They're delicious.'

'Doesn't Mrs Adamson want one?'

'She can't abide them. Says they're too fiddly and is too ladylike to pick them up.'

Mrs McDonald had not lowered her voice when talking about her mistress before, nor did she now. Sam heard Grace utter a harrumphing sound. He turned to see the two women smiling at each other and was struck by how easy their relationship must be. But he had long ago noticed what a comfortable atmosphere there was in this household. A fair and just relationship between master and servant that even allowed for friendship.

If Richard married Caroline Travers and brought her here things might change. He couldn't imagine the beautiful and well-educated Miss Travers allowing servants to speak thus, no matter how thoughtful and progressive she believed herself to be. But any man would surely be only too happy to suffer a little domestic tyranny from a wife such as Caroline. It would be a small price to pay.

Sam filled his plate, helping himself to a couple of the cutlets as Mrs McDonald had suggested. Just as she was about to leave the room, he asked, 'If Mrs Adamson doesn't like the cutlets why do you prepare them?'

'For Master Richard and Mr Munro, of course. And that's who those little potato cakes are for. Mr Munro loves them – but I'm sure he won't mind if you try one or two.'

'Mr Munro?'

'My nephew,' Grace Adamson said. 'Now off you go, Mary. I know you like your well-deserved cup of tea while I'm having breakfast. Mr Munro is an artist,' she told Sam when Mary McDonald had gone. 'You might have heard of him?'

'Oh, yes. He's set up a studio in the village, hasn't he?'

'He has. And my sister is convinced that, left to his own devices, her son will neglect himself. So I've persuaded him to at least have breakfast with me every morning. Sometimes he forgets but more often than not he honours me with his company.' Grace smiled. 'We shall see if he turns up this morning. And now, Sam, please sit down and eat your breakfast while everything is hot. Then, over our tea or coffee, you can tell me about the girl.'

Grace's smile had vanished and Sam picked up his knife and fork, grateful that he had been granted time to think. He wished he knew more about what was going on here. Had Richard simply found the girl in distress as he had claimed or was there more to it? And if there *was* more to it, did Richard's mother know? He got the impression that she wasn't pleased that Richard had brought her here.

So how much should he divulge? He would be able to say truthfully that Kate Lawson had a feverish cold. That in his opinion she should stay in bed until she was quite well. Otherwise she would be endangering two people: herself and the child he was sure she was expecting.

Chapter Fifteen

'Goodness, Betsy, this is an early hour to call upon a gentleman.'

Howard Munro, still struggling with a collar stud, stared at the bedraggled apparition on his doorstep. She was wearing a coat he'd never seen before, but she'd put her old shawl on top of it, tying it round her shoulders. If only she'd had the sense to pull the shawl up over her head, he thought. Her wet hair hung down like the proverbial rats' tails.

'Take me to see Kate,' she said.

The child looked anguished. Howard sensed that this was more than an example of Betsy's eccentric behaviour. 'You'd better come in and explain,' he said.

At the Adamsons' house Sam Phillips helped himself to the last piece of toast. He scooped up another spoonful of apricot preserve. 'This is delicious,' he said.

'Shall I ask for more toast and a fresh pot of coffee?' Mrs Adamson's dry tone was almost drowned out by the sudden jangling of the doorbell. The sound echoed through the house. 'Ah. I think my nephew has arrived.'

The door from the hall opened and Sam glanced sideways, expecting to see Howard Munro enter the room. However, the person who entered was a flustered-looking maidservant. She was alone.

Mrs Adamson frowned. 'What is it, Joan?'

'Mr Munro is here.'

'Well, of course he is. Why don't you show him in?'

'He's not alone.'

'Explain.'

'He's got that daft lass Betsy Smith with him and he says they want to see Kate Lawson.'

Sam understood little of this. Who was Betsy Smith and why had

Howard Munro brought her here? It was clear that the usually good-natured Grace Adamson was vexed.

'Tell Howard to come in here immediately,' she said.

'He won't come into the house unless I let Betsy in too.'

'You mean you've kept my nephew waiting on the doorstep?'

'It's his own fault. He won't come in without her.'

Sam suspected the young maid, driven by her own bad humour, was straying near the edge of her mistress's benevolent tolerance of her servants' eccentric ways. 'For goodness' sake,' the elderly lady snapped. 'Remember your place and show my nephew in – and the girl as well.'

'Yes, madam.' The young woman's tone was sullen.

'Joan,' Mrs Adamson called as the maid turned to leave the room.

'Yes?'

'I know you were trying to do the right thing, but show them in and then bring us a fresh pot of coffee and more toast.'

Howard Munro proved to be tall and good looking. His hair flopped over his forehead in a way that Sam imagined young women would find romantic. His clothes were well made and elegant – the only hint that he might be 'artistic' was the collar coming adrift from his shirt over the not-quite-properly-adjusted tie. But that could happen to anyone who dressed in a hurry, Sam supposed.

The artist wasn't given the chance to speak. 'What's this about?' his aunt asked even before the maid had closed the door behind her. She gestured towards the child who had followed him in and was now looking round the room and the people in it like a wary cat.

'I'm told you have Kate Lawson here,' her nephew said.

'The fish lass?'

'Yes. If you must describe her as such.'

'What is your interest in her?'

Howard Munro's slight hesitation aroused Sam's interest. 'She . . . she's been posing for me . . . I'm painting her portrait.'

'Ah, yes. Along with those of other village folk. Including this child's grandmother.'

'You know about that?' Howard was obviously surprised.

Mrs Adamson allowed herself a slight smile. 'I know about many things that go on in the village. Servants are a great source of gossip, you know. So, you have heard that Kate Lawson is unwell and was brought here—'

'By Richard.'

198

'— by my son, and because you are concerned about her welfare, you have hurried along in a state of undress to enquire about her.'

'Undress?'

'Your collar and tie.'

Howard frowned and his hands rose to his neck. He began to fiddle with his collar.

'Leave it,' his aunt snapped, 'and have your breakfast.' She sighed and bestowed a less forbidding look on Betsy. 'And I suppose this child had better have some, too.'

'Mrs Harrison gave me bread and dripping.'

It was the first time the girl had spoken and Sam looked at her properly. Wet and bedraggled though she was, he could see that she was beautiful. But there was a look in her cat-slanted eyes that was not quite – how could he phrase it – not quite 'right'.

'The cobbler's wife?' Grace asked.

'Yes.'

'Well, I won't ask you what you were doing there. The answer might take too long. But are you so full of bread and dripping that you are unable to eat anything else?'

Sam was surprised by her kindly tone and then he remembered that she had been a schoolteacher before she married. He suspected that her pupils might have regarded her as a 'tartar' but she had obviously been a tartar with a kind heart.

'Do I help meself?' the girl asked, glancing at the dishes still being kept warm on the sideboard.

'Yes you do – there are some clean plates there, too. But I'd be grateful if you would remove your coat and shawl before sitting down. Mr Munro will take them and hang them in the hall with his own coat.'

Mrs Adamson gave a nod of command in her nephew's direction and Howard did as he was bid. Then he shepherded his protégé to the sideboard and helped her to fill her plate.

'Now tell me why you have brought Betsy here,' his aunt said as they took their places at the table.

'Betsy is a friend of Kate's. She is worried about her, as I am.'

'Well, no doubt the whole village knows she is here by now so I might as well confirm it. This is Dr Phillips, by the way. Your unorthodox arrival prevented me from introducing you properly. Sam, this is my nephew, Howard Munro.'

The two men nodded at each other.

'*Dr* Phillips?' Howard asked.

'Yes. Richard insisted on hauling his poor friend out of bed at an unearthly hour to come to see to the girl. And before you get too concerned, I think he will assure you that all that is the matter with her is a cold. At least, that's what it looked like when Richard brought her here last night.'

'A feverish cold,' Sam amended.

'Very well,' her tone betrayed her irritation, 'a *feverish* cold. I've sent a message to her mother asking her to bring some clean clothes along, and as soon as she's rested she can go home.'

'Er . . .' Sam began.

'What is it?'

'That might not be for a while.'

'A while? Be more precise, please.'

'A week – maybe more.'

'And why not?'

'I mean that it would be best for Miss Lawson to stay here until I am satisfied that her condition will not worsen.'

'Worsen?'

'She could develop complications.'

'Such as?' Grace was terse.

'You know . . . bronchitis . . . pneumonia.' He tried not to flinch under her cool stare. 'Well, that's my professional opinion.'

Before Grace could answer, the strange child looked up from the plateful of sausage and bacon she was demolishing and asked, 'Can I see her?'

'No,' Sam said. 'She must rest.' He spoke to Betsy but he was looking at Howard. 'It's better if she sees no one.'

Howard inclined his head. He had understood. 'Anything she needs,' he said. 'Just tell me.'

'That's all right,' Sam replied. 'Richard has already offered to foot the bill.'

Sam watched as the American's eyes narrowed and his open boyish expression became that of a man with dark thoughts. Suspicions? Was he jealous of his cousin and, if so, why? Until now Sam had been inclined to suspect that his upright friend might have been conducting some sort of affair with the girl. He would be disappointed if that turned out to be true but, after all, Richard was a man and the girl was beautiful. It could be a simple case of sowing his wild oats before committing himself to marriage and Caroline.

But what should he think now? Here was Howard Munro in a state of great agitation because Kate Lawson was not only sick but had been brought to his cousin's house. Were both men involved with the fish lass somehow? How distasteful if that were true.

However, the arrival of Howard and Betsy had saved him from an embarrassing conversation with Richard's mother. He would not have had the right to discuss what he thought to be Kate's condition with Grace Adamson unless she had revealed that she already knew about it. He had already decided to tread carefully until he'd had a chance to quiz Richard. But now he couldn't even do that. The situation was more complicated than he had first imagined. Either man could be the father of the child the girl was expecting, and the other might know nothing about it. Or they might, and that was disturbingly unsavoury.

Worried that his expression might reveal too much, Sam picked up his napkin and made a show of dabbing at his lips. 'That breakfast was first rate,' he mumbled over the crumpled square of damask linen. 'But now I'd just like to go up and check on Miss Lawson before I go.'

'You're leaving?' Grace Adamson's tone revealed how frustrated she was that she had been denied a chance to question him alone.

'I have other patients, and I must get back to take morning surgery.'

'Of course. Ring for the girl and she'll show you upstairs.'

'There's no need. I know the way.' He bade a speedy farewell and escaped from the room.

Although he knocked on the bedroom door before entering, his patient did not awaken. She lay with her magnificent hair spread out across the pillows, and the faint feverish flush colouring her fine-boned face only enhanced her beauty. Sam closed the door and crossed quietly to the bed. He picked up the arm that lay across the eiderdown and, holding her wrist, took his watch from his fob pocket and measured her pulse.

Still too fast, he thought. Whatever the situation is here I cannot in all conscience let this girl go home. He lowered her arm and laid her hand gently on the eiderdown. She moaned and stirred but did not open her eyes. Green eyes, as he remembered. Yes, she was ravishing. As well as the high cheekbones she possessed long graceful limbs and Sam had been surprised by her speaking voice. It was not quite that of a lady and yet neither was it that of a rough village lass. Her tone was well modulated and her speech correct.

Had Richard been grooming her? Sending her for speech and deportment lessons? It was not unheard of for gentlemen to treat their mistresses so in the hopes that the women might be accepted by society

201

and even become their wives. But surely not. Not his old friend Richard. He was not the kind of man to be so devious – and it would have been devious indeed to have carried on like this while he was courting Caroline Travers.

Sam felt a stab of anger. Caroline was elegant and well educated and if there was a slight haughtiness in her manner it was solely because of her upbringing as the only child of a wealthy magnate. Caroline would bring wit, beauty and a considerable fortune to the man she married. If she so wished she could make a brilliant match, perhaps even gain a title, and yet she seemed to have set her heart on Richard. She did not deserve to be treated so callously.

The young doctor was honest enough to admit to himself that his thoughts were prompted by jealousy as well as concern. He admired Caroline himself but knew that his position was hopeless. Although not poor, his scholarly father had devoted most of his inherited fortune to medical research and the education of his son. Caroline Travers would never consent to be the wife of a humble man of medicine.

'What is it?'

Sam was shaken out of his reverie to find that the woman before him had opened her eyes and was staring up at him with a puzzled frown. Her hands fumbled at the bedclothes and pulled them up to her chin in an instinctive gesture of modesty. He was almost taken in by it.

'I am Dr Phillips,' he said. 'Remember? I came to see you before.'

'Yes, I remember.' She eased herself into a sitting position, still clasping the bedclothes. 'But I meant what is it that's troubling you? Am I very ill?'

'No, of course not.'

'But the look on your face . . . it was . . . disquieting.'

Her eyes were huge. He found himself wanting to comfort her and was prepared to prevaricate. 'That was just the everyday countenance of a busy doctor of medicine, I'm afraid. All the cares of the world on my shoulders – that sort of thing.'

She responded to his words with a gentle smile. 'And I have made your life more burdensome.'

'How is that?'

'I'm sure you do not usually visit patients before breakfast.'

'Not unless the case is urgent.' Her smile trembled and his heart lurched. 'And yours is not, I assure you. But Richard – Mr Adamson – insisted that I come.'

202

The young woman's smile vanished to be replaced by a look of anxiety. She could no longer meet his eyes and his heart hardened.

'That was . . . that was good of him,' she said.

'No doubt he had his reasons.'

She caught the cool edge to his voice. 'What do you mean?'

'Mr Adamson was obviously concerned about you.'

She didn't answer.

'Can you tell me why?'

'He is a good man.'

'That's not what the villagers think of him, is it? Particularly your own family.'

She seemed to shrink back and pull the bedclothes closer to her body. 'My family?'

'You are a Lawson. I read the report in the newspaper about the riot.'

'It was hardly a riot.' Her eyes flashed.

'The demonstration, then. But even if the newspaper reporters exaggerated, my friend ended up with stitches in his cheek. I know because I patched him up that day, and he still has the scar. The stone was thrown by a Lawson, I think.'

'Thomas. My brother.'

'And yet Richard is so concerned about you, the young criminal's sister, that he brings you into his own house when he finds you ill on the beach at night.'

He noticed how tightly she gripped the bedclothes when she replied, 'My brother is not a criminal.'

'He broke the law. He was the leader of an unlawful assembly and he was also the one who assaulted Richard Adamson. He could have gone to prison if Richard had pressed charges.'

'I know that. But Mr Adamson understands why my brother and the other men are so angry. He wants to help them—'

'He's told you this?'

'Yes, and I believe him. And I also believe him to be a good man. But as for why he brought me here instead of taking me back to my cottage, I have no idea.'

She raised her chin as she glared at him. She was good, he thought. If this was an act she ought to be on the stage.

'And if it disturbs you so,' she continued, 'I shall leave this house as soon as my clothes are returned to me.'

'I'm told your mother will be bringing some things for you later today. But you cannot go home.'

203

'Why not?'

'Because you still have a fever. You must stay in bed.'

'I can stay in bed at home.'

'Of course you can, but in the circumstances there is another reason why you should not be moved too soon after your ordeal, isn't there?'

'Circumstances?'

'I presume you don't want to endanger your unborn child.'

She caught her breath and one hand released its grip on the bedclothes and fumbled at her neck where it caught at a piece of loose ribbon. 'How do you know?'

'I couldn't be certain, but there are signs. I am a doctor, you know.' He smiled faintly when he said this. He could see how distressed she was and he found he couldn't harden his heart completely.

'Nobody knows,' she said and her voice was husky.

'Nobody? Not even—'

'My parents? Yes, but no one else.'

'I was going to say not even the father of the child,' Sam said. Suddenly he saw what was attached to the ribbon she was playing with. 'Are you married?'

Swiftly she tucked the wedding ring down the neck of her nightgown and raised her head to look him in the eye. 'No.'

'Are you going to be?'

'No.'

'But does the father . . . I mean does the man know he's fathered a child.'

'No.'

Her obdurate tone caused him to lose patience. Once more, despite the fact that there was something straightforward about her, something that proclaimed her honesty, he began to think that, after all, she was involved in something dishonourable.

'Are you going to tell him?'

'That would be impossible.'

What did that mean? he wondered. That whoever it was was not free to marry her? Or, worse, that she simply didn't know who the father was? Then he saw the sheer misery in her eyes and stopped himself from questioning her further.

'You mustn't tell anyone,' she whispered.

'Of course I won't. Whatever you say to me is in confidence.'

Sam flushed when he said this because he realized that, until he had met Howard Munro at the breakfast table and seen his concern for the girl, he had probably been going to tell Richard that Kate Lawson was with child. And that was because he had assumed that his old friend had taken the girl as his mistress and was the father. Now he knew that he couldn't take anything for granted, and he was glad that professional etiquette would bind him to keeping her secret.

He had done his duty as a doctor and would continue to call until he deemed it safe for her to leave this house. But, as Richard's friend, all he could do was step back and keep his own counsel. And be ready to help, when, in the nature of things, the girl's condition became a secret no more.

Joan Donkin showed Nan Lawson into the room and departed without a word. Kate, still in her nightgown, was sitting on the edge of the bed. She looked up and her eyes shone.

'Oh, Ma, I was expecting you nearly four weeks ago.'

'I came along the first day you were here but I was told that the doctor said you had to rest. No visitors. Not even me.'

Kate sighed. 'I know. I'm not blaming you. But, Ma, I've missed you so!'

'There, there, lass.' Nan looked pleased and a little awkward. 'Have you been here all by yourself, then?'

'The only other folk I've seen are Joan Donkin and Dr Phillips.' Suddenly Kate couldn't meet her mother's eyes. She dropped her head and examined her feet swinging to and fro. She had imagined that Richard Adamson would come to see how she was. She had been racked with embarrassment when she tried to conjecture what he would say – and how she would reply. Would he refer to what had happened in the few moments after he had rescued her from the cave? Or would he pretend it had never happened? And how would she respond to him?

But she hadn't been put to the test. He hadn't come. Neither had his mother. She had been well looked after but she had been almost completely isolated.

'Where shall I put your things?' her mother asked. She was carrying a large bundle wrapped up in brown paper and tied with kitchen string.

'Here on the bed. And then why don't you sit down by the fire while I get ready?'

Her mother did as she was bid, and looked around the room wonderingly. 'Isn't this grand?' she said. 'Pretty wallpaper, nice curtains, and the wardrobe and chest of drawers so highly polished.'

'Joan does that,' Kate said.

'The polishing?'

'And tending to the fire, and the dusting and the sweeping and the fetching and carrying for me all the time I've been here. It seems Mrs Adamson thought it better for me to see a "friendly face" while I was poorly. That's what Joan told me. But most of the time her face looked as though she'd just drunk a bottle of vinegar – especially when she had to deal with my chamber pot!'

'Let me see it.'

'What? The chamber pot? What on earth for?'

'I'll bet it's a bonny one.'

'As a matter of fact it is. And, as it's empty, I'll humour you!'

Kate slipped off the bed and knelt down. She pushed the hanging bedclothes aside and reached for the chamber pot. When she drew it out she heard Nan give a gasp of appreciation.

'Let me hold it,' she said.

Kate carried the chamber pot over to her mother, who took it as though it were something precious. 'Best china,' she said, 'not like our old pot jerries. Look at this – such pretty red roses. Why, they've even got a rose inside for you to water when you—'

'Ma! Stop it!' Kate said but she was smiling. 'But look over here – it matches the set.'

Kate walked over to a triangular washstand that fitted neatly into the corner of the room. On it there was a large jug standing in a bowl, a medium-sized jug, a lidded dish and two beakers. Every piece was white china decorated with the same pattern of red roses.

Nan Lawson rose from her chair and carried the chamber pot almost reverentially over to the bed. She knelt down and pushed it back into place. When she stood up, slowly, Kate noticed the fleeting expression of pain and the gasp for breath. But she knew if she asked her mother would brush it aside with some remark about her old bones. Kate knew it was the hard life her mother endured rather than age, for Nan was still in her forties.

'Now what are all these pretty things?' she asked when she joined Kate at the washstand.

Kate lifted the largest of the jugs from the bowl. It was full of water and was steaming gently. 'Joan brought the hot water just before you arrived,' she said. 'And in a moment it will be cool enough for me to start my *toilette*.'

'Your what?' her mother asked.

'It means I'll get washed. But that's what Joan calls it. "Here's the water for your *toilette*," she says. She's just showing off.'

'Aye, she's always thought a lot of herself, hasn't she? Ever since she was a great lumpy bairn. What's all these other things for?'

'The middle-sized jug is for the waste,' Kate told her. 'When I've washed my face I can empty the water into here and then pour some more for my other bits.' They grinned at each other. 'And this is the soap dish.' Kate lifted the lid.

'Let me see.' Her mother took the dish and smelled the bar of soap inside it. 'Mm, it's scented.'

'Carnation.'

'Eeh, our Kate, what luxury.'

'And this is the tooth mug – look, Mrs Adamson sent Joan up with a new toothbrush. And this,' Kate picked up the final item of the wash set, 'is a shaving mug. Which I don't need, of course.' She bent down to open the door of the wash stand. Inside there were two shelves filled with clean towels and flannels. 'So, if you sit down, again, Ma, I'll get myself ready.'

Kate's hairpins were in a small china tray on the washstand. She pinned up her hair and then opened the neck of her nightgown in order to wash her face and neck. Then, as she had always done in the crowded cottage at home, she became a contortionist as she washed the rest of her body under the cover of the nightgown.

Aware that her breasts were full and her belly rounded, embarrassment made her grateful that her mother turned her head to stare into the fire. Kate dried herself and pulled on half her clothes before taking off the nightgown and pulling on the top half. Her mother was quiet. Kate turned round as she did up the buttons of her blouse and saw the older woman's distracted expression.

'How are things at home?' Kate asked.

'As usual. Although . . .'

'Tell me. My father isn't bullying you, is he?'

'No. Most of the time your brothers keep him in check. But he's drinking more.'

'Is that possible?'

'It seems it is. More than once he's been brought home and dumped on the doorstep. He . . . he doesn't like the gossip, mind you.'

'Gossip?'

Her mother remained silent.

'About me?'

'Aye.'

'What are they saying?'

'Well, they don't like you being here at the Adamsons' house.'

'Would they rather Mr Adamson had left me in the cave to drown?'

'No, pet, don't get upset. Of course folk are glad that he rescued you but most of them think he only brought you here to curry favour.'

'Oh.'

That hadn't occurred to Kate and now she examined the idea. For Richard Adamson could easily have taken her back to Belle Vue Cottage and then, braving the Lawson menfolk, gone for her mother. But he'd brought her to his own home. Had he hoped to impress the villagers by looking after Kate and sending for his own doctor? Had he hoped that this gesture would give him a small advantage in any future confrontation?

But what about that moment on the beach? A timeless moment measured only in heartbeats when he had held her close and kissed her and roused her sleeping senses to a passion stronger than any she had ever experienced before. Had he simply been taking advantage of her helpless state? And then, regretting his action, had he made sure to stay away from her? To her dismay that thought brought nothing but anguish. Shocked by this revelation she turned away from her mother and faced the window. The sky was an unrelenting grey.

'Don't fret, Kate,' her mother said. 'Nobody thinks badly of you.'

Kate shrugged, not able to speak or even face her mother.

'No, it's your father they blame,' Nan said. 'They say it was wicked of Henry Lawson to turn his daughter out, especially as you had just lost your sweetheart, and that, after Meg died, he should have forgiven you for whatever it was that angered him. Most folk admired you for working so hard.

'The gossip this last week has been that you were so grief-stricken over the loss of Jos and then Meg that you neglected yourself. And that made you ill. They say your father should have relented and let you come home. Especially as . . .'

Kate was alarmed by the way her mother's voice wavered. She turned to face her. 'Especially as what, Ma?' She paused as alarm took over. 'You're not ill, are you?'

'No, pet, I'm not ill. Divven't fret about me. It's your great-grandmother. I think old Sarah is failing. She barely touches the broth I make for her and hardly ever opens her eyes these days, but that doesn't stop her muttering and moaning. I think it's her dreams.'

'What does she dream about, do you think?' Kate had often wondered.

'Who can tell? But sometimes she smiles and laughs just like a child – or a young girl. And she mutters a few words. Kate, it's uncanny. If you didn't know who it was who's talking, you would think there was a young woman in the room – greeting her man back from the fishing, or chiding her bairns. And then sometimes she cries – fair breaks her heart – just sobs and sobs until her voice is dry and cracked. If I try to comfort her, she'll open her eyes wide and say, "Where's my Kate? Where's me bonny lass?"'

'Oh, Ma, I wish I could come and see her.'

'Your father's forbidden you to set foot in the house again.'

'Would he have to know?'

'Kate, hinny, nothing that happens in the village goes unnoticed. Someone would tell him.'

'And then you would suffer for it.'

'Aye.'

'But it's so cruel!'

'I daresn't cross your father, pet. Besides, it wouldn't be right. He's my husband.'

'And you promised to love, honour and obey him!' Kate felt her anger rising. 'What about the part that says you must love and cherish each other? Has our da ever taken note of that?'

'Kate . . . don't . . .'

To Kate's dismay she saw that her mother's eyes had filled with tears. She rushed over and sank down on to the floor at Nan's feet.

'I'm sorry, Ma,' she said. She was almost crying herself. 'You've done nothing to blame yourself for. I was the cause of all this and it's my own fault that I can't come home and see my great-grandmother.'

Nan took her daughter's face in her hands. She leaned forward and kissed her brow. Then she said, 'Perhaps if old Sarah gets worse – perhaps if it looks like the end – then maybe your father will relent and let you say goodbye to her.'

'If I'm still here.'

'What do you mean?'

'Well it won't be long before I'll have to take myself off to the workhouse, will it?'

'Don't say that!'

'Why not? I can't stay in the village once the bairn shows, can I? If that piece of gossip got round my father would likely go berserk!'

Her mother was silent. Kate knew there was nothing she could say.

'I don't suppose there's been a letter from my Aunt Winifred, has there?'

Her mother sighed. 'No. I've been round to the cottage every day. I can't understand why she hasn't answered our letter.'

'Perhaps she doesn't know how to. I mean, perhaps she just doesn't want me.'

Her mother shook her head. 'No, that wouldn't be like Winifred. There must be a reason. She would answer if she could.'

The two of them stared at each other as they realized for the first time the implications of what Nan had just said. Kate shivered and reached for the warm shawl that her mother had brought along with her other clothes.

'I'm ready. I suppose we'd better get back to the cottage,' she said. 'I'm supposed to ring for Joan to see us out. She has to tell Mrs Adamson when we're gone. Then no doubt they'll fumigate the room.'

'Fumigate? Why?'

'Joan Donkin has made more than one reference to the smell of fish!' Kate reached for the bell pull near the fireplace.

'Wait, pet.' Her mother stopped her. 'There's something I have to tell you.' Nan's troubled expression filled Kate with alarm.

'What is it?'

'You can't go back to Belle Vue Cottage. Alice has moved her daughter and her family in.'

'Into the cottage? Of course . . .' Kate realized that her illness and the high fever had made her forget what it was that had upset her so that evening and made her go to the beach and take refuge in the cave. 'She told me Susan was coming home . . . that night I fell asleep in the cave.'

'So that's why you were so upset. Kate, Kate, it breaks my heart that you had no one to go to.'

Except Jos. The words formed themselves in Kate's mind. Had she gone to the cave intending to join Jos? That's what would have happened if Richard Adamson and his dog had not been on the beach that night.

'Well, Alice felt bad about it, I can tell you, but Susan and her man had nowhere to go and you have to look after your own family, haven't you?'

'That's the way some people feel.' Kate regretted the words the moment she'd said them. She saw the look in her mother's eyes and it almost broke her heart. Her mother didn't deserve to be spoken to like that. 'I'm sorry, Ma,' she said.

210

'No, you've a right to be angry – bitter.'

'Yes, I have. But not with you. Never with you. But now can you tell me where on earth I'm supposed to go?'

By the time he returned home from work she would be gone. That was how it should be but, nevertheless, Richard suppressed a groan. He turned the pages of the ledger that Len Dawson had placed in front of him and nodded as if approving. But in truth he was finding it hard to concentrate. The copperplate writing blurred as he remembered the night he had crept upstairs in his own house like a thief and opened the door of Kate's room.

He ought not to have done so. Kate was a guest in his house, a guest deserving of respect, but he had not been able to stay away. That night the moonlight had streamed across her sleeping form, her perfect face and her glorious hair spread out across the pillow.

Such pale beauty, he thought, and immediately remembered the moment when he had taken her in his arms and kissed her. He should not have done it. She had been vulnerable and he was supposed to be a gentleman, wasn't he? And yet, that night, when he had rescued her from the cave, relief had given way to an emotion as deep as the ocean itself. He had been unable to resist her.

Richard had closed the door quietly and returned to his room in turmoil. Perhaps that was the moment he had realized that Kate was as important to him, if not more so, as these neat rows of figures and the business he had worked so hard to make successful.

Chapter Sixteen

'This is your bedroom, Kate. Do you like it?' Alice Willis looked at Kate anxiously. The shopkeeper's greying hair was escaping from her usual neat bun and she looked tired. Kate's mother had followed them upstairs and stood beside, Alice smiling encouragingly.

'A room of your own, eh, Kate?' Nan said. Kate looked at the concerned faces of the two kindly women and managed a smile.

'It's at the back of the house,' the shopkeeper said, 'so it's quiet – although I admit there's not much of a view, only the back lane and the yards.'

Kate looked round the room, which was furnished with solid old furniture. The curtain rails were set so that the curtains almost covered the narrow window even when they were open. Perhaps this was deliberate in order to obscure the view of the roofs of the coal houses and the privies. On the surface everything was clean and tidy, but the lavender bag hanging from the brass bedrail did little to dispel the faint smell of ancient damp.

Alice had seen the direction of her glance. 'That's me best feather bed, mind. You'll be real comfortable.'

'I'm sure I will.'

'And there's extra blankets in that chest if you get cold. And you can light the fire,' Alice said. 'Look, I've set it ready. And there's plenty coal in the coalhouse; it's there for the taking.'

Kate glanced at the fireplace where paper twists, sticks and coal were waiting to be lit. A full coal scuttle stood at the side. 'I'm sure I'll be very comfortable, really I will. And it's good of you to take me in.'

'Well, I felt bad about turning you out of the cottage, but that's not the only reason as I'm sure your mother's told you. Now that Charlie's so bad I need someone to help me in the shop and I can't think of a better person than you. You're quick in the head and you're honest, and your ma says you'll work hard for your money.'

'Are you going to pay me?' Kate was surprised.

'Of course I am, what did you think? You'll get your room and board and a bit money besides. I wouldn't expect anyone to work for nowt.' Alice Willis turned to leave the room. 'Now I've told your ma that she can come round and visit of an evening whenever she can, and you can sit up here in private. Charlie hasn't been upstairs for months now and I've moved everything down so that I can be beside him. He's real bad, you know.'

'I'm sorry to hear that,' Kate's mother said.

'It's the nights I dread.' Alice responded to Nan's compassionate look. 'I have to go to him time after time to lift him up from the pillow so he can bring the phlegm up. And now he says he's got a terrible pain right here.' She placed a work-worn hand on the centre of her chest. 'Dr Fenwick was here just yesterday and he says there's nothing can be done. All the coughing has strained Charlie's heart.'

'I'm real sorry, Alice,' Nan said. 'You must be exhausted.'

'Aye, I'm getting by on cat naps.'

'Is there anything I can do to help?'

'No, hinny. There's nothing anyone can do except care for him and keep him happy. And I'm the best one for that. And you know it doesn't take much to please him, bless him. He likes to sit up in bed with the newspaper and a pack of Jolly Sailors. He says smoking a cigarette helps to get the poison up but I have me doubts. If you ask me it's the tabs that are making him worse.'

Kate felt sorry for Mrs Willis. She'd never known a married couple as close and as loving as the Willises, and now all his devoted wife could do for him was to ease his passing in any way she could.

Mrs Willis must have seen the concern on both their faces. She summoned up a smile and tried to banish her sombre mood. 'But, bless you, I'll manage fine now,' she said. 'With Kate working in the shop and Susan nearby to help look after her da, we should get by until . . . well, you know what I mean. And talking of the shop, was that the bell I just heard?'

'Shall I go down and see to it?' Kate asked.

'No, pet, I'll go. You stay and get settled in. Your ma will help you. And when you've done you can both come down and have a cup of tea with me. In the stockroom, if you don't mind. I don't want to disturb Charlie.'

When Alice had gone Nan took the box of matches from the mantelshelf and lit the fire. She watched until the flames were drawing nicely and then told Kate to sit down in the small armchair. 'I'll see to your things,' she said.

On the way here from the Adamson house Nan had told Kate that Alice had sent for her to clear out Belle Vue Cottage ready for Susan and her family to move in. She'd brought Kate's belongings here and taken Meg's bits and pieces, including the creels and the baskets, back to her own home. 'Of course, if there's anything you want, you just have to ask,' she'd said.

'No thank you, Ma, it's best if you keep everything. After all, I haven't a home to put them in.' Kate had smiled sadly.

'Well, at least you've somewhere to stay,' her mother had said, 'until . . .'

'Until Aunt Winfred's letter arrives?'

'Yes. And it will come. I'm sure of that.'

But her mother didn't sound at all sure.

'There now,' Nan said when she'd done putting Kate's things away, 'all neat and tidy. And here's your bit money. I found it in this jug on the dresser in the cottage. And as for that, Alice gave me a good price for it – the dresser, I mean, and the bed and the table and chairs. Susan and her man have come home with hardly anything to their name. I've put what Alice paid in the jug with the rest.'

'But shouldn't my father have the money for the furniture? Aunt Meg was his sister.'

'He'll never know.'

'But what about you, Ma?'

'I'm . . . making a bit money of me own, now.' She'd started hesitantly but now the words tumbled out. 'Kate, pet, I hope you don't mind but I've taken over your round.'

'Oh, Ma, you haven't!'

'Why shouldn't I have done?'

'Because it's hard work, that's why.'

'And do you think I'm afraid of hard work?' Nan sounded offended.

'No, of course I don't. But . . . at . . . I mean . . .'

'What were you going to say? "At my age"?' Nan smiled and the laughter in her eyes made her look years younger. 'I'm nowhere near as old as your Aunt Meg was, I'll have you know. And I've got a strong back and a head for figures. And, Kate, the customers seem to like me. Most of them were relieved that someone had taken over.'

Kate felt a twinge of guilt. She had to admit that she hadn't given a thought to her Aunt Meg's old customers. What had started as a

214

challenge had become a chore. It galled her that she might not have the stamina and determination of the other fish lasses but she acknowledged that too much had happened to sap her spirit. The loss of Jos, and then her aunt, and her thoughts and fears for the unborn child.

'And, Kate,' her mother continued, 'I'm really enjoying meself.'

'Really?'

'No doubt about it. I get out and I meet people and I have a bit chat and gossip. It's doing me the world of good.'

'But what about Da? What does he think about it?'

'He doesn't object, if that's what you're afraid of. I'm bringing money into the house. More beer money for him.'

'Oh, no.'

'Divven't fret. I'm not daft. There's no way he can find out what I've earned in a day and as long as I hand over a reasonable amount he's happy.'

Despite her mother's obvious pride and pleasure in what she was doing Kate felt depressed. From the very early days of marriage Nan had been forced to conceal the exact truth from her husband in order to keep the peace. It wouldn't have been like that between Jos and me, Kate thought sadly. We would always have been truthful with each other. And yet even as she thought it, unease stirred. Jos had been concealing something from her. Something he had been planning and which she had first learned of on the day of his funeral.

Would he have told me what he and the other lads were going to do? she wondered. Once we were married would he have taken me into his confidence or would he have proved to be like most of the men in the village in thinking that women are somehow a lesser race of beings? Surely not my Jos, she thought. But the doubt remained.

And what of Richard Adamson? she wondered. What kind of husband would he be? Would he be open and honest or would he, too, keep secrets from me like Jos did? I don't think so. I believe Richard would regard his wife as an equal. Kate stirred uneasily when she realized where her thoughts had taken her. She berated herself for being so foolish. It was pointless to speculate about a marriage that could never be . . .

'Cheer up, lass.' Her mother's voice ended her reverie. 'You really mustn't worry about me. Promise you won't.'

Kate smiled. She got up and gave her mother a hug. 'I promise.'

'Good. Now let's go down for that cup of tea Alice promised us.'

Alice had brought a tray into the stockroom, placing it on an upturned tea chest. She explained that if they sat here instead of the kitchen she could listen out for anyone coming into the shop. So they sat on wooden boxes amongst the clutter and the smell of paraffin oil. As well as tea she had brought a pile of sandwiches made with thickly cut bread and home-boiled ham and pease pudding. There was also a plate of rich fruit cake. It was like a picnic, Kate thought, a children's feast in a secret den.

'Charlie's asleep,' Alice said. 'So I can relax for a moment or two.'

But even in his sleep he had no ease. Every now and then they could hear him coughing. Alice would sit still and listen to see if the coughing got worse. If it died down straight away she would relax a little, but if not she would go and hover in the doorway until she was sure her husband was all right.

'This is real good of you, Alice,' Kate's mother said. 'And your best china and all.'

'No, it's a treat for me to have a bit conversation. Our Susan is always too busy with her bairns to be able to sit still awhile and talk to her mother. But she's very good,' Alice added quickly, as though they had thought she was criticizing her daughter. 'As soon as she gets the bairns settled at night and her man's safely home from work, she comes in to help me with her da.'

Nan smiled and nodded and Kate didn't know what to say. She remembered Susan as one of the older girls at school. Like Jane Harrison, Susan Willis was always better dressed than the other girls. But, unlike Jane, she had got on with the likes of Joan Donkin and her pals. Jane's deportment and elocution lessons had set her apart and made her the victim of name-calling until Kate had befriended her, but Susan had been happy to be one of the crowd. She had never wanted to better herself as Jane did. And why should she? But Kate had always suspected that Susan owed her popularity in part to the bags of sweets and cakes she brought to school and shared with the favoured few.

'Do you want another cup of tea?' Mrs Willis asked.

Nan said she would have one but Kate thanked her and told her she'd had sufficient.

'Well then, why don't we have a bit fun? Why don't I read your tea leaves?'

Kate smiled. Alice Willis's reputation as a teacup fortune teller had spread beyond the village and sometimes even well-to-do women from Shields and Newcastle would call at the shop to have their fortunes told. They were ready to believe anything Alice told them. They wanted

216

to believe. Nan, like some of the other village women, had sometimes watched the shop while Alice sat with her visitor behind the counter to read the cup. Her mother had told Kate with a smile and a laugh what went on. Kate had no idea how Alice did it but she didn't believe there was anything mystic about it. Alice made no charge for her readings but the sitter always spent generously in the shop. 'Alice Willis is not so daft,' Kate's mother had said.

'Shall I do it?' Alice asked her now. 'Shall I read your fortune?'

'Go on, our Kate,' her mother said. 'Let's have a bit laugh.'

Kate looked at the two older women's eager faces and realized she would be doing them a favour. It would be a distraction. A bit of fun in her mother's eyes, but she was not sure what it meant to Alice Willis. Perhaps she just wanted to forget about her own sad situation for a while.

'Have you finished drinking, now?' Alice asked.

Kate nodded.

'Nan, pet, go and put the closed sign in the door. Anyone's entitled to a bit break. And I'll try to be quick.' Kate's mother did as she was bid and when she returned Alice looked at Kate and said, 'Give me your cup.'

Alice took the cup and carefully dribbled the dregs of tea into a little bowl. Kate realized that the shopkeeper must have intended to do this all along. When she'd done she handed the cup back to Kate.

'Put the cup upside down on the saucer,' she said, 'and twist it round three times.'

Kate looked at Alice keenly. Her voice had changed and she had already adopted the air of a mystic – or a gypsy at the fairground. Was she acting? Or did she really believe in her own powers?

'Hold the cup firmly, mind,' Alice admonished as if sensing that Kate was half-hearted about the whole enterprise.

When she had done as she'd been told she looked at Alice for instructions but the older woman simply nodded and held out her hand. Kate lifted the cup carefully and saw that the twisting had spread the tea leaves round. They looked like nothing more than the used tea leaves they were. But now she knew she was going to be asked to believe that the pattern they made actually meant something.

Alice held the cup in both hands, her arthritic fingers spread around the delicate pattern of pale blue forget-me-nots. She gazed down at the leaves, her face impassive. She turned the cup one way and then another, playing out the drama, Kate thought. She realized her mother was

217

holding her breath. For a while nothing could be heard except an occasional cough from the back room and for once even that didn't disturb Alice.

The silence lasted a little too long. Kate began to feel uneasy. Tension coiled inside her.

Without looking up Alice said, 'I see happiness.'

The knot eased a little.

'And I see sadness.' Despite her words she looked up and smiled. 'But bairns always bring a mixture of sorrow and joy, don't they?'

Kate heard her mother gasp. They glanced at each other then looked at Alice aghast. The shopkeeper-fortune teller seemed only then to realize what she'd said and she frowned. Suddenly she lost her air of mystery and looked like Alice again.

'Well, I don't know where that came from,' she said. She peered into the cup again. 'No, no mistake, there's a baby there. Unless I'm losing the sight.'

A moment later she looked up and smiled. 'There's a wedding there, too. Look!'

Nan leaned forward and looked eagerly but Kate held back. Was Alice humouring them?

'I got things in the wrong order, didn't I, Kate, lass? I saw the baby before I saw the wedding. And that wouldn't be doing for a good lass like you, would it?'

Kate was aware of her mother's discomfort but Alice was happy again. Kate tried to hide her doubts. I'm sure this is all nonsense, she thought, but Mrs Willis seems to be sure of her own powers and I'm beginning to think my mother believes in them, too.

'That's it. A wedding and a baby.' Alice stared into the cup again and shook her head. She looked puzzled. 'But I can't say when this is going to happen. All I can say is that there's happiness ahead for you, Kate.'

Alice was just about to put the cup down when she stopped, stared into it again, and drew it back into the protective circle of both hands.

Oh, no, Kate thought. I wish she'd stop this. Now what kind of nonsense will she 'see' in the leaves? For Kate still thought this was nonsense. Even though she had been shocked just now by Alice's prediction of a baby, she believed that, tired as the poor woman was, she had simply produced the sort of prophecy that many young women would want to hear. A wedding and a baby. It had simply been a mistake to get them the wrong way round. But Alice was probably enjoying herself. She hadn't had any sort of relaxation for weeks now. No wonder she didn't want to stop.

'Does the letter R mean anything to you?' Alice asked, fixing Kate with a penetrating look. Kate felt the heat rise and sat back a little, so that her face was in shadow. Alice didn't notice; by now she was carried away with her performance again. She pointed into the cup. 'Can you see it? Look, R, it's plain to see.'

Kate lowered her head before leaning forward to stare into the cup. 'Yes, I think I can,' she said slowly as if she was concentrating. She could see no such thing but had decided to humour Alice in the hopes that this would soon be over with some cheerful prophecy about meeting a nice young man whose name began with that letter. But the tension began to knot inside her once again. Alice couldn't possibly mean Richard Adamson, could she?

'Turmoil,' Alice declared in a low sepulchral voice. The sort of voice that Kate used to adopt to frighten her playmates silly telling them ghost stories in the cave.

Kate heard her mother clear her throat and whisper, 'Turmoil, Alice?'

'Yes. Connected with the letter R.'

'Can you tell us what the turmoil is?' Nan asked.

'I can't.' Alice shook her head. 'I can't.'

She paused, and Kate took advantage of the moment to say, 'Well, thank you for the warning. I'll take care to avoid people whose name begins with R.'

'Divven't mock me, Kate.' Alice sounded sharp. 'There's more.'

Kate's heart sank. 'More turmoil?'

'This is different. It's a warning. There's a warning here for a W.'

Kate heard a soft cry of dismay. Her mother would naturally think Alice meant William. Kate felt her temper rising and wondered why it had taken so long. Perhaps she'd been too exhausted after her illness and too grateful for the home that was being offered. That gave her pause. She needed this home – this job. She mustn't alienate Alice Willis. Not now.

'Can you see the W?' Alice asked. 'Look in the cup.'

Kate leaned forward again. She wanted to bring this to an end. 'No,' she said, 'I can't. I'm sorry.'

'Are you sure?'

'I'm sure. Sorry.'

Perhaps Alice detected the sharp edge to her words. She was silent for a moment and then she sat back and looked into the cup again. 'But

219

as well as sorrow, I see joy,' she said, repeating some of the words she had uttered before. Her voice took on a cheerful tone as she said, 'You will have more than one child and find great success in life.'

Kate recognized this as the sort of thing Alice would say at the end of most of her readings. Her voice was already sounding almost normal. But then she added, 'But not without a struggle. And that's all I can see.' She put the cup down on the chest that served as a table and smiled. 'Now why don't I make us a fresh pot of tea?'

Later that night, as Kate's feet sought the stone hot-water bottle which she'd wrapped in a clean towel, she shivered, and not just with the cold. Alice had told her to bank the fire down but keep it going through the night and Kate was grateful for that. She'd put up the cinder guard before slipping into bed, accepting a slight loss of heat in the interests of safety.

She had come upstairs soon after tea because Alice had warned her that they would have an early start. In truth she was grateful; after all, she had been ill, and Dr Phillips had insisted on rest. Now she lay back amongst the pillows and watched the patterns the flames made on the ceiling. And shivered again. She thought she understood why the women of the village took Alice's readings so seriously. Their daily lives had so little comfort, so little cheer, that if for a moment they could dream that something good might happen, they would enjoy that moment to the full.

What was she to make of Alice's predictions? She was going to have a baby – that was true. But Alice also thought she was going to get married. And who would marry her after she had given birth to a fatherless child? A bastard? She made herself think the word, for that's what the poor bairn would be in this God-fearing and yet unforgiving community.

And what about the R and the W that Alice was supposed to have seen in the tea leaves? Well, it wasn't so strange when you thought about it. Alice knew very well that Kate had been staying at Richard Adamson's house, and she knew what the villagers thought about him.

As for the W, Alice knew that Kate's elder brother bore that initial. But why on earth should she have predicted trouble for William who was so sensible and so wise? If she'd claimed to have seen the letter T it would have made more sense. Thomas had already had a brush with the law and, knowing how hot-headed he was, anyone could have predicted trouble for him – and they wouldn't have needed a teacup. Kate had already sensed that the so-called 'riot' was not the end of the matter. But whatever the young fishermen had planned she was as certain as she could be that William would not be involved. Never William. No, poor Alice Willis, with everything she was living through, had got the Lawson brothers mixed up, that was all. And although that thought only brought small comfort Kate found herself giving in to her exhaustion.

I wish I'd never agreed to let Alice read the tea leaves, she thought drowsily. I believe the future should keep its secrets. That was almost her last thought before she went to sleep. Almost. For just as she felt herself drifting downwards into that warm secure place where you could escape from care, she felt a slight sensation in her lower body.

A fluttering, a gentle beating like that of small birds' wings. The movement brought with it an anguish comprising equal parts of sorrow and joy. Great joy. Tears came to her eyes. The baby in her womb had quickened, and, as soon as Kate realized that, she was overwhelmed by a surge of love. Such love as she had never known before.

Chapter Seventeen

'People will begin to talk about us, Betsy.'

'What do you mean?'

'Calling on me so early in the morning again. And alone. A beautiful young girl like you and a single man.'

Howard Munro stood on his doorstep and looked down at the child. She was wearing her new coat, which really was quite smart when he looked at it properly, but she still insisted on spoiling the effect by bundling herself up in her old shawl. To protect the coat from the rain, probably, he thought. For it was raining again; a steady driving rain that was keeping the cats indoors, all tumbled together on the hearthrug.

Betsy was staring at him blankly.

'I was joking,' he said.

'How was that a joke?'

Howard sighed. Suddenly losing patience and hating himself for it, he said, 'You're right. It wasn't a joke. It was a silly thing to say. Now what do you want?'

Startled by his abrupt change of tone, Betsy's eyes opened wide and she backed away like a nervous cat.

She believes I'm angry with her, Howard thought. He felt guilty. 'Have you a message for me?' he asked. 'From Kate, perhaps?'

The girl smiled. 'That's right, from Kate. Shall I come in and feed the cats? I've brought some fish heads. Sometimes they throw them away.'

She produced a newspaper parcel from her pocket – the pocket of her smart new coat – and Howard flinched.

'No, Betsy, give the fish heads to me. I'll feed the cats. Just tell me what the message is.'

'Kate can't come.'

'When – when can't Kate come?'

'Again.'

As patiently as he could he said, 'Can you remember exactly what Kate told you to say?'

'She said now that she's going to work in the shop she won't be able to get here until it's dark. So she won't be able to pose for the picture. She says she's sorry.'

'Tell Kate it's all right.'

The girl frowned. 'But what about the picture?'

'I've done enough work – I can finish it.'

Howard didn't know how he was going to explain it to Betsy but she surprised him by saying, 'All them drawings – sketches.'

'That's right. Tell her I'll call into the shop and see her when I buy my groceries.'

'Give me a list. I'll deliver them.'

'You're going to deliver groceries, Betsy?'

'Just bits and pieces. Mrs Willis says I can help Kate – sweep the floor and that.'

'Well, I think that's marvellous. And I will give you a list. But you needn't deliver them. I'll come and collect them.'

'I'll come in while you write the list. I'll feed the cats.'

Howard accepted defeat and stood aside, but he was careful to leave the door wide open. Despite the fact that he admired and respected the hardworking fisherfolk, he was aware of how narrow-minded some of them were. How ready to think ill of people. He did not want it reported that Betsy was visiting his cottage alone. He was by no means sure that even her youth and her difference would protect her from the malicious tongues of the more unpleasant among them. And besides, his own reputation as a promising artist of wholesome and uplifting paintings was already established and he did not want even a hint of scandal to attach itself to him.

Kate, wearing one of Alice's pinafores, looked around the stockroom. The boxes of soap, the casks of oil, the jugs and bowls, brushes, candles, chamber pots, coal scuttles and all the rest of the hardware were together at one end of the room, at least. All they needed was tidying. She thought she would enjoy the task. She had just cleared one shelf completely, putting the candles that had been there on an upturned box. She found a ball of twine and some scissors and began to cut the twine into lengths. She realized that Alice had come into the stockroom, and turned to see her looking worried.

223

'What is it?' Kate asked. 'Is Charlie . . .'

'He's sleeping. No, it's you I'm thinking about. You're doing things I didn't ask you to do.'

'I don't mind. In fact I enjoy it. And, at the moment, nobody seems to be venturing out in the rain.'

'As soon as it stops they'll all arrive at once like a flock of hungry gannets, and they'll all want serving at the same time.' Alice smiled. 'You'll be working long hours, you know, Kate. The folk round here have got used to me staying open late.'

'It'll be better than being outdoors in all weathers.'

'Like your ma, you mean?'

'Yes.' Kate sighed.

'Divven't fret. Nan's a tough one. And getting out and about will be good for her. What with looking out for your great-grandma, and all.'

'Oh, no! When my mother told me she'd taken over my fish round I never thought about that.'

'Divven't fret. She's got good neighbours. One or two of the wives round the doors have agreed to pop in. Everyone likes your ma, you know. They think she has a lot to put up with.'

And I've made her burden heavier, Kate thought. If a letter doesn't come from Aunt Winifred soon I shall have to think of somewhere else to go before my condition becomes obvious and my father makes Ma pay for my mistake.

'As there's no one about,' Alice said, 'shall I put the kettle on?'

'But we've just had breakfast.'

Kate had come down to find a bowl of porridge and a pot of tea set out in the stockroom. The chest they used for a table now sported a tablecloth. Alice liked to sit with her when she could and, as she'd told her, this way they could listen out for customers.

'Breakfast was an hour and a half ago,' Alice said, 'and I like to sit and rest a bit while Charlie's sleeping.'

'Of course,' Kate said. 'I'd love a cup of tea.'

The tray Alice brought back didn't just contain the tea things; there was a plate of fancy biscuits, too.

'I'll get fat, Mrs Willis,' Kate said as she bit into her second one.

'You'll work it off. And call me Alice.'

'Mrs Willis – I mean, Alice – I'm sorry about Betsy.'

Kate had opened the shop door first thing in order to sweep the pavement clear of the ever-present sand. As the door opened, the bell jangled, and a huddled form almost fell into the shop. Betsy had been

224

crouched in the doorway, goodness knows how long for, and she must have fallen asleep.

'No need to apologize,' Alice Willis said. 'I've noticed that if a body can find the right way of talking to the lass, she can make sense of things. If she wants to help you, run errands, do a bit cleaning, make a few deliveries, then she's welcome. I'll give her a penny or two, and her ma will be glad to have her out of the way.'

Charlie started coughing and the older woman finished her tea quickly, but Kate noticed that already the strained look on Alice's face was easing. The knowledge brought a further stab of guilt. What will she do when I leave, as leave I must? Kate wondered. May the Lord forgive me but it would be better if poor Charlie dies before that happens. She resolved to do as much as she could to help while she could.

The shop door opened and Kate went through to serve two women who complained about the weather and confided various worries as they bought the few things they needed to keep them going. Kate found that she enjoyed serving in the shop. The rows of packets and tins and bottles reminded her of the days when Jane and she used to play shops when they were children.

An upturned box at the mouth of 'their' cave and a collection of rocks, shells and bits of seaweed served as the counter and the goods for sale. Thomas and Jos were persuaded to be the customers, paying with pebbles for imaginary groceries and confectionery. As they grew older, Jos would tease the girls by slipping other items on to the 'counter'. Smooth bits of glass washed in by the tide were all right. Some of them were quite beautiful, and to Kate and Jane they became 'ornaments'.

But then Jos took to plonking down smelly fish heads and long-dead crabs. Sometimes the crabs would be alive and they would scuttle frantically about, scaring Jane witless. One day he brought an old shoe that he'd found in a rock pool. Despite the salt stains it was obvious that it had once been a smart shoe, an expensive shoe – a gentleman's shoe, Jane, the shoemaker's daughter, had proclaimed.

'Some passenger on the way to Norway or Germany must have dropped it over the side,' she said.

'But why would they do that?' Thomas asked.

Jane shot him an irritated glance and picked the shoe up to look at it more closely. And then she screamed and dropped it again. Kate would never forget that scream.

'There's something inside!' Jane wailed.

And indeed there had been. Inside the shoe were the remains of a foot. They had never played shops again.

Kate was still thinking about that day when the bell jangled and someone came in, pausing in the entrance to shake her umbrella before closing the door and making the bell jangle again.

'Jane!' Kate said. 'I was just thinking about you.' She was so pleased to see her old friend that, at first, she didn't notice that Jane's greeting was subdued. 'Did you know I was working here?'

'Yes, my mother has kept me informed. I'm sorry you were ill.'

'It was just a cold.'

'And yet you stayed at the Adamson house for nearly four weeks.'

'Dr Phillips was overcautious, I think.'

'Dr Phillips?'

'He has a practice in North Shields. He's a friend of Mr Adamson.'

'So old Dr Fenwick wasn't good enough for you?'

'Dr Fenwick would have suited me fine. I had no choice in the matter. In fact I didn't even know that they'd called a doctor until the next morning. For goodness' sake, Jane, why are you quizzing me like this? If your mother told you what happened—'

'It's all round the village. Mr Adamson found you in the cave. They say you'd fallen asleep and the tide was coming in. He waded in and saved your life.'

'Well, yes, but I suppose it was really his dog who found me. He takes him out every night.'

'But why did he take you home to his house? I mean, he could have taken you to the cottage.'

'I don't know.'

'Haven't you asked him?'

'I haven't seen him since that night.'

'Do you mean you were in his house all that time and you never saw him?'

'That's what I said.' Kate tried to control her rising irritation. Why was Jane – her friend – behaving like this? 'In fact I didn't see Mrs Adamson either, even though I was her guest. I saw no one but the doctor – oh, and Joan Donkin. She works there, you know. Mrs Adamson told her to look after me.'

'Joan Donkin? Oh, poor you!' For the first time since she had entered the shop Jane sounded sympathetic. She smiled and her whole demeanour softened. She seemed to make an effort to banish her

226

disapproving crosspatch manner. 'Well, I'm pleased to see that you look quite well now.' She stood back so that the light from the window in the door fell across Kate's face. 'In fact you look more than well. You look positively blooming. There's something about you . . . I don't know . . .'

'It's probably because of the rest I had,' Kate said swiftly. 'Lying around like Lady Muck, as Joan called me.'

That made Jane laugh. 'Do you like working here?'

Kate was surprised herself by answering promptly, 'Yes, I do.'

'I don't care much for the pinafore you're wearing. It's far too big.'

'As a matter of fact it's not long enough – but I agree, it's much too wide.'

'Mm. Why don't you pull the ties tighter?'

'I've got them as tight as they'll go. The whole waistband needs adjusting. It's a needle and thread job and you know how much I hate sewing. Besides, it belongs to Mrs Willis and I'd only have to alter it again when I leave.'

'Leave? You've only just started working here.'

'I know, but . . . I mean, the job is temporary. I'm just helping out until – I mean, it's just while Mr Willis is so ill.'

And that was the truth, Kate thought. She couldn't tell Jane the real reason why she wouldn't be staying either in the shop or in the village. And that was wrong. Best friends ought to be able to confide in each other, oughtn't they? But her mother had begged her to tell no one, and Kate would never break a promise made to her mother.

Just then the door opened and two small boys came in with a written request for half a pound of broken biscuits. Their faces were wet and shining, their clothes gave off a damp and not too clean smell, and the note was sodden and barely legible, but the boys were smiling. Kate scooped the broken biscuits from the tin behind the counter, put them into a paper bag and weighed them. The older of the two lads handed over the money and stuffed the bag of biscuits inside his jacket, and they both said, 'Thank you, miss,' before leaving the shop.

'You gave them good measure,' Jane said.

'Alice is soft on the children. She won't mind.'

Jane looked round at the jumbled shelves. 'It's a bit untidy, isn't it?'

'I intend to sort things out. I enjoy doing that kind of thing, I don't know why. It's good for the soul.'

'Perhaps because we can't bring order to our lives so easily,' Jane said. Her smile had faded and Kate was dismayed to see that there were tears in her eyes.

'Jane . . . what is it? What's the matter?'

'It's William.'

Kate was immediately anxious. Was this going to prove to be something to do with Alice's warning?

'I can't get him to name a date for our wedding.'

'Oh, is that all?'

Almost before she had finished speaking the words Kate wished she could recall them. Jane was furious.

'So you think it's a trivial matter, do you?'

'No, of course not. But I thought it might be something serious.'

Oh, no. That also had been the wrong thing to say. How could she explain to Jane that she had thought it might be a matter of life and death and not merely the matter of setting a date for their wedding. Kate suppressed a groan when she realized that even the way she was thinking would upset her friend.

'It is to me,' Jane said icily. 'My wedding is a very serious matter to me even if it isn't to the man who is supposed to love me.'

'I'm sure he loves you, Jane. I know he does.'

'He loves his mother more.'

Kate was shocked. 'Of course he loves his mother. He's a good son and he always will. But he loves you in a different way. It's not a matter of degree.'

'If he loved me he wouldn't be risking losing a good job with Mr Rennison.'

'Mr Rennison the Newcastle fishmonger?'

'Yes. He needs a general manager. He interviewed William last week. Mr Rennison explained what the job entailed and said the job was William's if he wanted it. He gave him time to make up his mind. And William still hasn't decided.'

'A week isn't a long time for such a big decision,' Kate said.

'It is when the matter is so important to m— to both of us.'

'You want William to leave the fishing?'

'You know I do. And you must know that the way things are with Adamson's trawlers taking away the local men's livings it would be for the best. It's such a respectable job, too, and we could get married and live above the shop.'

'The fish shop?'

Jane was losing her patience. 'You're being deliberately stupid. I mean my shop – my dressmaking business. I'm almost ready to take over.'

'Of course. I'm sorry. And you believe William is delaying things because he feels he ought to look after our mother, do you?'

'Yes, I do.'

'You're probably right. William takes his responsibilities as the elder son seriously.'

'But why can't Thomas look after your mother? Why shouldn't he be responsible?'

'I agree. He should be. But you see it's not just that William feels responsible for our ma, it's our father, too.'

'What's wrong with him?'

'You know what's wrong with him. He drinks too much. He's becoming a danger to himself and to others.'

'So William thinks he has to stay here – give up his chance of happiness?'

Kate looked at her old friend. The tears had started flowing. She had never seen Jane looking so distressed. She wished she could avoid what she was going to say next but it had to be said.

'You love William, don't you, Jane?'

'How can you ask that? I think I've always loved William, ever since we were children.'

'Well, have you ever considered that you could be together – be happy – if you gave up the idea of having your shop in town and lived here in the village?'

Jane stared at her aghast. 'Give up my dream? My dream of owning my own dressmaking business?'

'Which dream is more important to you?'

'What do you mean?'

'Your dream of married happiness or your dream of a successful business?'

Jane's eyes widened. She looked so distressed that Kate felt sorry for her. She hurried on, 'You could easily live here—'

'As a fisherman's wife? In that cottage with your mother and your father and your brother and Sarah?'

'There's nothing wrong with that. I grew up in that cottage and so did William, the man you're supposed to love.' Jane's face drained of colour and Kate felt guilty. 'But there would be no need for you to live there. There are cottages to rent – folk are leaving the village. William could be near his family and you could—'

229

'I could do what? Bait the lines? Go down to the beach and help land the fish? Sort it? Gut it and then sell it from door to door like—' Jane stopped and covered her mouth with her hand.

'Like me, you mean?'

'Kate . . . I'm sorry. I don't think less of you for doing that.'

'Thank you,' Kate said drily. She wondered why she hadn't lost her temper, but decided it was because Jane's anguish was so obvious. 'But there wouldn't be any need for that. My mother is still strong and capable of the work – as well as doing a fish round.'

Jane looked uncomfortable. 'Yes, my mother said she'd taken over the round.'

Kate continued, 'And if they needed more help then William would just have to pay some lass. You could run your dressmaking business from the cottage.'

Her friend stared at her for a moment and then she asked, 'And who exactly would my clients be?' Her tone was chilly.

'Well, the village women for a start. Some of them hate mending.'

'*Mending.*' Jane's voice was dangerously low.

'Not just mending. There's bonny frocks for weddings, for christenings—'

'*Bonny frocks.*'

'And . . . and it wouldn't just be for the village women, would it? I mean when word gets round you'd get the well-off folk from the big houses – and from Shields, probably, and Whitley-by-the-Sea.'

'Very sophisticated, I'm sure.'

'Jane—'

'Have you no idea of the sort of business I have planned? Of the clients from Jesmond and Gosforth and the sort of clothes they want? The velvet, the silks and the satins, the latest styles from Paris? Do you think I could ever be satisfied with plain wool and cotton and perhaps a bit of taffeta for a lady from Monkseaton?'

'But you would still be making clothes. That's what you love doing, isn't it?'

Her friend began to shake her head. Slowly at first and then faster and faster as the tears welled up and streamed down her face. 'You don't understand!' she said. 'You'll never understand!'

Jane turned and yanked the door open. The bell jangled furiously as she flew out and almost knocked over the younger girl who was just about to enter. Betsy turned and watched as Jane hurried away, struggling to put up her umbrella as she went. Then Betsy came in and shut the door, setting the bell jangling again. Kate's nerves jangled, too.

'That was your friend,' Betsy said. 'She's sharp but she's kind.'

Kate stared at the girl and thought that she had summed up Jane's character perfectly. Jane was sharp in two ways – she was clever, and she could offend people with her impatient manner. And there was no denying that she was a little self-centred. But, at heart, she was kind.

'Here's a grocery list,' the girl said. 'It's from Mr Munro. He'll come and collect the things later.'

'Thank you. Now, Betsy, would you like to help me?'

'That's why I'm here.'

Kate looked at the girl's determined expression and was overtaken by a rush of affection. 'I know, pet,' she said, 'and I'm very grateful.'

'Are you?' Betsy's eyes shone. 'Am I a real help to you, not just a hindrance?'

Kate was moved by the vulnerability Betsy's words revealed. 'You're a *real* help,' she said. 'In fact I don't know what I'd do without you.'

Betsy's answering smile touched Kate deeply. She didn't know what she had done to deserve the child's devotion but she would always cherish it.

'And now,' she said encouragingly, 'I want you to go into the stockroom. There are some candles on the chest. Do you think you could tie them up in bundles of six?'

For an answer Betsy held up one hand with thumb and fingers stretched and the other hand with only one finger raised. 'Six,' she said.

'That's right. And you'll find some pieces of twine. I've already cut them to the correct length.'

'Divven't you trust me with the scissors, then?' She grinned as she said this. There was no need to answer her question.

'Put the bundles of candles on the shelf. You'll see which one – it's empty.'

Betsy went through into the stockroom and Kate found a cardboard box and began to put up the artist's groceries. She was sure he didn't need so many items and wondered if Betsy had 'helped' him to make the list. Soon, lost in a world of pickles and jams, tea and sugar, butter and cheese, bacon and cooked meats, she found she was able to forget her problems for a while.

When that job was done she looked round for something to do and found a small blue notebook by the till on the front of which Alice had written 'Tick'. Kate didn't feel like opening it – she didn't want to know which of the villagers needed to buy on credit, although she supposed she would have to ask Alice eventually who was allowed to do this.

Another notebook proclaimed 'Christmas Club'. Kate knew that many of Alice's customers made weekly payments so that they would be able to afford extra luxuries at Christmas. Her own mother did so and Kate smiled at the remembrance of oranges and sugared almonds and chocolate pennies that Nan had saved for and put in the three stockings hanging by the fireplace.

Then her smile faded when she remembered the Christmas her father had come home in a drunken rage, accused her mother of being extravagant and, seizing the stockings from his children's hands, had hurled them in the fire.

The bell over the door jangled, banishing the memories, and Kate closed the book. She looked up with a smile to serve the customer, and found herself facing Richard Adamson.

Chapter Eighteen

'I've finished the candles. Is there anything else I can do? Oh.'

Betsy walked through into the shop and stopped when she saw the two people staring at each other over the counter: Kate on one side and Mr Adamson on the other. Neither of them took any notice of her. They were just staring as if they'd never seen each other before. And that was daft. Betsy could hear voices coming from the back room where Mrs Willis was trying to coax her husband to take some soup. But, here in the shop, nobody was talking. And that was daft, too. Had her friend forgotten what she was supposed to say? She made a decision and went to stand next to Kate.

'Can I help you, sir?' she asked.

'I beg your pardon?' Mr Adamson said. But he didn't look at her. He was still staring at Kate.

'I said, can I help you? Do you want to buy anything? I'm allowed to help.'

At last, very slowly, Kate turned to look at her. 'Oh, Betsy,' she said, as if she was surprised to see her.

'I've finished the candles.'

'That's good.'

'What shall I do now?'

'Well . . . I suppose . . .'

Her friend sounded really strange, Betsy thought. As if she was thinking of something else and didn't know what to say.

'Yes, there is something you can do.' Thank goodness Mr Adamson seemed to have remembered where he was. 'I want to buy some biscuits,' he said. 'A tin of biscuits.'

'A whole tin?' Betsy's eyes strayed to the deep tins arranged along the counter top. People bought half a pound or a pound at a time. They never bought a whole tin.

'Yes.' Mr Adamson smiled at her. 'But I mean one of those

233

smaller fancy tins. Look, on that shelf. I'd like the one with the tartan pattern.'

Betsy frowned.

'Look, there, there's a picture of a Scottish piper on it.'

'Shortbread!'

'That's right, Betsy, and if Miss Lawson would wrap it up I'd like you to deliver it.'

'Where to?'

'To my house. My mother is very partial to shortbread biscuits.'

'Why can't you carry it home?'

For a moment Mr Adamson looked as though he hadn't thought of that. But then he said, 'Because I'm taking my dog for a walk on the beach.'

'So you don't want to carry anything.'

'That's right.'

While they'd been talking Kate had been wrapping up the tin of biscuits in brown paper. She'd tied it neatly with string.

'It's like a present,' Betsy said.

'For my mother.'

'Well, you should put a card with it.'

'Of course. Thank you for reminding me. I'll use one of these.'

Betsy watched as Mr Adamson took a small white card from a pocket in his waistcoat. He put it on the counter and began to write something. Then he took another card from his pocket and wrote on that, too. He tucked the first card under the string of the parcel and gave the other to Betsy. 'This one is for the maid who will answer the door,' he told her.

'I'll get my coat on,' Betsy said, 'and me shawl. But remember you have to pay for the biscuits.'

'Betsy . . .' Kate began.

'It's all right, Miss Lawson. Here you are. And perhaps you would give tuppence from the change to Betsy for her trouble.'

Betsy knew what to say to that. 'It's no trouble, sir.' But nevertheless she took the tuppence and soon was on her way.

They stared at each other again but, now, they were smiling. Kate had recovered from her shock at seeing him. Betsy, bless her, had given them something to talk about.

'What did you write on the cards?' Kate asked.

'On the card for my mother I simply asked her to be kind to the child and perhaps give her some milk and a piece of cake.'

'And the second card?'

'I instructed Joan that Betsy was to be allowed to give the parcel to my mother in person.'

'Ah.' Kate smiled at him. 'Thank you.'

'Why do you thank me?'

'Because I can imagine what sort of reception Joan would give her.'

Richard laughed. 'She's not the sunniest of persons, is she?'

'She never has been.'

And then they seemed to run out of things to say. Richard Adamson moved nearer to the counter and Kate backed away. Ridiculous, she thought. He's hardly going to leap over and take me in his arms . . .

'Did you really come to buy biscuits?' she asked.

'No. I wanted to see you. To ask how you are.'

'I'm fine.'

'I've been worried.'

'Why? You know I wasn't allowed to leave your house until Dr Phillips was satisfied that I was quite recovered. And you could have asked before now. I was in your house for nearly four weeks.'

'I wanted to come and see you, believe me. But I thought you might not want to see me. I mean, after what happened when I . . . Kate – may I call you Kate?'

'Yes.'

'Do you remember what happened on the beach – after I carried you from the cave?'

'Yes.' It was barely a whisper.

'I'm sorry.'

'Why sorry?'

'You were hardly yourself. What's more you were vulnerable.'

'That's true.'

'Do you despise me?'

'No.'

'Then I don't regret it. But I had to stay away while you were ill – in my home – I didn't want you to think I was taking advantage of the situation.'

'And now?'

'I'd heard that you'd lost the cottage. I was – I am – concerned.'

'I'm not homeless. Mrs Willis has taken me in, and I like working here.'

'Why can't you go home, Kate?'

'My father has forbidden me to go home. He's angry with me. We . . . we had a disagreement.'

'I suppose I have no right to ask what it was about?'

'No, you haven't.'

'Then all I can say is that I find it sad when families are split apart in this way. If you had been living at home with your mother you would never have been allowed to go alone to the cave that night. I still have nightmares thinking about what might have happened if I had not found you.'

'But you did.'

Without thinking Kate moved nearer to him again. Richard Adamson had taken hold of the edge of the counter with both hands and he gripped it tightly as he leaned forward. Kate breathed in, and as well as the odours of tea and coffee and cheese and bacon she could smell the lemony tang of his hair dressing.

'It was meant to be.'

He had spoken softly – so softly – and yet Kate shivered at the intensity of his voice. 'Meant?' she whispered.

She looked into his eyes, so dark, so deep, so different from eyes she had looked into before. She shivered again, violently, and wrapped her arms across her body, hugging herself tightly.

'What is it?'

'Someone walked over my grave,' she whispered.

The moment of stillness that followed was broken by the jangling of the bell above the shop door. Kate and Richard sprang apart as Howard Munro walked in.

'I've come for my groceries,' he said cheerfully, but his smile faded quickly as he recognized Richard. 'Oh. Doing some shopping, are you?'

Richard shook his head. 'I just called in to see how Miss Lawson was.'

'Ah, well, I suppose having acted the hero, you feel somewhat responsible for her.'

'Are you mocking me, Howard?'

'No, of course not.'

Richard said no more but he looked vexed. The two of them are on the verge of quarrelling, Kate thought. And she was not so naïve that she could not guess why. Disturbed and flustered, she was glad to turn away from them while she sought the box of groceries and lifted them up on to the counter.

'Here are your things,' she said as cheerfully as she could. 'It was kind of you to give Betsy a list. I'm sure you don't really need all this.' She gestured towards the box. 'But it makes her feel useful. She would have delivered them, you know.'

Howard shrugged. 'I wanted to see you. To ask if you have quite recovered.'

'Thank you, I'm fine now. But I'm glad you came.'

'Are you?' Howard smiled brilliantly.

'I wanted to apologize in person for not being able to pose for the picture any more.'

The smile faded slightly but he adopted a teasing tone. 'Is that the only reason?'

'Well, of course I'm always pleased to see you.'

Kate found herself responding to his flirtatious manner, although she knew very well what he was doing and was also aware that Richard was becoming irritated. He had moved away and his face was in shadow.

'As I told the child, you needn't worry about the portrait,' Howard said. 'I'll be able to finish it without asking you to sit again. Although I hope very much that you'll come and view it when it's finished.'

'Perhaps I will.'

'*Perhaps*?'

'Well, to tell you the truth, I don't know what to expect. I might not like what I see.'

'But you must view it. And you need have no fears that I haven't done you justice. In fact I think it might be the best portrait I've ever painted. Please say you'll come.' Howard stepped forward and took hold of Kate's hand. 'I'll tell you when.'

At that moment the shop door opened and closed; a strident female voice said, 'What's going on here?'

Kate tried to withdraw her hand but Howard hung on to it as he turned to face the newcomer. 'And you are?' he asked.

'This is Susan Armstrong, Mrs Willis's daughter,' Kate told him. She pulled furiously and freed her hand. 'Hello, Susan. This is Mr Munro, the artist. I'm sure you've heard of him,' she added lamely.

Susan barely nodded. 'And does my mother know about this?'

'I beg your pardon?' Howard said.

'I'm talking to Kate,' Susan said. 'Does my mother know about this?'

'About what, precisely?' Kate said with as much composure as she

237

could muster. She noticed that a raindrop was about to fall from the tip of Susan's sharp nose.

'About the way you're carrying on while you're supposed to be working?'

'I'm not . . . I mean . . .'

As Kate stumbled over her words Richard Adamson stepped forward. 'What happened was entirely Mr Munro's fault,' he said. 'I can assure you that Miss Lawson is not to blame.'

'Oh . . . Mr Adamson.'

It was clear that Susan had just become aware of who the other gentleman was. She bit her lip and looked discomfited. 'Well, if you say so,' she said.

'I do say so. I was about to admonish my cousin for embarrassing Miss Lawson.'

'Well, in that case . . .'

'And how is your husband?' Richard continued smoothly. 'Seth, isn't it? Is he enjoying his job in the warehouse?'

Susan struggled to adjust her expression to one of gratitude and Kate almost felt sorry for her. 'Yes . . . thank you. It was very kind of you to find the position for him.'

'Not at all. But now we must go. Come along, Howard, you have caused enough inconvenience for Miss Lawson.'

Throughout this exchange Howard Munro had kept silent. But now, and Kate could have cursed him for it, he decided to have the last word. 'Mrs Armstrong, I apologize if I have offended your sense of propriety. But Miss Lawson and I are good friends.'

'Friends? You and Kate?' Susan frowned.

'Certainly. We have become close while I have been painting her portrait.'

Susan's astonishment was almost comical and unfortunately it spurred Howard on to further devilment. 'I understand you have only just returned here so you may not know that it was my intention to paint both the village and its inhabitants.'

'Oh, yes. I heard.'

'And once I saw Kate I knew that if I never painted another portrait in my life I must paint hers. I can only hope that I have done justice to her beauty.'

Kate could have hit him. Susan was goggle-eyed and Richard was obviously furious. He took hold of Howard's shoulder. 'That's enough, Howard. Mrs Armstrong does not understand that your artistic

238

temperament gives you licence to speak this way – or at least you believe it does. Now apologize to Miss Lawson for embarrassing her and pick up your groceries.'

'Have I embarrassed you, Kate?'

'You know very well that you have,' she said tersely.

'Then I'm sorry.'

Without more fuss Howard paid for his groceries, picked up the box and allowed Richard to guide him – forcibly – out of the door. Through the shop window Kate saw Prince greet his master enthusiastically but Richard barely noticed the poor beast. The two men walked off together quarrelling furiously. Kate felt drained. She leaned forward to grip the counter and face Susan. But before the enraged young woman could speak her mother came through from the back shop.

'Susan, pet,' she said. 'I thought I heard your voice. Hev you been talking to Kate?' She hurried on without giving Susan time to answer, 'Eeh, you'll never know how grateful I am that Kate has agreed to help out. You know I was beginning to think I'd have to close the shop. But with Kate here I can look after your poor father. Come on, Susan, come through. Your da's awake and I know he'll be pleased to see you.'

Susan lifted the flap in the counter and walked through. She let the flap drop so carelessly that it would have banged forcefully if Kate had not caught it. Once she was alone again she turned her attention to tidying the shelves. If she was finding it difficult to make sense of what had just happened – the feelings aroused by Richard Adamson's mere presence and the rivalry that had sprung up between him and his cousin – at least she could put the shop in order. Jane was right about finding peace in such tasks because they were easier than bringing order to life.

Poor Jane, she thought. She loves my brother so and yet her ambitions might be coming in the way of a happy ending to their problems. But at least it was still possible for them to marry if one or the other of them would give way.

But what about me? There can be no solution to my problem. I have fallen in love with Richard Adamson whilst I am carrying another man's child. And the admission Kate had finally made to herself brought heartache instead of joy.

The shop door opened and the bell jangled, fraying Kate's nerves. But she turned to face the next customer with a smile.

* * *

'Were you deliberately trying to cause trouble for Kate?'

Richard Adamson and his cousin were still quarrelling when they reached the artist's cottage.

'Of course not.'

'Then what were you doing talking like that?'

Howard opened the door and went in. Before Richard could follow, Prince, no doubt determined not to be left out in the rain, dodged round his legs and preceded him. Richard heard a cat yowl and take flight, but once he'd gained the centre of the room Prince stopped and looked back at his master with liquid eyes, the picture of innocence.

'All right, boy, you can stay,' Richard said. 'But go and lie down. And leave the cat alone.' He pointed to the hearthrug where another, older cat was sleeping. It raised its head, opened one slanted eye and hissed. Prince backed away to the very edge of the rug and lay down, his head between his paws as he watched the cat warily.

Richard looked up to find that Howard was equally wary. 'Are you angry with me?' his cousin asked.

'Yes.'

'You think I've caused trouble for Kate?'

'Yes. And I can't think why.'

'I didn't mean to. It was that woman I took exception to. Mrs Armstrong . . . Susan. She was so determined to put Kate in her place. Or rather what she thought was Kate's place.'

'Susan Armstrong is Mrs Willis's daughter,' Richard reminded him. 'I imagine she thought she had the right to reprimand someone who works for her mother.'

'Reprimand? Reprimand her for what, for goodness' sake?'

'Do I really have to explain it to you?'

'Yes you do.'

'It's not hard to see that in Mrs Armstrong's view Kate was behaving totally inappropriately while she was supposed to be working.'

'Well, she wasn't.'

'That's right. She wasn't. You were. But Mrs Armstrong was not to know that Kate had not encouraged you, was she?'

'I suppose not.'

'And then you went on to anger the woman further.'

'I couldn't help myself. There she was, that squat, sharp-faced scold trying to make out that she was better than Kate. I wanted her to know that Kate is my friend – and furthermore that she is beautiful. Something Mrs Susan Armstrong must know she will never be.'

240

Howard was pacing the room. Richard had never seen his normally easy-going American cousin so agitated. 'Are you in love with Kate?' he asked.

Howard stopped pacing and smiled disarmingly. 'I suppose I must be.'

'And Kate? Is she . . . does she . . .'

'Return my feelings?' Howard shrugged. 'I think she may. But she doesn't know it yet.'

'That's nonsense.'

'No it's not. We became friends while she was sitting for me. We got along so well . . . she's easy to talk to. She's intelligent, has a sense of humour, is curious, hungry to know things.'

'Have you spoken to her?'

'Spoken to her? Oh, you mean asked her to marry me? Yes, I have. I told her I wanted to take her home to America with me.'

'And her answer?'

'She . . . she promised me she would think about it.'

Was that true? Richard wondered. And if so why couldn't Howard meet his eyes?

'And what about you, Richard?' his cousin said suddenly. 'Why are you so interested in the girl?'

'I found her in the cave. Naturally I was concerned – am still concerned – for her welfare.'

'Ah, her welfare. And what does Caroline think?'

'I beg your pardon?'

'I said what does Miss Travers think of your "concern" for Kate's welfare?'

'Caroline? I haven't asked her. Why should I?'

'Because you are courting her, aren't you?'

'What makes you think that?'

'For God's sake, Richard, what do you think you have been doing if not courting her? She comes to your house—'

'She is a friend of my mother.'

Howard raised his eyebrows. 'You go out together—'

'In family parties.'

'And what do you suppose your mother and Caroline's parents make of these family excursions? Why have there been so many if you do not intend to propose to her?'

'I . . . don't . . . know.'

'In other words you can't make your mind up. What is it you want,

241

Richard? Caroline is beautiful, accomplished, rich. She obviously adores you.'

'Stop this!'

'You're not being fair to her, you know. Don't frown. You must know what I mean. So long as other possible suitors think that the rich and successful businessman, Richard Adamson, is courting her, they'll stand back. And if this sad state of affairs goes on much longer and then you decide that Caroline isn't for you, you will have made things impossible for her.'

'What are you talking about?'

'Well, apart from the fact that her reputation might be compromised, people will think that there must be something wrong with the poor girl. Can't you see that?'

Now it was Richard's turn to avoid his cousin's eyes. 'Yes, I can.'

'Then make up your mind. Personally I think you'd be crazy not to marry her.'

Either Prince sensed his master's unease, or he'd decided that he'd waited long enough. He got up and came over to Richard, nuzzling his nose into his master's hand. Richard was glad of the interruption. 'All right, old boy. We'll go now.'

Howard laughed. 'I missed the signal but I guess you've trained the dog to rescue you.'

'Stop talking nonsense.'

Richard took his leave, aware that Howard had turned the tables on him and had managed to gain the superior ground. He knew very well that he had been unfair to Caroline. He had been attracted to her in the beginning, but as he got to know her he had realized that the attraction had been merely physical. And now even that had faded in comparison with the passion that Kate Lawson had aroused in him. Much as he admired Caroline it would not be fair to marry her when he had given his heart to someone else.

'My, you've got the cottage looking grand, Susan,' Joan Donkin said, turning from the sink where she was washing the dishes and speaking quietly so as not to wake her friend's three small children.

The two boys were sleeping together in a truckle bed by the wall and the youngest child, a girl, was still small enough to fit into a low cot with rockers. Susan was rocking it gently with her foot. Susan's husband Seth sat by the fire with his pipe and a newspaper. Every now and then he looked up and smiled contentedly at his wife.

242

It was late and they had already had their supper. Joan had joined them and had insisted on clearing the table and washing the pots.

'Yes, it's nice, isn't it?' Susan replied just as softly. 'My mother gave me some bits and pieces from the house – the rugs and the pictures. Oh, and that vase on the dresser and the dinner service, too.'

'It's lovely,' Joan said. 'I swear it's as good as anything in the Adamson house – and I should know. I can't think of anyone else round here who will have plates as grand as this. Not even that stuck-up Jane Harrison's mother.'

Susan smiled with satisfaction but then she sighed. 'My mother has no need for some of her things any more. Not now that my father is so poorly.'

'Your poor mother. I feel for her, I really do.'

'Well, I'm here to help her now,' Susan said. 'As soon as Seth gets back to mind the bairns I go to see what I can do.'

'She must be grateful for that. Managing all on her own, the way she is.' Joan began to dry the plates, treating them with exaggerated care.

'Hmm.'

'What is it?'

'She's not on her own, is she? She's got Kate Lawson working for her.'

'Aye, I know. In the shop. But I suppose she had to have someone.' Joan put the last of the plates on the dresser and brought a chair up next to her friend.

'Pity it had to be that stuck-up Lawson lass,' Susan said. 'And furthermore my mother's taken her in. She's living there.'

'Be fair to your ma, Susan. She put her out of this cottage so that you could have it. I suppose she felt obliged.'

Susan looked down into the cradle and, satisfied that the little one was deeply asleep, she motioned Seth to come over and lift the cradle away and place it beside the bed. Susan went with him to make sure the blankets were tucked securely round her daughter and then came back to sit beside Joan. She took up the conversation where they had left off.

'Why couldn't Kate have gone back to her parents' cottage? Why was she living here in the first place?'

'Her Aunt Meg took her in when her father threw her out.'

'Threw her out?'

'Told her never to show her face at home again, so the gossip goes.'

243

'But why?'

'You know what the Lawsons are like. A quick-tempered lot, and that father of theirs doesn't get any better when he's had a drink. Kate was always standing up to him. She must have gone too far.'

Susan shook her head. 'It seems funny to me. A father throwing his daughter out and not even relenting when she was found half drowned in the cave. What could have made him so angry?'

'I think mebbes it was Jos Linton,' Joan said.

'Jos Linton? But he's dead, isn't he?'

'Yes, he is. But the wedding had already been planned.'

'Jos and Kate?'

Joan nodded. 'And I've heard tell her father wasn't even going to go to the wedding. He's supposed to have told Kate that once she was married to a Linton, he never wanted to see her again.'

'What are you two bonny lasses looking so serious about?' Seth folded his newspaper and tucked it behind the cushion. 'Are you putting the world to rights?'

Susan smiled at him. 'Oh, you know, just catching up with village gossip.'

Seth leaned over and tapped the bowl of his pipe against the grate to rid it of the tobacco ash. Then, standing up, he slipped the briar in to his pocket. 'In that case you'll enjoy yourselves better without a mere man around. I think I'll go and wet me whistle at the Queen's Head. Just a pint, mind, and I'll come back in time to walk Joan back to the Adamsons' house.'

Joan watched a little enviously as her friend's husband unashamedly gave Susan a kiss before wrapping a muffler round his neck and going out. There was no justice in a world where the likes of Susan, who, although not ugly, was certainly bordering on plain, could land a big bonny good-natured fellow like Seth Armstrong in her net. Although when you thought back to their wedding day, and then counted forward to when the first little lad had been born . . .

'What are you thinking?' Susan asked and Joan felt herself flushing.

'Nothing in particular.'

'You had a strange look for a minute.'

'Did I? I was just thinking about what you told me earlier,' she lied. 'About finding Kate Lawson carrying on with the American when she should have been working. And Mr Adamson in the shop.' Joan shook her head and pursed her lips. 'Disgraceful.'

'Shameless!' Susan agreed. 'And the way Mr Munro went on about her being his friend. *Friend*! That's one word for it. And telling me how beautiful she is!'

'Beautiful? Kate Lawson? With that hair! That's not my idea of beauty,' Joan said.

'Mine neither. And I've heard that she went alone to his house every day to pose for him. Pose, indeed.'

'Ah, well,' Joan said as if she were pretending to be fair. 'She didn't go alone. Betsy Smith went with her.'

'What? Betsy? That idiot child? She hardly counts as someone respectable.'

'Well, no, I suppose not.' Joan was enjoying this.

'And how come Kate Lawson got so pally with Mr Richard Adamson? Why on earth would he be bothered with her after what her brother did? We read about the riot in the newspaper, you know. And yet there was Mr Adamson, as large as life, standing up for her, and making excuses. He made Mr Munro apologize.'

Joan shook her head in wonderment. She lowered her voice even further. 'Do you think she's carrying on with both of them?'

They looked at each other knowingly. 'Who can tell?' Susan said. 'But the sooner I can get her out of my mother's house the better.'

'You'd have to find someone to serve in the shop,' Joan said.

'I know, that's the problem. But once my father's . . . I mean, once my mother isn't so busy . . .'

'I know what you mean. Your poor mother – and poor you,' Joan said solicitously.

'Well, when that's all over with, there would be no need for her to stay, would there?'

'You're right. And in any case . . .'

'What? What were you going to say?'

'Well, just that I could look about for a suitable girl to work in the shop, couldn't I?'

'That would be good of you. Now, shall we have a cup of tea? I think there's time before Seth comes back.'

Joan watched Susan as she rose to make the tea. She didn't offer to help. She sat and thought about what she had nearly let slip. She had almost said that Kate Lawson might very soon be forced to move. She turned her suspicions over in her mind. Kate had been at the Adamsons' house for nearly four weeks and in all that time she hadn't had her monthlies.

Well, she might have had them just before she came – or perhaps the fright she'd had might have driven them away. But there were other signs . . . signs that Joan had noticed when, in the first few days, she'd helped Kate wash. Her full breasts and her rounded belly. They had been obvious through the clinging fabric of Mrs Adamson's fine lawn nightdresses.

Joan would have loved to have told Susan what she suspected but if she was wrong she'd have made a fool of herself. No, better to keep quiet for the moment. But if she was right she knew how much she would enjoy seeing that stuck-up Kate Lawson knocked off her high and mighty perch.

Chapter Nineteen

The night was cold and the public bar at the Queen's Head was warm and welcoming. A wind had got up and, now and then, blew down the chimney sending gusts of sooty smoke out across the room to mingle with the fug of beer and tobacco fumes.

There was a blast of cold air when the door opened and William saw Seth Armstrong walk in, to be greeted by smiles of welcome. Armstrong seemed a good sort and William had nothing against him. He only wished that his coming back here hadn't meant Kate's losing the cottage, although she seemed happy enough living above the shop where she was now working.

'Drink up, William,' Thomas said. 'My treat this time.' The brothers were sitting next to each other on the wooden bench that ran along one wall. At Thomas's other side sat two of his pals, Matthew Linton and Jack Chisholm. A rough wooden table with a scarred top was before them. It carried its fair share of empty glasses.

'No, this is enough for me,' William said. 'And perhaps you should stop now, too.'

For answer his younger brother just laughed. William watched him lift the pint glass to his mouth and tip it back until every last drop of the Newcastle Ale had gone down his throat. He wiped his mouth with the back of his hand and turned to his two pals. 'Same again, lads?'

Before either of them could answer he got up and edged past William until he was free of the table. He shoved his way through the crowd to the bar and hailed the barmaid. 'Five more pints of the same, Florrie,' he shouted over the hubbub.

William stared glumly down at the sawdust that covered the wooden floorboards and returned to the problem that had been worrying him all evening. He knew that Jane wouldn't approve of his being here. They'd agreed to save every penny they could towards setting up home after they were married. Whenever that would be . . . His conscience stirred.

He wasn't being fair to the lass in not naming a date – but how could he? How could he leave his mother to cope with his father the way he was these days – worse than he'd ever been.

He loved Jane and for the life of him he couldn't imagine why such a beautiful and clever lass would want to marry a simple fisherman. But that was the problem. Jane wanted to change all that. And, when they were together, he was carried along by her enthusiasm. Just one look into those blue eyes set his senses spinning and he forgot everything he should have said. When she told him how clever and how wise he was, she inspired him with the confidence he would need to leave the fishing and work for the likes of Mr Rennison.

But as soon as he left her, the doubts came back. He had never told Jane, hard as he'd tried, that he found it difficult to imagine any other life but that of a fisherman. He'd been born into it as his father and generations of Lawsons had been before him. He looked down at his hands, red and callused and scarred from being cut by the fish hooks. How could he have dealings with respectable tradesmen with hands like that? Would putting a smart suit of clothes on make him a different man?

Thomas was still at the bar. William glanced along at the other lads; their hands were the same as his. And they wore their fishermen's ganseys of oiled wool. He was wearing one, too, as was Thomas; they'd been knitted for them by their mother in the intricate local pattern. Each fishing community on the Northumbrian coast had its own pattern so as better to identify the bodies of the drowned. They were all born to be fishermen. And most of them expected nothing more than to die as fishermen.

These lads, like him, were born to the sea – and they didn't want things to change. It was no wonder Thomas was so bitter and ready to fight for the way of life he believed in. William hadn't wanted to come here tonight, but Thomas had been in such an ugly mood after the fishing that morning. Their father had been even more of a liability than usual and they'd landed the poorest catch ever.

'We might as well have stayed in bed,' his younger brother had said angrily. And later, when he'd talked about getting together with the lads to cheer himself up, he'd asked William to go with him. William had refused but their mother, not liking the mood Thomas was in, had begged him to go along to keep an eye on things. Especially as Henry had decided to join them.

Henry Lawson was sitting by himself, further along the bench, almost in the corner of the room. He liked that corner. For some reason he thought of it as his place, and no one had ever had the temerity to challenge him for it. He was staring into his beer. Even in the crowded bar no one was willing to sit too near him. He had long been known as a troublemaker. He would pick fights which ended with both him and his unfortunate victim being thrown out. William guessed it wouldn't be long before he was barred from every public house in the village. If he hadn't drunk himself to death first.

'Take a hold of these, lads.'

Thomas returned and put three pints of beer on the table and went back for two more. He gave one to William and took the other over to their father, who didn't even look up.

'You shouldn't have done that,' William said when Thomas resumed his seat next to him.

'Hawway, drink up, man, it'll do you good. You're becoming such a miserable beggar, William, that I hardly recognize you these days. You haven't spoken a word all evening – I don't believe you've heard a thing we've said.'

William let that go. 'I meant you shouldn't have bought another drink for Da.'

'Not buy a drink for my own father? What do you think I am?'

'A fool, that's what I think you are.'

Thomas bridled. William saw the telltale flush of temper begin to rise up. 'Now listen—' Thomas began.

'No, you listen. You know our father can't take his drink.'

'Can't take his drink? You must be joking. There's no man in the village that can down as many pints as Henry Lawson.'

'But look what it does to him. Do you want him to go home and take his temper out on our ma?'

'Well, no, but we'll be there, won't we? We can keep him in hand these days.'

'And that's another thing,' William said. 'These days he doesn't always get home safe, does he? Our mother thinks he's ill and I agree. But I believe it's an illness brought on by the drink. Whatever sort of father he's been, do you want to be the one who finishes him off?'

Thomas fell silent. He looked along at their father and then back at William. 'You're right. Damn it, you usually are. I won't buy him any more drinks tonight if you promise not to speak to me like that in front of my friends.'

William looked hard at his younger brother. Thomas couldn't stay serious for long. He was smiling now and looking a little shamefaced.

'Don't worry, I doubt if Matthew and Jack heard me. They're too deep in conversation.'

Thomas glanced over his shoulder. 'Aye, so they are. They haven't even noticed that I've brought them another beer.' He turned his whole body round to face his friends. 'Right, lads, drink up,' he urged, and picked up his own glass. He took a long swallow from his pint and then said quietly, 'Are we agreed? If we don't do something to stop Adamson soon, we might as well burn the cobles and seek work in the pits.'

Oh, no, William thought. So that is what tonight is about. William felt uneasy. After the demonstration outside Richard Adamson's house he had promised Jane that he would steer clear of any protests about the fishing and he'd been glad to. In all honesty he couldn't see how action of the sort Thomas preferred would do any good. Mr Adamson had made it clear that he would be happy to talk to the men.

But Thomas and his pals wouldn't listen. After the so-called 'riot' they had behaved themselves. But their anger had seethed on and William had suspected that they had something else planned. Now he was annoyed with himself for allowing Thomas to persuade him to come along tonight. But at least his brother had turned his back on him for the moment and was talking quietly to his two best pals. They were listening intently to what he was saying and in spite of himself William found himself straining to hear what they were talking about.

'Now this is how I see it,' his brother said. 'We've got to hit Adamson in the pocket. See how he likes it.'

'Aye, that's right,' the other two said in unison.

William wondered where this was leading.

'And how do you think we could do the most damage?' Thomas asked.

Matthew and Jack shook their heads.

'Hawway, think about it. The steam trawlers are taking away our living. And which is the biggest and the best of the trawlers? The pride of Adamson's fleet?'

'The *Tyne Star*,' Jack Chisholm said softly.

'Aye, that's right,' Matthew said. 'Adamson spent a fortune on it, I'm told.'

'Right.' Thomas lowered his voice and leaned towards his two friends. 'So what have we got to do, lads?'

William realized he was holding his breath.

Matthew and Jack frowned

'Come on – it's not that hard,' Thomas said. 'Use your brains. What we've got to do is sink her.'

Matthew was the first to speak. 'You're mad.'

Jack Chisholm said nothing. William could see he was uneasy.

'Mad, am I?' Thomas said. 'Well, I'll have you know that it wasn't me that thought it up. It was your own brother, Jos.'

'How could that be?' Matthew asked. 'Jos was drowned before Adamson took delivery of the *Star*.'

'Yes, but not before news of it got out. We knew what Adamson was planning – and that there would be other boats just as big if not bigger. Jos wanted to hit him straight away. Show him that we wouldn't stand for it. And if Jos had still been with us, we'd have done it by now.'

'Jos never told me about this,' Matthew said.

'No. There was only me and him knew. He planned to tell you all once the boat was delivered.'

William wondered if this was the truth and decided it probably was. Thomas was a hothead but he wouldn't have had the brains to think of something like this. Jos had been a clever lad and, what's more, a natural leader. Thomas was right about one thing: if Jos hadn't been drowned it was more than likely that the deed would have been done by now.

'And did Jos tell you how we should go about it?' Matthew asked.

'Well, we're not going to follow the bloody boat out to the fishing grounds and blow a hole in its side,' Thomas said. He laughed.

'That would be murder.' It was the first time Jack Chisholm had spoken since Thomas had revealed the plan.

'You mean the crew?'

'Aye. If they caught us they'd string us up.'

'I told you – that's not the plan!' Thomas flared.

Heads turned at the sound of his raised voice and Jack glared at him. Matthew looked uncomfortable.

'Keep your voice down,' Jack said, 'and tell us what the plan is, then.'

Thomas leaned over the table and lowered his voice, forcing his friends to lower their heads too. William couldn't help moving closer to his brother. He had to know what he was going to say.

'We'll sink it at its mooring at the fish quay.' He planted his hands so firmly on the table to make his point that it shook, slopping beer from the glasses.

Matthew and Jack looked at him doubtfully.

'Look, I'm telling you, it'll not be hard to do. We get on board in the middle of the night—'

'What if there's a watchman on board?' Matthew asked.

'We knock him on the head and throw him in the river.' Thomas paused and shook his head. 'I wish you could see your faces,' he said. 'Of course we wouldn't drown the man. We'll . . . we'll find some other way of dealing with him.'

Jack Chisholm hunched forward over the table. He looked down into his beer. 'So we get him out of the way?' He raised his head and looked at Thomas. 'And did Jos say how you were going to sink the boat?'

'Well, that's easy, isn't it? Like I said, we get on the boat in the middle of the night and we open the seacock. Then, down she'll go.'

William had listened with growing consternation. He hoped that the other two lads would reject the idea there and then as being too risky. But he could see that, although Jack seemed to have reservations and Matthew was just plain scared, they were half convinced that the plan would work. He knew very well that was because Thomas had told them it was Jos's idea. And perhaps it was. But it didn't seem as if his sister's sweetheart had got much beyond considering the possibilities. William couldn't believe that he had made any definite plans.

'Do you think we can get away with it?' Matthew asked.

'Aye, I do.' Thomas turned towards William. 'What about you, William? You've sat here saying nowt. What do you think of the plan?'

A voice in William's head urged him to speak out and put an end to this madness. The enterprise was far too risky and those involved would almost certainly end up in prison doing hard labour for a very long time. And what would they have achieved? They certainly wouldn't have done anything to help their families.

The demonstration outside the trawler owner's house had left Mr Adamson in no doubt of the men's feelings and yet he had done nothing to change his fishing methods. And nor would he. He had offered to help them find other jobs – even working for him. William believed the offer was genuine, but would he still feel that way if a bunch of young hotheads sunk the pride of his fleet?

He glanced at his brother and the other two lads. Their eyes were bright and their movements unsteady as they picked up their glasses. Their bellies were full of beer. It would do no good to speak now. Thomas would not thank him for disagreeing with him in front of his friends. It would seem disloyal. His younger brother would grow

252

belligerent and William would lose any chance there might be of talking him out of the idea.

'I don't know what I think of it,' he said slowly. But Thomas was already on the way to the bar to order another round.

Just as well. He wouldn't say any more now, William decided. He would tackle Thomas when they were alone and try to convince him to drop the idea. And as for the other two, he had sensed they were not entirely happy about the plan. He could only hope that in the cold light of dawn their half-hearted enthusiasm for the idea would peter out completely.

The rain of the last few days had stopped and the air was fresh. It was late evening and Alice had told Kate to close the shop and go for a walk.

'Go on, pet,' she'd said. 'It'll do you good. You've been shut up in the shop for days. You need a bit break. And you can borrow my good cloak. It's cold out there.'

Alice's cloak was old fashioned, but it was good quality and heavy enough not to flap about in the freshening breeze. As Kate walked along the cliff-top path she was pleased to be able to pull the velvet-lined hood up over her head. She'd decided to walk along to the Long Sands at Tynemouth, the lovely stretch of fine pale sand where it was said the Vikings had beached their long boats when they came to rob the monks at the priory of their treasures.

Once down on the beach she was less exposed and she let the hood fall back as she walked along the shoreline. The sky was darkening and there was a scatter of early stars and a pale disc of a moon rising over the sea and sending a silvery path across the gently lapping waves right to the shore. If only I could step out on to that path, Kate mused. Where would it take me?

Kate remembered a poem that Jane had brought home from one of her elocution lessons. They had learned it together. It was a short poem – a sonnet, Kate remembered.

'With how sad steps, O Moon, thou climbst the skies!
How silently and with how wan a face!'

She spoke the first two lines out loud as she looked up at the moon. Was the moon sad? It was a fanciful idea. She knew that poets had written about the moon since time began but she believed it was their own feelings they were describing as they looked up into the night sky.

Kate had thought she was alone on the beach so she was startled to hear a noise behind her. She turned just as a black shape hurtled into her and jumped up excitedly, giving every sign of being pleased to see her.

'Prince,' she said. 'What are you doing here?' Then, 'Down,' she commanded and the dog obediently sat and looked up at her with its head cocked on one side. 'Where's your master?' Kate asked.

Trying to control a surge of hope she looked up in the direction of the cliff path and saw a figure making its way down the moonlit beach towards her. It was not Richard Adamson.

'I'm sorry,' Caroline Travers said, 'did the dog annoy you? Oh, it's you, Miss Lawson.'

'There's no need to apologize. Prince did no harm.'

'Oh, but he has. Look at your cloak.'

Kate looked down and saw that Prince had left a mess of sandy pawprints. 'That's nothing. The sand will brush off easily.'

'Even so you must give it a good shake before you go back inside,' Caroline said. 'You don't want to trail sand into the house, do you?'

Kate wondered why Caroline Travers thought she had the right to speak to her like this. Did she use the same manner with her friends or had she classed Kate as a servant who needed to be told how to behave properly? Kate decided it was the latter.

While they had been speaking, Prince had dashed headlong into the sea.

'Oh, no!' Caroline said. 'Come back, you wicked dog.' She raised her voice. 'Do you hear me, Prince? Come here at once!'

The dog obeyed, but as soon as he had reached their side he began to shake himself vigorously. Kate stepped back and watched as he flung a curving shower of water droplets and wet sand in all directions. Caroline had not been as quick to escape and now her fashionable coat was in a much worse state than Kate's cloak.

'Oh, dear,' she said. 'Now I shall have to follow my own advice.'

For some reason this reaction made Kate like the young woman better. She couldn't help being Caroline Travers, with all that meant, any more than Kate could help being Kate Lawson.

'Come here, beastie,' Caroline said to the dog. She stooped gracefully to attach a lead to his collar. 'I think you have had enough fun for one day. And Mrs Adamson will not thank me for bringing you home in this state. Or rather Joan will not. That's the maid who answers the door,' she explained to Kate. 'I don't think she likes the dog – or at least the mess he makes.'

'Understandable, surely, if she has to clear it up?'

'But that's her job.'

Kate was reminded of the gulf between them. 'Ah, yes,' she said. 'That's her job.'

Perhaps sensing Kate's sudden coolness, Caroline changed the subject. 'And are you quite better now, Miss Lawson?'

'Better?'

'My mother and I have been to London to visit friends and do some shopping. Mrs Adamson told me that, while I was away, Richard found you in a cave – quite soaked through – and brought you home with him and summoned Sam Phillips to attend you. You stayed for nearly four weeks, in fact.'

Was there a hint of accusation in Caroline's tone?

'I would have left much sooner but Dr Phillips insisted I stay.'

'And Richard – Mr Adamson? What did he say?'

'I have no idea. I never saw him – or Mrs Adamson.'

'Ah.'

Did Kate imagine it or had her answer pleased Caroline?

'Well, now, Miss Lawson,' the young woman said. 'I'm glad we met tonight. I feel I know you better.'

Maybe she does feel that, thought Kate, but surely the real cause of her gladness is that she has discovered Richard did not come to see me while I stayed in his house.

'Shall we walk together?' Caroline asked.

'If you like.'

'Good. Let us go as far as those rocks, but as it's getting darker I suggest we walk back along the top where the street lamps are lit.'

Kate was not given the chance to agree or disagree. Caroline set off, seeking the dry sand above the tideline. Kate followed. Why not? she thought. Prince resigned himself to the lead and slouched along with his head down. When Kate glanced at him she chuckled.

'What is it?' Caroline asked.

'Look. Now I understand where the expression "hangdog" comes from.'

Caroline looked at the dog and laughed. 'He does look miserable, doesn't he? When in fact he ought to be happy and grateful.'

'Why is that?'

'His master is working late at the office. I came to keep his mother company. She likes me to visit. We share a passion for literature, you know. That's novels, poems, theatrical dramas—'

'I know what literature means.'

'Do you? Ah, well, in any case I decided to bring Prince out for his evening walk to save Richard from that task. He'll be tired enough when he comes home for his supper.'

It all sounded cosy and domestic. Caroline keeping Mrs Adamson company, reading books together, taking the dog for a walk. And would she be staying to have supper with Richard? Just the two of them, perhaps, by the fire with trays on their laps? A surge of jealousy rose in Kate's throat like bile. She gulped in a breath of cold air in an attempt to quench the bitter taste it left.

'I understand you are no longer posing for Mr Munro?' Caroline changed the subject.

'No. I have no time now that I'm working in the shop but Mr Munro said he would be able to finish the portrait without me.'

'And do you like working in the shop?'

'Yes, I do.'

'I imagine it's a little step up in the world for you.'

'I don't know what you mean?'

'Well, it must be better than selling fish from door to door.'

Kate gripped the edges of the cloak and said nothing. As they walked up the slope at the south end of the beach Kate pulled up her hood. A sensible measure, but it also meant that the other girl could not easily see her expression. She told herself that Caroline had not meant to insult her. It was simply that her upbringing had led her to believe that a young woman who had nothing more demanding to do all day than read books, play the piano maybe, and perhaps take drawing lessons, was in some way superior to a mere fish lass.

Soon they were walking along the cliff-top road back towards the village. The wind was strong enough now to make talking difficult so they lapsed into silence. Kate kept the edges of her hood drawn together with one hand. Caroline was not wearing a hat and Kate, glancing at her, noticed that the wind was busy unravelling her elaborate hairstyle. I wonder if she uses curling tongs, Kate mused.

Then Prince, who had been trailing behind on his lead obediently but morosely, suddenly shot forward, jerking Caroline's arm out in front of her.

'Goodness me!' she gasped and the wind caught her words and tossed them away. 'Prince! Stop this!'

But the dog ignored her. Long before the figure was recognizable, the dog had sensed who it was who was approaching them. Soon Caroline realized who it was too. She let the dog have his way and, keeping tight hold of the lead, she began to run. Kate watched her helter-skelter progress and heard her laughter.

'Richard!' Caroline exclaimed as she collided with Prince's master and fell into his arms.

Richard had seen the two women walking towards him. They appeared in one pool of light from a street lamp, disappeared into dimness for a few steps, then appeared again. Caroline was immediately recognizable because of the dog and he assumed that the other woman in the old-fashioned cloak must be one of the housemaids. He was pleased Caroline had had the sense to ask one of them to accompany her. When his mother had told him she had taken Prince out he was vexed. Normally this was a peaceful and law-abiding community and there would have been no harm in her strolling on the beach, even in the dusky hours of twilight.

But times were not normal now. Not with the men of the village hating him the way they did. And Caroline had been seen at his house – by his side during the demonstration. Did she not realize that she might be a target?

Now he was glad she was safe. She looked up at him, her lovely dark hair blowing wildly round her face. She smelled of fresh sea air with an underlying hint of *Muguet des Bois*, her favourite perfume. Richard experienced the now familiar pang of anguish that he could not feel more for her.

'You were coming to meet me?' Caroline asked.

'To find you. Your father's carriage has arrived to take you home. Look, there it is, turned round and ready to go.' He pointed to where the carriage was waiting with its coach lamps illuminating the road ahead.

'Oh, I see.' She moved away from him.

Richard could tell she was hurt. He had given her the impression that he was keen for her to go. What would it have cost him to say 'Yes, I thought we'd walk together a little'? The carriage would have waited.

'Well, there's your dog,' she said and handed him the lead.

'Let the girl take it,' he said. 'We'll stroll along together.'

'The girl?'

'Yes – the maid. Is it Joan?'

'No. She's not one of your household staff, Richard.' Caroline gave him a strange look. 'Don't you recognize her?'

'No. Should I?'

The other woman had been hanging back, looking down at the ground. Richard had assumed that was because she was a servant who was expected to keep her distance and not eavesdrop on the conversations of her betters. But now he looked at her properly for the first time. She raised her head, and as she did so the hood of her cloak fell back a little. Her gaze was cool.

'Kate,' he said.

'We met on the Long Sands and she was kind enough to walk with me,' Caroline told him. 'We have had a pleasant conversation, haven't we, Miss Lawson?'

For answer Kate inclined her head and then said, 'I must go now.'

'Of course,' Richard said.

He stared at Kate in anguish. What was she thinking? Had she seen the way Caroline had fallen so intimately into his arms? That had not his choice, but how could he explain? All he could do was stand silently while Kate said goodnight to Caroline, who simply nodded. Then she walked on past them. She did not say goodnight to Richard.

Kate knew she had no right to feel so miserable about what had just happened. No right to have been so shocked when she saw Richard take Caroline in his arms. Richard Adamson was going to marry Caroline Travers. Howard had as good as told her so. And it was right that he should. Caroline was beautiful, well educated and, what's more, a lady. She was just the sort of woman that a successful man like Richard deserved. And what am I? Kate thought. I'm a fish lass. Of course he isn't interested in me. And if he were he would lose interest as soon as he discovered that I'm carrying another man's child.

But Kate found herself remembering that moment on the beach. The moment when he had carried her out of the cave, set her down safely and then folded her in his arms. She had never been so moved by a single kiss – not even when Jos had kissed her. She had clung to Richard Adamson, and he to her, as if their very lives depended on it. She felt her body heat rising – was it with shame? – and was glad of the cool air on her face.

But it wasn't just passion that drew her to him. Yes, he was attractive; a fine figure of a man, her mother would say. But there was more. Richard had an inner strength. He had integrity and a keen intelligence that would prove an exciting challenge to any woman. Especially to a woman who loved him.

And what was she to make of the way Caroline had questioned her? It was as if the young woman suspected her of being a rival. Surely not? A woman like that would not suspect such a thing unless . . . unless what? Unless she had sensed that the man she loved was cooling towards her. Women were wise about these things. Was it possible that Caroline had come to the conclusion that Richard's feelings had changed because of his growing interest in Kate herself? No, she could not allow herself to believe that . . .

Kate stopped walking when she realized she had taken a wrong turning. Instead of arriving at the village shop she found herself standing outside Belle Vue Cottage. She stared at the solid, low dwelling that had stood there for centuries, keeping its inhabitants safe and warm. She took in the whitewashed walls, the moonlight shining on the roof and the smoke curling up into the sky from the chimney. How welcoming the cottage looks, she thought, and she stood for a while lost in contemplation of what it would be like to have a home of her own and bring up her child there. But the wind from the sea caught at her cloak as if trying to tug her away. She turned round and made her way to the shop.

When she got there she saw someone standing in the doorway. Some man sent out by his wife to see if there was a loaf of bread left or maybe a slice or two of cooked ham for the supper. But the shop had closed early tonight because Alice had wanted her to go for a walk and get some fresh air. She supposed she could let him in and serve him. It would be a kindness. But as she got closer the man must have heard her footsteps and he turned to face her. It was Richard Adamson.

'Kate! I thought I'd missed you!'

Alice had left the shop light burning low and it shone dimly through the glass in the door and the windows. Richard Adamson's hair was ruffled. He looked as though he'd been running. There was something vulnerable about him that caused Kate's heart to beat faster.

'I've been . . . I've been walking,' she said. 'What are you doing here?'

'I wanted to see you. I didn't like the way we parted just now.'

'The way we parted?'

'Without a word.'

'But where's Miss Travers?'

'Gone home. Her carriage was waiting.'

'So you put her into it and set off after me?'

'Yes.'

Poor Caroline, Kate thought. But she said, 'Just because I didn't say goodnight?'

'I wanted to know why.'

'For goodness' sake!' She allowed herself a flash of temper. 'You were there with your fiancée—'

'She's not . . . I mean I don't—'

'Please don't say any more. I left quietly because there was no point in my staying. I met Miss Travers by chance. I was on the beach and Prince came racing up to me, otherwise she would probably have ignored me. Where is Prince, by the way? Did you send him home with Miss Travers?'

Richard laughed softly. 'No, I didn't. He's there in the doorway – look.' He moved aside so that Kate could see the faithful dog lying across the door and looking up at them with interest. It was as if he knew they were talking about him. Kate couldn't help smiling and the tension that had lain between her and Richard eased a little.

'Kate,' he said softly.

She turned her head to find he was staring at her intently. 'Yes?' she whispered.

'I . . . I want to see more of you.'

'What do you mean?'

'I don't know how to say it. I want to come courting, I suppose. Would you consider spending time with me?'

'No!' Her response was louder than she intended and Prince gave a bark of surprise.

'Why not?' Richard asked.

'*Why not*? I'm the daughter of a fisherman. My family live in a humble cottage. You – well, you live in a big house and you own a fleet of trawlers.'

'My family once lived in one of those cottages, too. My forebears were fishermen just like your family. We're the same kind of people, Kate.'

If only, she thought. If only Richard still lived in that cottage on the cliff top, a fisherman like his forebears. Then it might have been possible. But now . . .

'Maybe we are,' she said. 'But you have moved on. What you are doing now is destroying a way of life. The way of life my family still clings to.'

260

'I can't turn the clock back, Kate. I'm not the only man to own steam trawlers. I've said I'll do all I can to help the men of the village. I can't help it if they won't accept my offer.'

'I know.'

'And, as far as I can see, you are already at odds with your family. You've told me you can't go back. Would it be any worse if you married me?'

'Married!' Kate couldn't believe her ears. The man she'd thought could never be hers wanted to marry her.

'Of course. What else did you think I meant? I want you to be my wife. I think far too highly of you to make you my mistress.'

'You shouldn't!'

'Shouldn't what?'

'Think highly of me.'

'Why ever not?'

'Because I'm not what you think I am.'

Richard smiled. 'And what do I think you are?'

She stared at him, unable to answer.

'I'll tell you what I think. You're beautiful, clever, courageous – perhaps a little quick-tempered but that's because you're a woman of spirit. And I adore what you are. I'm not a fool. I know there will be difficulties but we're both strong enough to overcome them, aren't we?'

'Yes. I mean no . . . I *can't* marry you.'

'Of course you can.' Richard took hold of her shoulders. He pulled her close.

'No . . . please don't . . .'

Kate closed her eyes as his face came nearer. She ought to have stepped back, turned her head, but she did not have the will. His kiss was gentle, questioning, persuasive. But as soon as he sensed her response the kiss became more passionate. Her cloak fell open as she raised her hands to grasp his shoulders. He slipped his own arms inside the cloak so that he could hold her even closer. She gave herself completely to the pleasure of the moment. Then the spell was broken by the jangling of the shop bell followed by a yelp of pain from Prince.

They sprang apart. The shop door had opened and someone had stepped out and trodden on the dog.

'Stupid beast!' an angry female voice exclaimed. It was Susan Armstrong.

'Here, boy,' Richard said and Prince limped forward. Richard crouched down to soothe his pet. 'There, there,' he said, as if to a child. 'No bones broken, I think.'

'Mebbes the dog is all right but I nearly came a cropper. What a shock I got!' Susan said angrily.

Richard straightened up. 'I'm very sorry, Mrs Armstrong,' he said. 'My fault entirely; not the dog's.'

Susan stepped out of the doorway. The light from the nearest street lamp revealed her cross face. But there was something else in her eyes, Kate thought. Prurient speculation. She saw the way the woman was looking at Richard and then at her. What had she seen? Kate's heart was still pounding with the fright she'd received but she thought that she and Richard had reacted quickly enough to the sound of the bell. That blessed bell.

'And what was the animal doing in the shop doorway in the first place?' Susan asked. '*And*, if I might ask, what are you doing here, Mr Adamson?'

'I wanted to see that Miss Lawson had got home safely,' he said.

Kate supposed that wasn't an outright lie.

'Why should you do that?' Susan asked.

'Miss Lawson has been for a walk with my friend Miss Travers.'

'Miss Travers was out walking at this time of night?'

'She was exercising my dog. The two young women met on the beach and they may have stayed out longer than they intended. As I said, I just wanted to make sure Miss Lawson—'

'Got home safely. I heard you the first time.' Susan paused abruptly as if she had just remembered that she ought to be polite to the gentleman who had found a job for her husband. 'Well,' she said, and her tone was less combative. 'She's here and you can see that she's safe, so, if you don't mind, Mr Adamson, she'd better get inside and see if my mother needs her help with anything.'

'Of course. Goodnight, Miss Lawson.'

'Goodnight, Mr Adamson,' Kate said equally decorously. We have become play actors, she thought, all for the sake of propriety and Susan Armstrong.

'Oh – Miss Lawson?' Richard said as she was about to enter the shop.

She turned to face him. 'Yes?'

'Will you think about what I said? Will you consider it?'

'No, Mr Adamson. It's quite impossible.'

She glanced at Susan and saw the woman's frown as she no doubt tried to make sense of what had been said. Let her make of it what she will, Kate thought, and she entered the shop and closed the door before Richard could speak further.

Kate had lain awake so long that the stone water bottle had lost its heat. She could have risen and boiled a kettle on the fire but she hadn't the will. Her limbs were cold but that was nothing to the ache of regret and longing that had taken over her heart.

She had shed no tears. There was no point in crying for the moon. That's what her great-grandmother used to tell her when she was a little girl and wanted something she couldn't have.

And she couldn't have Richard Adamson – there was no question of that. But no one would ever know what it had cost her to turn him away.

Chapter Twenty

When Kate went down to the stockroom for her breakfast the next morning she found Alice sitting on one of the upturned boxes next to the tea chest they used for a table. The shopkeeper had her head in her hands and was weeping without making any sound. Only her shoulders, moving up and down convulsively, revealed her distress.

'Alice . . . what is it? Is Mr Willis . . . has he . . .'

The older woman raised her head. Her face was streaked with tears, her expression bleak. 'No, pet. Charlie is still with us, it's just that very soon I'm going to have to say goodbye to him and I don't know how. We've never been apart since the day we married. I really love the man, you know.'

'I know you do. And he loves you.'

'That's part of what's grieving me. I know it's selfish but I can't help thinking that there'll be nobody who cares so much for me when Charlie is gone.'

'But you have Susan and your grandchildren,' Kate said.

'Aye, that's a blessing, but they have their own life, don't they? Oh, I know Susan will look after me. She's a good daughter – and I'm sure she loves me. But that's not the same as the love of your own man, is it?'

'No, I suppose not.'

'There's no suppose about it, Kate. Take my word for it. You've had a hard knock losing Jos, but a bonny lass like you will find another man one day, I'm sure of it. And if you're lucky enough to get a good man and be happily married like I've been, you'll know what price you have to pay.'

'Price?'

'Aye. The price for such happiness is that one day one of you will be left alone in this vale of tears.' Alice lifted the edge of her pinafore and wiped her eyes. She smiled sadly. 'But hark at me, talking like the parson. Now sit down and have your breakfast before that porridge gets cold.'

Kate took her place on one of the boxes and poured them both a cup of tea. They had got into the habit of taking breakfast together in the stockroom and, although Alice never ate much more than a slice of toast, she always made sure that there was something more substantial for Kate. This morning was no exception. There was a bowl of porridge waiting for her, still gently steaming, a rack of buttered toast and a jar of honey.

Alice sipped her tea and kept quiet while Kate ate her porridge, but when Kate put the bowl aside and reached for a piece of toast she said, 'I'm glad you're here, lass. And I don't just mean because of the shop; it's good for me to have someone to talk to like this. I'm very grateful.'

'I'm the one who should be grateful,' Kate said. 'You've taken me in, given me a job.'

'Well, we're both lucky beggars, then, aren't we?' Alice said as she rose from the table. 'Now I'll clear the pots and you'd best get the shop open – in fact I can hear someone knocking, can't you? Some improvident soul who hasn't kept a bit bread back for breakfast and will want a loaf before it's even been delivered from the baker, no doubt. Some folk never learn.'

'Or it might be the baker's delivery man,' Kate said. 'I think we've sat here longer than usual.'

But it wasn't the delivery man. It was Susan who was knocking impatiently on the shop door. When Kate let her in she scowled and pushed her aside as she hurried in.

'About time,' she said. 'Lazing in bed no doubt after your shenanigans last night.'

'Shenanigans?'

'Your walk with Mr Adamson.'

'It was Miss Travers I was walking with.'

'So Mr Adamson said.'

'Are you saying that you don't believe him?' Kate's gaze was cool but challenging.

Susan backed down. 'I'm not going to stand here arguing with a shop assistant,' she said. 'Especially not when you've opened late. My poor mother—'

'What about your poor mother?' Alice had come through to the shop and she stood at the other side of the counter looking at her daughter questioningly.

265

'I was just reprimanding Kate for opening up late. I was about to say that my mother depended on her and she should not take advantage of you.'

Alice shook her head. 'You've got it all wrong, pet. It's good of you to worry about me but it was my fault that we opened late today. We lingered over breakfast because I needed a bit company. In fact Kate is a great comfort to me. I don't know how I would manage without her.'

Susan was stung. 'Then I'll just turn round and go home, shall I? You obviously don't need your own daughter.'

'Don't talk like that. Of course I need you. My heart's glad at the very sight of you. Now come on through and see your dad. He's just woken up. Come and gladden his eyes, too.'

Mollified, Susan followed her mother through into the back room. But a moment later she returned and thrust an envelope into Kate's hand. 'This letter came to the cottage,' she said. 'It's addressed to your Aunt Meg so I suppose you'd better have it. It's got a foreign stamp on. Seth says it's from Canada.'

The letter had remained in the pocket of Kate's pinafore all day. Only now, when she was sitting by the fire in her own room, did she open it. Her mother was with her. Somehow the news had spread amongst the women of the village that a letter with a foreign stamp had been delivered to Belle Vue Cottage and Susan Armstrong had taken it round to the shop for Kate.

'Just as well Susan didn't bring it to me,' Nan said. 'She could have done. Your da might have been there and I dread to think what would have happened if he had opened it.' Nan stood by the fire where a kettle was coming up to the boil on a small hob. The glow from the fire illuminated her kindly features.

Kate was resting her feet on the plump cushion she used as a footstool. Her ankles had swollen and she had taken off her shoes. The letter, still unopened, was in her hands. It must be a long letter because the envelope was fat. She turned it over and over restlessly.

'Well, why don't you open it?'

'I will. As soon as you've made that tea. I'm parched, Ma. I need a drink before I read it to you.'

Nan carried the kettle over to the small table near the window where there was a tray containing everything Kate needed to make a cup of tea. At the end of each day in the shop Alice would have a meal with Kate in the stockroom and then send her up to her room with this tray,

266

and there would always be a little treat or two on it. Today it was a big slab of rich, sweet gingerbread. Nan picked up a knife in order to cut it into slices.

'You can eat most of that, Ma, or take it home and share it with my brothers. I don't want any.'

Her mother looked surprised. 'But you've always liked gingerbread.'

'I know. But at the moment it gives me heartburn.'

'Pity,' her mother said. 'That's to be expected, I suppose. But otherwise you're all right, aren't you?'

'Yes. Apart from my back, which feels as if it's breaking – and look at these ankles. Lovely, aren't they?' Kate lifted her feet from the cushion and pulled her skirt up sufficiently to show her mother how swollen they were. 'Oh, Ma, I just hate being like this!'

'There, there, me bairn.' Her mother spoke to her as if she were a little lass again. She took a small cushion from her own chair. 'Here, put this cushion in the small of your back and settle yourself and drink this tea. And then, for goodness' sake open that darned letter and read it to me!'

When they were both drinking their second cups of tea, Kate did as her mother requested.

'It's addressed to Aunt Meg,' was the first thing she said.

'Well, it would be, wouldn't it?' Her mother shook her head. 'Poor Winifred, she doesn't know about the accident yet. We'll have to write and tell her.'

'She's hardly kept in touch with her family of late, has she?'

'There'll be a reason. You'll see.'

And Kate found that her mother was right when she began to read the letter.

'Dear Meg,

'You'll be wondering why I've taken so long to reply to your letter. Well, let me tell you that it's something of a miracle that I even received it. It must have travelled thousands of miles chasing after me, and all I can say is God bless all the folk who took the bother to forward it.

'Herbert and I have left America, you see. His shoe factory, which had been doing very well, began to fail. Progress and cheap labour meant that cheaper footwear could be made in the south. Well, anyway, Herbert decided that he must sell up before the situation became hopeless, take what money he could get together

267

and start elsewhere. Oh, how I wept when I realized that we must sell our beautiful home as well as the factory. But needs must. I'd married the man for better or for worse and now I had to prove I meant it.'

'Winifred always was a loyal little thing,' Kate's mother interrupted. 'If you made a friend of her you knew it would be for life. But please go on, pet.'

So Kate continued:

'Have you any idea how big this continent is, Meg? We travelled thousands of miles from the east coast to the west coast. We stopped many times along the way because Herbert had to establish addresses for various business papers to catch up with him. Thank God he did, or otherwise I wouldn't have received your letter! Each time we stopped, Herbert would investigate whether there was any local enterprise that might be worth investing in. After all, America is the land of opportunity. But, you know, I believe he knew all along where we would end up and why.

'Go along to the Fishermen's Mission, Meg, and look at the maps they keep there. Look for Canada and on the far west coast look for a region called British Columbia. Then look for the Fraser River. Because that's where we are, in a little town called Steveston. It might not be on the map. And it looks like this is where we'll be staying because, at last, Herbert has established a new business.

'We are the proud owners of a cannery. We process and can salmon. We are a small concern as yet; there are many well-established canneries here, but the sea is full of the redfish and Herbert says there's room for us. He is determined to make a success of the venture.

'Just think about this, Meg. I ran away from a fishing village and I have ended up in another one at the other side of the world. Fishermen are the same the world over. They take their living from the sea. And it's a hard life. Men can perish at sea here just as they do at home. But here there is such progress, such wealth to be made. It truly is a new world.

'A world fit for my great-niece or nephew to be born into. For, of course, Kate can come and live with me.'

'There now,' Nan said. 'I knew Winifred wouldn't let us down.'
Kate managed a smile before continuing.

'Tell Nan that I would be proud and happy to give a home to her daughter. Kate would be such good company for me. Herbert is a dear, dear man, but he is not from home. He was born in America, as were his parents before him, and although we speak the same language, I'm sure that at times we appear "foreign" to each other. How marvellous it will be to have Kate to sit and talk to of an evening. For me to ask about people I once knew and the sights and sounds of my beloved Cullercoats.

'But now I must ask a question. How far gone is the lass? This is important, for it will be a long and gruelling journey, whichever way she decides to come. If she chooses to come by sea all the way it means sailing round Cape Horn, and that could take fifteen weeks, maybe longer depending on the winds and the weather.'

'Fifteen weeks!' Nan said. 'But that means—'
'Whisht, Ma. Let me finish.'

'She could make for a port on the eastern seaboard, of course, and continue the journey by train and then coach. This will be very tiring and the winter weather will become bleak as the journey continues. I would very much like Kate to be here with me for the birth of her child, but if she feels she ought to break her journey she can stay with a very good friend of mine in New York. Sarah Rubinowitz owns the lodging house for young women where I stayed when I was working in Herbert's factory. It's clean and respectable and Sarah would take great care of Kate if I wrote and asked her to.

'Obviously resuming the journey with an infant would bring its own problems, so I would tell Sarah to find a trustworthy young woman who would like to make a life for herself in Canada, and I will pay her to accompany Kate and the little one. But, Meg, wouldn't it be even better if you would come too? Please, please think about it. You wouldn't have to work, but you could if you wanted to. Not selling fish from door to door but helping me to look after the young women who work in the cannery.

'The other papers I've enclosed are self-explanatory. One is a letter to a business contact of Herbert's in a shipping office on the quayside in Newcastle. It is a request to help Kate make the necessary travel arrangements. The other is a money order which Kate must present at the bank named, also in Newcastle. I have sent sufficient funds for both of you to come if you wish. And who knows, although two of you set out, it may be three who arrive!

'Give my love to Nan and to Kate.

'Love,

'Winifred.'

'Fifteen weeks or more!' her mother said as Kate put the letter and the two documents back in the envelope. 'And this is November,' Nan continued. 'When is the bairn due?'

'I'm not sure exactly, but it should be some time in April.'

'Fifteen weeks? That's nearly four months, isn't it?'

'Yes.'

Her mother counted up the months on her fingers. Then she looked up aghast. 'That's cutting it fine, even if you were to set off tomorrow. If the bairn comes early, as it very well could with all the travelling, the poor little 'un could be born at sea.' Nan shook her head. 'No, our Kate, you'll have to go the other way,' she said. 'And it's best if you set off as soon as possible. That way you might get to Winifred's before it's too late to travel on.'

'I can't.'

'You mean you can't go? Kate, you haven't changed your mind, have you?' Without waiting for an answer her mother hurried on, 'Your Aunt Winifred is offering you a home – a new life – a wonderful life by the sounds of it. You'll be able to bring up your bairn in a fine new country. There'll be work a-plenty – not like here.'

'I didn't mean I'd changed my mind about going.' Kate dropped her head, unwilling to meet her mother's eyes lest Nan saw the uncertainty in her own and realized that she had never been totally convinced that she should go. 'No, I didn't mean that,' she said. 'It's just that I can't go yet. Not until Mr Willis . . . this is difficult to say, but you know what I mean.'

'Until Charlie dies?'

'That's right.'

'I don't see what that's got to do with it.'

'Alice depends on me.'

270

'Maybe she does. But it would be easy enough to find someone else to work in the shop.'

'But not someone she's got used to – someone who's grown close. And apart from the shop, Alice likes to talk to me now and then. Whenever she feels low.'

'But she's got her own daughter.'

'I know. But I don't think Alice wants to burden her. After all, Susan must be sorrowing too, mustn't she? Can't you see, it would be cruel of me to leave Alice now, when Mr Willis is so very ill.'

Her mother sighed. 'Kate, you've got to think of yourself.' She sounded exasperated. 'Will you at least start making arrangements? The bairn won't wait to be born just to suit you, and you have a duty to Jos's child as well, you know. You've got to do your best for it.'

'Even if it means going to the other side of the world?'

'Do you think I want to lose you? Of course I don't. You're my daughter, my only daughter, and I wouldn't urge you to go unless I believed it was the best thing for you – and my grandbairn.'

'All right, Ma. I'll write to my Aunt Winifred. But I'll have to think about what I'm going to say.'

'And you'll start making arrangements?'

'As soon as I can. And please don't ask me when that will be.'

Nan insisted on seeing her into bed and as Kate slipped into her nightgown she felt the now familiar movements of her growing child. She stood very still.

'Is it the bairn?' her mother asked.

Kate nodded. She reached for her mother's hand and placed it with hers on her belly. They stood still while the child moved inside her and when they looked at each other their eyes were moist.

'I wonder if I'll ever see my grandbairn,' her mother said.

Kate was too full of tears to answer her.

The next day was Sunday and, with the shop closed, Kate borrowed Alice's cloak again and walked to the ancient graveyard on the headland. Betsy had wanted to come with her but Alice, perhaps understanding Kate's need to be alone, had found a job for the girl. She'd asked her to tidy the display in one of the windows, and when Kate left the shop Betsy was happily occupied with a supply of dummy tins and some brightly coloured display cards.

The air was cold but the sky was bright and there were quite a few people about. From the looks of them, in their carefully pressed Sunday

271

best clothes, some had come on the train from Newcastle to enjoy the sea air.

The ruined priory always drew visitors and often you would see them wandering about among the gravestones marvelling at the carved sailing ships and the names of the sea captains who had sailed the seven seas before coming to rest in this last harbour. Or they would pause and be saddened by a headstone listing a whole family of fishermen lost in one storm.

Kate was grateful that the wind was just sharp enough to keep folk away from the exposed graveyard today, and she made her way to Jos's grave without seeing anyone at all. It was the first time she had been since the headstone had been erected and now she stared at the carved letters recording the birth and death of her childhood sweetheart and wondered if this was all a man's life amounted to.

Jos was the first of his family to be buried here. His ancestors were buried far away on a hillside near the village of Burnmoor in the Cheviot Hills.

And I have to decide whether I should take your child even further away, she told Jos silently. If I stay here, people like my father, who did not welcome your family to the village, will not welcome your child either. If I go, the child and I will become interlopers, too, but in a land that has taken in many strangers and put them to work. That's why I'm here today, Jos: so that your child can visit your grave at least this once before we say our last goodbye. Otherwise I don't know if I would have had the courage to face you. And I want you to forgive me. I have fallen in love with the man you swore to repay for taking your livelihood. And yet in a way you have got your revenge. Richard Adamson cannot be with the woman he loves. How could you have known that woman would be me?

'Isn't that Kate?' Howard asked. 'Look, over there in the graveyard.'

Richard turned to look. The woman had her back to them. She was wearing a long cloak but the hood was down and the bright blaze of hair was unmistakable. 'Yes, I think it is.'

Howard had brought his sketch pad and was sitting at his easel on some sort of folding contraption while he sketched part of the ruins. He had chosen what he called a romantic-looking arch which soared above a tumble of ancient stones that resembled a giant's building blocks. 'Not my usual style,' he'd told Richard. 'A touch too Gothic, but my mother has asked me to do something dramatic for her. When I begin

272

the work proper, I shall add a night sky, a storm-tossed moon and a bat or two.'

Richard never knew whether his cousin was joking or not, but he acknowledged that Howard was a gifted artist and had even succumbed to his pleas to sit for him – or rather his mother had insisted. And today, again at his mother's request, he had accompanied Howard on his sketching expedition in order to make sure that he packed up his drawing equipment in time to go home with him for Sunday lunch.

'I suppose she is visiting her sweetheart's grave,' Howard said. 'That may be the reason she turned me down.'

'What are you talking about?'

'I told you. I asked her to marry me. I said I wanted to take her to America but she didn't seem keen on the idea. I should have realized it's too soon. She will still be mourning her fisherman sweetheart. Ah, me!' he said in the manner of an actor in a play.

Richard was taken aback by his cousin's casual tone. But perhaps he was deliberately trying to make light of it. Perhaps he truly loved Kate and his pride had been hurt by her refusal.

'We'd better leave her alone with her thoughts, don't you think? Best not to disturb her,' Howard said.

Richard had to agree, so while Howard concentrated on his drawing Richard tried very hard not to stare at the lone figure by the new headstone. He did not want her to be distressed in any way if she should turn round and see him watching her.

While he waited, shifting his weight from foot to foot on the cold slabs of stone, he thought about what Howard had just said, and cursed himself for causing her pain. Of course Kate was still grieving for her sweetheart. How could he have been so insensitive? He remembered with horror how he had kissed her on the beach the night he had found her in the cave. I am a monster, he thought. I imagined she shared my feelings because she responded to my kiss but now I realize that in her confusion and desolation she might even have mistaken me for the ghost of her drowned fisherman.

And yet what about the other night outside the village shop? Had he imagined her warm response simply because he desired her so much? Surely there was something there . . . surely she felt something that could grow into love if he gave her time. That's what he must do. He must give her time to grieve properly. He would have to be patient.

He allowed himself a glance in Kate's direction and saw that she had gone. He turned quickly and caught sight of her cloaked figure hurrying towards the substantial ruins of the fortified gatehouse that guarded the entrance to the priory. In spite of the decision he had just made it took all his self-control not to go after her.

Kate hurried back along the cliff road. She had seen Howard and Richard in the ruins but they had not been looking her way. She didn't think they had seen her. Why did he have to be there? she thought. Why today when I had come to say goodbye to Jos? Is this some sort of punishment? Someone had once told her that the dead faded from your life as the years went by. But what about the living? She wondered how many years and how much distance between them it would take before Richard Adamson faded from her memory and from her heart.

Chapter Twenty-one

Alice wasn't in the stockroom. There was a tablecloth on the upturned tea chest but that was all. Kate wondered if Charlie had had a bad night, leaving Alice exhausted. She went through to the door that led to the back room and stood there hesitantly. She wanted to see if Alice was all right but she didn't want to intrude. She raised her hand to knock on the door but then dropped it again. If Mr Willis was asleep she didn't want to wake him up.

Eventually she took hold of the door handle and turned it quietly, opening the door just an inch or two. She peered inside but couldn't see through the gloom. The curtains were still closed. 'Alice?' she whispered, but there was no reply. Kate wondered whether she should close the door again and simply open the shop. Alice would awaken sooner or later. But as she stood there and her eyes adjusted to the dim light she became uneasy.

A faint red glow from the fireplace told Kate that the fire was still burning – but only just – and the room seemed cold. She felt the hairs on the back of her neck rise. Something was wrong. Kate pushed the door open a little further and went in. She gagged a little at the sour-sweet smell. The smell of a sickroom, she supposed, of sweat and urine, of desperation and fear.

She had never been in this room before. Before the premises became a shop this had been a dining room. When Charlie became bedridden Alice had some of the heavy old furniture taken out and had his bed brought down. There was still room for a table, a few chairs and a large chest of drawers, and by the fireplace there was a big old wing-backed chair and a footstool.

When Kate looked at the chair she realized that it had been serving Alice as a bed. There was a pillow and an eiderdown but they had been pushed aside. Mrs Willis was not there. Kate held her breath as she crossed the room towards the bed. Alice was on top of the bedclothes, fully clothed, sitting up amongst a heap of pillows. She was cradling her husband in her arms. Her mouth was open and her breathing stertorous. She had taken the pins out of her grey-brown hair and it fell down on to her shoulders like the hair of a young girl. But her face was old and lined with worry.

In contrast Charlie's face looked peaceful and unlined. His eyes were open as he stared up at the ceiling. 'I'm sorry, I shouldn't have come in,' Kate said quietly, but he didn't shift his gaze to look at her. And then she realized that the eyes were unseeing. Charlie was dead. He had died in his wife's arms.

As Kate stared at them, wondering what to do, Alice stirred. She opened her eyes and, seeing Kate, she smiled sadly and eased her arms out from under the body of her husband. As she did so she whispered an endearment to him and apologized for disturbing him.

Kate was appalled. 'Alice . . . he can't hear you . . . he's . . .'

'It's all right, pet, I know,' Alice said. 'It's habit, I suppose. Now, will you go and get Susan for me?'

'Of course.'

'And, Kate, I know there's no love lost between you and my daughter, and I'm not blaming you, but you'll break it gently to her, won't you? She loves her da.'

Kate bent down swiftly and kissed Alice's brow. 'I know she does and I'll do anything to help you and her. You only have to ask.'

But Susan didn't want Kate's help. When she opened the door of Belle Vue Cottage she regarded Kate with open hostility. 'What is it?' she asked. And although it was a cold morning with frost coating the cobblestones, she did not ask her to enter.

'Susan – your mother needs you to come to her. It's your father. He . . . he died during the night.'

Susan Armstrong clutched at her neck and her eyes filled with tears. She didn't speak.

'What is it, Susan?' Seth appeared by her side.

Susan was shaking her head and making keening sounds.

'It's her father,' Kate said.

'Charlie's left us?'

'Yes. I'm so sorry.'

'Listen, pet, put your warm coat on and go straight to your ma,' her husband told her.

'What about the bairns?' she managed through gulping sobs.

'Don't worry about the bairns. I'll mind them.'

'What about work?'

'I'll take the day off.'

'No – that wouldn't be right – not when you've just started.'

'I'll look after the children,' Kate said. 'I'd be happy to.'

Susan stopped crying abruptly. 'No you won't. You'll get back to the shop. That's your job.'

'The shop? But I thought your mother wouldn't want to open today.'

'Well, you thought wrong. And whatever Ma might say, I'm telling you to open it. Seth, you must go to work. But first of all, go along to the Donkins' cottage and ask young Ellen to come along and look after the bairns. Now you,' she turned back to Kate, 'go back and tell my mother that I'll be there as soon as possible.'

Kate opened up the shop as Susan had told her to do. Alice, her hair now neatly pinned in its usual bun, came through to see what she was doing. She looked shocked. But before she could say anything Susan arrived. She must have seen the expression on her mother's face because she said, 'It's all right, Mother. I told Kate we should open as usual. We can't let folk down, you know.'

Weak with grief and exhaustion, Alice tried to convince her daughter that the shop ought to close as a mark of respect for Charlie.

'All right. We'll close at midday. That way folk will be able to get what they need,' Susan said.

Kate marvelled that although Susan appeared to be genuinely grief-stricken, she could still care about such matters. And she had noted the use of the word 'we'. Having watched this small exchange Kate envisaged many battles of will ahead between mother and daughter.

That night the walk home from Tynemouth station took William past the Long Sands. He'd just returned from Jesmond and an evening out with Jane. He was dressed in his best, as Jane always insisted when they went into town, and tonight they had been to Alvini's in the Haymarket. That is, they had been to the coffee shop on the ground floor, not to the high-class restaurant above.

Jane had ordered hot chocolate for herself, coffee for William and a selection of pastries. And although she had given the outward appearance of enjoying herself, William could tell from the nervous way she fiddled with the long-handled teaspoon that she was hiding her anxiety.

'Isn't this grand?' she said as she glanced round at the other smartly dressed customers. 'You know, William, once we live in town, we'll be able to do this more often. And even go to the Palace Theatre next door.'

William had never been to the theatre in his life but Jane had accompanied Mrs Coulson and her daughter now and then. The theatre and the department stores. To Jane these provided a very good reason for wanting to live in town and William, looking at the way her eyes were shining as she tried to share her enthusiasms with him, didn't want to deny her anything.

But eventually she fell silent. She picked up the teaspoon again and chased the froth around the bottom of the tall glass. When she'd popped it in her mouth she left a bubble or two of froth on her upper lip. William was entranced. He would have liked to lean across and take the froth from her lip with the tip of his tongue. He smiled as he imagined the shocked reaction of the respectable folk around them if he gave way to his impulse. But how were they to know that the big, strong, intelligent lad William knew himself to be could be vanquished in an instant by the flash of a particular pair of blue eyes?

'I'll be opening my shop before Christmas,' Jane said eventually. 'In time to make and alter party frocks. I've ordered some lovely new fabrics and style patterns of the latest fashion. But listen, William, I have to ask you. Mr Rennison . . . Mr Rennison wants to know . . .'

'Tell him I'll take the job,' William said.

At first it seemed as though she hadn't understood. She stared at him for a moment and then tears had gathered in her eyes. They were tears of joy. 'Now we can get married,' she'd said.

All the way back on the tram to the Coulsons' house in Jesmond she had talked of their happy future and all her wonderful plans, and William had smiled and squeezed her hand, but if the truth were known he had already been wondering if he had done the right thing.

Now, walking home alone, his doubts tormented him. When he was with Jane, everything was simple. He loved her, he wanted to marry her, and her belief in him convinced him that he could 'move up in the world' as Jane put it. When he was on his own, the worry returned.

He stopped for a moment and gazed out over the sea towards Bate's Island at the north end of Whitley. For generations, perhaps since the beginning of time, his family had been fisherfolk, and now Jane wanted to take him away from this life. Jane wasn't just beautiful: she was clever, cleverer than he was perhaps, and he trusted her judgement. She had told him that the days of the inshore fishermen were numbered.

278

The likes of Richard Adamson and his steam trawlers were the future. In his heart William knew she was right.

But could he live in the town with all its grime and the chimneys belching smoke? He would miss the tang of the sea and he would miss sitting at the tiller of the *Rock of Ages* as he crossed the harbour bar at first light on a fine summer morning, a friendly breeze filling the lugsail and a good day's fishing in prospect. But how long had it been since there had been a fine day's fishing?

He looked down at the moonlit harbour and the beached cobles. What would happen to his father and his brother when he left home? George Lisle could crew for them but he was getting on in years and not so able as he used to be. Thomas was popular with the younger lads and William supposed he would easily find a pal to make up the crew. One or two of the families had already sold their cobles and were looking for employment. But would Thomas be able to cope with Da? William sighed. He would have to. And, quick-tempered though Thomas was, there was nothing wrong with his judgement when they reached the fishing grounds.

The night was unusually still. A stillness that might cause a visitor to think that it was safe to put out to sea. But it was the sort of stillness that would make a fisherman wary. Nothing moved. There wasn't even a hint of a breeze. Weather like this was treacherous. It could change in an instant.

Moonlight reflected from a glassy sea that was dead flat, without so much as a ripple disturbing the shoreline. William stood very still and listened. His ears tingled with the cold. After a few seconds he heard it: a muffled wailing sound. It came from beyond the horizon, which was hidden by a low, dark sky. There could be no mistake; the sea was calling. He turned and walked away.

Light from the windows of the big houses along Beverley Terrace came into view although much of the village beyond was in darkness. The fisherfolk did not keep late hours unnecessarily. When their work was done they went to bed to save lamp oil.

At this late hour most of the activity in the village was centred round the public houses. No doubt his father would be in one of them along with Thomas and his pals. Not many of the older men would tolerate Henry Lawson these days, and if it weren't for his sons there would be no one for him to have a drink with.

William quickened his pace. He would soon be home and his mother would be waiting for him. She never settled until her boys came home.

If she was alone – for the presence of old Sarah hardly counted – he would take the chance to tell her of his decision. He knew she would be glad for him.

William turned the corner into Back Row and tripped over a figure lying on the ground. He fell headlong, instinctively thrusting his arms out to break his fall. He rolled over on the frosty cobbles, then sat up, more shaken by the shock than the fall itself. His hands were stinging and his shoulder throbbed with pain; he'd hit it on the wall of the end cottage as he'd fallen. It was dark in the lane and William could just make out the shape of the figure he'd tripped over lying slumped against the wall with its legs stretched out into the path.

William began to get to his feet and as he did so the figure on the ground moaned then fell over sideways and vomited. The overpowering stench of stale beer reached William's nostrils. So at least he hadn't fallen over a dead body; whoever it was who lay there retching his guts out was alive.

He squatted down and waited until a last great heave seemed to be the end of it, then reached forward and took hold of the man's shoulders. He pulled him up into a sitting position and eased him back so that he was supported by the wall again.

'What the hell . . . leave me alone . . .' As the man spoke he swung an arm in William's direction.

William recoiled, not so much at the sudden coming to life of the drunken man, nor to avoid the flailing arm, but because the slurred angry voice was that of his father.

'Da, for God's sake! Let's get you home.' William hooked both his arms under his father's armpits and hauled him to his feet, holding him upright.

'Who is it?' Henry said, lifting his head and then letting it slump back on to his chest. 'Is it Thomas?' he mumbled. 'I thought you were gone . . .'

'It's William, Da.'

'William? Where did you spring from?'

'Never mind. I'm here and I'm going to take you home. But where's Thomas?'

'Don't you worry about Thomas.' He tapped the side of his nose. 'He'll manage all right.'

William was used to seeing his father drunk and this wasn't the first time he'd passed out in the street. But it was a cold November night and the lane was dark. If Henry had lain there undiscovered he might have died. And where was his brother? What did his da mean, that Thomas would manage all right? He didn't suppose he'd get sensible answers with his father in this state. He'd better get him home.

'Come on, Da, put your arm over my shoulder.'

Henry did as he was told.

'Hang on.'

William hitched his father up against his hip and with his arm round his waist half walked, half dragged him along Back Row towards the cottage. By the time they reached home Henry had passed out again and had become a dead weight. His head lolled against his son's shoulder. He had lost his cap. No doubt it would be lying in the gutter. Well, it could stay there until morning, William thought. Congealed vomit matted Henry's hair and clung to the side of his face. Some of it had transferred itself to William's neck and shoulder and the stench almost made him sick.

He wedged his father into the corner of the doorway and leaned against him to prevent him from falling while he reached for the sneck and pushed the door open. His mother was sitting by the fire with knitting in her lap. She looked up and William could hardly bear to see the anguish in her face.

'Dear God,' she said. 'Where did you find him?'

'Don't fret, Ma. He wasn't far from home. I don't think any of the neighbours would have seen him.'

'Where's Thomas?'

'I don't know.'

'Well, bring him in. You can't stand there all night. Sit him over here.' She nodded to Henry's usual fireside chair. 'He'll need to be washed.' Nan looked resigned to the task. She'd done it many times before.

While William steered his father towards the chair his mother wrapped up her knitting in a clean linen cloth. It wasn't the usual sort of knitting, William noticed. It wasn't a fisherman's gansey or even a pair of socks. The wool was white and fine. His mother was knitting something for a baby. One of the neighbour women must be expecting. His ma liked to do good turns like that.

By the time he'd got Henry into the chair the knitting had vanished. Put away in a drawer no doubt to keep it clean. His mother had gone into the scullery. William looked round the room. His great-grandmother was asleep, as usual.

His mother came back with a flannel and an enamel bowl of water.

She put the latter on the table and added a little hot water from the kettle.

'Hold on to him, son, while I wash this muck off,' she said.

'I will, but first . . .' William took the flannel and dipped it in the bowl, then wiped his neck. He took off his jacket – his good one – and said, 'I'll sponge this down later.'

He held his father by the shoulders and had to keep pulling him up to prevent him from slipping off the chair while his ma began to take off his gansey. 'Lift his arms up,' she requested. William did so one after the other and his mother let the jumper drop to the floor. 'I'm ashamed of Thomas that he could let his da get in such a state,' she said.

'That's not fair, Ma. You know as well as I do that nothing Thomas could do or say would stop him.'

'You're right. But why didn't he at least see him home safely? They set off together so they should have come home together. And where do you think Thomas has gone? The pubs will surely be closed by now.'

William looked at the clock on the mantelshelf. 'They'll be calling time soon.'

'Do you think he's gone to Matthew's house?' Nan asked as she dipped the flannel in the water and then wrung it out.

William shook his head. 'No, I don't. None of the lads go there these days. Mrs Linton hasn't welcomed any of Matthew's friends since Jos drowned. Mebbes he's gone to Jack Chisholm's. He's been pretty pally with Thomas and Matthew lately.'

'Well, if he has, I just hope Jack's mother puts them out before much longer. I want a word with that young man before I go to bed.'

'And so do I,' William said. He was worried and he didn't quite know why. Since he had begun courting Jane he and Thomas often went their separate ways but they usually told each other where they were going, in case their ma asked. It bothered him that he had no idea where his younger brother might be tonight.

Henry had done no more than give a few irritated grunts since William had sat him in the chair, but when Nan put the wet flannel on his face and began to wipe away the vomit, he revived enough to protest.

'Leave it be, woman, I'm going to bed.' He put his hands on the arms of the chair and tried to push himself up but he soon collapsed again.

Nan ignored his protests and went on cleaning him up. 'You're not going to bed in this state,' she said, 'or I'll have the sheets to wash. If you sit still this will only take a minute. William will help you get your things off when I've got this mess out of your hair.'

If Henry had been sober, or even a little less drunk, Nan would never have dared talk to him like that. However, both she and William knew that by the morning he would not be able to remember a thing about his night out and its consequences. William's only chance of getting some answers was to question him before he went to bed.

He waited until his mother had dried his father's face and hair on a clean towel and then he asked, 'Why didn't Thomas bring you home, Da?'

His father frowned. 'Thomas?'

Oh God, William thought, his memory is already fading. 'Thomas,' he repeated. 'You went for a drink with him tonight.'

'Oh aye,' his father nodded, 'so I did. Don't you worry about your brother, he'll do the trick.'

What was his father talking about? Or was it just the beer talking? None of it made sense, William thought. Until the next words.

'Aye, he'll manage, even without that turncoat Jack Chisholm. He's got to do it, you know.'

'Thomas has got to do what, Da?' William spoke slowly and deliberately, as though he were speaking to a child.

'Fettle Adamson. That's what he's got to do.'

'And how is he going to do that?' But William was afraid he already knew the answer.

'Mind you, I never thought a Chisholm would let him down,' Henry said. 'Wouldn't go with them. Said it was criminal. Your brother told him that what Adamson was doing was criminal and he deserved it. So they're going to Shields. That's where they're going.'

'What's he talking about?' Nan asked. 'Why should Thomas go to Shields at this time of night?'

Henry didn't answer. He belched, and for a moment William thought he was going to throw up in the fireplace. 'Who's going with him?' he asked.

For a moment Henry looked scornful. 'Matthew Linton. One of the interlopers. I could hear what was going on, you know. They sat in the corner with me to put a distance between themselves and any nosy beggars. They thought they'd got me drunk but I wasn't so drunk that I couldn't make out what was going on. I could tell Matthew Linton didn't want to go but Thomas told him he owed it to his brother.'

'To Jos?' Nan said. 'Owed what to Jos?'

Henry shot William a look of contempt. 'Thomas knew it was no good asking you to help. You've had no stomach for it ever since that upstart lass, the cobbler's daughter, turned your head.'

'I never had the stomach for it, Da,' William said. 'It's nothing to do with Jane. I would have refused to go even if I wasn't going to marry the lass.'

'William.' Nan turned to her son in her frustration. 'If you know what this is about then tell me. Is Thomas going to cause some sort of trouble for Mr Adamson?'

Henry laughed and the wheezy laughter turned into a prolonged bout of chesty coughing. William and his mother could do nothing but wait until the coughing subsided.

'There'll be no trouble,' Henry said. He spat in the fire and the flames sizzled. 'No trouble. Thomas will manage fine – even if he's only got a Linton to help him.'

'Help him do what?' Nan was almost despairing.

Henry got unsteadily to his feet and stared blearily at the clock on the mantelshelf. 'Aye,' he said, 'they'll be on their way now. They had to wait until all the pubs were closed and the streets were quiet before they set off. Not daft, our Thomas. Didn't want anyone to see them.' He collapsed back into the chair and stared foolishly at the fire.

'Will somebody answer me for God's sake!' Nan cried.

William took hold of his mother's shoulders and drew her away from the fire and her husband before he answered her. 'Listen, Ma. Thomas and Matthew intend to sink the *Tyne Star*, and I've got to stop them.'

Chapter Twenty-two

'Keep to the shadows. For God's sake keep to the shadows!' The words were snatched from Thomas's lips by the ferocity of the gusting wind. He cursed. It had been a clear moonlit night when he and Jos's young brother had left the village. The sea had been calm, deceptively so, for now a squall had blown up, bringing icy rain up river and causing the boats to rock in their moorings.

They inched their way along the quayside, hugging the warehouse walls, seeking the security of darkness. The masts of the sailing ships moored alongside the quay swung wildly, creaking and groaning, the tangle of rigging slapping loudly against the spars.

The gas lamps set in brackets on the walls highlighted the slanting rain that swept the glistening cobblestones. In between each lamp there was a pool of welcoming darkness. Thomas used the back of one hand to wipe away the water that dripped from his hair and into his eyes and took a tighter grip on the bag of tools he carried. He was ready for this. No more talking, no more planning. He would not turn back now.

Having cursed the weather, Thomas now blessed the cover its ferocity afforded. There was not a sign of activity. The crews of the brigs and schooners were secure in the warmth of homes and lodgings ashore, the local lads with their wives and many of the others in the arms of the obliging ladies of Clive Street.

'There she is,' Thomas breathed. The trawler's bravely painted name was plain to see in the lamp's yellowish light. Thomas stopped and turned to Matthew. 'We'll wait a bit to be sure the watchman's not about. I warrant he's taking shelter in the quaymaster's office.'

Matthew leaned close. Thomas could see the fear in his eyes. 'What if there's a watchman on board?'

'There won't be. I checked with a lad that works on the quay. Adamson pays the quay watch well to keep an eye on things. And look around you – there's not one of those brave fellows in sight, is there?'

But even as he reassured Matthew, Thomas became aware of another problem. Something he hadn't thought of and, as a fisherman used to the ways of the sea, should have taken into account. Jos would have taken it into account. Thomas brushed away that irritating thought. The problem was that the tide was on the turn. The decks of the trawlers were some six feet lower than the quayside. This meant that they would have to jump out into the darkness and land on a slippery wet deck.

An added hazard to boarding in this way was the erratic movement of the boats in the strengthening wind which was blowing directly up the river from the east. Thomas knew that if they didn't time their jumps precisely they could break a leg – or end up in the river. If that happened Adamson would have the last laugh. But, perversely, it only made him all the more determined to continue.

He took one more look up and down the quayside. It was still deserted. 'Stay close to me,' he said to Matthew without turning his head. 'We'll board the boat at the for'ard where it's higher in the water. All right?'

There was no answer and Thomas looked round. One glance told him that Matthew was petrified. He hoped Jos's young brother wasn't losing the stomach to carry out what lay ahead.

'Are you all right?' He spoke as calmly as he could.

'Aye, but I'm bloody wet through,' Matthew replied. Then he gave a watery grin. 'Let's get it over with.'

Thomas told Matthew that to break cover and run would make them more conspicuous. So he walked the twenty yards to the quay's edge with Matthew close behind him. 'Now!' he hissed.

And they both jumped out into the darkness.

William saw the two figures clearly as they crossed the pool of light cast by a gas lamp and he knew who they must be. He'd run most of the three miles from the village and had reached the high embankment that overlooked the Shields Quay and the river. The flight of steps that led down to the quay seemed endless, and it was impossible to run down them in the dark without risking a headlong fall. The buffeting wind and the incessant rain helped to make the descent precarious.

Once at the bottom William made straight for the place near the edge of the quay where he'd seen the two figures. When he saw where he was standing, next to Richard Adamson's *Tyne Star*, he knew that the two men he had seen were Thomas and Matthew. Without a second's delay William jumped down on to the deck of the trawler. The jump plunged him into darkness, the deck of the boat being in deep shadow below the quay wall.

'Damn!' He cursed under his breath as his left leg hit an obstacle when he landed. It sent him over on to his side and he lay sprawled on the wet deck, stunned and with the wind knocked out of him. He lay there for a few seconds until it became less painful to draw breath. While he gathered his wits he allowed his eyes to adjust to the gloom. Clouds covered the moon and the light from the gas lamps on the quayside didn't reach deck level.

Gradually objects became visible and he saw it was a coil of rope that had caused him to fall. But where were Thomas and Matthew? They could only be down below. Then he saw that the hatch cover, just behind the wheelhouse, had been left open. That's the way they must have gone down, he thought. To the engine room.

He stood up and immediately pain shot up his left leg from his ankle. Gingerly he put his weight on it. Although the pain intensified nothing gave way. Thank God it wasn't broken. Perhaps the pain had provided a jolt of doubt, though, because now William hesitated and looked at the open hatch. Was it any use going on? Thomas and Matthew could have the seacock open by now.

His spirits sank. Was his attempt to stop them futile? With the seacock open the *Tyne Star* would start to take on water and slowly sink to the river bed. But damn it, he thought, I've come this far. They may not be finding the task as easy as they thought it would be. There may still be time.

He limped over to the open hatch and sat on the edge with his legs dangling inside. Then he eased himself down on to the metal grid through which he could see down into the engine room. A dim light flickered up from below. They must have provided themselves with candles.

William swung his legs on to the ladder that gave access to the engine room some six feet below. He could smell oil and grease and the dank odour of stagnant water. He was halfway down when he heard a dull knocking and the noise of metal on metal.

'Thomas. Matthew,' he called into the dimness through cupped hands. The noises stopped and William could almost sense the feeling of panic. 'Thomas,' he called again, 'it's William.'

He heard a gasp and then Thomas answered, 'What the hell are you doing here?'

'I've come to try to make you see sense. What you're doing is madness.' He gave his hushed voice as much authority as possible. 'For Christ's sake stop before it's too late.'

He reached the bottom of the ladder and groped his way along the trawler's bulkhead, past highly polished brass tubes, pipes and gauges that reflected the candlelight. Thomas and Matthew were crouched in the corner. They had one of the floor plates lifted. It wasn't too late to stop them!

'Come on, lads,' he pleaded. 'Get out while you can.'

'No, you get out,' Thomas snarled. 'I told the others you'd gone soft and I was right.'

William ignored his brother's angry response. 'Thomas, there's no sense in what you're doing. Adamson will hire divers and he'll have the boat raised within the week. And, besides, he's got other boats. And he's not the only trawler owner to convert to steam. Tonight's work won't make a ha'p'orth of difference to the fishing.'

Before his brother could reply Matthew said, 'We're going to do it. It's what Jos wanted.' He looked fired up with nervous energy.

'Are you sure?' William asked. 'Did your brother tell you that before he died?'

'No . . . but he told your brother. Didn't he, Thomas?'

'Aye.'

'Listen, Thomas,' William said. 'Adamson didn't even have the *Tyne Star* before Jos died.'

'Don't you think his other steam trawlers have done damage enough? Jos knew this one was on its way and he knew she would be the pride of the fleet. The *Tyne Star* would be able to stay out longer, in all weathers, and catch more fish, he said. He was so worked up about it, he said he'd like to sink it.'

'He'd like to sink it or he planned to sink it?'

'Stop trying to confuse me with your clever way of putting things. You're nearly as bad as Kate. Now, hawway, Matthew,' he said. 'Don't listen to him. We've got to get on with it.'

William looked at them in despair. Matthew was holding the candle. Thomas had a hammer and he'd wrapped a piece of cloth around the head to deaden the noise. They had the floor plate open and William could see the brass seacock glinting in the candlelight.

Ignoring William, Thomas put the hammer aside and, reaching down, grasped the seacock with both hands. His neck muscles bulged as he strained to turn it open. Suddenly it moved and the valve opened. There was the sound of water rushing into the boiler.

'That's got it.' Thomas was panting with the effort. 'Now to stop the bastards from closing the valve,' he said. And he swung the hammer again and again.

William knew it would be hopeless to try to stop his brother now. Thomas looked almost demented in the flickering candlelight as he rained blow after blow on the brass seacock. Then, as he began to tire and his movements became slower, the valve broke and water gushed into the engine room.

'Get out!' Thomas yelled.

Matthew, still holding the candle, ran to the ladder, followed by Thomas.

'William, you first,' his brother said. But William knew his injured ankle would only hold them back.

'No, you two go on.'

They didn't argue. They brushed past him and climbed the ladder. William followed and had reached the metal grille when he heard a commotion ahead of him. Just outside the hatch by the sound of it.

'Who the hell are you?' A voice he didn't recognize was shouting and cursing. The voice was thick, the words were slurred; either with sleep or drink, William decided.

Then there was a scuffling. He poked his head out of the hatch into the open air in time to see two men on the deck swinging punches at each other. A third man stood watching. He recognized the third man by his slighter figure as Matthew. Which meant that it was his brother, Thomas, who was in the thick of the fight. He also realized that the rain had stopped and a pale moon was emerging from the clouds.

So who could Thomas's assailant be? One of the watchmen, or perhaps a member of the crew who had been sleeping in the wheelhouse or the fo'c's'le quarters and had been disturbed by the hammering?

William was still half in and half out of the hatch when the fighting men reached the side of the boat further away from the quay. The other man, even though he seemed to be staggering a little, was getting the better of his brother. He had his arms up behind his back as he manoeuvred him towards the gunwale. In a heart-stopping moment, William realized that he intended to throw Thomas over the side.

'No!' William shouted and heaved himself up. But Matthew got there before him. The other man already had Thomas dangling over the water when Matthew leapt on him and pulled him back with all his might. Surprised, the man let go of Thomas, who fell on to the deck, and turned on Matthew. The fight should have been uneven, but

289

Matthew was fired by anger and fright and he fought back fiercely.

Then the bigger man, attempting to avoid a blow, seemed to lose his balance. He let out a despairing cry of rage and fear as he toppled over into the river. William rushed forward. Matthew, who a moment ago had been fighting for his life, was reaching down over the gunwale in an attempt to rescue his adversary. But, all too soon, he sank back and fell on to the deck, where he kneeled and moaned with despair.

'I had him,' he told them between sobs. 'He reached up and I grabbed his arm. And then . . . and then I felt him trying to drag me in after him. I shook him off. I let go. What else could I do? I saw the current take him. I've killed him.'

William rushed to the side and looked over. There was no sign of the man. Thomas had risen to his feet. 'Never mind that now,' he shouted. 'The boat's sinking. It's time to go.' He grabbed Matthew by the shoulders and dragged him to his feet.

William realized that Thomas was right. The *Tyne Star* was settling in the water. They had to get ashore. Thomas and Matthew turned to go. William stayed a moment longer, leaning out over the water and straining his eyes in the pale light to see if he could catch sight of the man who'd gone overboard. His hopes rose when he saw a dark shape break surface about ten yards away, but from the wake it left as it swam by it soon became obvious it was too small to be a man. It was a water rat. He hoped that the man, whoever he was, had managed to swim to safety. But he knew the hope to be forlorn.

'William, come on!' Thomas turned and yelled.

With a final glance over the side William limped after the other two as they ran to the bow. By climbing on to the gunwale they were able to reach up and hook an arm round a quayside bollard then pull themselves up, one after the other. First Matthew and then Thomas. William heard them running along the quay as he reached for the bollard.

He got his arm round it but he was bigger and heavier than either Thomas or Matthew and it was not so easy for him, especially with the trawler sinking in the water.

At last he managed to swing one leg over the edge of the quay and then, pulling as hard as he could on the bollard, he eased himself up until, finally, he lay face down on the wet ground, panting with the effort.

The other two would be well away by now, he thought, but they might be waiting for him at the top of the embankment steps. He put both hands on the ground, ready to raise himself, and lifted his head.

The shock of what he saw almost stopped his heart. There, not more than three feet away, were two sturdy boots, the toecaps glistening in some sort of light from above. William rose to a crouching position.

'What are you up to, lad?' a voice said. The man was carrying an oil lamp and as he spoke he held it out towards William's face.

William didn't answer. He scrambled upright and lashed out with one arm, catching the lantern and sending it skittering across the cobbles. The light went out and, with the curses of the watchman and the smell of burnt oil filling the air, he ignored the pain in his ankle and ran as fast as he could.

Thomas and Matthew had waited at the bottom of the embankment steps. When William reached them they each hooked an arm under one of his and dragged him up. The steps were steep and slippery but panic made them sure-footed. They were exhausted by the time they reached the top and they flung themselves down. Lying on their stomachs, they peered down at the quayside. There was no sign of chase.

'We've got away,' Thomas said.

'No we haven't. He saw me,' William told him.

'He doesn't know who you are.'

'He'll soon find out.'

'How's that?'

'How many people have hair this colour? When he reports the incident someone will tell him that's it's likely he caught one of the Lawsons.'

'But that could be me!' Thomas lost a little of his bluster.

'It could be but you've nowt to fear.'

'Why?'

'I told you. He got a good look at me. He saw my face.'

'What the hell are we going to do?' That came from Matthew and he sounded scared. 'When they come for you they'll ask you if you acted alone. What will you tell them?'

'William won't tell them anything. Will you?' his brother asked and William sensed the pleading in his voice.

'You're right. I won't tell them anything because I won't be here.'

'What do you mean?' Matthew asked.

'I mean what I say. I won't be here. I'll have to run.'

'No!' Thomas gasped.

'Use your head, man,' William said. 'If I don't run for it, it won't just be prison; they'll hang me. There's a man drowned, remember?'

'Oh, God, oh God, oh God,' Matthew began to moan.

'Stop that,' William said. 'It doesn't help.'

'But it was my fault he went overboard,' Matthew said.

'He was trying to shove you over the side, remember?'

'Aye, and me too,' Thomas added.

William raised himself on his elbows and reached out and gripped his brother's arm. 'And if this fiasco is anyone's fault it's yours, isn't it? It was all your crazy idea—'

'No, it was Jos's.'

'Stop trying to blame a dead man. You have no idea if he would have carried out his plan to sink the trawler. If he'd lived, and if he'd gone ahead with the plan, then we could lay the blame squarely at his feet. But he didn't and what happened tonight is entirely your responsibility.'

'We'll have to own up,' Matthew said. 'We can't let you take the blame alone.'

'What good would that do? We'd all hang. Do you want to break our mother's heart, Thomas? And you, Matthew, your mother's already mad with grief because she's lost one son; what would it do to her if she lost another? No, I was the one the watchman saw and if I vanish there's no way they can get to you. But you'll both have to keep quiet about what happened for the rest of your lives – quite a burden. And you, Thomas, will have the extra burden of making sure that our da keeps his mouth shut. Your lives won't be easy, either of you.'

'But where will you go?' Thomas asked.

'Right now we're going home and you're going to get a few things for me from the cottage.'

'What shall I tell Ma?'

'Nothing.'

'She'll ask.'

'Tell her I'll make sure she finds out all she needs to know.'

'How will you do that?'

'For God's sake stop blethering and let's get home. I'll wait in the lane until you get my things and then I'll be off.'

'You haven't told me where you're going to go,' his brother said.

'That's the way it'll have to be. If you don't know you can't tell anyone.'

'As if I would!'

'You might not mean to but you're just like our da when you've had a drink or two. I won't change my mind, so let's go.'

* * *

Alice had insisted on sitting up all night to watch over Charlie. Mrs Hewitson had been to lay him out and the undertaker would be coming today. And Kate knew that Alice would keep her vigil when Charlie was in his coffin until the hearse came to carry him to his last resting place in the graveyard on the headland. Kate made Alice a cup of tea and sat with her while she drank it.

When Alice dropped her head and began to doze Kate eased the cup and saucer from her hands and took them through to the scullery. Then she slipped quietly out of the living quarters. She wanted to open the shop well before Susan arrived. She would give the young woman no cause for complaint. It would only upset Alice, who would be torn between her love for her daughter and her growing affection for Kate.

No sooner had she opened the shop door than the muffled figure of a man pushed his way in, took hold of the door and closed it quickly. Kate looked at him in surprise. His cap was pulled low on his forehead and the collar of his jacket was turned up. But despite this there was still a glint of red hair showing. He was carrying a bundle wrapped in sacking and tied with string. And she thought that when he entered he had been limping.

'Lock up again,' her brother William said. 'I won't stay long.'

Sensing his urgency, Kate did as she was told. 'What is it?' she asked.

'Is there somewhere we can sit where no one can see us?'

'Yes, for the moment. We could go to the stockroom. But . . .'

'But what?'

'Susan Armstrong will be arriving.'

'How soon?'

'We've probably got about half an hour. Maybe just a little less.'

'That'll have to do.'

'Come through then, but I'll unlock the door. If an early bird arrives they'll expect me to be open.'

William followed Kate through, and once they were seated in the stockroom she urged him to talk softly. 'I don't want Alice disturbed,' she said. 'Now, what is it? There's something very wrong, isn't there?'

'I don't know where to start.'

'At the beginning.'

As concisely as he could William told Kate what had happened just a few hours ago and what he intended to do. 'I've been skulking in the shadows until you opened up,' he told her. 'I thought it best not to go home. I can trust our ma but I don't want Da to know too much.'

Kate was appalled.

'You're leaving Cullercoats?' she said.

'What choice do I have? I don't want to hang. And I don't want to lead the law to Thomas and Matthew, either.'

'I'd find it hard to be sorry for them if you did!'

'No, Kate, you wouldn't want them to hang either, would you?'

'Between them they killed a man.'

'It was an accident.'

'An accident that wouldn't have happened if they hadn't been there!'

'You're right. And you're right to be angry. But . . .'

'What is it?'

'You mustn't put all the blame on Thomas.'

'Don't tell me it was Matthew Linton's idea. I wouldn't believe you.'

'No, it wasn't Matthew.'

William looked as though he'd rather be anywhere than sitting opposite her in the close confines of the stockroom. Kate stared at him, trying to make out what it was that he was finding so difficult to tell her.

'*Jos*,' she breathed.

'Yes. I'm sorry, Kate, but it was Jos who first put the idea into Thomas's head. We'll never know whether he would have carried out his plan if he'd lived.'

'Not if I'd had anything to do with it!'

Her temper flared and she didn't know whom exactly she was angry with: her twin brother for sinking the trawler or her dead sweetheart for dreaming up the idea in the first place. She knew William was telling the truth because this was just the sort of thing Jos would suggest. He had been hardworking and clever but there had been a wild streak in him that had eventually led to his death. It was that wildness that brought us together in the first place, Kate thought. We were both wayward bairns and no one else was a match for us. But now, months after Jos had drowned, his words had caused another tragedy. She wondered, not for the first time over the past few months, whether she had really known the man she had loved so much.

'Kate,' William said. 'You know I have to go? You know there's nothing else I can do – not if I want to stay alive.'

They stared at each other and suddenly Kate reached out and took William's hand. 'Does this mean I'll never see you again?'

He nodded, too full to trust himself to speak.

'Is there anything I can do to help?' Kate asked.

'That's why I've come. I've told you the truth, the full story of what happened last night. I want you to tell Ma. I've told Thomas to say nowt. You're the best one to do it.'

'Where are you going to go? What are you going to do?'

'I'm going to leave the country. I'll sign on to some ship heading far away. That is if any master will take me with this limp.'

'I can help you there.'

'How's that?'

'Wait here.'

Kate left him and went upstairs to her room. When she returned she handed him an old purse. He looked inside.

'I can't take this,' he said.

'Why not?'

'It's too much. It looks as though you were saving up for something.'

'Most of it is what Aunt Meg left me,' she lied. She could not tell William the whole truth although she would have liked to do so. If he knew she was expecting a bairn he would have insisted she keep the money. 'She would want you to have it. You'll be able to buy a passage to America, and once you're there – well, it's up to you, but I have a suggestion.'

William grinned. 'Good old Kate. You could always be trusted to come up with a suggestion. Especially if we'd done something wrong and explanations were called for.'

Kate took a letter out of her apron pocket and a clean sheet of notepaper. She put them on the upturned tea chest and copied something out. She gave him the piece of paper. 'Don't lose that address.'

He looked at it and his eyes widened. 'I didn't know you'd been in touch,' he said.

'I can't explain now. It would take too long. But don't write home, whatever you do. Ma and I will write to you. Now, you must go. William, do you want me to tell Jane what has happened?'

Her brother's eyes filled with tears. 'My bonny Jane. She thinks we're going to get married.' Quite unashamedly he wiped the tears from his eyes with his handkerchief. 'No, you don't have to do that, Kate. I'll tell her myself.'

'When?'

'I'll go there now – to the Coulsons' house in Jesmond. It's still early. I'll catch the workmen's train.'

'I don't think that's wise.'

'Wise or not, I can't leave without seeing her – telling her . . .'

'Of course you can't. But this is what we'll do.'

Kate had just finished explaining to William what her plan was when they were interrupted by the jangling of the shop bell. Her brother started up and almost overturned the box he'd been sitting on. 'Susan Armstrong!' he exclaimed.

'Whisht!' Kate put a finger to her lips. 'Wait here. I won't be a moment.'

Kate opened the door quietly and saw that Alice was still asleep in the chair by the fire. She was snoring gently. Charlie was laid out on the bed in his best suit. It was like a dream, Kate thought. Or a nightmare.

She went back for William and beckoned him to follow her. She took him along the cold passage that led to the kitchen and the scullery and the door to the back yard, which she opened. 'Off you go,' she said.

William hugged her. 'Tell Ma I love her.'

'Of course I will.' Then, 'Wait!' she said.

She took down a scarf that was hanging on a hook on the back of the door along with a couple of outdoor coats. It would be one of Charlie's. Kate leaned forward and wrapped the scarf round her brother's neck. He looked surprised.

'To hide your bonny hair,' she said and felt the grief rise in her throat.

She watched him cross the back yard, open the door and slip out into the lane. She'd advised him to keep to the back lanes as far as he could on the way to the station. When the yard door closed behind him she hurried back along the passage to the shop. She hoped against hope that it wasn't Susan who had arrived; always suspicious, she might ask awkward questions. But fortunately it was Betsy.

'Oh, thank goodness you're here,' Kate said. 'I want you to run an errand for me.'

The girl grinned. This was what she liked to do. 'Do I have to remember anything?' she asked.

'Yes, but it's easy. Go and tell my mother that I want to see her. Don't speak to anyone else. Ask her to come to the shop straight away. Can you remember that?'

Betsy gave Kate a scornful look and ran for the door. 'Course I can.'

Chapter Twenty-three

Nan got on the Newcastle train along with the other fishwives. They were surprised to see her. 'I didn't know you did a round in town,' Mary Coxon said.

'I don't.' Fearful of upsetting the regulars she added, 'But one of my customers in Whitley is looking after her sister who's just had a bairn. The sister lives in Jesmond.' This raised a few eyebrows. Jesmond was even more select than Whitley. Nan hurried on, 'She left word I was to bring up a nice bit of turbot. I won't be coming up here again.'

'I hope she'll pay your train fare,' Mary said.

'I didn't think of that.'

'Well, ask her for it. You can tell you're new to the game. All this way for bit of turbot. You must be daft,' Mary added scornfully.

Nan felt herself flushing. She only half remembered the story that Kate had made up for her – lies, she supposed, but surely God would forgive her in the circumstances – but ever since she had left Kate earlier she had been in turmoil.

'Leave her be,' Mary's sister Edith said. 'We all had to learn. And in any case it pays to keep in with a good customer.' She turned to Nan and asked kindly, 'Where do you usually go today?'

'Wallsend.' Well, at least that was true.

'There now, you'll be able to go back there on the train, so it's not quite a wasted journey.'

The only comfort Nan could take from the exchange was that the news of what had happened the night before had not yet got round the village. If it had, the other fish lasses would have been asking her much more difficult questions. Nevertheless, she was glad when Edith nudged her arm and told her that the next stop would be the best one for Jesmond. She managed a smile and a thank you before she got off the train.

Kate had drawn her a map but, nevertheless, Nan got lost and she had to ask the way twice before she arrived at the Coulsons' house. House, she thought, it was more like a palace with its gardens set out like a park, and its tall bay windows giving glimpses of luxuriously furnished rooms. No wonder Jane had got a little bit above herself, she thought, and immediately felt guilty when she remembered why she was here.

At the same time she realized that she ought not to have come in this way at all. She should have followed the high red-brick garden wall until she found a turning into a lane which led to the back entrances and the stable blocks of these grand houses. She hesitated, half deciding to retrace her steps, and then deciding not to.

She had spied the way the drive divided before the pillared porch and veered round to the sides of the house. One way seemed to end at a glasshouse set back a little and bigger than Nan's own cottage, and the other way looked as though it might lead to the back premises. She went that way and, to her relief, discovered that she had guessed rightly.

But even then her quest had not ended. There were all sorts of outhouses, the green-painted doors looking identical. She chose the door which had the most well-worn step below it. There was also an enamel notice nailed to the door which she read and ignored. Hitching her basket safely over one arm, she raised the other and knocked as loudly as she dared.

Iris, the Coulsons' scullery maid, was frowning. 'Mrs Roberts, there's a fishwife at the back door,' she said.

The cook-housekeeper was seated at the scrubbed table. She looked up from her cup of tea. 'Tell her we get our fish from Rennison's. And – wait – ask her if she can read.'

'Read?' Iris said. Her frown deepened.

'The sign on the door,' Mrs Roberts said. ' "No hawkers, no circulars."'

'Mebbes she can read but mebbes she doesn't know what a hawker is – or a circular come to that,' Iris ventured.

'Pert, aren't you, miss?' But the older woman was smiling. 'All right, just tell her we don't want any fish.'

Iris disappeared through the door that led to the scullery. Mrs Roberts helped herself to another fancy cake left over from teatime the day before and told Dora, the tweeny, to pour herself a cup of tea and sit down. Iris returned looking baffled.

'Well, child?' Mrs Roberts said.

'She says she doesn't want to sell no fish.'

The cook-housekeeper shook her head. 'You mean she doesn't want to sell any fish.'

'That's what I said.'

'No you didn't, but never mind. What does she want?'

'She says she'd like a word with Miss Harrison.'

'With Jane?' Mrs Roberts showed her surprise.

'She says she has a message from home.'

'Oh, of course. Jane's parents live in Cullercoats. I hope this isn't bad news for the poor girl.'

'What sort of bad news, Mrs Roberts?' Dora spoke for the first time.

'Well, maybe something's happened at home – her mother may be ill. But it's no use speculating. Iris, tell the woman to come in. She can leave her basket in the scullery and come and sit here while she waits. Dora, go upstairs and ask Miss Jane to come here. Now don't say anything to frighten her. Just say that I want to see her. Understand?'

The girl nodded and left the room swiftly. Her eyes were wide with the excitement of bearing what might prove to be grave tidings. Without rising from her seat Mrs Roberts told Iris to top up the teapot and fetch a cup and saucer from the dresser. 'Make that two, Iris. Jane might appreciate one, too.'

When Jane appeared and saw the woman sitting at the end of the kitchen table she went white. She literally drained of colour, Mrs Roberts thought, just like the heroines in the romantic novels she loved to read.

'Mrs Lawson!' she gasped. 'Is it . . . is it William?'

The woman nodded and Mrs Roberts thought the girl was going to pass out. 'Iris – Dora – catch hold of Jane!' she commanded. The girls flew to Jane's side. 'That's right, now sit her at the table – not there, you muddle heads – put her next to her visitor.'

'Is he . . . is he drowned?' Jane asked.

'No, not that.'

Thank goodness for that, the cook-housekeeper thought. She had realized by now that the haggard-looking woman sitting at the table must be Jane's sweetheart's mother. And she had brought some sort of news about the lad. Mrs Roberts only hoped that it didn't mean he was going to turn down the position as buyer for her brother's fish business. Perhaps some illness – or, no, surely the young man couldn't be thinking of breaking off the engagement and have sent his mother because he was too cowardly to come and tell her himself ? Poor Jane.

'Dora, get a tray and take that plate of fancy cakes along to my sitting room together with some fresh cups and saucers,' she said. 'And Iris, get another teapot and milk jug down and make us a fresh pot of tea.' The girl opened her mouth. 'And before you ask why, it's because you and Dora are going to have a special treat. You're going to enjoy your morning cuppa with me in my lovely sitting room.'

'Why?' Iris asked.

'You'll be the death of me, lass,' the cook-housekeeper said with a sigh. 'Because I believe Mrs Lawson wants to talk to Miss Harrison in private. And it suits me to oblige her.'

'The *Tyne Star* sunk?' Jane whispered. 'A man overboard and maybe drowned?' She felt herself begin to shake.

William's mother reached over the table and covered Jane's small white hand with her own work-worn brown one. 'He tried to stop them, Jane, you must believe me.'

Jane shook her head. Nothing Nan Lawson said made sense, at least not in her own ordered world. This was a nightmare. She was still in bed and dreaming.

'And William is leaving the country?'

'Aye, there's nowt else for it.'

'But we were going to get married.'

Nan looked at her helplessly.

'We had such plans . . .'

'I'm sorry.'

Jane looked at William's mother and saw the pain in her eyes. 'But he wants to see me?'

'Aye, it's in the note Kate sent. Here you are.'

'Kate. Always Kate.'

'What do you mean?'

'Ever since we were children we went to Kate if things went awry. She always tried to put things right.'

'Aye, well it's a pity she couldn't have put things right for herself.' Nan sounded bitter.

Jane frowned. 'Oh, you mean Jos.'

'Aye, that's right, I mean Jos.' William's mother got to her feet. 'I have to go. I still have a day's work to do.'

Jane saw her to the door. Then she managed to keep her composure long enough to inform the cook-housekeeper that Mrs Lawson had gone.

'Does he still love you?' Mrs Roberts asked jokingly.

'Yes, of course,' Jane said.

'Well, that's a relief. I thought his mother had come to tell you that he'd run off with another. For God's sake, Jane, don't look at me like that! I was only joking.'

Jane turned and hurried away. It wasn't until she reached her own room that she gave way to a storm of weeping. She thought she wouldn't be able to stop and she watched helplessly as all her hopes and dreams were swept away on a tide of grief.

The cathedral clock struck three as Jane walked through the gateway that led into the church garden, or Amen Corner as it was known. A damp mist hung in the bare branches of the trees and the public seats were unoccupied. The only other person in the garden on this last day of November was an old woman wrapped up in a voluminous shawl. Jane watched as she spread a newspaper out on the damp wood of one of the benches and then sat down. There was a bulging patchwork bag at her feet. Goodness knows what was in it but Jane suspected it was all her worldly goods. From the look of her the old woman was one of the many homeless souls who lived on the streets of Newcastle.

Then, as Jane watched, the old woman reached down into her bag and brought out a crust of bread, curled and stale-looking. She began to crumble it up between her gnarled fingers and scatter the crumbs to the sparrows who had gathered in anticipation. Jane guessed they must have been waiting for her.

She was distracted by the sound of footsteps. They were unmistakably William's, even though they seemed to be limping. The way he walked, the way he talked, the way he laughed, the way he breathed, all were familiar to her. Part of her. They would be for ever and yet now he was proposing to leave her. She turned to face him.

The old woman shuffled off and Jane noticed, inconsequentially, that her swollen feet were protected from the cold weather by nothing better than an old pair of carpet slippers with newspaper showing through the ragged tears in the fabric. When she had vanished into the mist-filled streets of the city William spoke.

'I'm sorry I'm late,' he said.

'Is that all you're sorry for!'

'Jane, please don't. You know I'm sorry for all of this mess. But if my mother told you what happened you know there's nothing else I can

301

do. I've just been to the shipping office. My bundle is already on board. I sail tonight on the midnight tide.'

'So soon! Do you really have to go? Isn't there any alternative?'

'The alternative is the gallows.'

'But you're innocent!'

'Don't you see, to prove my innocence would be to condemn Thomas and Matthew to hang. And they'd probably hang me anyway. But at the moment no one knows there was anyone else involved except me.'

'That man might not have drowned. He could have washed up safe somewhere.'

'Even if that were true – and I hope with all my heart it is – I think they'd still hang us for attempted murder.'

'But, William, just think. If he is alive he would tell the police there were more than one of you.'

'I've thought of that and I don't think he would be able to identify the two he was fighting with. It was dark on deck. And another thing . . .'

'What?'

'There was a smell of drink on him. He was staggering.'

'He was fighting!'

'I know, but I'm pretty sure he didn't have all his wits about him. So long as they can't find me, Thomas and Matthew are safe.'

Jane sighed. 'You've made up your mind, haven't you?'

'Yes.'

'So where are you going?'

'I can't tell you. It's best that you don't know in case the police question you.'

'I wouldn't tell them!'

'Of course you wouldn't. But I wouldn't want you to have to tell lies for my sake.'

'William – take me with you. I could buy a passage – I have the money.'

'I can't ask you to throw in your lot with a fugitive.'

'I'd do that gladly so long as we could be together.'

'We will be one day, whichever way things turn out. But now you must continue with your plans for your shop. It's what you've always wanted.'

Jane could have told him that what she'd always wanted was William himself but that she had baulked at the idea of being a fisherman's wife. She had planned a better life for both of them. But now that everything was being snatched away from her she realized that she would go anywhere, live anyhow, if it meant she could be with William.

'I'll open the shop, William. I'll work as hard as I can and save money for us both until I hear from you.' She panicked when she saw the bleak look in his eyes. 'I am going to hear from you, aren't I?'

'Yes, but I don't know when that will be.'

'So I can't write to you and you can't write to me? William, I can't bear this!'

As she spoke, the birds who had been pecking up the crumbs flew up as one to perch in the bare branches of the trees.

'Whisht, whisht, my bonny lass,' William said. 'You're frightening the little birds. And don't despair. Kate is going to write to me—'

'Oh, so your sister will know where you are but I am not to!'

'I've told you why. I don't want you bullied. Kate will tell you when it's safe to write to me.'

'And when it's safe to come to you?'

'If you still want to.'

'How can you say that!'

William took hold of her arms and drew her close. He looked into her eyes. His own were full of pain. 'I must go now, sweetheart,' he said and she noticed how his breath misted in the cold air. He kissed her only once and then broke away.

'I love you, William,' she whispered and watched how her words, too, turned to vapour and vanished in the air between them.

Without looking back William walked out through the gateway and turned to walk downhill towards the river and the ship that would soon be taking him away from her. A sudden shaft of sunlight pierced the mist to bring a little warmth to Amen Corner. And in the quiet that followed William's departure the birds hopped down from the trees again to garner the last few crumbs. But Jane didn't see them because her eyes were full of tears.

The undertakers had come and gone discreetly through the little-used house door at the side of the shop, and now Charlie Willis lay in his coffin on a black-swathed trestle table erected in the room where he had passed his last months on earth. Alice and her daughter were sitting at the kitchen table and Susan was trying to persuade her mother to eat some of the broth she'd made.

'I'm not hungry, pet,' Alice told her.

'Hungry or not, you need something inside you if you're going to keep vigil tonight.'

'You're a good lass. I can see you'll look after your mother.'

'Of course I will. And, Ma, I've been thinking about that. What if Seth and me and the bairns moved in with you after all this is over? This is a big house. I know most of the ground floor is taken up with the shop, but think of all those empty rooms upstairs. Seth and me could have our own sitting room up there so's you could have a bit of peace and quiet.'

'Peace and quiet?'

'Well, you're not used to the bairns, are you? You'd want your own place to sit.'

'I suppose you're right.'

'I could help in the shop whenever I could and Seth could chop the wood, make the fire, do the heavy work.'

'I thought you liked living in Belle Vue Cottage.'

'Oh, I do. But families are important, aren't they? And if we move in here, you'll be able to rent the cottage out again. Bring some more money in.'

'I'll think about it, Susan, but not tonight.'

Susan could see that she would get no further tonight but she was satisfied that she would get her own way sooner or later. 'Whatever you say, Ma.'

Her mother picked up her spoon and began to sup her broth. In a little while she said, 'Eeh, this broth is lovely, Susan. I'm glad you persuaded me to have some.'

Susan saw that her mother was trying to please her so she took the risk of adding, 'And just think, if we did move in, I'd be able to do all the cooking. Make sure you eat properly. You'd have gone without tonight if I hadn't been here, wouldn't you?'

'Eeh, no!' Her mother had put her spoon down and raised a hand to her mouth.

'What is it? Was the broth too hot? Have you bitten on a bone?'

'No, it's not that. We've forgotten about Kate, haven't we? She usually has a bite to eat with me before she goes up to her room. Susan, you'd better go up and get her.'

Susan looked down at the table. She didn't want her mother to see how much this displeased her. 'She eats in the stockroom, doesn't she? Do you want me to put something out for her?'

304

'If you wouldn't mind, pet. But there's no need for her to eat alone. Tell her to come and join us.'

'Well, you know, when she closed the shop I thought she looked very tired. And upset and all.'

'Upset?'

'About her brother.'

'I don't know what you're talking about.'

'Well, of course you don't. You've been back here all day. You haven't heard the talk in the shop and I didn't want to bother you.' The truth was that Susan had been waiting for the right moment to bring this up and now it looked as though it had arrived.

'It's nothing bad, is it, Susan?'

'Very bad, I'm afraid. Her brother has run off, God knows where.'

'Why on earth would he do that?'

'Because he went and sunk the pride of Mr Adamson's fleet, the *Tyne Star*, and mebbes murdered a man while he was about it.'

'Murdered a man?'

'Aye. The watchman said he heard an almighty yell and a splash. That's what brought him to the scene. He couldn't see anyone in the river but he could see the trawler sinking. And who should be climbing up on to the quay but Kate's brother!'

Her mother shook her head. 'Poor Nan,' she said. 'Ever since the demonstration outside Mr Adamson's house she's been worried that Thomas would cause more trouble. Do something rash. But she couldn't have foreseen this.'

'It wasn't Thomas, Ma. The man the watchman saw was William Lawson.'

'William? I don't believe it!'

'Well, it's true. And that's why he's run off. And that's why I said Kate had better go straight up to her room. She might not want company at the moment, might she? Ma – what's the matter? Have you taken a turn?'

'No, pet, but I've just remembered something. I saw this when I read Kate's cup. I saw it in the tea leaves.'

'What did you see?' Susan had never been sure whether to believe in her mother's gift of sight but she knew that others in the village were impressed by it. And it brought custom to the shop so she didn't want to disparage it.

'I saw a warning – saw the letter W clear as clear. I asked Kate to look and she said she couldn't see it. But it was there, I swear it was. I warned Nan about it. And now look what's happened!'

'Yes, well, perhaps they should have taken notice of what you said.'

'Some people never do.' Alice sighed. 'But now you must take something up for Kate.'

'Take something up?'

'Make some nice sandwiches – enough for two in case Nan calls to see her. Use the boiled ham and cut a slab off the Madeira cake.'

Susan was vexed that what she had told her mother had only made her more sympathetic to Kate but she set about cutting the cake and making the sandwiches. She kept quiet as she did so but her mind was working. She wanted to move in here and she wanted to be sure that her mother had only her to rely on.

Seth was a good-natured, happy-go-lucky fellow but he wasn't all that keen on going to work and he might end up losing this job just as he had lost the last one. But if they lived here with her mother they wouldn't want for anything and Susan would gradually take over the running of the shop – and she'd be able to make Seth help her.

So now she would do as her mother had asked and set a generous tray and make sure her mother saw it before she took it up.

Kate had hardly moved since she came up to her room. She hadn't even taken off her pinafore before sitting down by the fire. She was tired, but then she always seemed to be tired these days. But most of all she was worried.

Her mother had called into the shop just before it closed to tell her that Jane had promised that she would go to meet William. Kate could hardly bear to think of how heartbroken her old friend must be. Almost as heartbroken as Kate had been herself when Jos had drowned. The sea was taking William away, too, but in this case to a land far away and an uncertain future.

Jane must be wondering whether she would ever see William again. Ever marry the man she loved, make a home, have children . . . What torment she must be suffering. But I will do my best to see to it that they are united in the future . . . as soon as William is settled . . . as soon as he is safe.

And what about my dreams? Somehow I must make a better life for my child even though it means I must give up any idea of happiness with the man I love.

The child moved within her and for the first time the movement caused her pain. She placed both hands over her belly and sat motionless until the spasm passed. But her reflective mood had been broken and she realised that as well as being tired she was hungry. Susan had sent her up to her room as if she was a child to be ordered about and had not even thought about providing her with a meal.

So it was just as well that she had the means to make a cup of tea and a lump of rich fruitcake in the tin. She would risk indigestion and have a feast by the fire. She leaned forward and, using the poker, she nudged the kettle nearer to the fire so that it would start to boil. She decided that before eating anything she would wash herself and get ready for bed. Once out of her clothes she would feel more comfortable.

Kate poured water into her wash bowl from the large jug of cold water she brought up to her room every morning. Then she took the kettle over to the washstand and added some hot. The steam rose and curled upwards into the dark corners of the room. She had not lit the lamps.

Before taking her clothes off she knelt by the fire and built it up a little. Why not be comfortable? It won't help William if I sit here as cold as charity just because he is leaving to sail across a wide cold sea to a country that would soon be in the grip of winter. But when the fire sparked and flared and began to give off a warm, cosy heat, she felt guilty nevertheless. Even the journey across the Atlantic would be rough. If storms delayed the vessel would William spend Christmas at sea, all those miles away from his family and the woman he loved?

She sat on the edge of the bed to take off her shoes and stockings, then stayed there while she undid buttons and hooks. Finally she rose to take off her underwear and stood naked in the firelight. She caught sight of her shadow thrown on to a wall. There was no mistaking the curve of her belly and the fullness of her breasts and what that fullness meant. She was just about to turn and go to the washstand when the door of her room opened.

Susan Armstrong had not bothered to knock and now she stood there with a tray and stared at Kate open-mouthed. Kate snatched up her shift and covered her nakedness but it was too late.

'You shameless bitch,' Susan said. 'Does my poor mother know what kind of a whore she's sheltering in her home? I'm sure she doesn't. How could you deceive her like this? And which one of those fine gentlemen friends of yours is the father, I wonder? Adamson or the American? Or mebbes you don't even know!'

Chapter Twenty-four

'I think this is your man,' Sam Phillips said.

He had sent word to the office for Richard to come to the infirmary. They stood at each side of one of the narrow beds in the long high-ceilinged room and looked down at the pale, unshaven patient who, although sleeping, still managed to look ruffianly. Sam thought Richard looked as pale and as gaunt as the man on the bed.

'It could be,' Richard said. 'I recognize him and there's no other crew member missing. Will he live?'

'Probably. He was lucky. He drifted out with the tide and fetched up on Sand End at the river mouth. He was found there the next morning and brought here.'

'He didn't travel far, then.'

'No, and I don't think he knew much about the journey.'

'Why's that?'

'Just smell the man! Even now when he's been cleaned up he still stinks of alcohol.'

'Has he said anything?'

'Only that he can't remember how he got in the river.'

'You say that as though you don't believe him.'

'Well, he must have been drunk, I'm fairly sure of that, but I believe he's hiding something.'

'If this is the man who went overboard he wouldn't want to admit to being on board the *Tyne Star* at all. He's a fine worker when he's sober but the drink seems to madden him. He'd become a troublemaker and a liability. The skipper had paid him off that very day.'

'So what do you think happened?' Sam Phillips asked.

'He probably spent all his pay on drink at a pub in Clive Street and then staggered back to the *Star* to sleep it off.'

'You think he was woken up by the noise of what was happening?'

'That would make sense.'

'And, still drunk, he went out and got involved in a fight?'

'Yes.'

'Well, he's not going to admit to that, which means that apart from the watchman you haven't got a witness.'

'That hardly matters. The culprit has flown.'

'William Lawson?'

'So it seems.'

'The elder brother of the man who led the riot, I understand.'

'It was hardly a riot.'

Sam sensed that Richard was unwilling to talk about the incident, even though it would cost him a considerable amount of money to have the trawler raised. And Sam thought he knew why. The man who had done the damage was a Lawson. The brother of the man who had led the riot. And also the brother of Kate, the beautiful flame-haired girl whom Richard had taken back to his own home and who was expecting a child.

'Has the man's family been told?' Richard asked.

'Yes, poor wretches. One bag of bones of a wife and three starveling children. They looked as though they hadn't had a good meal in years. The head of the miserable household spent his pay on drink, no doubt.'

'I'll see they're looked after,' Richard said. 'The money will go straight to the woman. And I'll find a place in a refuge for them if you think I need to.'

'That might be for the best. But make it as far away from this villain as possible. I don't trust him.'

After Richard had gone his old school friend reflected that, in his opinion, even the sinking of his trawler had not made a pennyworth of difference to his feelings for Kate Lawson. Poor Caroline, Sam thought. I can't bear the way that Richard is making a fool of her.

The black-plumed horses set off bearing Charlie's coffin in a glass-sided hearse. The sound of their hoofs rang out on the cobbles and echoed round the narrow streets. Mutes in tall hats led the procession, walking in step as if they were listening to some funeral march that no one else could hear. This was not like any other village funeral. Alice was determined that Charlie should go out in style. And her daughter had not opposed her.

Kate was not going to the funeral. Susan had told her to keep away. 'You're a disgrace,' she had said the night before, 'and I don't want you defiling my father's memory. I'm not going to say anything to my mother tonight, obviously. But you'd better spend tomorrow packing your bags because I want you out of here.'

On the day of the funeral the shop was closed. Even Susan had to agree that it wouldn't be proper to open. Kate didn't have much to pack so she tidied out the drawers and put everything in neat bundles ready to be parcelled up when the time came to leave. She had no idea when that would be but at least now there was nothing to stop her arranging her own passage to America and her journey on to her Aunt Winifred's home in Canada.

Charlie was dead. Alice did not need her. There was no place for her here or anywhere else in the village where she had been born. She had given most of her savings to William, as well as the money Howard Munro had finally paid her for posing for the portrait. But she still had her aunt's money order to take to the bank and the letter for the shipping office. One trip into Newcastle was all it would take and she could say goodbye to Cullercoats.

She looked round the room. She had been happy here. As happy as it had been possible to be in the circumstances. She had worked hard but Alice had treated her well. Susan's words came back to her. Had she deceived Alice? She supposed she had. She had never told an outright lie, she simply hadn't mentioned the fact that she was with child. Susan had leapt to the wrong conclusion about the father of the child and Kate had not wanted to demean herself by contradicting her. She had too much pride to enter into a shouting match and, in any case, she knew that she wouldn't have been believed.

Most of the villagers would be at the funeral and a fair number of them would be going to the funeral tea at the church hall. The village would be quiet. Kate decided to go out. She still had Alice's cloak. She hoped the kindly soul wouldn't mind if she borrowed it for one last time.

It was the first of December and frost sparkled on the ground. The air was bitingly cold, so much so that it actually hurt to breathe. Poor Charlie, Kate thought. All those years of being warmed and cosseted by his devoted wife and now he was about to be lowered into the iron-hard ground.

The beach was deserted, too, and Kate walked down the slope wondering if this might be the last time she would come here. She paused at the entrance to the cave, their cave, not just Jos and hers but Jane's and Thomas's too. Thomas, Thomas, what have you done, she thought. You took a half-formed plan, a crazy idea and turned it to tragedy. You've caused your brother to flee the country and have broken the heart of the girl you once loved. But even in her grief and anger with her brother she knew that none of this would have happened if it hadn't been for Jos . . . Kate tried hard to visualize him and found his face had faded from her mind. She'd thought she'd known him so well but now she realized she hadn't really known him at all.

By the time she walked back up to the village, small groups of people were hurrying towards the church hall. Most of them kept their heads down to avoid the knife-sharp wind but one or two of them looked at Kate curiously then put their heads together as if they were talking about her.

She realized with a dreadful certainty that Susan had spread the word about her condition. She decided to go back to the shop but, suddenly, a group of young women barred her way. She looked up to see Joan Donkin and her sister Ellen, along with Ann Watson and Sally Dodd.

'I hear you're expecting?' Sally simpered in her silly, squeaky voice.

'Is it really true?' Ann asked. She had always been prepared to give folk the benefit of the doubt.

'Of course it's true,' Joan said. 'I'd already guessed, you know, when Mr Adamson brought her back to his house. Why else would he bother with a common fish lass?'

'But I'm told the bairn might not be his,' Ellen Donkin said. 'She's been carrying on with the American, too, hasn't she?'

'Surely not,' Ann said.

'No question about it,' Ellen told her. 'That's why Susan wouldn't let her anywhere near her innocent bairns. And now she wants her out of her mother's house.'

All this time Kate stood quite still and kept her head high. She looked into their faces one by one as they spoke and didn't flinch. She felt her temper rising but hung on to it. Not one of them, even doubtful Ann, was worth compromising her reputation for.

Reputation! Susan Armstrong had seen to it that she had none left. But she still had her pride and she was not going to engage in a street brawl like a . . . like a common fish lass! She laughed when she realized what words she had chosen. For, of course, fish lasses were far from common. They were hardworking, brave and loyal. Not like these four harpies.

Her laughter had surprised them and, momentarily silenced, they were waiting for her to say something – to deny her condition, defend herself. But she wasn't going to. She wasn't even going to tell them the truth that the baby she was carrying was that of her old sweetheart, Jos, whom she'd been planning to marry. Even if they believed her they would still find some reason to scorn her. Just like her own father they would call her a loose woman. Not one of them – and she included her father in this – knew anything of love.

'Excuse me,' she said, 'would you mind stepping aside?'

'Oh, la-di-da,' Joan said. 'Just listen to my lady talking posh. Are you practising for when you'll be Mrs Adamson? Well, you'd better not hope for too much from that direction. Do you think Mr Adamson would marry the sister of the man who sank his trawler? Of course he wouldn't. Especially when he has the beautiful Miss Caroline Travers just waiting for him to pop the question.'

'What about the American?' Ann asked. 'Do you think he will marry her?'

'I suppose he might,' Joan said. 'He's an odd one, after all. But even he would want to be certain that the bairn was his, wouldn't he?'

'You . . . all of you,' Kate said, looking from one to the other, 'you disgust me. Now step aside before I knock you to the ground. And don't think I couldn't!'

Her tormentors were so astonished that they backed away and Kate stormed past them. She hadn't gone far when she felt a hand on her shoulder. She turned, her eyes blazing, to find herself staring into the troubled face of Howard Munro.

'Is it true, Kate?' he asked.

She stared at him uncomprehendingly.

'I was walking up behind you. I heard most of what was said.'

'True that my brother sank the *Tyne Star*?'

'You know I don't mean that.'

'Oh, the other. Yes, I am.'

She saw his eyes widen with shock. 'And is . . . is my cousin the father?'

'Goodbye, Mr Munro,' Kate said.

Turning round, Kate walked back past Joan and her friends. She continued along the cliff road, ignoring the curious glances of the returning mourners, until she came to the graveyard on the headland. Only the gravediggers were left as they shovelled soil into Charlie's grave. She heard the thud as each clod landed on the coffin. A heap of floral wreaths waited to be arranged over the freshly disturbed earth. But that was not where Kate was heading. She had not come to say goodbye to Charlie.

'I've made my mind up,' she said aloud when she reached Jos's resting place. 'I cannot stay here with these mean-minded people. I shall take your child to a new land. A better land, and I will not be alone there. There will be other folk from this village, other folk who will teach your bairn the old ways.'

She had thought she was alone and when she heard a sound behind her she turned with her eyes blazing to find herself facing Mary Linton. Jos's mother. Kate's anger faded.

'Is it true, Kate?' the older woman asked. This was the second time someone had asked her this question.

'My, doesn't news travel fast,' Kate said.

'I can see you're angry. But you owe me an answer.'

'What kind of answer?'

'Are you with child?'

'Yes I am, and before you ask—'

'I don't have to ask. Jos is the father, isn't he?'

Kate's eyes widened and Mary Linton smiled at her. Her spare features were etched with sorrow.

'Don't look so surprised, Kate,' she said. 'I know you, and I would never believe what those wicked women are saying. And I know my Jos – or rather I knew him – and I'm ashamed.'

'Ashamed? You? Why?'

'Because I've neglected you. I believed there was no one who had ever suffered as much as me. I had lost my firstborn and I think I became a little mad. I've barely crossed the door since.'

'I know. I'm sorry.'

'But I'm the one who should be sorry. You should have been able to come to me when your father threw you out. I should have guessed why he did it, but I was only thinking of myself.'

'That's natural.'

'No, I've been an unnatural mother. If Jos is looking down on me from heaven he'll be very angry that I've let it come to this.'

Mary Linton only had her shawl to protect her from the keen wind blowing in from the sea. 'All the way from the steppes of Russia,' Jos used to tell Kate. 'No wonder it's so cold!' She could hear his voice in her head. It was the first time it had happened since he'd drowned. She found herself smiling at the memory.

'What is it?' his mother asked her. 'You smiled. Did you hear him too?'

Kate shivered when she saw the look in the other woman's eyes. 'Hear him? No,' she said. 'I remembered something he said.'

'Well I heard him plain as plain telling me what I have to do. Kate, you must come to us. And when the bairn is born I'll raise it as my own. I'm sure that's what Jos would have wanted.'

'You want to raise the child?'

'Yes. You're a young woman. You must get on with your life. Perhaps you'll marry. You won't want a bairn to hold you back.'

'But I do! I mean I want this child. It's my child as well as Jos's. I could never give up a bairn of mine!'

'Kate – I'm begging you – it would mean so much to me. And I heard what you said just now when you thought you were alone. You mean to go away, don't you? Far away?'

'Yes, I do.'

'You can't take my grandbairn from me like that! You mustn't! Imagine growing up and never knowing your own folks!'

'My child will have me and—' Kate stopped herself just in time.

'Oh, I know you'll be a good mother. You would have made Jos a good wife. None better. I always thought he was lucky to have won your heart – a clever, beautiful lass like you. You could have had anyone. You still could – if you give the bairn to me.' Mary Linton started to cry.

'Please don't,' Kate said. 'Jos wouldn't want you to be upset like this. Come on, I'll walk home with you. We can talk on the way.'

'What's the use?' Mrs Linton said. 'You won't give up the bairn, will you?'

'No. I'll never give up my bairn.'

That night Kate's mother called to see her. 'I've heard the gossip,' she said. 'It's wicked. Why didn't you tell them it's Jos's child?'

'Do you think it would make any difference?'

'You were going to marry Jos. If he hadn't drowned no one would ever have known. You're not the first lass to be caught out and you won't be the last.'

'Ma, listen, some of those women hate me.'

'They're jealous, that's why.'

'Jealous of me?'

'They always have been, ever since you were a small child.

314

Sometimes I used to wonder where you came from. You were like a fairy child, a changeling, so bright and so bonny and so brave. Naturally those other great lumps were jealous of you.'

'And now they can pay me back. Ma, it's time for me to go.'

'I was afeared you were going to say that. I know it was Meg and me who came up with the idea of writing to Winifred, but that hasn't stopped me dreading the day you would leave me.'

'Ma, you must never mention Winifred again – not in any circumstances.'

'But why?'

'Because if anyone finds out where she is, or that we've been writing to her, they'll know where to look.'

'Oh, Kate. How could I forget! But that Susan Armstrong knows there was a letter from Canada to Meg.'

'I know, and that's a pity. But Canada's a big country. You can have no idea how big. And now, my darling ma, I'm going to tell you exactly what I'm going to do so that you won't be worrying about me. And what I tell you—'

'I know.' Her mother smiled. 'That's a secret, too.'

Not long after her mother had gone there was a knock at the door. Kate braced herself for Susan's abrasive presence and called for her to come in. But it wasn't Susan. Kate should have known that, for Susan wouldn't have bothered to knock. She would have barged straight in. It was Alice.

Alice, all in black, and looking tired, seemed almost apologetic. 'Can I come in, pet?'

'Of course.'

'Fancy putting the kettle on? I'm parched with all the talking I've done today.' Mrs Willis sat by the fire and watched as Kate made the tea. She took the cup gratefully. 'Well, then,' she said. 'What are we going to do?'

'Susan's told you?'

'Aye, and half the village an' all. Kate, pet, I'm real sorry.'

'And I'm sorry, too. But you don't have to worry. I'm leaving.'

'You don't have to, you know. I wouldn't mind a bairn living here with you.'

Kate felt emotion welling up as she looked at Alice in grateful astonishment. 'I can't tell you what it means to me to have you say that,' she said. 'But the last thing I want to do is cause trouble between you and your daughter.'

'Aye, I can't deny there'd be trouble. But she'd have to learn that she can't always have her own way.'

'Thank you, Alice. I'll always remember this, but it's all right. I have somewhere to go.'

'Well, you don't have to hurry. Take as long as you like to make your arrangements. I'll fettle Susan.' Alice had finished her tea and she raised her cup a little and looked at it. She smiled. 'Do you mind the day I read your tea leaves?'

'I do.'

'I got the impression you didn't believe any of it.'

'Well . . .'

'Don't try to deny it. But don't worry, I'm not offended.' She smiled. 'Well, I was right, wasn't I?'

'About what?'

'About the baby.'

'Yes, you were.'

'And remember I also saw a wedding. I thought I'd got them in the wrong order at the time, but I hadn't, had I?'

'No.'

'And I still think I'm right about that wedding.' Alice heaved herself up. 'I'm for me bed – and I won't be sleeping in the chair tonight. I've moved into the bedroom at the front of the house, just along from you. Susan's had the hot-water bottles in it all day.' She paused as she reached the door. 'Oh, and Kate, hinny, don't think I believe for one moment all that nonsense about you carrying on with Mr Adamson or Mr Munro. I know you too well. And anyone who can add up should have realized that the father of your bairn is Jos Linton.'

When she was alone Kate sat and stared into the fire, trying to lose herself for a short while in the game of seeking pictures in the flames. There were none. She was pleased that Alice had not mentioned the other predictions she had made that day when she had read Kate's tea leaves. The warning for someone whose name began with W and the turmoil connected with another whose name began with R.

How could anyone have foreseen that good, kind William would end up taking the blame for the sinking of the *Tyne Star*? And Richard Adamson had certainly had his business affairs thrown into turmoil. Or had Alice been hinting at another sort of turmoil? The turmoil Kate herself now felt? No, there wouldn't be a wedding. How could there be when the only man she wanted to marry would never want to see her again. Not only had one of her brothers sunk the pride of his fleet but she was carrying another man's child.

Wearily Kate rose and went over to sit at her small table. She turned up the oil lamp and opened her writing pad. Before she went to bed tonight she must write to her Aunt Winifred. And then find some way of coping with the unbearable realization that she would never see Richard again.

Chapter Twenty-five

When Richard Adamson got home that evening he found his mother waiting in his study. She was standing looking up at the portrait of her late husband, Richard's father. It had been painted by a local artist but it was as good as any her sister's son, Howard, had produced. At least that was her opinion.

'I thought you would come straight here,' she said without looking round. 'You usually do, and I want to talk to you before we have our evening meal.' Then she went on to say musingly, 'You look like your father, you know. Although perhaps not quite so handsome.'

'Thank you,' Richard said drily.

His mother turned to look at him. 'Have I offended you? I didn't mean to. It's just that nobody would ever be as handsome as your father in my eyes. And now we must see what Howard has done with your likeness; whether it will be fit to grace the wall next to your father. He sent word that he will leave it at the cottage when he goes.'

'He's leaving?'

'Yes. Tomorrow he will begin his journey to Paris. All artists must go there, apparently.'

'But why so suddenly?'

'He didn't say. In fact he didn't have the good manners to come and tell me personally. He sent a letter along with that strange child, Betsy. But at least he had the grace to thank me for helping to make his stay in Cullercoats comfortable.'

'Is that what you want to talk to me about?' Richard asked.

'Partly. You see, the reason for his hasty departure also concerns you.'

'I don't understand.'

'You really have no inkling?'

'None at all.'

318

She sighed. 'Then I think I'll sit down before I start,' she said. 'And I request that you will do so, also. I have no wish to end up with a crick in my neck.'

Richard settled his mother in the most comfortable chair and then sat down facing her. His father's portrait was on the wall behind her, and suddenly he felt like a schoolboy again, facing his parents with his latest school report.

'I think you know, Richard, that one of my weaknesses is to listen to the gossip of servants?' Richard smiled. 'It livens my day. I was lonely after your father died.'

'I'm sorry. I know I've neglected you.'

'No, I'm not complaining, you've been a good son. And since Caroline Travers started coming to the house my existence has been much more lively.' Richard stirred in his seat uncomfortably and his mother looked at him keenly before continuing. 'But old habits die hard. And, in this case, Joan thought I ought to know what was being said. She thought it her duty to tell me – although she gave every appearance of enjoying that duty immensely.'

'Mother, what is this leading to? Is it something to do with the sinking of the *Tyne Star*?'

'No, although the whole sorry mess is connected – connected to the Lawson family, that is.'

'And how is Howard involved?'

'He painted the girl's portrait.'

'Kate's portrait. Yes.'

'And he says he'll leave it at the cottage with your own. He thinks you'll want it.'

That surprised Richard. He knew how much Howard valued the portrait and he had imagined that he would want to show it in exhibitions. But he was glad he was leaving it for him – although one look at his mother's face warned him that, for some as yet unexplained reason, he had better not say so.

'Do you know yet what I'm talking about?' his mother asked.

'Apart from the facts, I have no idea.'

'Then, first, I will tell you that Mrs Travers has withdrawn her invitation for us to spend Christmas with them. She and Caroline will go to their friends in London. Then, when the winter is over, Caroline may travel a little. They think it best in the circumstances.'

'Circumstances?'

'Yes, they've heard the gossip, too. Although I'm sad to say from an

319

entirely different source.' She shook her head. 'I thought better of Sam Phillips.'

'What has Sam got to do with this?'

'He realized straight away that the girl was pregnant. After all, he is a doctor, but he has been perfectly discreet about it until now. I can't imagine why he has behaved so unprofessionally – unless he is in love with the girl himself.'

Richard Adamson came as near to losing his temper with his mother as he had ever done. All this nonsense was apparently supposed to mean something.

'Who is pregnant, Mother? Caroline?'

'Richard!' His mother was shocked. 'Of course not! No, it's the fish lass, the girl you brought to our house. Kate Lawson. And the gossip in the village is that she's been carrying on with both you and Howard, and that one of you is responsible for her condition.'

A moment later Grace Adamson was staring at an empty chair. Richard had risen and stormed out of the room without a word. She guessed he had gone to see Howard. And he was obviously angry with him. But why, exactly? The anger only made one thing certain: Richard cared for this girl. But she still didn't know which one of them, her son or her nephew, was the father of the child the lass was carrying. Whatever the answer it seemed she was to become either a grandmother or a great-aunt. Oh, Lord, she thought, as something else occurred to her, how will my sister react to this?

Lights shone from every window of the cottage his cousin had been staying in. The door was ajar and Richard could hear the sound of sobbing. A young woman's sobbing. Could it be Kate, heartbroken because Howard was leaving? Richard pushed the door open and entered and was met by the evidence of a hasty departure. Old papers and discarded laundry had been left carelessly on the floor but, apart from that, Howard had removed his belongings. It was Betsy, Richard realized now, who was kneeling on the floor nearby and doing the sobbing.

She looked up when she heard him and stopped crying long enough to tell him that Mr Munro had gone.

'How long ago?' Richard asked. Betsy frowned and Richard realized the accurate measurement of time might be difficult for her. '*About* how long?' he added.

'It was while they were having the funeral tea in the church hall.'

Richard realized that the 'tea' had more likely been held at lunchtime,

320

or as soon as the ceremony was over. 'How do you know this, Betsy?' he asked.

'I came here with some fish heads for the cats. He was packing like a madman. Just grabbing things and throwing them in. He sent me with a note to Mr Brunton.'

'Brunton?'

'At the wood yard.'

'Oh, yes. The horse and cart.'

'That's right.' Betsy looked surprised that Richard had guessed the purpose of the note. 'He paid Mr Brunton to take his trunk and his boxes – crates he called them – to the station and load them into the guard's van of the train. I suppose there'd be porters at the Central Station in Newcastle,' she added. 'He said he was getting the night train to London. Fancy travelling through the dark like that.'

There was a question Richard had to ask. 'Did Mr Munro go alone?'

Betsy started to snivel and Richard guessed what that might mean. The child was very fond of Kate. But she was nodding. 'Yes, he went alone,' she said. 'Isn't he cruel?'

'Cruel? Because he left . . . I mean because he didn't take . . .'

'The cats. That's right. The poor creatures think they belong to him. Look at them asleep on the hearthrug and in the chair. They have no idea their master has deserted them.'

Richard found himself relaxing a little although he wasn't sure why. He knew that he wasn't the father of the child Kate was supposed to be expecting – he still hoped the rumour was ill founded. But if it were true and if Howard was the father then it looked as though he had seduced her and abandoned her. Richard wasn't sure yet what he wanted to do about that. But now he distracted himself with Betsy's distress.

'Mr Munro couldn't take the cats, Betsy. They would be frightened on the train and even more so on the ferry.'

'Ferry? Is he going to Norway? Why is he going to London first?'

'No, not Norway. I think he's going to France. But wherever he's going the cats would hate it, believe me.'

'So what will become of them?'

'You can go on feeding them.'

'How? Where?'

'You've been bringing them fish heads and tails, haven't you?'

'Yes, they love them.'

'And what do they drink?'

'Water or a bit of milk. Mr Munro gave them the milk.'

321

'There's a coal house and a storehouse in the back yard, isn't there?'

'Yes, and a netty – I mean a water closet.'

Richard smiled. 'Well, here's what we'll do. I want you to make a comfortable place for them in the storehouse—'

Betsy was ahead of him. 'Can I take a blanket or two from the bed?'

'Take the best. But you'll have to leave the door just a little bit open so that they can get in and out. And I want you to come to the back yard each day, use the door in the lane, and put the fish down for them. Milk and water, too.'

'Where will I get the milk?'

'You'll buy it from Bains's dairy. Take a jug. I'll make sure you get the money. In fact I'll pay you to look after the cats. How does that sound?'

'I divven't want much.'

'I'll decide what's proper.'

'And can I take some dishes to put their food and drink on?'

'Of course you can. In fact we'll make their little house now, shall we?'

Her face fell. 'Tonight?'

'I'm afraid so. I'll have to lock up the cottage now that there's no one living here.'

'But it's cold and they like lying by the fire.'

'I know they do. But don't worry, Betsy. They were used to living on the street before Mr Munro encouraged them to come in, weren't they?'

'I suppose so.'

'Come on. Why don't we take the eiderdown, too? Let's make their new home as cosy as possible.'

The cats did not want to be moved. They made disgruntled noises, but they knew Betsy so they didn't protest too much. While Richard was helping the child to settle them he tried to decide what he was going to do. He had to see Kate but he didn't know how he was going to face her. He tried to remember exactly what had happened the last time they'd been together. She had given herself up to his kiss, there had been no doubt of that, and yet, almost immediately, she had erected some sort of barrier between them. And he had sensed regret and sadness. As if she would have liked to respond further but there was a reason why she couldn't.

What if that reason was that Howard had seduced her and she was indeed pregnant? It almost tore Richard apart to think that might be true. But one thing he knew for sure. He had to have some answers before he could put it all behind him and get on with his life. It was too late tonight, but he would seek Kate out in the morning and demand to know the truth.

Betsy was crying again. Richard met her as she was leaving the shop the next morning and tears were streaming down her face.

'What is it now?' he asked.

Perhaps sensing the weariness of his tone she shot him a resentful glance. 'Kate isn't there,' she said. 'She's gone and they won't tell me where.'

'Kate . . . gone?'

'Will you ask her? She might tell you.'

'Ask who?'

'Ellen Donkin. She says she's working in the shop, now.'

'Wait here.'

Richard went into the shop, setting the bell jangling, and found that it was indeed Joan Donkin's sister who stood facing him across the counter. She looked surprised to see him. In fact her mouth dropped open unattractively. But she remembered her manners and said, 'Yes, sir, Mr Adamson. Can I help you?'

'I'd like to speak to Miss Lawson, if you don't mind.'

'She isn't here.'

'Then can you tell me where I can find her?'

'No, I can't.'

'Why not?'

The girl frowned. 'Because I don't know. I only know that Susan – Mrs Armstrong – came for me first thing and offered me the job. I took it,' she added unnecessarily.

'Is Mrs Armstrong here?'

'No, sir, she's at home with her bairns.'

'Thank you.'

Richard was just about to turn and leave when Alice Willis came through the doorway from the back shop. 'Wait a moment, Mr Adamson,' she said. 'Would you like to step through?' She lifted the hinged section of the counter. 'Hold that for us, Ellen,' she said. And then she beckoned Richard to follow her.

They sat in a room that must once have been the dining room of the house, Richard guessed. But now it was in a state of upheaval. A bed was half dismantled and there was a pile of gentleman's clothes on an armchair.

323

'Charlie's,' Alice said when she saw his glance. 'Mr MacAndrews at the mission will see they go to folk who need them.'

'May I offer my sympathy?' Richard said.

'You may. But that's not why you've come here, is it?'

'No. I came to speak to Kate – Miss Lawson.'

'And Ellen told you she'd gone.'

'That's right.'

'And you'd like to know where?'

Richard nodded.

'Well, I can't tell you. No, before you say anything – I don't know where she's going. And anything Kate did tell me was in confidence. So I'm sorry but I can't help you. I mean that. I really am sorry, but I promised. And now, if you don't mind, I want you to do something for me.'

Richard sensed that for all she couldn't help him she was not entirely antagonistic. 'I'll help if I can,' he said.

'It's the girl,' Alice Willis said. 'Betsy. She's heartbroken. I've noticed you've been kind to her and I'd like you to go on looking out for her even though Kate isn't here.'

'Of course. I've already asked her to look after the wretched cats that my cousin encouraged to live with him and then abandoned. I've told Betsy I'll pay her.'

'Good. And I told Kate that I'll try to find an errand or two for her to run. That is if my daughter doesn't mind.' Richard sensed some family tension here but Mrs Willis didn't explain. 'And Nan's going to ask her to help with the old woman. To sit with her when Nan's on her round.'

'Nan?'

'Kate's mother.'

'Ah.'

'Don't do it, Mr Adamson.'

'Don't do what?'

'Don't go to the Lawson house to ask after Kate. Nan won't tell you anything and you'll just cause trouble. You must know you're not welcome there.'

After he had gone Alice sat for a while and recalled the turmoil she had seen in Kate's teacup. Of course the R must have stood for Richard Adamson. And as for the turmoil, he had caused grief and heartache in the village in the name of progress. But she sensed that he was a good man for all that. And he was in love with Kate, that was plain to see. She wondered if he believed the story about Kate and the artist. She

324

hoped not. She would have liked to set his mind at rest but Kate had forbidden her to even mention the subject – to anyone. Her pride would not allow it, she said.

But Alice couldn't help speculating. Was Richard Adamson man enough to bring up another man's child – let alone overlook the trouble Kate's brother had caused him? And even if the answer to both those questions was yes, what of Kate herself? The lass was proud and mostly that was a good thing. But in this case, Alice suspected that Kate's pride was only going to serve to make two people unhappy. Herself and Richard Adamson.

Richard let himself into the cottage and went straight to the upstairs room that Howard had called his studio. The only two portraits left there were his own and Kate's. He would take them home but first he must bring himself to look at them. They were propped up against the whitewashed wall, side by side. Had Howard arranged them deliberately so that the figures seemed to be facing away from each other?

Wanting to delay the pain he knew he would suffer, he glanced at his own portrait first. He saw, not the man who looked back at him from his shaving mirror every morning, but a dark authoritarian figure who was saved from total austerity by a hint of controlled vitality and, furthermore, a rugged look that was barely tamed by the fine gentle-man's clothes. It seemed his cousin had seen him as a man of action rather than an office-bound businessman.

Then, reluctantly, he let his gaze fall on the other portrait. Kate. The pain that seared through his body left him weak and close to tears. The woman standing on the cliff top, with the wind lifting her lustrous hair as she gazed out across the sea, was beautiful, of that there was no doubt. But Howard had perceived in her more than mere beauty. He had infused the slender lines of her body with an inner strength, a valiant fearlessness that defied fate to do its worst.

Such a woman was a prize worth fighting for; worth dying for. And Richard had hoped and believed that he could make her his own. But now it seemed he had lost her, and he knew that he would live for ever with the torment of what might have been.

The old woman's eyes moved restlessly behind closed lids. Was she dreaming? Betsy guessed that she was. But what did old Sarah dream about? Things that had already happened or things she wished would happen, like the dreams Betsy had?

Her favourite dream had come to her more than once. She was living in a cottage with Kate. But it was not a cottage by the sea. It was in the country, Betsy thought, although she had never been to the country. But in the dream there was green grass and flowers and trees with blossom. And she was sitting with Kate under one of the trees and they were drinking milk and eating raisin cake. Betsy wondered if dreams could come true.

Sometimes the old woman smiled in her sleep but sometimes she looked so sad that Betsy wondered if she should wake her up. But Kate's mother had told her not to do that. She said it might frighten her.

Today they were alone in the cottage, Betsy and old Sarah, and there were tears streaming down the old woman's face. All Betsy could do was kneel by the bed and hold her hand.

Chapter Twenty-six

Paris, April 1896

Richard sat with his coffee and a cigar at a table in the courtyard of a café in Montmartre and tried to pretend that he was simply on holiday. That was difficult, not only because the task that had brought him here was distasteful, but because he had never been on holiday and was not sure what people on holiday did. He had bought a guide book. The English was quaint but readable.

The book had directed him to some public parks and he had seen straight away how different the Parisian parks were from the municipal parks in England. Here there were no swaths of green, no winding pathways, exuberant flower beds, or romantic groupings of trees. In fact these parks did not look green at all. The Parisian parks were laid out in a formal manner with gravel pathways and obedient avenues of chestnut trees.

The parks in Paris seemed to be for smart public display rather than somewhere where working people could relax and enjoy a breath of fresh air. However, they were decorated with monumental statues and fountains and there were plenty of benches for visitors to sit quietly and view the passing scene.

Richard had allowed himself to sit now and then and be warmed by the spring sunshine. He had deliberately put the purpose of his visit out of his mind, but could not so easily suppress the deep longing to have someone sitting here beside him – someone who had put herself out of his reach. Who had vanished from the face of the earth, it seemed. When he saw the young couples walking by sedately with their pretty children he thought he would give anything – his entire fleet of trawlers – just to be part of one of those family groups. His own family...

Quite alone, he had visited Notre Dame, the Eiffel Tower and the Arc de Triomphe. His mother would want to know his impressions. And now here he was in Montmartre. Once a village, it was situated on a hill soaring high above the city; a place that took its name from the slaughter of early Christian martyrs, but was now the favoured district of artists from the world over – including his cousin Howard.

The waiter appeared with a smile and asked m'sieur if he would like more coffee. Luckily the man spoke English. Richard had no wish to make a fool of himself by exercising the French he had learned at school and not spoken since.

'Yes, please,' he said. 'And I'll have a glass of cognac, if you please.'

His mother would be shocked if she knew he was drinking alcohol at such an early hour, but somehow, away from home and duties, normal time and routines seemed to have lessened their grip on his life. And, besides, he wanted to fortify himself for the confrontation to come.

He sipped his cognac and sat back, closing his eyes as the light streamed in over the grey slate rooftops to dance on the pavements of the little square. He could hear low voices and muffled laughter from the open windows of the buildings all round him. He already knew which were the windows of Howard's apartment. He had come here the day before and actually seen his cousin looking down and along the street as if he was anxious for someone to arrive. Howard had not seen Richard sitting at the café table. Why should he think to look there? And Richard had baulked at the last moment. One more day, he promised himself. I can live in peace for just one more day.

With his eyes closed his sense of smell seemed to become more acute. There was a bakery nearby, he was sure of it. Someone else was smoking a cigar – a cheap one – and, of course, there was the coffee. And the perfumes. They wear more perfume here, he realized. Both the men and the women. And, as that thought flitted through his mind, his nostrils were assailed by a delicate refreshing scent that he thought he recognized. But it was gone too quickly for his memory to recall the name.

He opened his eyes just in time to see two women cross the road towards the building where Howard lived. They wore dresses of some soft, cream material that flounced and swayed as they walked. But, just like yesterday, he couldn't see their faces. They both carried parasols low enough to obscure their heads. And again, just like yesterday, they entered the big old door of the building that contained Howard's apartment.

One of them would come out again soon. The smaller of the two. And now she would make no attempt at concealment. He was right. No more than five minutes later a plump, fresh-faced young woman emerged and sauntered off in the sunshine. And, as she did so, a woman's laughter echoed down from an open window of his cousin's apartment.

This was why he had come to France. His aunt had written to his mother saying that Howard had extended his stay in Paris and had given no good reason. Something about his letters had made his mother suspect there was a woman involved. Richard had thought this nonsensical and had told his mother so. But Grace Adamson had assured him that a mother senses these things and that she, for example, knew very well that he, Richard, was pining for someone, no matter how much he tried to conceal it.

Not wishing to have his own emotions discussed Richard had agreed, reluctantly, to go to Paris and seek Howard out. 'Just to put my sister's mind at rest,' his mother had said.

But what about his own peace of mind? He could not remember the precise moment when the idea that the woman might be Kate had come to torment him. But, ever since, he had not been able to rid himself of the notion that Howard had somehow persuaded Kate to join him in Paris and that she was the woman who was with him now in his apartment. Today he would find out if this were true.

The lobby was cool. The marble floor was clean, perhaps freshly mopped by the old woman he had seen emerge now and then to shoo away the pigeons. The staircase must have been grand at one time. Richard realized that this house had once been home to one wealthy family, but that must have been long ago for now there was a distinct impression of many lives lived here, different voices seeping through the doors, different cooking smells of dishes prepared for different tables. All this was a distraction until he reached the top floor and the moment when he must face his cousin.

He could hear two voices: a man's and a woman's. He could not hear what they were saying, but the moment he knocked on the door the conversation stopped. He heard the sound of suppressed laughter, and after a moment or two Howard opened the door. His shock was comical.

'Richard! What on earth are you doing here?'

'May I come in?'

'Of course.'

Reluctantly, it seemed, his cousin backed away and allowed him to enter. While Howard closed the door Richard looked round and saw a large sun-filled room that served as sitting room, dining room and artist's studio. There was a table near the window where croissants and coffee were waiting – for two. A parasol rested against a chair, and draped over a chaise longue was a cream-coloured lace shawl. However, there was no sign of the owner of these things. Richard's eyes were drawn to a door that stood ajar. The bedroom? He frowned. There was that scent again . . . delicate and fresh . . .

'Well, then,' his cousin said. 'Why are you here?'

'Have I interrupted something?'

Howard's eyebrows rose. 'Yes, you have as a matter of fact.' His grin was like that of a guilty schoolboy.

'I'm here because your mother is worried about you. She wrote to my mother who ordered me to come to find out what was going on.'

'Going on?'

'Your mother feels that you are reluctant to come home.'

'She's right. I am. I'm enjoying myself here. My painting has taken on a different dimension. Let me show you . . .' He started walking towards an easel but Richard stopped him.

'It's not the painting, Howard, is it? Your mother believes that there may be a woman involved. Her words.'

Richard expected his cousin to be angry but, instead, he smiled and began to laugh. 'Does she indeed? I never could fool her. Yes, I am in love, again.' For a moment Richard imagined his cousin looked shamefaced. 'Truly in love.' Did the words 'this time' hang unspoken in the air? 'I suppose I'll have to write to tell her.'

'Why haven't you told her before now? Is it . . . is it someone of whom she wouldn't approve?'

'My God, Richard, do you know what you sound like? You're getting remarkably pompous as you get older. And I can assure you that my mother will be delighted with my choice of wife.'

'Wife?'

'Yes. And the only reason I haven't told my parents up till now is that I wanted to wait until the lady in question accepted my proposal. And now, I'm delighted to say, she has.' Howard walked towards the screen. 'Come along, my dear, I suppose you'd better come out now.'

And then, incredibly, Richard remembered what the scent was. The scent of lilies of the valley. The name, *Muguet des Bois*, came to his mind just as Caroline Travers emerged from the other room. Caroline – but a Caroline he'd never seen before. Her long dark hair was loose

– had Howard taken out the pins? – and it framed her face and hung down on to her shoulders in gypsy fashion. The bodice of the cream-coloured dress was moulded to her figure, making her look voluptuous, and her eyes . . . her eyes were shining as he, Richard, had never made them shine in all the time he had known her. This was a different Caroline. A Caroline he decided he hardly knew. And most wonderful of all – this vision of happiness wasn't Kate!

Caroline laughed softly when she saw Richard's expression. 'It's Paris, you know,' she said.

'Paris? What do you mean?'

Howard answered for her. 'Just being here – especially in the springtime – it does something to people. You discover things about yourself – and others – that you never suspected were there. I won't go on. I risk making a fool of myself. Suffice to say that I have fallen in love with Caroline and she with me. But now let us sit at the table and talk over coffee and croissants. There's sufficient for the three of us – and love makes me hungry.'

Richard wanted no more coffee but he sat at the table with them and listened to their explanations. 'We met by chance,' Howard said. 'Caroline is staying in Paris with an old school friend Jeannette who is half French and has come to live with her grandmother for a year. The two of them decided to visit Montmartre one day and we bumped into each other.'

Caroline laughed. 'I suppose it's time I made my confession,' she said.

'Confession?' Howard asked. 'What could you possibly have to confess?'

'We did not meet by chance. I knew you were living here and we had been walking round for days in the hope that we would find you. Poor Jeannette, I tested her friendship severely.' She turned to smile at Richard. 'And it's still being tested, because each time I visit Howard she has to pretend to her grandmother that we have been out walking together. But, fortunately, Jeannette has a secret of her own.'

'And that is?' Richard was intrigued.

'She visits a small convent nearby and spends her time in prayer and contemplation with the nuns.'

'But what could be wrong with that?'

'Her family are not Catholic. Her parents want her to return to England at the end of the year and marry some prosperous and respectable businessman just like her father. They would not be at all pleased if they thought their daughter had discovered a vocation to become a nun.'

'Ironic, isn't it?' Howard asked. 'They are both in love. One young woman with a religious ideal and the other . . .' he reached across the small table and took Caroline's hand, 'the other with me.'

Richard was happy for them but he could not bear to see the way they looked at each other. The bliss they had found made him feel more lonely and despondent than before. He would have left there and then, but there was still the other question to be asked and, as he remembered the day Howard had left Cullercoats, his anger returned.

'What's the matter?' Howard asked suddenly.

'The matter?'

'Your face. You have an expression like a thunderstorm just about to break over the German Ocean. Surely you are not angry because I have asked Caroline to marry me? After all, you had more than enough time to ask her yourself.'

Caroline withdrew her hand from Howard's and looked uncomfortable.

'No. I acknowledge my fault. But there's something else . . .' He glanced at Caroline who responded immediately by rising from the table.

'I must go soon. I'll retire to pin up my hair.' She left them alone.

'Why did you leave Cullercoats so suddenly?' Richard asked. He saw no point in delaying the matter further.

'Because I was angry with you.' All traces of good humour had vanished from Howard's tone.

'*You* were angry with *me*?'

'Of course. I'd heard the rumours – in fact I'd heard a quartet of harpies taunting Kate about the baby she was expecting. They believed she'd been consorting with both of us, and as I knew I couldn't possibly be the father, I assumed you were.'

'Couldn't possibly?'

'No question about it. So as I knew I hadn't seduced the girl, that left you.'

'But I didn't – and I thought you were responsible.'

They stared at each other as each absorbed the fact that they had wasted time and energy being suspicious of and angry with each other.

'When I left I thought you might do the decent thing. Marry the girl. But when Caroline arrived she told me you hadn't.'

'Caroline talked about it?'

'Oh, don't worry, she was discreet. I had to coax the information out of her. She was angry, too, at first. Angry for a different reason. But now I'm pleased to say that is all in the past. But, in any case, how is Kate?'

'I have no idea. She's vanished. She's left Cullercoats and if anyone knows where she is, they're not saying. But I have an idea . . .'

'What is it?'

'I think she may be with her brother. He ran off after he'd sunk my trawler.'

'Oh, yes. Her elder brother William, wasn't it? I was surprised when I heard that.'

'So was I, and I have my suspicions about what really took place that night.'

'You haven't pursued the matter further?'

'No, and I'm not going to. The man who went overboard didn't drown. The *Tyne Star* is back in action, and there's been no more trouble. I think it best to let sleeping dogs lie. I'm hoping the fishermen and I will learn to live together in peace.'

'Very wise. A lesser man would be motivated by revenge. But you're a good man, aren't you, Richard? Much better than I could ever be.'

Richard was saved from having to respond by Caroline's coming back into the room. With her hair pinned up she looked almost respectable again. Almost. She picked up her shawl and draped it around her shoulders. 'I must go now and rescue Jeannette from the nuns,' she said.

Howard hurried over and picked up her parasol. 'I'll walk down to the street with you,' he said.

Caroline turned to Richard. 'Give me time to write to my parents before you say anything to your mother.'

'Of course.'

'I really am fond of her, you know. I would hate you to think I made friends with her for . . . for any other reason.'

Richard nodded.

'And now there's something I must say to both of you,' she said. 'I could hear what you were talking about just now and I marvel at how stupid we've all been. About Kate, I mean. Just think back to last summer. There was a tragic accident in the village, wasn't there? A drowning.'

'Two young fisher lads,' Howard said.

'One of them was Kate's sweetheart,' Richard added.

Caroline smiled sadly and shook her head. 'That's right. How could we have forgotten. Her sweetheart drowned just days before their wedding.'

Four passengers alighted from the train at Burnmoor. Two middle-aged women, a young woman and a girl. They made their way through the streets of the village to a track that wound up into the hills, the Cheviots. As the two older women chatted companionably the young woman and the girl looked about them with interest. One of the older women nodded and smiled now and then to curious passers-by. It was obvious that they knew her but were not sure about her companions. Soon the little group left the neat rows of houses behind them and headed towards open countryside.

As the track began to climb they passed a tidy inn nestling against the rise of the hills. When they reached a place where the track diverged the woman who was not a stranger led them along the left-hand path, which dipped down again towards a sheltered valley. The track was wide enough for a cart and deeply rutted at the sides with rough stones in the middle, some of them big enough to turn your ankle. But the leader of the group was surefooted, as if she'd trodden this way many times before. She guided her little party safely.

The May day was warm and the grass at the sides of the track was long and lush. It smelled sweet. Birds sang high overhead and insects buzzed. The girl took in a deep breath of the clean, fresh air and began to run ahead. When she spied a dwelling in the sun-filled valley below she stopped and clasped her hands together. This was just like her dream. A slight wind ruffled her hair and she took flight, racing down the path to stop at a gate. There was someone there to meet her. A young woman whose hair shone bright in the sunshine. She held a tiny infant in her arms.

'Kate!' the girl said.

By the time the rest of the party reached the gate Kate and Betsy were sitting on a bench set before a sun-warmed wall of the farmhouse. Betsy was staring with awe and delight at the child in Kate's arms. Kate looked up and saw her mother, along with Mary Linton and her friend Jane, and her eyes filled with tears of happiness.

She rose and went forward to meet them. 'Your grandchild is pleased to see you again,' she said to the two older women. Then she turned to the young woman. 'Jane, this is my daughter Josephine.'

Baby Josephine obligingly opened her eyes and Kate turned a little to protect her daughter's face from the sun.

'Her eyes are blue,' Jos's mother said.

'No, I think they're green,' Nan Lawson said and Kate laughed.

'I don't think we can tell what colour they are yet,' she said, 'but there's no mistaking the colour of her hair, is there?' Kate eased the shawl back a little to reveal a soft mass of red-gold curls and for a moment all five of them stared at the child in wonder.

'She's beautiful,' Nan said. 'Just like you were. And how she's grown since Mary and I were here last.'

'Yes, the bairn's thriving,' Mary Linton added. 'And she's the image of Jos, isn't she?'

Kate and Jane's eyes met and they smiled at each other.

'Hawway, then! Aren't you lasses going to step inside?' Mrs Linton's brother had appeared in the doorway of the farm. 'Hilda has a fine spread waiting for you.'

Mary Linton led the way with Nan, and Kate and Jane followed. Betsy was hanging on to Kate's skirt and staring up at both her and Josephine as if she never wanted to lose sight of them again.

'So you've been here in Burnmoor all the time?' Jane asked Kate quietly as they sat at the table. 'You know I thought you and William might be together.'

Josephine had fallen asleep and been placed in her crib. Kate was enjoying the farmhouse tea along with her family. 'Why did you think that?' she asked.

'The messages your mother gave me, I suppose. One from William along with one from you. But, tell me, are you happy here?'

'They're very good to me. They couldn't have been kinder.'

'For Jos's sake, I suppose?'

'More for Mary's sake. She begged me to let her raise the child, you know, and when I said I couldn't part with any child of mine, she suggested that instead of going to . . . some other place, far away, I should come to her family so that she could stay close to her grandchild. I searched my conscience and I found that I couldn't deny her that. And I made the right decision. Mrs Linton's brother sent one of the lads to fetch her when my pains began and she was here when her first grandchild was born. My mother came with her.'

'Jos's child,' Jane said quietly.

'I'm sorry I didn't tell you that I was pregnant, but my mother made me promise not to,' Kate said.

'No, I should be the one to say sorry. There was something your mother said in an unguarded moment that made me think . . . something about your condition . . . and I didn't pursue it. I was too wrapped up in my own problems. But we're still friends, aren't we?' Jane sounded anxious.

'Yes, and we always will be.' Kate smiled at her old friend and Jane relaxed. Then Kate said, 'I wish you could have seen Mary Linton and my mother when they first saw the baby. My little Josephine has brought them such joy.'

Jane looked troubled. 'Kate . . .'

'What is it?'

'What about your father . . . does he know?'

'No.'

'But he must have realized that your time will have come.'

'Even if he has, he won't care. He told my mother he never wants my name mentioned again.'

'That's wicked.'

'It is. But in any case they hardly ever speak to each other these days. He's . . . he's failing. My mother thinks the drink will kill him. Thank God she has Thomas to help her.'

'My mother says your brother has changed.'

'Yes, he's more serious – steadier.'

'And does he know about Josephine?'

'He does and he wants to come to see his niece as soon as it can be arranged.' Kate broke off and smiled.

'But tell me, Kate,' Jane said. 'If you hadn't come here, where were you going to go? Where was that "other place"?'

'I'll tell you later, I promise you. But now I think we had better stop gossiping and do justice to Hilda's table.'

'I've been here in my dreams, you know,' Betsy told Kate after the meal. They had wandered out into the sunshine again and Kate and Betsy were sitting on a rug spread under a tree in a small orchard. The younger girl looked up into the branches above them. 'What are they?' she asked.

'They're apples,' Kate said. 'But they're still very small. They have to grow much more before they'll be ready to pick.'

Betsy looked up in wonderment and Kate found her thoughts returning to that time nearly a year ago now when Jos had changed their lives for ever for a sackful of unripe apples that had dropped too soon from Farmer Bains's trees. She looked over towards the farmhouse where her mother was sitting on the bench cradling Josephine in her arms. Mary Linton and Jane sat at each side of her rapturously engaged in baby worship.

'Betsy, will you do something for me?' Kate asked.

'Course I will.'

'Go and tell Jane I want to talk to her. Just Jane. You must stay with Josephine.'

Betsy rose swiftly and ran towards the farmhouse. Kate watched her deliver the message and plonk herself down on the bench in the place Jane vacated.

'What is it?' Jane asked a moment later.

'Sit down. I have something for you.' Kate took an envelope out of her pocket and handed it to her friend. 'It's from William. I'll leave you alone while you read it.'

Kate looked back and saw that Jane's hands were shaking as she tore at the envelope. She could guess what William had to say and she wondered what decision her friend would make. She would soon know.

The letter for Jane had arrived enclosed in the latest missive from William. Her Aunt Winifred had also enclosed a letter – and a money order. She had been offended when Kate had sent the original money order back and now she begged her to cash this one and buy something for the bairn when it arrived. Kate had written to inform them of Josephine's birth but the letter would not have reached Canada yet.

Her mother saw Kate coming and looked up and smiled. 'I'll come and visit whenever I can,' she said. 'Me and Mary will come together – that is if Mary's brother doesn't mind.'

'Of course he doesn't,' Mary Linton said. 'Kate's been a grand help while she's been here. Joe says that she's been like a daughter to him and Hilda. It's nice for Hilda to have a lass living here she can have a bit gossip with. Her four big lads never say much – just eat them out of house and home.'

'I'm not much help at the moment,' Kate said.

'Never mind that, pet,' Jos's mother assured her. 'Hilda says it's a joy just to have a new baby in the old place. Her sons don't show much sign of bringing wives home!'

'Mebbes she makes them too comfortable,' Nan said and the older women smiled at each other.

Kate had suckled Josephine before they came out and she was

sleeping peacefully in her grandmother's arms. A movement under the apple tree made Kate look over to see Jane waving to her.

'I'm going to see what Jane wants,' Kate whispered to Betsy. 'Come and tell me if Josephine wakes up.'

Betsy looked up at her and smiled. 'I'll sing to her,' she said. And as Kate walked away she heard the girl begin to chant softly, 'To and fro . . . to and fro . . . I'll rock the cradle to and fro . . .'

'Well?' Kate said to Jane.

'You knew what he was going to say? To ask me?'

'I guessed.'

Jane smiled. Folding the letter, she put it back in the envelope, then clutched it tightly to her body.

'Well, aren't you going to tell me what your answer will be?' Kate asked with a flare of her old spirit.

'Kate who always knows everything. Can't you guess?'

'Stop trying to annoy me. You'll curdle my milk!'

'Well, I'd better tell you my answer, then. It will be yes. It seems I am going to be a fisherman's wife after all.'

'So he's told you?'

'Yes. Your aunt's husband offered him a job in the cannery and William tried it for a while. But the call of the sea was too strong. He's working for a skipper at the moment but he's saving up to buy his own boat. That's his dream. And do you know what, Kate? When I sell my business I think I might just have enough to make his dream come true.'

'Jane, I'm so pleased. But . . . I have to say this . . . what about your parents?'

Her friend's smile faltered. 'They won't be happy that I'll be going so far away. But they won't stop me. And William has thought of that too.'

'What does he suggest?'

'Apparently your Aunt Winifred has never forgotten how much she enjoyed designing shoes. She says that if my father wants to set up business as a cobbler and shoemaker in Steveston, she'll back him.'

'Do you think he would agree?'

'I'm not sure. My mother loves her home and they're happy living in Cullercoats. But you never know. If William and I were to present them with a grandchild . . .' Jane's eyes filled with dreams and the moment was so intense that Kate had to look away.

Then, 'Kate,' Jane said, 'I don't suppose you have any notepaper and an envelope, do you?'

'Of course I do.'

'Good. Because I think I'd like to sit down and answer this letter straight away.'

At the end of the visit Betsy could only be persuaded to leave when Kate assured her that every time her mother or Mrs Linton came to visit they would bring Betsy too. Then, before they set off for the station, Jane took Kate aside.

'You didn't answer my question, you know.'

'What question?'

'I asked you if you were happy here.'

'And I told you I was.'

'No, you didn't. You said that Joe and Hilda were very good to you. That's not quite the same thing.'

'Josephine makes me happy.'

'Of course. But I believe there's someone who could make you happier still.'

'Jos is d—'

'I don't mean Jos. I mean someone who came to see me knowing that I was your friend and hoping that I would know where you were. He came to see me and begged me to speak for him. I think you know who I mean.'

Kate's eyes widened but she didn't answer. She saw Jane's eyes go to the wedding ring she still wore on a ribbon about her neck.

'Maybe it's time to put that away?' Jane said.

'Maybe. But I'll keep it for Josephine.'

'Of course.'

Jane bent down and kissed the brow of the babe in Kate's arms and then hurried to catch up with the others who were already walking up the track. When they reached the top of the rise Jane looked back and saw that Kate still stood at the gate, watching them.

The mild weather held, the sun warmed the little valley, and the apples ripened on the tree. Kate was walking across the grassy patch in front of the farmhouse towards the orchard with Josephine cradled in her arms. She noticed that some of the fruit had fallen. A June drop they called it. Joe had told her that it was just nature's way of thinning the crop so that the remaining fruit could reach full size. She looked down at the small green apples lying in the grass then moved on towards the gate. She thought she might walk up the track a little way.

The sun was in her eyes as the track climbed and at first she didn't see the figure walking towards her. And when she did make out the outline of the man, she thought it was one of Hilda and Joe's sons returning from the village. She smiled a greeting. And then a cloud covered the sun and she saw him more clearly. She saw his face. Her smile froze.

He had seen her coming up the track towards him. Even though she was carrying an infant her graceful stride had not changed. Except that now she walked more slowly, more circumspectly, her arms enfolding the child protectively. She looked more beautiful than she had ever looked before. Instead of her workaday clothes she was wearing a soft green summer dress that clung to the lines of her body and fluttered behind her as she walked into the slight breeze. This was her colour. She should always wear pale green; the colour of the new tender shoots on an apple tree.

And she had smiled when she saw him. Richard would swear later that his heart almost stopped when he saw that smile. But then a cloud moved across the sun and her smile disappeared to be replaced by an expression of shock and dismay. At first he thought she was going to turn and run. But then something, probably concern for the child in her arms, made her stay. He had stopped in his tracks when her expression changed.

'Kate?' he said. She didn't move so he began to walk towards her.

When he was within arm's length of her she spoke. 'Who told you where I was?'

'Will you hate that person for ever?' He smiled, but there was no answering smile.

'Probably,' she said and the corners of her mouth almost turned upwards.

'Then I can't tell you.'

'You must.'

'Must?'

'Otherwise I shall turn round and go back to the farm, shut the door and ask Joe and Hilda's four big sons to keep you out.'

'The person who told me did it because she loves you and wants you to be happy. For some reason she thinks you will be happy with me.'

'Do you mean my mother?' She sounded disbelieving.

He shook his head. 'No, it was Jane.'

'And here was I thinking the girl was a friend of mine.'

'She's never been a better friend, believe me.'

Kate looked at him askance and while she stared at him he came closer and looked down at the baby in her arms. 'She's beautiful,' he said. 'Jos would have been proud of her.'

340

'You know?'

He would have liked to have said that he had never doubted it. But he couldn't because his love for her and his jealousy of his cousin had blinded him to the truth. So he had to content himself with saying, 'Yes, I know.'

'There's something else you should know,' she said. 'My brother William did not sink the *Tyne Star*.'

'I believe you.'

'And whatever happens now, I do not want to speak of it again.'

'So be it. As far as I'm concerned the matter is ended.'

She smiled and the tension that had lain between them ebbed away. 'I love you, Kate.'

He saw her eyes fill with joy as she replied, 'And I love you. You can have no idea how much I have longed to tell you that.'

At last she had said the words he had despaired of ever hearing and his heart was filled with elation.

They stared at each other, overwhelmed by the knowledge of the happiness that could be theirs at last.

And then, 'It won't be easy,' he said. 'There will be many who oppose our marriage.'

'Our marriage? I don't believe you've asked me to marry you yet. You really shouldn't take me for granted.' Her voice hinted at laughter.

'I'll never do that. Not for as long as I live.'

'I hope I don't have to remind you of that some day.' She was teasing him now, and he felt a surge of desire.

'Where do you want to live?' he asked her. 'Here in the country? I could find us a comfortable house. A family house.'

'No, I want to go home to the village where I was born. I want to be able to look out over the bay and watch the boats coming into the harbour as they have always done. And be joyful that you and I are living there together.'

Richard could hardly conceal his emotion. 'Kate . . .' he breathed.

'What is it?'

'I want to kiss you but I'm afraid of disturbing the baby.'

She smiled and turned her face towards his. 'You'll have to be gentle, then.' And there, on the hillside, he leaned towards her and covered her mouth with his. He kissed her softly, tenderly, with an achingly sweet passion. Neither of them knew that Josephine had opened her eyes and was looking up at them in wonder.

* * *

341

'Kate's coming home,' the strange child had told her. 'It won't be long now.' And Sarah smiled in her sleep as if she had heard and understood.

It was a fine summer's morning and the men would be back from the fishing. It was time she went down to the beach and helped Rob beach the coble and unload the catch. She stirred her bones and was confused for a moment by a cruel twinge of pain, but she knew her duty and she got out of bed. Her bones which somehow had got shrivelled and twisted seemed to grow and strengthen as she bent down to kiss the sleeping bairns. The Lord would keep them safe until her return.

She tied her long copper-coloured hair back with a ribbon and left the cottage to hurry through the quiet streets. Then halfway down the slope she stopped; the beach was deserted. There were no cobles, no men, no women come to greet them. She closed her eyes and stood for a moment letting the sun warm her face. Had she made a mistake? Was it not yet time?

But when she opened her eyes again she saw him standing waiting for her by the shoreline. As tall and as fine and as bonny a lad as he had ever been, wearing the new gansey she had just finished knitting. The light faded a little. When had that been? When had she put away her needles? But it didn't matter. The light grew strong again and she began to run across the glistening sand. He looked up and smiled at her. Her heart leapt as it always had at the sight of him.

'Sarah!' he cried and she stopped and looked up into his dear face. He hadn't changed. And the light of love was still there in his eyes for her. He took her in his arms and held her for one long moment of joy. Then they drew apart, but only a little, and they turned to face the sea.

The rising sun was lighting up the sky and tracing a fiery pathway across the sea from the horizon to the shore.

'Are you ready, lass?' he said.

'Aye, Rob. I'm ready.'

He took her hand and together they stepped out on to the surface of the water, their feet barely skimming the gently lapping waves as they followed the path of light. The gulls saw them go and circled high above the bay, their cries getting fainter and fainter the further the young couple went from the shore.

Sarah gave one last sigh. She knew the time of dreaming was over. Rob and she were together at last.